Caragin Farm

Sweet Friendship, Volume 2

Renée Hodges

Published by So Shine Press, 2024.

To my family - not nearly as many as in the Caragin family, but every bit as fun, loving, and supportive. I love you beyond measure.

Cover design Hannah Linder Designs

ISBN:

Print ISBN 979-8-9885206-2-7

Digital ISBN 979-8-9885206-3-4

He could have been my son. Stop it. Work . . . don't think.

Liz Caragin hovered over the strawberry plants, hands on autopilot, folding back vines, plucking bright red fruits, and tossing them into the bucket beside her. At the end of the row, a Caragin Farm branded wagon with two other buckets brimming over with lush, ripe berries waited.

The face of the delivery man at her door this morning pulsed like a strobe light through her brain. Scribbling the date beside her signature on his device jolted her memory. May 15. The due date of her first child. That young man would be about the right age. And his dimples creased his smooth, dark skin when he smiled, just like the baby's teenage father. The cobweb-covered secret smacked her heart, and her deep brown eyes watered as she worked.

What else could I have done? I was just a baby myself. Still . . .

Resting back on her heels, Liz wiped a worn leather glove across her sepia-brown cheeks. Gauzy spring clouds allowed the late morning Alabama sun to fulfill its purpose. Sweat beaded her forehead. Wet circles splotched her light denim shirt. She closed her eyes and slowed her breaths. Her attention turned from the hole in her heart to the ache in her back. Garden therapy was working.

God's forgiven you already, Liz. Kick the devil out of your head.

With a shake of her head, she pushed herself up and brushed the dirt from her jeans. She'd just snugged the third bucket into the wagon when she spotted her husband coming her way. As he'd done for the last twenty-eight years, Jim smiled as if she were an oasis in the middle of the desert.

Would he still smile at me like that if he knew? No time to dwell on that. Had she gotten all the tears? She pivoted to give her face a final swipe, staring out into the field. Game face on. His hands landed firmly on her waist and turned her body. She tilted her head into his to accept his kiss on her forehead.

"Hey, baby." His mouth brushed past her ear and grazed over her cheek. Stepping back, he pulled a smackerel of soil from his lips with his white, farm-callused fingertips. "Mmm, you taste like dirt. And your mama didn't think you'd ever be a farm girl." His blue eyes sparkled with the tease, but his smile faded when she didn't respond with the giggle he probably expected. "You okay?"

"I'm fine. Just trying to get the ripe ones before it gets to eighty-five." Avoiding his eyes, she forced a smile and turned for the house. "I better get in and get lunch going. You can grab the wagon."

Jim took the wagon handle in one hand and her hand in the other. "Just a little warning . . . the kids already started working on lunch."

As the sprawling white farmhouse came into view, Liz counted four of her brood spreading cloths over picnic tables beneath a centuries-old oak. Wait. Was that? She gasped at the unexpected sight of one of the girls, smacked Jim on the shoulder, and rushed to embrace their oldest daughter.

• • • •

"Oh, yeah." Jim snickered at the breeze left in her wake. "Did I mention Laurel's home?"

Jim grinned as he pulled the wagon nearer the tables. Liz still had Laurel in a tight grip, rocking back and forth and cooing exuberant mama words. Laurel craned her head past her mother's arms and mouthed, "Help me." He shrugged his helplessness to interfere as he continued to the house.

Familiar strains of discontent wafted through the kitchen's screen door before he opened it. He deposited the berry buckets in the farmhouse sink as a roomful of voices pleaded with him to take their sides in the lunch prep controversies.

Jordan, the fourteen-year-old self-appointed catering queen, implored. "Dad, tell him it has to be set up so everyone moves clockwise."

"It . . . is . . . lock . . . wise!" Ten-year-old Sam yelled in the clipped syllables his autism speech therapist had taught him. He further defended himself by swirling his arm around in a definite counter-clockwise circle.

Peanut, their youngest, blinked her big, brown eyes and whined, "Dad, Coop's putting mustard in the tater salad. I'm 'lergic to mustard."

"You aren't allergic. You just don't like it. There's a difference. Dad, tell her." Cooper, the oldest in the kitchen, paused with a squirt bottle of French's yellow in the grip of his prosthetic hand and a mischievous glint in his eyes as he awaited his father's judgment.

Over Cooper's shoulder, Jim caught sight of Beth loading her twin sister down with sandwich fixings at the fridge. He opened his mouth to shout a warning as he watched the missed handoff. The industrial-size pickle jar slipped through their hands to the floor. The sound of shattering glass—not at all strange in a home that raised fifteen kids—silenced the room.

Jim took control. "Everyone, move slow, be careful. It's okay." He winked at his eleven-year-old twins, grabbed a towel, and began corralling the pickles and glass. "Jordan, get the broom and dustpan. Darius, bring the trash can over. Sam, your sister is right about how the food goes, and Cooper, for goodness' sakes, scoop some salad out for Peanut before you put in the mustard. You know she hates it."

"Uh, Dad?" Marshall's voice came from the doorway to the living room. "There's someone here to see you."

Jim raised his head to see his twenty-year-old next to an Asian-American thirtysomething man. With his round glasses, half-shaved hairstyle, designer satchel, and skin-tight khaki capris, he looked like an alien from another world in the chaotic country kitchen.

"Mr. Caragin, I'm so sorry to interrupt." The man smiled, stepped into the kitchen, and extended his hand. "You said I could drop by anytime today. I'm L. Chandler Lee. We spoke on the phone."

Recognition set in. "Oh, yeah, yeah, I remember now." Jim stood and offered a hand with a pickle juice-soaked towel to the visitor. He rolled his eyes as all the kids laughed.

Jim made his way to the sink with the dripping towel. "Sorry about that. Guess we can shake hands in a minute. We're just getting lunch ready. I would say it ain't normally like this, but that'd be a lie. Marshall, why don't you show Mr. Lee out to the patio until we get all cleaned up?"

The newcomer offered another option. "Actually, I'd be happy to help. I've cleaned up my share of messes. And you can call me Chandler."

Without waiting for a reply, Chandler dropped his satchel, grabbed a towel, and bent down to work. Jim exchanged glances with his kids and nodded his approval. Lunch prep resumed, minus the fussing and bickering.

Jim noticed Sam staring at the visitor. No telling what was running through his mind, but Jim knew he only needed to wait a minute to find out. Sure enough, after some processing, Sam sidled up to his father and not-so-subtly voiced his concern, "Dad, what's . . . wrong . . . with his . . . pants?"

• • • •

If not for the windshield, Elliot Caragin would have bugs in his teeth because nothing could stop him from smiling. He drummed on the steering wheel of the new-to-him Jeep Wrangler, the sun warming and the breeze cooling his face as he whizzed by farm after farm on the highway he knew pothole by pothole. Johnnyswim blared from the speakers as he and Bekah headed to Caragin Farm.

Bekah. The best part of his happy place. Elliot kept his eyes on her more than he did the road. Her shoulder-length raven hair swirled around her face as she closed her green eyes and leaned into the seatback, soaking in the springtime sunlight. Her feet, propped up on the dash, tapped in rhythm to the music while she sang, not caring which key she landed in.

When she attempted for the umpteenth time to tuck her hair behind her ear, he studied the fingers he'd held as often as possible during the last ten months. The one he intended to put a ring on soon had a sliver of dirt beneath the nail, a leftover from her morning spent transplanting the seedlings they were taking to his parents. Or could it be chocolate from the pies she made last night? Regardless, he loved that finger.

She dropped her hand to the gearshift between them, and he covered it with his right hand. With her early spring tan, her white skin almost matched the latte shade created by his black and white genes. She opened her eyes and pulled her hand from beneath his to stroke the dimple of his right cheek.

"I like your Jeep." She returned his grin, flashing her own dimples.

"I think it likes you." Elliot's cheeks warmed and he turned his attention to the road. Would flirting with her always have this effect on him? At least he didn't lose his words anymore—like he did last summer when they first met.

He nodded to a sign indicating an upcoming rest area. "You need to stop?"

"I'm good. Just about an hour to go, right?"

"Yep. Hopefully, right after they start eating."

Bekah laughed. "I know you *hate* missing out on the prep time."

"Yeah, you know it. My least favorite part of growing up. Well, except for waiting for a bathroom. You'll see what I mean."

"I don't know. I'm kind of excited about spending the summer with them. My family's so small. Guess every family's small compared to yours, though."

"Truth. I think you'll like it for a little while but, girl, the bathrooms are an issue. Especially since you grew up with your own suite."

"Stop it. You make it sound like a Hilton. The reason I had my own bathroom was because I was the only girl."

"And the baby."

"Don't be jelly, oldest child."

"You'll be the jelly one when I leave you at the farm and go back to Whitman, to my own place with my own fridge and my own bathroom and my own bedroom. You're gonna miss your apartment over the Bait Shop."

"Don't you worry about me, Elliot. A crowded house is a small price to pay. I'm just thankful your dad's letting me work there this summer. I could be stuck working garden centers at Wal-Mart or Lowe's to finish my landscape design certificate like most of the others in the program."

"Well . . . I did put in a good word for you." Elliot raised and lowered his eyebrows.

"Hmmm. Yep, I guess you do deserve something for that." Bekah unbuckled, leaned over, and kissed him on the cheek. "How's that?"

"It's a start, I guess." Elliot tousled her hair. "Now, put your seatbelt back on, lawbreaker."

• • • •

Elliot grinned at the sight of Jim hurrying to meet them as soon as the tires crunched the first bit of gravel in the parking area. Sure, his dad had a definite gift for making everyone feel like the most important person in the room, but he always seemed to smile bigger for Elliot.

Bekah had mentioned she noticed this several times and teased him now. "Daddy loves him some Elliot."

"True. But he may be coming for you. I think you're gaining ground on me."

"Let's see." Bekah raised her eyebrows and hopped out.

Elliot joined her at the front of the Jeep, and they waited to see who his dad would come to first, a silent bet hovering in the air.

He couldn't be mad that she won this one. She pointed to herself with a huge open-mouthed smile as she accepted his dad's solid hug. "Hey, Jim. So good to see you."

"Great to see you." He enveloped Elliot in a backslapping man embrace. "Hey! Nice Jeep. Think your church may be overpaying the youth pastor."

Elliot laughed. "Yeah, small-town ministers making bank. It's a used Jeep . . . very used."

Bekah overruled from the back of the vehicle. "It's great and fun. And it comes with treats." She beamed as she leaned over the tailgate and brought out a flat of geraniums for Jim's approval.

"Nice, very nice." Jim took the tray from her and inspected the fledgling flowers. "But when you said 'treat,' I kinda hoped Miss Ida sent a chocolate chip pie."

Elliot smiled, knowing Ida's signature pie had made such an impression on his dad. He and his family had only discovered his birth mom last year, and all had embraced her without hesitation. Her pies were an added bonus. Luckily, Ida thought enough of Bekah to teach her the secret recipe. "No, Dad. Ida didn't make a pie." Elliot lifted two pies from the back of the Jeep and held them in the air. "But Bekah made two!"

Liz arrived with a squeal. "Oooh, Bekah, those look so good!" She gave the younger woman a tight hug, then scooted to Elliot, hugged him, and relieved him of the sweet offering. "We'll save these for dinner. Come over and get some cobbler, unless you want to go inside for a sandwich first."

"Y'all through with lunch already?" Elliot asked his mother as he eyed the picnic tables where his brother, Will, sat with a man he didn't recognize. "Who's that?"

Liz rolled her eyes in Jim's direction. "Someone your father let in."

Jim placed a hand on Elliot's shoulder and steered him toward the tables. "Come on. I'll introduce you."

Will dropped his cobbler spoon and got up to meet Elliot and Bekah, fist-bumping them while he stated the obvious. "You guys don't want a hug right now. I been in and out of the nurseries all morning."

Elliot wasn't about to argue with him. Will was two years younger but had five inches and forty pounds on him. And even though he'd been in the shade for probably over an hour, sweat still streaked down both sides of his face and neck. His deep ebony skin only made him look hotter.

Jim introduced the visitor. "Elliot, Bekah, this is Mr. L. Chandler Lee. Elliot's our oldest."

Chandler shook hands with Elliot and Bekah. "Yes, I know. The son who started it all. Please, call me Chandler."

The man's over-the-top excitement contradicted his mom's tense body language, putting Elliot a little on edge. He appraised the stranger as everyone sat, a list of questions exploding like popcorn in his mind.

"Mr. Lee is from LA." His mom spoke in a tone she most often reserved for strangers who asked rude questions about her super-sized family or about one of her kids' disabilities. To Chandler, Elliot thought, it probably sounded like a simple statement, but the terseness sounded thicker than country-sliced bologna to him.

"You don't say?" Elliot settled onto a bench and made eye contact with Chandler. "Where you from, Mobile?"

"Mobile? No, I'm from LA."

"Yeah, I heard. Lower Alabama, right?" Elliot flashed his best smile at Chandler while Will, Bekah, and Jim muffled their giggles.

Chandler smiled, cocked an eyebrow, pointed to Elliot, and made a tally mark in the air with his index finger. "I get it. Funny."

Will, between mouthfuls of peach cobbler, let the cat out of the bag. "Chandler wants to put us on TV."

"What?" The word sputtered from both Elliot and Bekah.

Elliot regained composure first. "Like for a personal interest story on the news?"

Chandler leaned in, his eyes glowing like a four-year-old's in the light of a Christmas tree. "Actually—"

Will stole his thunder again. "A reality show. On Cartoon Network." He grinned ear to ear as he scraped the last of the cobbler from his bowl and shoved the spoon into his mouth.

Elliot glanced between his parents. Dad returned his look with a relaxed wink. Mom tilted her head down and turned her gaze toward the barn.

Chandler continued with enthusiasm. "And one for you, Will." He made another tally mark in the air with his finger before turning his attention back to Elliot. "Actually, it's for Over the Moon Network. We showcase inspirational documentaries, original series, and movies designed to promote understanding and empathy in our culture."

Bekah chimed in. "We watch *This Land*. It's fun seeing the hidden gem cities in the country."

Chandler straightened his shoulders, pushed his glasses up on his nose, and beamed. "That one's my baby! And funny you should mention it, Bekah, because *This Land* is the show that led me here. As you know, we try to find little delightful pockets of America you can't find by Googling 'what to do in fill-in-the-blank this weekend.'

"Our scouts spend a lot of time driving around, scoping out opportunities. They never drive on interstates, always smaller highways and back roads. As fate would have it, they stopped at a diner in your little town of Fairview. The server there told them the biggest thing in the county is Caragin Farm and happened to mention what lovely people Jim and Liz are and how they'd adopted so many kids.

"So the team came to scout it out, pretending they were ordinary plant-shopping people. The first person they met was Will, here. Then, when Will pointed to Jim and said he was his father, they were super intrigued. I mean, obviously, no one would ever *assume* that."

Light laughter from the others at the table validated the statement.

Jim laughed loudest of all. He reached across the table, his flour-white arm colored with only a smattering of freckles and a slight sunburn, to clasp Will's dark-as-night arm. "No. No one's ever assumed that."

Chandler plowed on. "My guys poked around the nursery, saw a few more of the kids working and playing around, and loved it. Different colors, different abilities."

"A people quilt." Elliot offered a well-used family phrase. "That's what Mom calls it."

Chandler's eyes brightened. "A people quilt. *The People Quilt*. Hmm . . . we could have a working title!"

Elliot saw a shudder work through his mom. His dad must have noticed it, too, because he placed a hand firmly on her arm. Elliot knew the move, a quiet way his dad tightened the valve on her emotional pressure cooker to keep her from saying things she might regret. It didn't always work, but this time it did.

Liz took a slight breath and made clear eye contact with Chandler. "Mr. Lee. You seem like a very nice man, but I'm afraid we don't have a working anything. This family is *my* people quilt. We been stitching it every day for twenty-eight years. I don't see us letting a bunch of Hollywood cameras in here filming us like we're zoo creatures."

Chandler opened his mouth—to object, Elliot assumed. Liz shushed him with an uplifted finger and continued. "Jim and I are no strangers to being stared at. We were the first interracial couple to get married in the county. But folks got used to that. When our family got bigger, people started staring again. But folks around here are used to that now. I don't intend to put these children back in a spotlight like what you're talking about."

If he'd been Chandler on the receiving end of his mom's mini-rant, Elliot thought he would politely say goodbye and be on his way. What would L. Chandler Lee do? Obviously, this wasn't the man's first pitch to an unreceptive audience. He softened his posture, removed his glasses, and stared off in the direction of the pond for a moment before he spoke.

"I understand. Or, I guess I can't really understand since I'm not a parent. What I want you to see, though, is my heart. I think you and Jim have done a remarkable thing here, and it deserves a spotlight. Seeing the way you've withstood prejudice and trials to build this beautiful family can inspire others."

Elliot could see by the way his mother's lips tightened and chin dropped as she rolled her eyes that the compliments weren't working. Credit to Chandler, though. The man didn't give up.

"I promise our intent is not to make your family a sideshow. We want to show your best light, and you can have loads of input into what we air. What if we film one experimental pilot and see what you think? The network will pay $25,000, and, if you don't like the final product, it sits on a shelf."

Liz pushed herself from the table and extended her hand to Chandler. He took it with an exuberant shake that slowed as she issued her next words. "I mean what I said. It was nice to meet you, Mr. Lee." Without another word, she gathered some plates from the table and sauntered toward the house.

· · · ·

Stars speckled the late evening country sky, and the breeze from an approaching storm made the oak leaves dance over the deck. Elliot breathed it all in, enjoying the background chatter. Bekah, Laurel, Marshall, and his dad lounged around him on miscellaneous chairs. Will and his wife, Tamika, swayed in the glider with their one-year-old daughter, Zoe. On summer break after completing her freshman year at the local community college, nineteen-year-old Victoria—nope, she wanted to go by Vee now—sat on a pillow near his dad's feet. Her eyes were locked onto the glowing screen of her laptop, fingers flying in intermittent spates across the keyboard.

"So . . ." Marshall, his long legs stretched out and head tilted back, drawled the beginning of the conversation Elliot guessed was on most of their minds. "Think she'll change her mind?"

Will mimicked his mother's earlier words, "Mr. Lee, you *seem* like a very nice man."

The others laughed as Laurel jumped in. "Yep, that's the death knell right there."

Jim defended Liz. "You guys, cut your mom some slack. She's had to watch out for you, for us, for most of her life. No surprise that she wants to protect us. Seems her mind's made up. However . . . I wouldn't rule out her being persuaded to at least try it."

Vee took a break from her laptop trance. "Oh, Dad, we *have* to do it. I'm already getting loads of feedback from my Veeps that they'd watch a show about our family."

Jim's face scrunched up like he smelled a skunk. "Your what?"

Vee sat up straight. "That's what I call my followers. I'm Vee and they're my peeps, so Veeps. Get it?" She looked proud of her cleverness.

Their dad's face hadn't relaxed. "Yeah, I get it. But what—"

"I posted on my Insta. Look!" She turned her screen so everyone could see hearts and smiling emojis floating in a constant stream over her post.

Jim put on his glasses to examine the screen. "Victoria Lynn, why would you post such a thing?"

Marshall rolled his eyes at his natural half-sister. "Because she has Veeps, Dad. You have to say whatever you're thinking to your Veeps."

Tamika came to her rescue. "She has five thousand followers. How many you got?"

Vee stuck her tongue out at Marshall and blew a kiss to Tamika.

Elliot brought the conversation back to his father. "What do you really think about it, Dad?"

Jim exhaled loudly. "I don't know. I ain't saying I think it's a bad idea. Done right, it could inspire other people to be more accepting of folks who are different from them. I'd want our faith to be a big part of it so people could see the real reason we're able to make this whole thing work."

Marshall stuck his foot in the crack Jim made in the conversational door. "Dad, if you think it's alright, why don't you just tell her that's what we're going to do? You're the head of the family. She has to do whatever you say."

Elliot and the women cracked up as Will spewed the tea he'd just gulped. Jim walked over to Marshall and thumped him on the forehead. "Son, what house you been living in? Being the head of the family don't mean the wife does whatever the husband says. It means I'm responsible for her well-being and have to love her as Christ loves the Church. We are a team, a team of two, in the process of raising fifteen kids.

"Besides, I said what could happen if it's done right. It could go all wrong. You know, the version where we come across looking like ignorant country bumpkins or worse. Anyway, I ain't saying it's out of the question, but I don't see it happening anytime soon. And that's all I got to say about it. Y'all gonna stay up all night?"

Jim kissed little Zoe on the head before he turned toward the house. The others watched him go into the kitchen. Through the window, they could see Liz busy at the sink, coring strawberries with two of the younger sibs. Jim wrapped his arms around her and nuzzled his face into the nape of her neck.

Will blew out a low whistle. "They really got it figured out." The others agreed with various nods and murmurs. Will stood and held his hand out to his wife. "Come on, woman, bring your baby and get in the truck. You got washing to do before we go to bed." He winked at his younger brother. "See, Marshall, that's how you do it."

Tamika leveraged herself and Zoe out of the glider and played along. "Yes, sir, just ten paces behind you like a woman should be."

Elliot shook his head. "I can't imagine how Dad could think this family being on TV could be a bad thing."

Bekah pressed into Elliot beside his Jeep, safe in the shadows of the overcast evening sky. She nuzzled his face with her forehead. He dropped his hands to the small of her back and pulled her another inch closer. The muggy night that would have kept older lovers separated proved no match for the pheromones of young passion bouncing between them like a million tiny magnets.

She whispered, "Stay."

"You're killing me, girl."

"Yeah, I know." Pleased with the power she had over him, she intended to make sure he remembered what he would miss when they were apart. She drew back enough to make eye contact. The edges of his green eyes crinkled as he returned her grin. She remembered how those eyes riveted her when they first met. A biracial man with eyes as green as hers. They were showstoppers. She traced a finger around his face. "I'm gonna miss those eyes."

He kissed her finger when it trailed to his lips. "Not for long." Taking his arms from around her, he held both of her hands between them creating a little more space. "Whew, you are not making this easy."

"That's my specialty."

"I'm aware. But I," he swallowed hard and straightened his back increasing the distance between them by a fraction. "I have tremendous discipline." He said it as if he were Captain America. Cute, but a feeble attempt to convince himself he could resist.

"Yes, it's one of your best traits." She lifted their entwined hands to her lips and kissed his fingers as she batted her lashes.

He blew a little air out and resumed his superhero imitation. "I must lead the young minds of the future tomorrow."

"Yes, you're a stellar example of Christian leadership." She continued to kiss his fingers, teasing him with her smile.

"This could go on all night."

"Mmm-hmm," she purred.

"But it can't." He kissed her and forced his body off of the Jeep enough to open the driver's door. "We will talk and text and Facetime until you're sick of me, then I'll be back on Friday night for the Memorial Day weekend."

She pouted her acquiescence as he hoisted himself into the Jeep and closed the door. Another tease hovered on her lips when her ringtone infringed. She pulled the phone from her pocket to decline the call. The name on the screen stopped her for half a second, all the time it took for Elliot to notice.

His eyes narrowed and his brow furrowed. "Sonny's calling you?"

She kept her face neutral, but her stomach tightened. "Can't imagine why."

"You should get it. It might be about Mom."

She knew he didn't mean Liz. He'd guessed Sonny, his half-brother, could be calling about Miss Ida, the mother they shared. The assumption provided a good out, but fear of pressing the green button paralyzed her.

Elliot pushed her. "Well, answer it."

She pressed the speakerphone button. "Sonny, hey. I'm here with Elliot. Gotcha on speaker. What's up?"

Silence.

"Sonny?"

He stumbled with his words. "Yeah, uh, hey, Rebekah . . . and Elliot . . . sorry. Uh, I thought I was calling Mom. Don't know how that happened. Okay. Well, I guess I'll try again. Talk to you later."

Elliot spoke up. "Everything okay, Sonny?"

"Yeah. Sure, everything's fine. What about you guys?"

With her eyes, Bekah prodded Elliot to answer. He'd talked often about seeking doors to conversations with his newfound brother. He seized the chance.

"We're good. We're at my folks, but I'm about to head back to Whitman. Bekah's staying here to intern at the nursery. Last thing she needs to complete her design certificate."

"Well, that's great. I know you'll enjoy life on the farm, Rebekah. Well, listen, I'd better go. Want to get Mom before she goes to bed. Have a good night." He hung up before Bekah or Elliot could say goodbye.

Bekah turned the volume off, tucked the phone into her pocket, and leaned into the open window in an effort to restart the flirting. Elliot's dimples weren't showing at all, though. The mood had passed.

"That was awkward." He tilted his head and squinted as if he expected an explanation.

"Totally."

"He call you often?"

"What? No." Heat crept up the back of her neck. "I'd even forgotten I had his number. We exchanged contact information last year when we met."

Elliot raised his eyebrows in a silent question, which she answered with a laugh and a deflection.

"He is so neurotic. Did you know he had me investigated when he found out Miss Ida let me move in over The Bait Shop?"

"Seriously? No, I don't remember hearing that. I guess you passed inspection."

"Guess so." She batted her eyes and turned her smile on. "Let's talk about something else. Where were we?"

Elliot laughed and cupped her face in his hand. "We were saying goodbye. I gotta go, girl. And you need some rest too. Getting ready for church in the morning's gonna be like living in a beehive. You'll see."

"I love you, Elliot."

"Love you, Bekah."

They kissed, and she watched him drive away. She wandered to a swing suspended from the strong arm of a pecan tree and let herself fall onto it. The crescent moon and a handful of stars broke free from the clouds and played on the surface of the pond at the bottom of the hill. Tree frogs and katydids sang from the trees, joined by an occasional owl hoot. Jim called it the country symphony.

Her phone vibrated, prompting a smile. Elliot often called soon after they parted company. Her smile vanished when her eyes hit the screen. Not Elliot. A text from Sonny.

He gone yet?

Really? What was wrong with him? She stared out toward the pond for a moment, gathering her thoughts. Maybe the best thing to do would be to ignore it. No, not a good idea. Sonny wasn't the kind of man who would be ignored. She typed, *What do you want?*

Just a chat. Can you talk?

The smiley emoji on the end did nothing to relax her. She typed and deleted, typed and deleted, her fingers unable to keep up with her brain. Yes, she could talk. No, she didn't want to. The lie she told Elliot festered.

Why hadn't she screwed up the courage to tell Elliot? He knew she was an emotional wreck when he met her, floundering amid an excruciating divorce from her college sweetheart. He would've understood how she could've been swept away by Sonny's attention. But then Miss Ida spilled her confession about giving Elliot up for adoption. It's one thing to confess a relationship gone bad to a new boyfriend. It's a nightmare to think about saying, "Oh yeah . . . did I mention? I slept with your brother."

Her chickens, as Miss Ida would say, were coming home to roost. Bekah pictured herself standing in the middle of the coop, flailing her arms around to keep them away. Her phone vibrated again. Sonny's name popped up on the lock screen. She hung her head and swiped the green bar.

"Sonny . . ."

"I kept seeing flashing dots. Are you writing a manuscript?"

Bekah could hear the smile in his voice. The left side of his mouth would be forcing that little scar to move. His ice-blue eyes would be dancing. He knew how to use both features to his advantage. Good thing they weren't on Facetime.

"Just thinking," she said.

"Funny that. I've been thinking too. I think you should give me another chance."

She opened her mouth but couldn't form the right words, or any words for that matter.

He gave her a moment. "I can hear you thinking it over. Take your time." He had his charm turned on high. "We could go back to New Orleans."

She had to stop him. "No. We can't go back to New Orleans. I mean, we could, of course, if I wanted to. But I don't want to, Sonny. You and I, we—"

He finished her sentence. "We were a mistake. I knew you'd say that. I prefer to think the timing was off."

"The timing was what it was. I'm not saying it didn't all feel good at the time, but it was never right. Even though I know you don't believe in right and wrong."

"Well, that's a gross oversimplification of my personal outlook." He slurred his *Ss*.

She noticed. "Are you drunk?"

"No, I'm not drunk. I am having a drink. Okay," he giggled, "maybe I'm a little drunk."

Unbelievable. "Dialing while drunk? This isn't like you."

"She left me, Rebekah."

"Who left you?"

"Arielle Simone."

"The pop singer?"

"Yep. Met her at a club in Miami. It's been two glorious months, but now I'm yesterday's news. She said I'm too possessive. Me! Can you believe it?"

Of course, the truthful answer would be yes. Anyone who knew the number five guy on *Forbes Young Entrepreneurs to Watch* list for more than thirty minutes could believe it. Bekah took the high road. "I'm sorry, Sonny."

"And tomorrow's my birthday. Did you know it's my birthday?"

"I didn't." Compassion softened her shoulders. Sonny's call didn't really have anything to do with wanting her. He just didn't want to be alone. "Come on, Sonny. You're still going to have a great birthday. Just put the bourbon down and get some sleep. You can have anything you want tomorrow."

"Can't have you," he murmured. "'Cause Elliot has you."

Warning! Warning! Her brain screamed as the tightness returned to her shoulders. Maybe he did want her back. This had the potential to go south in a hurry. Her next words were critical.

Sonny plunged into the verbal void. "Elliot. What a stand-up guy, huh? I mean, not many men would be okay knowing their girlfriend and their brother—"

"Sonny, stop it."

"How did he take it when you told him, Rebekah? Did he cry?"

Hot tears filled her eyes. Of course, it wasn't honest of her to keep the truth from Elliot, but there would never be a good time to drop this bombshell. She couldn't take it if he left her now, even though she wouldn't blame him if he did.

"You promised." She summoned the words past the golf ball-sized lump in her throat and out through tight lips. "You said we'd keep it between us, and I quote, 'To the grave.'"

He laughed without the charm that had marked the beginning of the conversation. Bekah assumed he used the same tone with underlings he'd lost patience with and was preparing to fire. "So you haven't told him. You know, I think Jesus would want you to."

He mocked her faith because it was the reason she told him they weren't a good match. Even though she knew he used it as a club, in all sincerity, the point kept her awake at night.

"I know. I know. I should tell him. I will tell him. I just haven't figured out how. Please, Sonny."

"Please don't tell him? I wouldn't do such a thing to you, Rebekah. I kinda like sharing a secret with you."

Tears trailed down her cheeks. "I have to go." She pressed the red button before he could protest.

Lightning bugs hovered above the grass between Bekah's feet and the pond, their tummies glowing in the early dusk. Tonight, there were only a dozen or so. In a month, they'd be uncountable. Her eyes darted around to find them, memories of Mason jars with ice-picked holes in the lids granting a wistful solace.

Simple times. She swayed in the swing and wished for a time unstained by secrets and lies, heartache and worry. Focusing her eyes on the far side of the pond, she prayed. *God, forgive me and guide me. Help me find your way through this mess I've made.*

A lightning bug flew a few inches from her nose, breaking her concentration. The sound of footsteps and ice clinking in a tea glass entered her sanctuary.

Jim stood beside her a moment later. "Mind some company?"

She smiled and scooted to one side of the swing. "I like it out here."

"A little less noise than the house, huh?"

"Elliot said it would be like a beehive on Sunday mornings."

"And?"

"And he wasn't wrong." The morning buzzing as she and thirteen others filtered in and out of two bathrooms lingered fresh in her mind. "Pretty impressive how everyone makes it all work."

"They grew up with it. If it's too much for you, you don't have to stay."

The thought hadn't occurred to her. "You're kicking me out?"

He looked a little flustered. "Nah, that ain't what I meant. There's a little apartment over the barn I made so workers can stay sometimes. Would give you a little privacy. Has its own bathroom." He winked and slurped his tea.

Its own bathroom. Sounded like luxury. Tempting, but she didn't want to appear rude or high-maintenance. "I'll be fine. Thanks, though."

"Talked to Elliot today?"

"Some texts. He'll probably call in a little bit."

"I'm sure he will. Seemed like a sad puppy when he left. He's pretty crazy about you."

A satisfied smile spread across Bekah's face. "It's mutual."

"Good. Real good." Jim stood and drained the last of his tea. "See you in the seedling house at seven?"

"Yes, sir. I appreciate the chance."

Bekah's phone rang.

Jim turned toward the house. "Tell him I said hey."

Bekah's smile faded when her eyes hit the screen. She made sure Jim had moved out of earshot before she answered. "Well, happy birthday," she said in as unenthusiastic a tone as she could.

Sonny answered as if she had just given him a surprise party. "You remembered!"

Make boundaries without antagonizing him. They were likely to be in each other's lives for a long time the way things were going with Elliot. The man was no doubt the poster boy for self-centeredness but, looking back with less glossy eyes, she saw a kind of sharp edge to his conceit. A warning that Annie, Miss Ida's best friend and Sonny's practical second mother, gave her last year played on the periphery of her mind.

She responded with her guard up. "You sound . . . sober."

He laughed. "Of course, I'm sober. It's been a beautiful day in the Magic City. You'd love Miami, Rebekah. Shopping, beaches, food . . . sorry I never brought you here."

"I'm glad it's been a good day."

"You sound tense."

"You think? You were pretty rude last night."

"Was I? I'm sorry. How can I make it up to you?"

Bekah knew him well enough to know two things. He didn't forget, and he wasn't sorry. This was pure charm offensive. After sobering up, he must have remembered the catch-more-flies-with-honey adage. She didn't appreciate being the fly.

"Look. I think it's best if we don't do this. No more calling. No more texting. Especially when you've been drinking or just broken up with a celebrity."

"Ouch. Harsh, Rebekah."

"You know what I mean. I'm with Elliot. You do understand we can't be friends on the side?"

"Yeah, yeah. I get it. I'll leave you alone. We'll see each other every now and then at Mom's and have a nice side hug. It'll be great. Until you tell him."

She closed her eyes. Should she say it?

"You said you were going to tell him."

She released her breath and trusted him with her most secret thought. "What if I don't?"

"Rebekah? You're thinking of keeping our secret 'til death do us part?"

"Sometimes. I mean, I just think it won't do anything other than hurt him. And, truth is, I don't want to lose him. He's so awesome. And you and me were over even before he came into the picture. I mean, you've moved on . . . happy with your life. Right?"

He hesitated. "Totally. Yep, moved on. Living the good life. Don't let the screen door hit ya."

"Sonny."

"Kidding. I get it. I mean, I don't really get what you see in him, but I get what you're telling me. If this is what the universe has given you and you want to hold on, that's what you should do. The secret is yours to do with as you please."

"I can trust you?"

"Scout's honor."

"No more drunk dialing."

"Taking you out of my phone as soon as we hang up."

"Thanks."

"My pleasure, Rebekah. Mazel tov."

Pizza night provided as big a treat for Liz as for the kids. No cooking. No washing. Time was too precious for Liz with all of her kids home at the same time. She knew full well this would be happening less as her babies grew, married, moved, and had babies of their own. She and Tamika and Jim were sliding stacks of paper plates and pizza bones into the trash when Sam and Emma bounced into the room, yelling with glee. "Family meeting! Family meeting!"

They each took a parent by the hand before a question could be asked and pulled them into the living room. All of the other children, plus Bekah, filled every piece of furniture and most of the floor. Sam and Emma herded Jim and Liz to their favorite overstuffed chair-and-a-half. Vee stood at the TV with a remote control in hand. A kaleidoscopic "Family Meeting" graphic filled the screen.

Liz scoped out the faces around her. They were giddy, kind of how they looked as little ones when she put them to bed on Christmas Eve. Jim's face told her he had no clue what this meant, but he was grinning. It irritated her a little. He always loved anything smacking of a fun conspiracy. She never appreciated surprises.

Her mind flashed back to the kid-organized ambush years earlier that roped her and Jim into accepting not one, but three puppies into their home. The mutts sprawled out now on three of the kids, and she could swear they were laughing at her. *You're doomed, lady.*

She shifted in her seat as the muscles at the tops of her shoulders tightened, forcing her shoulder blades together. "Alright. What's this—"

Vee interrupted. "Thank you for coming to our family meeting. We," she waved her hand like a *Price is Right* model from one side of the room to the other, "the citizens of the family called Caragin, have a proposal for the parents."

She used the remote to move to the next graphic. The most recent picture of the entire family graced the screen. Beneath their mostly smiling faces, the Caragin Farm logo and the title, *The People Quilt*, glowed in neon green.

"We propose that we allow Over the Moon to film a reality show pilot based on our family."

Favorable hoots and applause rippled through the room. Liz cocked her head and raised her eyebrows, regretting the decision to pay for the extra social media presentation courses Vee had whined for. Well, at least she appeared to be learning.

Vee let the hubbub die down before she continued. The next screen contained memojis of the kids in various costumes, all smiling and giving thumbs-up signals. "Fifteen out of fifteen Caragins agree: we should allow the pilot for the following irrefutable reasons."

A bedazzled heading "Reasons to Say YES!" appeared next. Vee read as each point shimmered onto the screen.

Prompt racial understanding..
Promote Christian values.
Teach flawless parenting skills.
Increase business for Caragin Farm.
Expand social influence.
Make extra money (for cars and college) from merch sales.
Showcase our beautiful mother to the world!

The last bullet elicited whistles and cheers from everyone under thirty. Jim leaned over to her and whispered, "Can't argue with that one."

"We understand," Vee said as she made eye contact with her mother, "there are objections. So if the parents agree to the proposal, we promise . . ."

Cooper stood and said, "To not play practical jokes on my siblings while the cameras are on."

Darius said, "To clean up anything the TV people leave behind every day."

Amy had a more generic offer. "To help more with all the chores."

Will laughed. "To stay at my house unless requested."

One by one, each child rose to make their promise from Peanut committing to brushing her teeth twice every day without being asked to Laurel agreeing to act as liaison with Chandler and the production crew.

When they were done, the family photo appeared on the screen again, this time with the caption, *PLEASE SAY YES!*

All eyes rested on Liz. She scooched to the front of her chair and straightened her back.

"The people of Israel wanted a king." She ignored the collective groan from her children, who had heard this cautionary tale more than once. "God had been leading them through prophets and judges, but they wanted to be like the other countries. God warned them of all the bad things that would happen, but the people insisted. The Lord relented and gave them a king and, through the years, all the things God warned about happened.

"I've talked to almost all of you in the last week about all the things that could go wrong with letting cameras in our house, holding every bit of our lives out for people we don't know to edit and play out for the whole country."

"But, Mom," Cooper spoke, "it's just a TV show, not a government takeover. Besides, they said if we don't like the pilot, it'll never be on TV."

Laurel added, "And if you and Dad agree you don't want to allow the show after you see the pilot, we won't argue with you at all. We just think it could be a good thing. At least a fun experience to try."

"And all of you," Liz waved her hand across the room as Vee had done to begin the meeting, "citizens of the family called Caragin, agree with this?"

Peanut bounced up. "It's anonymous!"

Liz couldn't help but smile but then immediately felt sorry for her youngest as the laughter of her siblings shrank her back to the floor.

"Peanut," Emma corrected with the disgusted air of an uptight grammar professor, "that's not even a word."

More laughter as various forms of affirmation came from all of the kids. Marshall blurted, "Dad thinks it's a good idea too!"

Liz whipped her head to face the traitor. Enveloped in the cushiness of the chair, Jim's eyes grew wide. She'd glanced at him several times already and knew this amused him. But she could tell he hadn't planned on being pulled into the fray. His face flushed red. He maneuvered himself up to the edge of the chair and pointed a finger at Marshall.

"That ain't exactly what I said."

Liz pounced like a prosecuting attorney. "Well, what exactly *did* you say?"

Jim stuttered, "I just said I could see positives, but there were also negatives." He clasped her hands. "You know . . . the things you and me been talking about, hon." His wink let her know he had her back.

"Well." Liz brushed her jeans as if she had crumbs on her hands. "Your father and I, the king and queen of the family called Caragin, will take your proposal under consideration." She stood and changed the subject. "Who wants popcorn?"

She strode from the room with Jim close behind, but not without hearing Sam's frustrated question. "What . . . does . . . that . . . mean?"

Vee answered, "It means they'll think about it."

Jim pressed his hands on his lower back, arched backward to stretch out the tightness, and used the moment of rest to study his wife across the sun-drenched yard. *God, I don't know what I did to deserve her, but thank you.* He smiled as he watched her adjust their granddaughter on her hip while she slathered butter on the latest batch of steaming corn on the cob.

Even with zero makeup and wearing a baked bean stained t-shirt, she still took his breath away. Sure, she'd put on some inches since she caught his eye under the Friday night lights during their senior year in high school, but he loved every inch. Besides, he wasn't one to talk. He patted his midsection. His waistline had expanded, too, *and* his hair was disappearing.

As if she could feel his stare, Liz looked up from her busyness and winked at him in a way that made the years disappear.

• • • •

Thirty years ago, it had been a bold move for blond-haired, white-skinned Jim to approach Liz, even though her deep brown eyes invited him. He waited until she was alone, unsure if he was reading her look right, and worried about what her friends would say. Even though forced integration happened before they were born, most of their personal worlds remained segregated. They grew up in different neighborhoods, attended different churches, and hung out mostly with kids who matched their own complexion.

In classes, on teams, and in clubs, they mixed and became friends, but there was no hint of crossing racial lines to date at the county high school. Until that September night, when Jim left his gawking buddies to talk to Liz. He could still hear the buzz of the stadium lights, a referee's whistle blowing, and his best friend hooting, "Her brothers are gonna *kiilll* you."

• • • •

"I'll get it, Dad," Jim stepped aside as Will reached over his shoulder to take the twenty-gallon stew pot from the burner, hoisting the pot of simmering water as if it were nothing.

Jim had gotten used to Will towering over him, but every so often, like now, it made him shake his head with amazement. Not bad for the baby born to a crack-addicted teen they'd adopted twenty-four years ago. He'd love to introduce Will to the pediatrician who told them the baby was stunted for life and they'd never be able to make a Mack truck out of a Volkswagen Beetle.

Jim nodded in Liz's direction. "She's never as happy as when she has a baby on her hip."

"I'm sure Tamika's happy for the break. Little princess kept us up all night." Will grinned the satisfied smile of a proud parent and took the stew pot from the patio.

While Jim still had the strength to do it, he was relieved Will took the pot away. *That's a chore for a young back.* He fished a can of Mountain Dew from the cooler, popped the tab, and lowered himself into an Adirondack chair. From here, he had the most open view of their property and, in a few hours, he would be able to see the sunset at the edge of the woods.

The perfume of freshly mown grass blended with the mouth-watering aroma of pork that had smoked over the pit since last night. Older men and women lingered at the picnic tables under the shade trees, digesting their first helpings. The younger ones flitted around the grounds from the barn to the catfish pond.

He loved Liz's description of their extended family get-togethers as a people quilt. The pet name painted a beautiful word picture of the mishmash of skin tones, every shade from lily white to mahogany brown. Not that there hadn't been hurtful comments, nights of tears, and at least one fistfight in the making. The determined love of two stubborn and naïve teenagers had stitched the whole thing together. *I don't know what I did to deserve this either, God, but thank you again.*

He pulled the brim of his baseball cap to cover his eyes and leaned his head back. The next thing he heard was his wife's sweet teasing.

"Just resting your eyes?" She perched on the arm of the chair and lifted his cap. A rain-scented breeze scurried across his face.

Jim took the cap back and smiled. "Maybe." He stroked her arm.

"Well, come on, Mr. Caragin, we got a big announcement to make before folks start leaving. Rain's coming." She stood and extended her hand.

He pushed himself up and took her hand. "You're sure about this, babe?"

"Sure would be an overstatement. But you made a compelling case, and I'm willing. Come on."

They strolled to the picnic tables and Liz rang a monster-sized iron triangle hung from the nearest sweet gum tree as dust-colored clouds softly obscured the sun.

Once everyone assembled, Jim smiled at Liz and opened with his usual. "I guess you're wondering—"

Almost all helped him finish the sentence, "—why I called you here today."

He feigned surprise. "Seriously, though, before y'all go back for seconds, or thirds as the case may be, Liz and me need to tell you something. We been asked to let Over the Moon Network make a reality show about our family."

Liz's two brothers guffawed.

Several of the kids informed them that Jim wasn't pulling their legs. Liz nodded and the tittering died down.

Jim grasped Liz's hand. "It's been a serious thing to think about. We talked about it a lot and prayed about it. The kids already put in their two cents." He'd never seen such attentiveness from his family. Backs were straight. Several sat literally on the edges of their seats. Eyes were wide, and a couple of mouths hung open. The scamp in him considered milking it for a few moments, but the plop of a cool, tiny raindrop on his face convinced him to get on with it.

He winked at Peanut. "It's anonymous. We're gonna do it."

The last syllable hardly left his mouth before the younger kids sprung up, whooping and dancing. His chest warmed watching the celebration. He hadn't seen them all so happy since the puppy purchase. Liz smiled, too, with three of the girls almost knocking her down with their hugs.

After a few minutes, he whistled to get their attention. "The thing that pushed us over the edge was something the pastor said yesterday. He talked about Jesus saying we should let our lights shine so others would see our good works and give glory to our Father.

"He said that means we're supposed to live our days striving for excellence for the glory of God in service to others. I never thought about it that way before, but that's really what we been doing with the nursery all these years. I guess that's why he's blessed us so much."

Several voices saying "amen" affirmed him.

He took off his baseball cap and crumpled the brim between his hands. Overwhelming gratitude enveloped him as he scanned the smiling faces. "Well, Liz and me, this family is the most excellent work we've done. Better than the farm. We think God can get a lot of glory from it, but we don't have much idea how this is all gonna work. We appreciate your prayers and support."

"Especially," Liz added, "your prayers."

A soft thunder rumbled like an ocean wave from the barn in the west to the patio. Practiced hands gathered dishes from the tables and hurried toward the house as the sky released its cool load like a child dumping a bag of mini marshmallows.

How does so much dirt get inside my gloves? Bekah used her index fingernail to pry potting soil from underneath the others as she trudged toward the farmhouse. The late afternoon sun lowering to the west made long pecan tree shadows on the lawn. She focused her sights on the house and her immediate goal of a glass of water. She hadn't taken time to fill her hydro flask in hours. Her tongue stuck to the roof of her mouth as if she'd swallowed a spoonful of flour.

Goal number two, a shower. Residue from the pine straw and potting soil she'd flung around all day made the sweat on her temples and around her neck grainy. Her blue jeans felt five pounds heavier than this morning and had completely lost the ocean breeze fabric softener scent they had when she pulled them on. She should be able to squeeze in a rinse before dinner.

Liz's grandmother sat on the patio in the shade of the jasmine-covered pergola, a plastic bucket of black-eyed peas in her lap. Her honey-colored fingers sliced the hulls open, and her thumbs flicked the tiny balls into the bucket before she dropped the empty hull onto a respectable mound already beside her chair. Bekah grinned. *How many thousands of peas this woman must've shelled.*

"Who's there?" The shelling paused when Bekah stepped onto the patio.

"It's Bekah, Miss Rosamond." Bekah raised her volume as she moved closer and bent to place her face in the older lady's peripheral vision where the macular degeneration had yet to corrupt.

Gramma Rosamond lifted her weathered hand to stroke Bekah's cheek and smiled brightly. "Oh, Bekah, you one of Lizzie's friends? You call me Gramma. All Lizzie's friends call me Gramma."

"No, I'm Elliot's girlfriend. From Whitman."

"Elliot? No . . . Elliot ain't old enough for a girlfriend." She chuckled and wagged her head. "You teasing me, ain't you?"

"Yes ma'am. Just teasing." Bekah raised up and turned toward the kitchen. "I need to get cleaned up before dinner. I'll see you inside."

"Can't you sit a spell?"

Bekah fingered her empty water bottle and willed her mouth to produce enough saliva to knock the edge off the dryness. Gramma Rosamond wouldn't remember their conversation in ten minutes. Still, it would be the height of rudeness to refuse her. She dragged a chair close and reached for a handful of peas.

Gramma Rosamond pulled the bucket away. "You take off your gloves? You know Missus don't want you getting purple all over your pretty white gloves."

"Yes, ma'am. My gloves are off."

"Okay, then."

How quickly she tumbled in and out of decades past. Bekah guessed the white gloves memory came from Gramma Rosamond's time as a housemaid for an affluent Birmingham family. She'd probably be appalled if she could see clearly how dirty this white girl beside her was from doing manual labor all day.

The repetition was calming. Pick up a pea, pull the string from the toughest end, open the pod, and scrape the tiny cool orbs from the hull. Funny how the peas were cool to the touch even when they'd been outside on the patio since morning. The two women worked in silent unison until Gramma Rosamond began to hum. She rocked ever so slightly as she continued her work.

Something meditative in her voice and movement spoke of a treasure trove of experience. At eighty-seven years old, she seemed a paradox—stately and frail, care-worn and joyful. Bekah, though loath to interrupt the moment, wanted to glean what she could while she had the opportunity.

"What's that song you're humming?"

"Hmm? Oh, I didn't know I was doing that out loud." She furrowed her brow and hummed a little more, her mind, Bekah imagined, searching for the words like pulling a water bucket from the depths of a well. "Oh, I know." She raised an empty hull and sliced the air in time with it while she sang. "*O they tell me of a home far beyond the skies, O they tell me of a home far away; O they tell me of a home where no storm clouds rise; O they tell me of an uncloudy day.*" She chuckled again and admitted, "That's all I remember."

"You sing it at church?"

"Back in the day. It was Reverend Cross's favorite."

"That at Fairview Second Baptist?"

"Oh, no. At 16th Street Baptist. In Birmingham. Before that day, of course. We moved to Fairview after that. Woodrow insisted."

"What day was that?"

Gramma Rosamond drew back and stared at Bekah as if she had three heads. "What day was that? Child, where you been? The bombing. Sunday morning. We wasn't there because my Addie, that's Lizzie's mama, was feeling poorly, but we felt it at the house." She paused, and her clouded eyes seemed to peer clearly into the past.

"My Addie's best friend was named Addie too. Addie Mae Collins. That bomb took her and three other precious baby girls. If she hadn't been sick, my Addie probably woulda been in that basement with her friends, putting on their choir robes for the service."

One word from Bekah's Alabama history class surfaced in her mind with a sobering weight. "Bombingham."

Gramma Rosamond nodded. "That's what they called it."

"I didn't know you went to church there. That must have been terrible." The words were inadequate but all Bekah could get out.

"Woodrow . . . he went flying out the house while it was still shaking. I pulled the young'uns to the hall 'cause there weren't no windows and fell on top of them like a mother hen. Well, I tried. They was a little too big for that. John was squirming out when I squeezed too hard, but he still didn't move far from me. I just prayed and prayed. Jesus, I said, don't let them blow us all up."

Bekah saw a shudder work its way through Gramma Rosamond's body when she paused her story and her shelling. With a shake of her head, the old lady picked her memory back up.

"It seemed like forever before Woodrow come back. He said it looked like a war zone. And he knowed about such, being in Paris when we took it from the Nazis. He said they was smoke and ashes and people bleeding all over the place. Cars by the church all burnt up. The police tried to keep the whites and blacks apart, but they was fighting and yelling. It wasn't the first bomb them Klan did, but it was the worst. Lawdy."

"Is that when you moved to Fairview?"

Gramma Rosamond squinted as if the memory came hard for her, then nodded slowly. "I didn't want to move, wanted to stay with my family. My church family. But Woodrow said he couldn't live with hisself if we stayed and something happened to one of our young'uns. His family had some acres out in Fairview. They had a good colored school. Suppose it was the right thing to do."

Out of unshelled peas, Gramma Rosamond raked her fingers through the shelled ones, lifting them and letting them fall like mini waterfalls back into the pan.

Bekah leaned back in her chair. "I don't know how you got through it all."

Gramma Rosamond harrumphed. "Not by my power. Standing on the promises of the Lord. You know, in the middle of all that madness, Reverend Cross was walking around calling out Psalms 23. 'Yea, though I walk through the valley of the shadow of death, I will fear no evil: for thou art with me; thy rod and thy staff they comfort me.' No matter what happens, you have to remember the good Lord is always there."

The screen door behind them squeaked open. A little voice yelled, "Mama says it's time to wash up!"

Gramma Rosamond shifted her weight. "Wash up? They ain't even time to cook these peas now."

Bekah took the bucket and helped her leverage out of the chair. "I guess we'll have to eat them tomorrow night."

"Well, I guess so. Thank you for helping me . . . what's your name, honey?"

"Bekah."

"Oh . . . Bekah. You one of Lizzie's friends?"

• • • •

"She's amazing," Bekah gushed to Elliot on Facetime after relaying the pre-dinner conversation. "Do you think she's got all the facts right?"

"Oh yeah, I've heard all of those stories. She may not remember what she had for breakfast, but things from years ago . . . yeah, sharp as a tack."

"I hope she gets on the TV show. Hey, and Miss Ida could get her story up in the Foundation."

Elliot seemed to warm to the thought of Gramma being a part of Civil Rights Foundation his birth mother managed in Whitman. "Not a bad idea. They're always looking for new ways to show the history."

"The Foundation seems to keep her busy."

"And you know she loves being busy."

"I think it's so cool she's found something new she loves. Had to be hard switching gears from running the diner since she literally grew up doing that."

"Yeah, but she really seems happy. And I'm pleasantly surprised to see that she seems to be giving more and more control of the Bait Shop to Cynda and Reuben."

"I like some of the changes they're making."

Elliot laughed. "That's where they may be pushing their luck. Cynda's trying to get Mom to agree to have the booths reupholstered."

"What?" She raised her hand to her chest in faux shock. "Is the duct tape wearing out?"

"You know her so well."

Bekah changed gears. "What about you? Think you'll be on the show?"

Elliot shrugged. "I don't know. Not thinking so. I'm not there much and don't know what I could add."

"L. Chandler Lee seems to think you're the golden child. And, you know, he's a rock star maker." She flayed her hands in firework explosion fashion.

He grinned. "Well, I know you don't know me very well, but I'm not much of a rock star wannabe. Seriously, though . . . I didn't say anything much because I didn't want to rain on everyone else's parade, but I don't feel a hundred percent good about the whole thing. I don't care to have everybody knowing all my stuff."

"Like?"

"Like how I feel . . . being adopted, growing up in a Brady-Bunch-on-steroids house, meeting my birth mom, trying to find my birth dad—"

Bekah hadn't heard him mention this in a while. "Wait, what?"

He shrugged. "I think it might be time to check it out more. I got some info from Mom, been Googling. It's all just thinking right now. What do you think?"

"I think what I think doesn't matter, babe. I mean, I try to put myself in your shoes, but growing up with both my parents, I can't really. I understand if you want to try to connect. I understand if you never want to see him. Whichever you choose, I got your back. Hope you know that."

"I absolutely know that. Can't believe how blessed I am to have you in my life."

Tears puddled in his eyes, which made Bekah misty-eyed. "I'm the blessed one. Love you, El."

"El?" Elliot grinned. "You been hanging out with my mom. She's the only one who calls me that."

"Well, I kinda like it. It's cute and saves on syllables."

Liz took in the new look of the pastor's study while he and Jim small-talked about the weather and their kids. Recent renovations had improved the office and the rest of the building, but there were some things that couldn't be overcome with sheetrock, paint, and new flooring. Narrow vertical windows didn't allow nearly enough light in, and the dropped ceiling with metal grids and fiberglass tiles hung way too low. *Wonder if we could take those out and open this place up more?*

Jim brought her back into the room with a clearing of his throat. "We know it's your off day, Ricky, so we don't want to take up a lot of your time."

The pastor's smile showed he was in no hurry. "I'm happy to help but not sure how much good I'll be. Even though I am still a licensed attorney, all of my work has been in real estate, not contract law, and certainly not entertainment law. Not much call for that around here."

Liz grinned. No argument there. She moved her paper copy of the contract—dog-eared pages, highlighted sentences, and one coffee stain on page nine—from her lap to the desk. "We know that. But we really appreciate you looking and praying through it with us."

Ricky swiveled his monitor so they all could see and tapped on his keyboard to open his pdf of the contract. "I've actually had a little fun looking into it. Guess law school habits die hard. I'd say from what I've learned it's mostly boilerplate provisions."

He scrolled to one of the sections Liz had marked. "Including this one. You guys need to be very aware that you're basically saying they can do anything they want to with anything they produce—pictures, video, audio. They can edit it any way they want, and you can't do anything about it, including suing to keep from airing it on TV or any and all social media platforms."

A shudder worked its way from her head to her toes. "Keeps me awake at night."

Jim said, "But Chandler said we have the choice to shelve the whole thing if we wanted to after we saw the pilot."

Ricky scrolled some more. "You told me that. I found a reference to it, but it took some looking. It's buried here in the midst of a lot of legalese. You have twenty-four hours after you see the pilot to decide to stop production without being in breach of contract. And there are several steps you have to take to assert your right to do so. Any attempt to stop after then will open you up to litigation."

Liz thumbed through her paper copy and scanned the paragraph. "Can we change this to give us more time or less restrictions?"

Ricky shook his head. "We can try, but I'm not hopeful they would accept. Frankly, from what I've read, I'm surprised they're giving you an out at all. Must be because they're a young network and hungry for new shows. It also says if you cancel, you waive the twenty-five thousand they've agreed to pay."

A shrug of her shoulders. "That's not an issue, for-us personally at least. We've already decided the money's going to Foster & Adopt Alabama for the work they do. Can we write it in so the money goes directly to them instead of us? And any chance we could get more than that for them?"

"Honestly, Liz, I wouldn't think so. That kind of money is crazy out of line with anything I've been able to see financial information about. Most people who agree to a reality show are doing it for the publicity and don't care that they get little or no upfront money. And, again, of these kinds of things I've been able to look into, the network most often takes away all of your rights with zero regard for your input or concerns. Unless you're already a celebrity of some kind with more of a platform."

Jim asked, "What you're saying is once we sign, we're stuck?"

"Well," Ricky smiled, "that *is* why contracts exist."

Liz felt her lips tighten. The way the contract read, it sounded like the network could edit video to suit any angle they wanted. And, even if it weren't edited for effect, they weren't a perfect family. The cameras were bound to catch moments she wouldn't be proud of. One of the main reasons she'd allowed herself to be convinced to do this was so they could present a good witness for their faith. What if they wound up doing the opposite?

Ricky broke into her thoughts. "Let's talk about some other things I want to make sure you're okay with." He scrolled to the filming provisions that filled the last three pages. "These are the provisions referred to in Section

Three. The nuts and bolts of what you will allow in the filming process. Again, mostly boilerplate."

Jim flipped through their copy and pointed out another highlighted clause. "Here, they say cameras mounted near the ceiling in all areas of the house and grounds and nursery except for bathrooms could be on all day and night. Marta, our live-in, has specifically asked that we leave her out of this, so we want to add her suite as an exception."

"And," Liz added, "we don't want to allow those things on twenty-four seven in the bedrooms. Can we make it so we have some kind of off switch, or they have to ask for our permission at least? We do need some privacy, right?"

Ricky typed into his document. "Those certainly seem like reasonable requests. What about allowed hours of manual filming? That's when camera people, and all the crew that comes with them, can be in your house. They say here 5 a.m. until 10 p.m."

Liz looked where he pointed. "Can we make it six 'til nine?"

"We can try. Anything else?"

Jim flipped to the next page. "What does this one mean? It says they can make necessary alterations to our house and grounds for filming. I thought this was supposed to be a reality show. They gonna change it to make it look like something it's not?"

Ricky shook his head. "I don't think so. The way I read it is that they may want to move furniture around to get everything in any camera shot they need. Or to fit the crew in without being noticed. You have to know it's going to be tight when they're filming. For example, I know your kitchen is large, but by the time they add another camera or two and a director and makeup people, there may not be room for your kitchen table. It is a little vague, though. I think we can add some exceptions in. You wouldn't want them, say, cutting down your bodock tree for a better camera angle."

Jim held up a hand. "Wait a minute. Go back. Makeup people?"

A laugh flew from Liz's mouth with a life of its own. "Jim Caragin. Ricky's talking about saving the oldest tree on our land, and you're worried about someone putting makeup on your face?"

Jim blushed. "I just ain't thought about it is all. You mean, I'd really have to wear all that gunk on my face the whole time this thing is going on?"

More scrolling by Ricky as he grinned. "There is a whole page of hold harmless agreements, including any 'adverse reactions to makeup products used by licensed cosmetologists on talent.' That's you . . . the talent. You should ask about how often that would be, but I would guess it would only be for the times they have you give specific interviews. Vignettes, they call them, back in the filming provision section."

Jim's obvious discomfort tickled Liz. "So foundation, powder, eyeliner . . . *now* do you want to pull the plug on this whole thing?"

Jim squirmed as he defended himself. "I just said that I ain't thought about it yet." He shrugged with a new thought. "I guess there could be worse things than having a pretty girl dabbing makeup on me. But I ain't getting none of them manicure or pedicure things."

The three of them shared a laugh that broke the prior tension.

Ricky brought them back around. "We can spend some more time going over individual items and mark them up for submission to the network. But I really think it would be a good idea for you to consult an attorney who has experience in this field. I do have a friend at a firm in Atlanta who owes me a favor. Any objection to me sending it to him, at least for a quick once-over?"

Liz nodded. "Sounds reasonable."

"But . . ." Jim leaned back in his chair. "We asked for your help because we trust you. Not only as an attorney, but as our pastor and friend. Your sermon on letting our light shine was a big reason we both agreed to this thing. Tell us, do you really think this is a good idea for the Kingdom?"

Ricky leaned forward, elbows on his desk, and looked between Liz and Jim. "As a pastor and a friend . . . I haven't only reviewed this contract—I've prayed over it. Prayed you would make a wise decision and, if you decided to take this on, you do it as a mission to share God's love.

"I have no doubt that, if you do this, there will be trials. But you are two of the strongest warriors I know. Everything you've overcome, all you've accomplished in your lives . . . you've done it faithfully and with a kind of humility and honesty I would like to see in the rest of my congregation and in my own life."

Liz bowed her head. Hearing those words humbled her. "I don't know if I'd say all that."

Ricky smiled. "I know you wouldn't. That's precisely why I think you're the right people to take this opportunity. The decision, of course, is yours. If you decide it's not the right thing, no judgment at all here. The Kingdom will carry on. If you decide to do it, I can promise you I'll be behind you all the way and here for anything you need me for."

Liz glanced at Jim. His eyes were as watery as hers. "Thank you. Guess we got some more praying to do."

Shrimp shells and hollow crab legs filled the metal bucket in the middle of the plastic tablecloth at Momma and Em's Seafood. A bite of creamy coleslaw would be perfect, but Bekah didn't want to have to clean her hands to pick up the fork. Without a word, Elliot lifted a forkful of the mayonnaise-smothered cabbage to her mouth. She smiled and accepted the assist.

"You get me." She winked, peeled a shrimp, and popped the cocktail-sauce-laden morsel into her mouth.

"Yes, I do." He saluted her with his tea glass before getting back to work on his cluster of crab legs.

"How's the knee?"

Elliot examined the open wound on his left knee. "Stings a little. I've had worse."

"Well, you looked like a champ sliding into home plate."

Elliot laughed. "Thought I was going to have to take out their catcher. What a monster."

"Yeah, *she* was tough. You think she's in what . . . tenth grade?" She teased with a huge grin.

He pointed at her with a crab claw. "It's *adult* co-ed. Don't make me tell you again."

Bekah gave him credit. "Church league softball ain't for sissies."

"You should play."

"Would, but I got a job on the farm. My boyfriend hooked me up."

"Sounds like a nice guy."

"He's okay." Bekah smiled, pushed her plate away, and grabbed a wipe package. Getting to an open edge with shrimp-covered hands turned out to be a chore.

Elliot took the pack from her, opened it, and handed her the lemon-scented wipe. "Seriously, you're helpless."

"Seriously, how do they expect you to clean up this mess with a one-inch square?"

"You could go to the bathroom."

Bekah shook her head. "Nope. I'll take the challenge. And I don't want to be away from you. It seems like a lot longer than two weeks since we've been alone together. Been missing you."

She watched the color flood his cheeks. Cute. He missed her too.

He leaned toward her and whispered, "I don't believe you."

Bekah leaned to meet him. "Take me home and I'll show you."

• • • •

A few steps inside the door to her apartment, Bekah stopped short, knowing Elliot would happily run right into her. His hands were strong on her waist as he bent to nibble her neck. Motor running, she cooed and turned for the kisses that flooded her thoughts since they parted on Monday. In one swooping movement, he lifted her and took her to the couch where he gently settled her and snuggled up close.

She moved her lips to his neck, kissed for a moment, then pulled away. Sitting up, she wiped her mouth. "Thought you took a shower."

"I did."

"Well, you taste like third base." She scrunched her nose, pushed off the couch, and headed to the bathroom.

Elliot protested. "I was in a hurry to get you to dinner. Hey, try the other side. Think I did a better job there."

Bekah returned with a warm, wet washcloth. "Who's helpless now, hmm? Hold still." She pressed the cloth to his neck and moved it up behind his ear. "Let me see if I got it all."

She bent to kiss his neck and moved her lips to mimic the trail of the cloth, pressing closer to him with every inch. His body relaxed as he allowed her to push him into the pillows. The time apart amplified the electricity between them. Bekah purred involuntarily as their hands and lips traveled around familiar territory.

Elliot took a deep breath. He forced her hands still on his stomach. "Wait."

Here we go, again. Bekah blew out a breath. "You're starting to give me a complex."

He maneuvered them upright, but still cuddled, and squeezed her against his chest. "You know it ain't like that."

"I know. You want me more than you can say but want to wait until we're sure. What's it going to take? I love you, Elliot."

"I love you, baby. I just need it to be really, really right. You know I made a mistake before."

"Lesia."

"You remember her name?"

"Yeah, I'm a woman. We do that." She felt his chest tremble with a repressed laugh.

"Let me ask you something." Elliot paused as if he were trying to formulate the question in the right way. "You were sure about Jeff, right?"

Bekah flinched at her ex-husband's name. "Well, yeah, at the time. It seemed like such a fairy tale. Marry your college sweetheart. Live happily ever after. I did love him, of course. But with twenty-twenty hindsight, I can see how naïve I was."

"So doesn't that make you want to be a hundred percent sure about the Prince Charming who waltzed in next?"

Tell him! Tell him, now! With her face still pressed against his chest, she kept him from seeing the slugfest between her heart and brain. Fever of guilt and embarrassment washed over her with thoughts of a stupid one-night stand with a man she barely knew and, after that, her relationship with Sonny. There would never be a good time. *Keep the analogy going. Tell him that he wasn't next. That you kissed a couple of other frogs. Get it over with.*

She scooted to the end of the couch. "Elliot." He shifted to lock eyes with her. Her heart pounded as her confession thudded in her mind like a rodeo bronco against the stall gate. The countdown to release ticked in her head. *Three . . . two . . .*

Tears invaded her eyes. No doubt, he would leave her. Who wouldn't? Her mouth opened to provide an exit for the dreaded words, but shut again when Elliot reached to the corner of her left eye to brush a tear away. She closed her eyes and kissed his palm as it lingered on her cheek. Before she could think another thought, his hands cradled her face, his lips caressed hers.

His words shocked her more than the kiss. "I'm sorry."

She opened her eyes and stared at him. *What?* Did he just say he was sorry?

Elliot gushed an apology. "You think I doubt you. I don't. Honestly, I don't. I love you more than I thought I could ever love anyone, and I one-hundred percent believe God brought you into my life. That's why it's so important to me we do this thing right. You know you make me cray, girl, with those lips and those hands and everything else you got. But if you'll just trust me and wait a little while, I promise it's all going to come together for us. I don't want to mess this up."

"I don't want to mess it up either. I couldn't bear losing you."

"You're not losing me. I'm sorry I made you think that for a second. Let's just forget I even said what I said. We'll put it in the box of stuff we never mention. That's alright . . . to have a box like that?"

"Yes." She nodded as she tucked her secrets into the imaginary box. "It's alright."

Tuesday, June 4

Bekah smiled despite her sore arms and weak legs when she spotted Gramma Rosamond on the patio. Liz had found the constant motion in the house frayed her grandmother's nerves so tried to give her something to do outside. Their vegetable garden wouldn't be ready for harvest for another few weeks, so the farmer's market supplied the current crops.

Snap beans were today's bounty in the bucket. With the same deftness with which she handled the peas, Gramma made quick work of the beans. She pulled the strings, snapped the beans in half, and dropped the beans in the bucket and the strings onto the newspaper beside her rocking chair in fluid movements.

"Hi, Gramma." Bekah dragged a chair near enough to chat. "Can I help?"

"Well, I suppose so, little miss. I done snapped about half a bushel, but they's some left. Gonna be a good winter once we get these put up."

"Yes, ma'am." Bekah snuck a photo of Gramma then turned the video recorder on and placed her phone on the table between them. *Hope the battery holds out.*

Bekah broached the subject she hoped would be as interesting as their last conversation. "I've been reading about Birmingham back in your day. Did you grow up there?"

"Born and raised. My mama and daddy moved off the farm when the cotton dried up, so daddy could work at the steel mill in the early twenties. Since he come in before most farmers, he kept his job when the Depression hit. I came along in thirty-two, number five outta six. Lawdy, I ain't got no idea how they fed all us, but they managed somehow."

"Your parents came from farmers?"

Gramma laughed. "Yes, child, we all came from farmers and farmers come from slaves."

Slavery. Bekah expected more scoop on recent history but found herself instantly fascinated. "How far back do you know about your family?"

Gramma's arthritis-gnarled fingers stopped snapping beans and hovered over the bucket. "I know my great-grandmother come over in the last slave ship to hit Mobile in 1860."

46

"Eighteen sixty? I thought the slave trade was abolished in the early 1800s."

"Just 'cause it ain't legal, don't mean it stopped. My great-grandmother, Henrietta, was in her mama's belly on the ship. Cotton man bought her mama and a man the traders said was her husband as a pair. Didn't know they was getting a third one at the time."

"So Henrietta was born just before the Civil War started?"

"Born a slave, freed as a child. Her and her mama don't know what happened to the man. Stayed on the plantation grounds long after the war. Owner went back to his family in the North. But there weren't no way for the slaves to go back to they families. Most of them just stayed and lived on the land best they could."

Bekah did some quick math in her head. If Henrietta was born in 1860 and Gramma was born in 1932 . . . "Did you ever meet Henrietta?"

"Sure did. Daddy took us down to visit most he could. I believe she lived 'til I was ten or so."

"That means she would've been around eighty-two when she passed."

"Sounds about right." Sudden laughter burbled from her mouth. "I thought she was so *old*. I done outlived her by five years. Lawdy."

Gramma cracked herself up and her deep, raspy chortle was contagious. The two of them laughed until the familiar sound of the screen door opening interrupted their moment.

Liz stepped out to join them and knelt beside the older lady. "Y'all having way too much fun out here. Want to share?"

Gramma smiled sugary-sweet and delivered a mock scolding. "Me and this young lady just talking and snapping. You shoulda been out here with us if you wanted to hear."

Liz gave Bekah a smile. "Well, I guess I'll try to join you next time. But right now, I got a pot with bacon drippings ready for those beans and a bunch of hungry mouths to feed."

• • • •

Liz stepped onto the front porch into the breezy evening air and let the screen door fall shut. "Ah, you found my favorite spot."

Bekah stopped the motion of the cushy glider swing. "It is peaceful."

"Around here, front porches are usually places where everyone gathers. You know what makes this one peaceful?"

"The sheer curtains? The palmetto ceiling fans? The jasmine trellis?"

"Nope, the glider. It's the only thing out here to sit on. I planned it this way. Backyard's the gathering place here. Front porch is private."

Bekah closed her iPad and uncurled from her spot. "I'm sorry. I'll let you have your alone time."

"No, you stay right there." Liz sat beside her. "Private and alone don't mean the same thing." She sighed as her head fell onto the back cushion.

"Littles in bed?" Bekah used Liz's collective term of endearment.

"Everyone under fifteen is upstairs. That's all I can confirm."

"I don't know how you do it."

"It's easier now than when they really were littles. Diapers, bottles, tears. *That* . . . I don't know how we did. Have to credit grace and dumb luck—and a lot of help too. I'd forgotten how much. I had to ask the Lord for a lot of forgiveness this morning."

"What for?"

"For taking everyone he's placed in our lives for granted. Those TV people been like hummingbirds around a feeder the last week, getting everyone who might possibly be in the show to sign non-disclosures."

"Signed mine yesterday."

"Making that list for them, every local family member, customer, therapist, pastor, teacher, friend, even the one who comes out once a month to cut all the hair that needs cutting . . . seeing all of those names reminded me of how many people love us, sacrifice for us, have made this journey with us."

"Hadn't really thought about all that."

"I hadn't either, not enough. I'm so grateful for everyone, and I don't show it enough. So I asked the Lord to forgive me, and tomorrow, I'll start showing those folks how much I appreciate them."

"That is a lot of blessing you have."

She couldn't suppress the giggle. "With this family, sometimes it's a messy blessing."

"I love your family."

"Especially one of us?" Liz's eyes were closed, but she conveyed the wink in her tone.

She thought she heard a blush in Bekah's reply. "Maybe. But, honestly, there's a lot to love with everyone."

"Like Gramma?"

"Yeah. She's awesome."

"I appreciate you spending time with her. It was sweet watching you today. And it's good for her."

"She's good for me. She told me about her great-grandmother. Henrietta? Has someone else gotten all that history recorded?"

"Oh yeah, there's a big box of it in my closet. My mother, you know, is a history professor, so she lives for this stuff. She got a lot of info from Gramma and Gramma's parents before they passed."

"I recorded her on my phone. Last week she talked about the 16th Street Church bombing. I thought we might talk more about that today, and it might be good for Ida and Annie at the Whitman Five Foundation. Then she went back to 1860 on me."

"You never know what she's gonna talk about."

"Maybe they'll interview her for the TV pilot."

Liz laughed. "She could have her own show."

Haley propped against the cool stone outside her LA Fashion District apartment building and freed her copper-highlighted brown hair from its scrunchie with one hand. With the other, she pressed an oversized cup of vitamin-packed smoothie to her cheeks. The frozen, beaded droplets cooled her face as her heart rate slowed. Six miles in a little over an hour. Not bad. She deserved a treat so allowed herself an extra pump of turbinado. Since she'd dropped below her 120-pound goal weight, she could spare an ounce or two.

The smog wasn't overpowering today—clear by LA standards—and the chatter of full sidewalks wafted past her on the lightest of breezes. Unable to keep her mind from working on her TV production skills, she lost herself in visualizing the best camera angles to frame stories of the passersby. There was the cliché power couple who seemed to fall out of bed with every possible status-wielding accessory draped on their tanned, toned bodies. Tourists—by the look of them mid-westerners—gawking at the sights unseen before they arrived in her adopted hometown. The homeless person, hidden in a mountain of blankets across the street, moving occasionally while desensitized locals maneuvered around the pile.

"There you are!" The cheery British accent interrupted her imaginings.

"Vanessa!" Haley squealed and hugged her roommate. "I thought you were getting in tomorrow. Where's your suitcase?"

"Already in the flat. I arrived more than an hour ago. Needed to walk to combat the jet lag. Assumed you were running. How'd you do?"

"Better than my worst, worse than my best." Haley stepped into the revolving door.

Vanessa followed with a shake of her head. "Sounds like a saying you moved here with. Let me guess . . . your dad."

"Amazing how you know him so well without ever meeting him."

"Well, you do talk about him quite a lot. I feel like he's some sort of Texas legend. Billboards everywhere with his toothy grin and a Stetson." She affected her idea of a Texas accent as they climbed the stairs. "Hey y'all. My name's Billy Bob Simmons, and I'm the most interesting man in the Lone Star State."

Haley unlocked their apartment door. "You need to work on that accent. And Randall, his name's Randall."

"Randall, then." Vanessa winked, dropped her tiny red Louboutin bag on the sofa, and unzipped the suitcase that took up most of the living area floor. "I brought gifts!"

She glowed like Santa Claus. A stunning, six-two, mahogany-skinned Santa Claus with high cheekbones and silver extensions to her mid-back. Haley adored this side of Vanessa. The woman truly loved giving. She rummaged through the suitcase, pulled a pair of leopard-print pumps and a copper-colored shoulder bag from the depths, and held them over her head like a prizefighter who just won a new belt. "Stella McCartney, baby!"

Haley dropped to the floor beside her and hugged the bag. "It's gorgeous! And so soft."

"And it matches your new balayage."

"Ooh, which reminds me, I saw a model with copper contacts the same color as my highlights. It looked pretty cool. Like some new Avengers superhero. What do you think?"

"Leave it to Hollywood, darling. Don't ever think of masking your gorgeous blues." Vanessa leaned back onto her elbows.

Haley kicked off her sneakers and replaced them with the pumps. "I love them." She stood and paced the tiny living room. "Wow, I love the perks of living with a globe-trotting supermodel."

"Well, I love having the best roommate-slash-wine buddy-slash-cat sitter . . . hey, where is Archibald the Great?"

"Sunning on the terrace." Haley opened the balcony door and Vanessa's flat-faced Persian cat sauntered into the room, passing Haley with head held high as if the human were a subordinate lackey.

When he spotted Vanessa, he belted a loud meow and scurried to her. She scooped him up, nuzzled her face in his bluish-white fur, and the purring commenced. "Oh, Archie, your mum missed you!"

"And he missed you. He skulked around for days wailing and looking at me like I was some Bond movie villain who kidnapped you. I even tried to call him 'Ahh-chee,' like you do. Nothing worked until I brought him some salmon from the market. You two can enjoy reconnecting while I'm gone."

"Oh, right. When are leaving?"

"Monday."

"Mississippi?"

"Alabama. Same thing basically." Haley sighed as she stepped out of her pumps and moved to the kitchen sink to rinse her cup. "Won't be needing heels there."

Vanessa allowed Archie to slink out of her arms and joined Haley at the island. "Oh, come on . . . I thought you'd be excited about going back to your part of the world."

"Please. Alabama is as far from Dallas as LA is. Distance and culture. We're going to be out in the country recording with a family with fifteen kids, thirteen adopted. They probably haven't even heard of Starbucks, or a juice bar, or Stella McCartney."

"Fifteen? Wow. That should be interesting."

"Chandler's excited about it. Thinks it could be his next big series."

"Which means it could be your next big series too. Climbing up the ladder. Just get in there and do that thing you do that makes them cry."

"Emotional TV is good TV." Haley grinned as she repeated her boss Chandler's mantra. "Took me a while to get it down. I just make myself think of something sad so I tear up a little. Almost always makes the people do the same thing. Empathetic impulse."

"I don't know how you do that. I can't force it. If they want my eyes watery for a shoot, they have to wave a jalapeno in my face."

Haley's nose scrunched. "My way sounds better. Maybe I can work with you on it when I get back."

"Is the boyfriend going?"

Haley rolled her eyes. "As a production assistant. And you can say his name."

Vanessa shook her head as if she'd given it a lot of thought. "No, I don't think I can. You'll come to your senses soon, and I can say the name of your *new* boyfriend. The one you deserve."

"Nessa . . ."

"He's a hothead, darling. You deserve better. And that's all I'm going to say about it." She picked up her cat and sauntered toward her room. "Come, Archie, let's go unpack."

Liz glanced at the clock as she slid out of bed. *2:43 a.m.* "I got it," she whispered to stop Jim from getting up. Pulling her robe on over the thin, faded t-shirt and shorts that had served as her pajamas for years, she hustled upstairs toward the sound of the retching.

When she reached the girls' bathroom, she saw she wasn't the first caretaker on the scene. Peanut clung to the porcelain toilet, her small body heaving out acidic chunks of last night's dinner. Amy stood over her, holding her hair out of her face and telling her she would be okay. Beth soaked a washcloth in cool water at the sink.

She brought the cloth to Liz and held it to her at arm's length, turning her face from the toilet. Splotches covered her face, and her eyes watered as she made the handoff. "Sorry, Mom. I just can't stand it."

"You go on back to bed, baby. Thanks for trying." Liz folded the cloth, pressed it on her baby girl's neck, and took her hair from Amy's hand. "You, too, Amy. You're a good sister. I can take over now."

Liz sunk to the floor and massaged her youngest child's trembling frame. When it seemed as if her stomach had to be empty, Liz flushed the toilet and pulled Peanut into her arms. She hummed and rocked as she pressed her cheek to the eight-year-old's forehead. *Good. No fever.*

"You okay, Peanut?" She'd have to stop using the pet name soon as their youngest hit her tween years, but not tonight. The apropos nickname was given by eight-year-old Amy as she cooed into the tiny baby's face the day Jim and Liz brought her home from the hospital. Except for Hope, who had Down syndrome like Amy, Amy had shown little to no interest in any of her other younger siblings, but she quickly took to mothering the four-pound preemie born to a teenage meth addict.

Liz smiled at the memories of Amy bestowing boundless love on their Peanut from that first day through tonight. No one could avoid the responsibility to care for others in a household their size. All of the children looked out for one another, but the Amy-Peanut bond stayed strong.

"I'm okay, Mama," Peanut whispered.

"Alright, let's stand up." Liz pushed them both from the floor. "Just a rumbly tummy, baby?"

"I guess. I was just lying in bed thinking about the TV show and, all of a sudden, I needed to throw up."

The TV show. Why did I ever agree to this?

Liz kissed her forehead. "It kinda makes me want to throw up too. But right now, you need to go back to bed and try to sleep. They'll be here by seven. And remember, you don't have to have anything to do with it if you don't want to. That's part of the deal I made with Mr. Lee."

"Mama, why don't you call him Chandler like Daddy does?"

Liz chuckled. "You sure are observant, little one. I guess I'm not quite sure yet whether we're going to be friends."

· · · ·

Hour by hour, Liz empathized with Peanut more. Sleep did nothing other than tease her after she settled back in beside Jim. Adding to her annoyance, he slept soundly, despite her quiet hopes he would wake up and hold her. At five-thirty, they were out of bed, going about their routine as if it were any other Monday.

The first eighteen-wheeler rumbled up the driveway at six-thirty, waking anyone who wasn't already up. After that, chaos. Even more than normal. Excitement became a larger-than-life character of its own, infecting everyone in the house. Even the dogs seemed buzzed.

"I guess we better eat inside today." Liz wiped her hands, then placed the mammoth bowl of chicken salad in the center of the kitchen island. "Jordan, start rounding up your brothers and sisters."

Jordan took her attention away from her view of the backyard commotion. She smiled at her mother and sing-songed, "Yes, ma'am. But it ain't gonna be easy."

"*Isn't* going to be easy. You let them know this family still eats together. Mama says."

"Even Vee?"

"Especially Vee."

Jordan knew her sister well. All the others had already said grace and were eating by the time Victoria flounced in to fill her plate. Liz noticed her newest accessory right away. "What in the world is that?'

Elation oozed from every pore as Vee modeled her new body camera. "It's a GoPro! Marshall gave it to me this morning. This thing is the jam! It's so much better than using my phone."

Liz rolled her eyes toward Marshall. "You've created a monster."

"Not created," Marshall grinned at his mom. "Just feeding it."

Liz supposed a word of caution, even if in one ear and out the other, couldn't hurt. "Well, you just remember this isn't your TV show, and don't be getting in the way."

Vee raised her hand as if swearing in court. "I won't. But Chandler said I can record as much as I like as long as he approves anything before I post. I'm working on a TikTok for today. Day One."

Jim stopped mid-bite. "Tick what?"

Twelve-year-old Emma answered with an educated air. "TikTok, Dad. Everyone knows TikTok."

All the kids laughed as Liz exchanged glances with Jim. *Don't let them see you sweat, but we're out of our depth.*

Jim tapped his watch. "Yeah, I know. It means hurry up and finish eating. We got trucks coming in. Everyone who's not helping Mom clean up needs to be helping me and Will. Tick tock."

Wednesday, June 12

"Why do you need all these lights out here in the daytime?" Liz questioned Chandler while a stylist flitted around her face, adding makeup and fussing with her hair. Vee hovered next to her, recording the entire process.

Chandler chuckled as he walked between the huge umbrella lights flanking the cameras on the patio. "I know. It's crazy isn't it? The sun is so bright, but it makes shadows. These keep your faces from being shaded. And they're different sizes and outputs so we can balance both you and Jim in the same shot since you're toned differently."

Liz caught Vee's eyes and laughed. "Toned differently. That's the nicest way I've heard it said."

The African American stylist admonished her. "I know black's not supposed to crack, but try not to laugh. You're crinkling." She dabbed around Liz's eyes with a foam blotter.

"Yeah, Mom. Don't crinkle." Vee winked at her mother and moved into the yard to get a long shot of the hubbub.

Jim emerged from the kitchen, his favorite Alabama Tide baseball cap in his hand. Close on his heels hurried another stylist, a young man who wore the expression of a man who'd spent the last hour trying to put pants on a donkey. When he locked eyes with Chandler, he threw his hands up, shook his head, and rolled his eyes, an unmistakable *please, do something with him!* written all over his face.

Jim crossed the patio to Chandler in three strides. "You did say you wanted us to be normal, right? Well, I been wearing this cap for almost ten years, and Bama's going to the College World Series next week."

The stylist stopped right behind him. He stage-whispered to Chandler. "And he's not happy about his hairline."

Jim plunged an imaginary dagger into his heart. "Harsh, man." He rolled his eyes and laughed before admitting, "Maybe a little true."

Chandler wrapped an arm around Jim's shoulder. "We definitely want you to be yourself in all the daily life interactions we film, whatever you would normally do and wear."

Jim brightened.

"However," Chandler continued, making Jim's smile fade, "what we're filming today is different. We call these vignettes. They're interviews with your family we'll scatter through the episodes. We want them to stand out as being different. If we do it right, they'll come across like you're having a conversation with the viewers. So let's try it Chad's way. He's one of the best. You can trust him."

"Alright, Chad." Jim nodded his reluctant compliance to the stylist. "Good luck."

Jim turned his attention to his wife. "Well, hello, Halle Berry!" He wolf-whistled, moved to her, and bent for a kiss. Her stylist gasped and Liz drew back. She circled her face with a finger in explanation. "Kobi's worked hard on this. We better wait."

He plopped beside her and picked up her hand. "Is this okay?" he questioned both stylists. "Can we hold hands? Sheesh, I'm starting to wonder about this whole thing."

Liz pushed him away from her and teased. "*Now* you're wondering? Too late now, James Monroe Caragin. You made this bed."

"Yep, guess I did. As long as I'm in it with you, Elizabeth Pearl Gaines Caragin, it'll be good."

"You just had to throw that in there? You know I don't want that one getting on TV, bless Gramma Pearl's heart."

"You started with the whole names. I thought it was gonna be a thing."

They laughed and touched foreheads, sneaking a chance to be alone in a crowd with a knack they'd developed as their family and business grew. A coo from a twenty-something brunette with copper-highlights bounding toward them intruded on their moment.

"You two are adorbs!" She extended her hand. "I'm Haley Simmons. Nice to meet you."

Chandler expanded the introduction. "Haley's one of our producers. She's in charge of the vignettes, so she'll be the one asking the questions off-camera."

"I'm so pumped!" She exuded the energy and enthusiasm of a puppy on Red Bull. "I've learned all I could about you, but I am so looking forward to learning more." She clapped her hands and raised her voice. "Are we ready?"

Jim and Liz nodded before they realized her question was more for the crew than for them. The bouncy young lady transformed into the commander of the patio. Kobi and Chad went behind the cameras. Lighting techs hovered with devices to check the light balance. The cameraman took his post. Chandler stood beside the camera and smiled at the Caragins, giving them a thumbs up.

Haley settled into the Adirondack chair and faced Jim and Liz. "Tell me about Elliot."

The open-ended question left Liz searching for a starting point. After a few silent seconds, Jim answered. "Well, Elliot's our oldest, turning twenty-six next month. He's a youth pastor at a church in Whitman. Is that what you're asking?"

Haley smiled at him with her whole face. "And cut."

The red light on the camera went dark, and the operator stood up straight. The person holding the fuzzy boom mic overhead relaxed. Haley leaned toward them and spoke with the kind tone of a kindergarten teacher explaining the rules to her new class.

"I should have explained better. These vignettes are interviews, but they need to come off as if I'm not really here. Like you're having a conversation with the viewer. So, I'll ask a question or give you a prompt. If you'll wait a moment before you answer and start with a complete sentence, that will help. Also, try not to ask me a direct question. At least not until you pause a little so we can have a clean edit if needed. Make sense?"

Liz understood, but in a somewhat foggy way. This thing was more complicated and uncomfortable than she realized. Regardless, her head nodded. Out of the corner of her eye, she could see Jim's head bobbing in tandem.

Haley clapped again. "Ready?" This time Liz noticed her glance to be sure the mic was back in place and the red camera light was on before she gave a more specific prompt. "Tell me how Elliot came into your life."

Liz gazed past the camera as the cobweb-covered day made its way to the surface. "It was Jim and his good Samaritan bent. I would've never stopped." Light tears came to her eyes as Jim squeezed her hand. "It'd been a rough morning. There was this car on the side of the road, man in a shirt and tie looking under the hood. Never the kind of thing he could pass by, so I knew we'd be stopping.

"I stayed in our truck while they worked. Lord, it was hot, but the heat felt kinda good to me and this little breeze blew through the windows. They were taking forever. I'd look back, and they were talking more than working on the car. Finally, I heard the hood close and some goodbye talk and Jim came back."

Jim picked up the story. "He was a minister . . . Samuel Taylor. Showed up at our house the next day and told us the Lord had broken his car just so we could meet each other. Him and his wife ran a ministry taking care of unwed mothers. A woman they'd taken in, white girl carrying a mixed-race baby, wanted to give the baby up for adoption. He said the Lord told him we was meant to be the parents."

Haley's mouth dropped open. "Wow, quite a leap."

"Well," Jim continued with a shake of his head, "it wasn't such a humongous leap after all we talked about." He looked at Liz to gain her permission, and she nodded. "Liz said it'd been a rough morning. We were on our way home from the hospital . . . just miscarried our second baby. She was still crying, saying maybe God didn't mean for us to have a baby, when I saw Samuel pulled over.

"Maybe it wasn't the nicest thing to do to Liz, stopping to help him, but I was just feeling like I had to get out of the truck and do something."

"He's a fixer." Liz added. "Couldn't fix me, but he knew he could fix a car." She stroked his bicep and tilted her head onto his shoulder.

"I guess that coulda been part of it. Anyways, two seconds after I got my head under his hood, he asked how my day was going and, I have no idea why, but I just went to telling him everything about me and Liz and the two babies we lost. I'm not big on sharing most of the time. I guess I needed to talk about it.

"I got the car patched up enough to make it into town. He told me he'd be praying for us and God had a way of working things out. But, you know, that's just something people say a lot down here. Did seem like he meant it, though. Gave me what I needed to get back in my truck and be there for Liz instead of just being mad about it all."

"So," Haley prompted, "you exchanged contact information, and he came to see you the next day."

Jim shook his head. "Nope. I'm not even sure I told him my name. He noticed the Caragin Farm logo on the truck. That's how he found us."

"And," Haley asked, "you obviously said yes to taking the baby."

Jim chuckled. "She did. Before I could even register exactly what he meant, she was crying and saying, 'yes, yes, it's a miracle, yes.'"

"It *was* a miracle!" Liz defended herself. "We picked him up from the hospital a month later. He was a month early but healthy and white . . . so white. We thought Samuel got it wrong about him being mixed, but his skin darkened as he got older.

"Honestly," Liz closed her eyes and swallowed hard, "Elliot saved me. Inside my head, I thought I must not deserve to be a mom. We'd only told a handful of people about the two others. Folks just didn't talk about it the way we do now. It was like they really weren't babies since they weren't born. But they were real. I had real babies inside me, and all of a sudden, I didn't. I just kept it all to myself. I've always been a happy person, but it weighed me down."

"I'm sure I wasn't much good neither," Jim said. "I could see how sad she'd been getting, but I didn't know how to help. Elliot brought the light back to her eyes." He reached over and cupped her cheek in his hand, and she kissed his fingers. "Samuel had it right. God meant for us to have Elliot."

Haley allowed a moment of silence before she let out a breath. "And cut." She turned to Chandler and mouthed the word *gold*.

Jim squirmed as Chad pressed paper towels onto his face to blot the sweat. Who would've ever thought he'd be in front of his rustic nursery storefront with a Hollywood makeup professional fluttering around? Who'd have ever thought he'd even be thinking of the word *rustic*? Dang. These people were wearing off on him already.

No amount of admonition to relax, however, could make him truly comfortable with foundation and eyeliner. *Hope my friends never find out about this.*

"Nothing personal," he muttered to Chad. "I just don't like no one messing with my face."

"Really? You've never had a facial?

"Nope."

"Or a shave where they wrap a nice steamy towel around your face before they lather you up?"

"Nope."

"What about getting shampooed when you get your hair cut?"

"I *wash* my own hair. The lady who comes to cut the kids' hair takes care of mine with a number two shaver."

Chad's clucks of disapproval made him chuckle. The look of disbelief on the young man's face made him laugh harder. "You ain't never met no one like me, have you?"

Chad affected a Southern accent as he shook his head. "No, I ain't."

From behind them, Haley laughed. "I see you two are communicating."

Jim winked at Chad. "Like two black-eyed peas in a pod."

"Good. We'll get ready while you finish primping."

Jim submitted to Chad's artful touch as Haley conferred with camera, lighting, and sound techs. She moved with complete confidence for someone he supposed wasn't much older than Elliot. Impressive.

He surveyed today's backdrop, the front of the nursery. Haley chose the spot after they finished their golf cart tour of the property. From here, she said she could be sure to get the Caragin Farm sign in the shot. While the faded, non-descript sign seemed acceptable to the location crew, other changes were obvious. A bright-striped awning shaded the metal door and petunia-laden baskets hung beneath each window.

Jim nodded to the wooden cart loaded with an elaborate display of hydrangeas, geraniums, zinnias, and most all of his best summer sellers. "I guess the crew wasn't happy with the metal rolling racks I had here."

Chad dabbed a foundation sponge under Jim's eyes. "Just trying to zhuzh it up a little."

"Zhuzh? What in the world is that?"

"You know. Adding a little pop of wow to something that's already nice."

Haley called to him from the front door near an old-timey soda shop stool. *No idea where that came from either.* "Jim, ready to join us?"

One last instruction from Chad. "Close your eyes." A fluffy powder brush skimmed his face. "There you go, honey." Chad pulled the makeup bib off and patted his shoulder, letting Jim know with a raised eyebrow that his work was done.

A tech had her hands around Jim's neck, attaching a lavalier mic before he quite sat down on the stool. Fuzzy boom mic guy poised for duty off to the side. The lighting girl took readings with her meter and gave a thumbs-up to the camera operator.

Haley took a spot under the camera on an armless camp chair. Her kindergarten teacher's grin lit up her face. "All set?"

"Yeah." Jim sat up straight. "Chad got me all zhuzhed up." He laughed along with the entire production crew, proud of himself for amusing them.

Haley laughed the loudest. "Whew! Good thing I wasn't drinking anything. It would've spewed everywhere." She shook her head as the laughter died down.

A clap of her hands. "Okay, everyone. Ready." With her lifted finger, the red light on the camera shone. She inhaled and tilted her head toward Jim with a smile. "Tell me about Caragin Farm."

Hoping she appreciated that he was a quick learner, Jim paused a moment and formed a complete sentence. "Caragin Farm started with me working at a nursery my Uncle Ray owned on the other side of town. His was mostly shrubs and trees. Not as big as we've grown but pretty good-sized. I worked there every summer since I was about fifteen."

"You've always enjoyed working with plants?'

Jim smiled. "I can't say I *enjoyed* it, least not back then. It was hot, hard work. But there wasn't a lot of jobs to be had around here, so I was grateful. Still am. I learned a lot. Uncle Ray and Aunt Virginia didn't have kids, so they treated me like their own. When me and Liz got married, we moved into a little Jim Walter house on their land."

"Jim Walter?"

"It's what you'd probably call a modular now. Stick-built. Kinda like building a house with a kit. They used to be everywhere in the county. Very simple, inside and out. Liz took to fixing up the inside, and I would bring up shrubs that didn't sell or were kind of puny to plant around the outside. That's when I really started getting the landscaping bug and learning more about plants and flowers and irrigation."

"I'm sure your uncle appreciated that."

Jim smirked. "Can't say he always appreciated it. Ray wasn't big on change. When I started toying around with the irrigation system or pushing to buy different varieties, he balked a little. Then again, it was his money I was trifling with. Guess it's understandable."

"When did you start Caragin Farm?"

"We opened in 2000. Y2K. Ray loaned us the money to buy this land and get started."

"No ill feelings that you were starting up some competition?"

The thought had never occurred to Jim. "No, nothing like that. First, it was just annual flowers and bulbs. Not the kind of inventory he was selling. But even if . . . he wouldn't have never looked at it as competition. Never met a more humble, generous man. He even came to work for me in '06. Just retired two years ago."

Haley tapped on her tablet for a couple of seconds, then returned her attention to him. "Tell me how your family looked then, in 2000, when you opened the nursery."

Jim's fingers played through the air as he back calculated. "Elliot was six. Will, just shy of five. Laurel, two going on thirteen." The memory caught in his throat and prompted a wisp of melancholy. *How have those babies gotten so big?*

He blinked it away. "Liz's folks gave us a fifty-year lease on the twelve acres out here that Rosamond deeded to them. At the time we opened, we was living in a doublewide. Had the sheetrock up in the farmhouse and working on finishing it. Good thing, 'cause Marshall and Victoria came along pretty soon."

"How old were you and Liz then?"

"Twenty-seven." *Oops, full sentences.* "We was twenty-seven."

The number seemed to boggle Haley. "New business, building a house, married with three kids at twenty-seven?"

"Too young to know any better, I guess."

A laugh from the crew. Haley took a slurp of her smoothie. "Just makes me feel a little lazy is all." She waited for the quiet to return. "You and Liz and your unique multi-racial family. Get much opposition?"

Not quite sure what she's looking for. "Opposition?"

"Any racism causing trouble for you?"

"Oh . . . that kind of opposition. By then, most anyone with a gripe about us had settled down. I don't remember anything bad going on then."

Haley studied her tablet. "I found this article from 2003. Says there was a fire set here that was racially motivated. A hate crime."

Oh. That. Jim nodded. "The fire. Me and Liz took the kids, there was five of them then, for a long weekend to the beach. First and last time we did that. Whoo, boy." He could practically feel the sand in the low pile carpet of the cinderblock mom-and-pop motel, hear the wheezing window unit that barely took the edge off the Florida heat.

Haley's stare brought him back around. Of course, she couldn't see why he'd be amused right now. Back to the story. "Third day, before the sun was up, we get a call from Ray. There's been a fire. Now, gotta tell you this here. Ray and Virginia were staying at our place because of Elliot."

"Elliot? Wasn't he with you?"

"Yeah. But the night before we was set to leave, Elliot comes and tells us he doesn't have 'peace' about leaving. Nine years old. But I'm telling you, really upset. Crying. We thought it was silly, of course, but asked Ray and Virginia if they'd come stay just to calm him down. Else, we could tell he was just gonna be miserable.

"They'd brought this big mutt of theirs, and he was barking his head off. Ray heard trucks on the gravel and thought he smelled smoke. Virginia called 911 while he set off for the nursery. Fire trucks got there real fast. If they hadn't been here, it woulda been a whole lot worse. Could've lost most everything."

Haley leaned forward in her chair. "So Elliot saved the day?"

Jim nodded. "Yep. In a big way."

"The articles I read said there were racist slurs spray-painted on the walls."

"Mmm, hmm. Bad ones. Couple of swastikas. By the time we got home, there was two news trucks from Birmingham. More came in overnight. Everyone was on edge because a black church down south of here had a fire a couple months earlier. Fear peddlers . . . almost seemed to be wanting 1963 all over again. Rosamond stayed in tears. We was worried too—especially for our kids."

"So when I asked about opposition . . . you didn't remember this?"

"I get why you're confused. But there's more. Something that didn't make the headlines. Those feds who got called in because of the hate crime issue found out who done it real quick. They weren't racists at all. They owned a nursery between here and Birmingham. Seems we'd been growing fast enough to make them lose some business, so they wanted to stop us. Thought the racist angle would throw suspicion somewheres else. Idiots."

"You're right. I didn't read anything about that. What happened to them?"

"Two of them went to jail for a few years. Wound up losing the business they was trying to protect by eliminating competition. Shame, really. But can't say I felt bad for them. Sorry if that ain't the story you was looking for."

Haley's shoulders relaxed. "Still a good story. While I'm sorry that happened, it's honestly good to know it wasn't racism. You can understand why people are interested in that angle though . . . wondering if the South has really changed or not."

"Not perfect yet. No place will be this side of heaven. But there's been a lot of good change just in my lifetime."

"But there are still times, like the church you mentioned that burned the same year."

Hate to pop her bubble, but . . . "Electrical fire. Didn't run that story much either."

"You're kidding."

"Look. I ain't saying there's no hate, no racism. I'm sure you can find it just about under every rock you turn over. Problem is, I think more people want there to be trouble than want peace. Trouble sells more newspapers, if there are still newspapers. You know what I mean. I'd rather look at the progress we've made and the ways, imperfect as they may be, we try to get along."

Haley smiled. "You're a wise man."

Jim shook his head. "Shoot, I wouldn't go that far. Just seems to make the most sense to me. Want my kids to live that way, so I need to show them what it looks like."

Another smile from Haley. "And cut."

The breath Bekah held came out with a quiver. Thick mist in her eyes trailed down her cheek as one tear as the Jeep taillights faded into the night. *Whew. Barely held it together that time.* No need to make him feel bad for going back to Whitman every week. He had to be there. She needed to work at the farm. The idea of the summer spent in different cities seemed much more manageable before they started living it.

The text tone from her back pocket made her flinch. Elliot or Sonny? *Please be Elliot.* Amazing how many thoughts can spill through your mind in the time it takes to retrieve a phone and look at the screen.

Miss you.

Good. She typed the same words in reply to Elliot, thankful it wasn't Sonny. Sonny had sent the same kind of brief messages for the last several weeks. A few words saying he missed her, a sad-faced selfie, a funny gif. None of the texts were salacious, but they were more than a little suspicious and almost impossible to defend if anyone, especially Elliot, ever saw them.

Most of the time, she didn't even reply and always deleted them as quickly as she could. Hopefully, he'd be distracted by someone or something else soon. Otherwise, how could she make him stop? She wandered down toward her new friend, the swing by the pond, counting on the starry sky and chirping crickets to soothe her frayed nerves.

Someone else had beaten her there. Laurel? Vee? No.

The young lady startled from the swing when Bekah said hello. She smiled and extended a hand. "Hi. I haven't met you. I'm Haley."

"Oh, hey. I've heard about you from Jim and Liz. I'm Bekah."

"Bekah . . . a daughter? I don't remember seeing your name."

Bekah laughed. "Oh, no. I'm not a Caragin. I'm Elliot's girlfriend. I'm working here this summer to get credit for a landscaping certificate I'm finishing up at Whitman U." Bekah sat in the swing. "Mind if I join you?"

"Not at all." Haley sat beside her unable to hide the beer bottle she'd held behind her back. "Do you mind?"

"Of course not." Bekah smiled and kicked off her flip-flops. "Wouldn't mind having one myself."

"I have some more in my trailer if you want."

"No, I'm fine. Don't get up. Maybe some other time." Bekah closed her eyes and breathed in the muggy magnolia-scented air.

Haley sipped from the amber-colored bottle and giggled. "I thought everyone here would be a teetotaler. Most of the religious people I know are."

"Not to excess."

"What?"

"Don't drink to excess. It's what the Bible says about wine. Don't see why that wouldn't apply to beer or other alcohol too."

"Definitely not the way I was raised. Alcohol is the pathway to hell, according to my parents. Mom would have a fit if she knew I drank, even now that I'm an adult."

"Well," Bekah turned her head to look at Haley. "I don't want to contradict Mama. I just don't see anything unbiblical about having a drink now and then. Now, I wouldn't drink in front of the Caragin kids because I don't think Jim and Liz would appreciate it. We haven't directly talked about it, but I think they have enough on their hands without worrying about their kids being tempted by alcohol."

"Truth." Haley pulled one tanned leg onto the swing as she idly pushed against the ground with the other. "Jim and Liz. Do they really have it as together as it seems?"

A warning flag popped into Bekah's relaxing brain. Haley wasn't some new friend of the family. She was a producer with a Hollywood TV crew. Was this a chat or an interview?

Bekah opted for a question. "What do you think?"

"I think they *seem* genuine and loving. But I've only been here a week, and I know everyone has multiple sides. You can keep up a façade for a while but having cameras around every day? When people start to relax, that's when you see true colors—tempers, hypocrisy, bad habits, secrets."

"Wow. Cynical much?"

Haley laughed. "Hmm, I guess so. Sorry, maybe I've worked in this industry too long. People just aren't usually what they seem."

"Sure, I can see that. But, you know, I don't think it's always hypocrisy. Everyone wants to make good first impressions. I mean you don't ever start a relationship by spewing out your faults, do you?"

"Nope. Guess not. It might make things easier, though. Rip the Band-Aid off."

"That would be honest, but, sheesh, how would anyone ever get a second date?"

The ladies giggled, and Bekah fidgeted with the swing chain. "Seriously, though . . . I think you'll find after you've hung out here a while that what you see with Jim and Liz is what you get. I've never seen two people who live out their faith more on a daily basis."

"Sounds churchy."

"You say that like a bad thing." Bekah pulled a leg onto the swing to face Haley more directly.

"Like you said . . . I'm a little cynical." Haley shook her head before she made eye contact. "Let's just say my experiences haven't been the best with good ole church folks."

The corners of Bekah's mouth lifted. "Now, that accent is *not* California. Where are you from?"

Haley giggled. "Oops, my Texas slip is showing. I've lived in LA for five years, but I grew up in Dallas. What about you? Alabama native?"

"Yeah, but I grew up on the coast. Came up here for college. Moved to Atlanta for a bit and came back."

"Big city life not for you?"

"Kind of. Needed a fresh start. Sometimes I miss the city, though."

"You mean where there's more to do at eleven o'clock on a Saturday night than drink beer by the pond?"

"Yeah," Bekah answered before she reflected. "But then again, making a new friend by the pond compared to killing myself in three-inch heels just to hang out in a club with people I barely know but want to impress . . . maybe it's not so bad here."

Haley's smile made her nose crinkle. "Maybe not."

Bekah's text tone interrupted. She slid the phone from her pocket, scanned the screen, and tapped delete.

"You need to answer that?"

"No. Not right now." Bekah clicked the ringer off and dropped the phone into her lap. "Hey, I bet I know someone in the Caragin fam you haven't met."

"Oh, yeah? Who?"

"Gramma Rosamond. Liz's grandmother."

"She lives with them?"

"Lives with Will and Tamika up the road. But she's on the back porch every Tuesday afternoon. Trust me, she could have her own show."

The dead air allowed for no respite from the stifling heat. Bekah rolled the last fragment of ice inside her mouth. The more surface it touched, the more she cooled down a little. On the walk from the greenhouses to the swing, she must've sweated a gallon. Haley, on the other hand, looked like a mirage floating across the desert toward her with bouncy steps, ponytail swinging like a cheery pendulum, and not a bead of sweat anywhere visible.

"I think I hate you right now." Bekah screwed the top back on her empty bottle.

"What?"

"You look like a shampoo commercial, and I look like . . . the girl in the flu commercial who didn't take the right medicine."

Haley laughed. "You've been working hard. I've been in the editing bay in a freezing cold trailer. Probably don't want to hear this, but the heat feels kinda good to me."

Bekah nodded her head toward Haley's accessory. "You brought a camera?"

"You said she could have her own show. I want to be ready. It's okay, right?"

"Sure. I recorded her with my phone last time. She didn't even see it. She can only see things in her peripheral vision, and I think that's not even great. And she can't hear well."

"Anything else?"

"Yeah, she also drops in and out of time. Seems like the farther away, the better she remembers."

At the edge of the patio, Bekah stopped when Haley paused to take a few snaps of Gramma in her rocking chair. Flowered apron over her plain cotton house dress. Pink Skechers. Fingers working rhythmically on the vegetable of the day.

Haley's eyes shone. "I love her already."

"I know, right?"

"Who's there?" Gramma halted her pea shelling when her spidey senses picked up on the visitors.

"It's me, Gramma." Bekah knelt beside her to get into her field of vision. "Bekah, remember me?"

"Oh, yes, I remember." She chuckled as if they shared a private joke.

"I brought a friend." Bekah motioned for Haley to come in closer. "Her name is Haley. She works for the TV show."

Haley followed Bekah's moves, squatting near Gramma and raising her voice. "Pleased to meet you."

"You gonna put me on the TV?" Another chuckle burbled out.

"Would you like to be on TV?" Haley stood and grinned at Bekah.

"Lawdy! I don't think so." Gramma dropped the pea in her hand and smoothed the white hair from her face. "I must look a mess."

Bekah pulled two chairs up close. "You look fabulous. But we just want to talk. Is that okay? We can help you shell."

The two young women sat when the older lady hummed her approval. Haley steadied her camera on the chair arm, making sure Gramma was in the screen. Bekah pressed record on her phone and propped it on the table beside their subject.

Gramma raked her hands through the bucket on her lap and lifted a few black-eyed peas. "I think I'm about done with this batch. You two sisters?"

"No, ma'am," Bekah winked at Haley. "Haley's my friend. She's from California."

"California? Lawdy. You a long way from home."

"Yes, ma'am."

"What you doing in Alabama?"

"I'm helping make a TV show about Liz and Jim and their family. Bekah said you might have some stories to tell."

A mischievous grin spread across Gramma's face. "Oh, I got stories."

Haley shifted her weight forward and opened her iPad, a subtle posture change that seemed to transform the conversation from friendly talk to an interview. "Well, tell me a little bit about your story. You were born in . . ."

"Nineteen and thirty-two. Birmingham, Alabama. Fifth out of six. My brother Waddell came along two years later."

"That was right after the Depression. Times had to be tough as an African American family with six kids."

"Tough as nails. But we only knew what we knew then. Other folks had it much worse. My daddy had a job, worked in the steel mill, and my mama took care of us and took in washing too. We had a little house just inside the city limits."

"Do you have a favorite memory from then?"

"Hmm." Gramma tilted her head to her left shoulder as the memory curled her lips up. "I used to love going to the movies. We called it the picture show back then. We could walk to the theater. It cost thirty-five cent to get in on Saturday afternoons. I met Woodrow there."

"Woodrow?"

"My husband. He hadn't been back from the war long when I first saw him. I was only sixteen. My, he was handsome. I guess he thought I was pretty too. Wasn't long before he was walking me home after the show."

"He was how much older than you?"

"Eight years."

"What did your parents think about him?"

"Oh, they loved Woodrow. He was at the theater because it was his second job, cleaning up and being the usher to the Negro section in the balcony. He worked at the funeral home, too, while he went to college on the GI Bill. He had potential, my daddy said."

"You said the Negro section in the balcony. How hard was it growing up in the segregated South?"

"Maybe not so terrible as you might think. Because everything was so segregated, we didn't even see white folks much. We had our own stores, schools, pool halls, funeral homes, churches of course."

"No separate water fountains, bathrooms, waiting rooms?"

"Oh, yes. In town, all those things." Gramma rocked a little harder, her hand patting her chest in time with the movement of the chair. "There was worse things too. Things make you see that some people thought our people were less than they was. My daddy, he was a kind of 'keep your head down and work hard' man. So that's what we did . . . until fifty-five."

"Nineteen fifty-five?"

"Miss Rosa Parks got arrested for not giving up her seat to a white man."

"Very brave."

"I read later she said she wasn't brave, just tired . . . tired of giving in."

"That changed things in Birmingham?"

"Lawdy, yes. Woodrow and me been married five years by then, had Addie and John. Woodrow made professor at Miles College, but it didn't pay like you might think today. I'd leave my two with my neighbor and take care of Dr. Speight's girls. They was three and five when I started."

"You rode the bus to their house? Like Rosa Parks?"

"Oh, no. Dr. Speight, he sent his driver to fetch me after he got dropped off at the hospital."

"Chauffeured around town? Not too bad."

Gramma wagged her head. "I didn't get to sit in the back. Rode up front with the driver. His name was Henry. Missing three fingers on his right hand."

Bekah smiled. *Amazing . . . her recall of decades-old details when she won't be able to remember my name in five minutes.*

Haley looked amused too. "That family, the Speights, they treated you well?"

Gramma pushed off with her foot to rock a little. "They was good white folks. From Pittsburgh, so not used to all the ways down here. The missus, Jane was her Christian name, she wanted to fit so much with the society crowd, but it was hard for her to get in with them Southern garden club ladies. We both learned a lot about what was expected."

"Like?"

"Like how to put on a tea, when to wear which gloves, how the children are to only speak when spoke to, how to not be too friendly with the help."

"What do you mean?"

Gramma took a moment, as if flipping through the aged pages of a mental photo album. "One day, I remember I had to bring my two to the Speight house because my neighbor was sick. Missus, she said it would be okay. Her girls was a little older than them, but they took to playing in the backyard, having a good time. A couple of the garden club ladies came over for tea, and when they saw Miss Joanna and Miss Kathryn running into the house with my Addie and John, they let my missus know that was not proper."

"What did they say?"

"I don't know exactly what was said, but she brought my babies into the kitchen where I was cutting the crusts off the tea sandwiches and told me they needed to stay there the rest of the day. I asked did they do something wrong, and she said no, but she wouldn't look me in the eye. I never took them back after that."

"That's horrible."

Gramma smiled. "It ain't so bad. She just did what she thought she needed to do for her children. A lot of pressure on her with all the talk going around about our folks 'getting out of our place.'"

The screen door banged closed as Liz came out on the patio. "What y'all doing out here?"

Haley glanced up. "Gramma's telling us about working for Dr. Speight in Birmingham. Life in high society."

Gramma handed her bucket of peas to Liz. "High society. Low society. I think it was better to be poor and happy with my family and thought worse of than be so high and mighty and miserable. Trying so hard to be something you ain't. I always say Southern ladies are like magnolia trees. Pretty and glossy and sweet-smelling on the outside but a little trashy underneath." She chortled at her joke.

Bekah and Haley burst out laughing. Liz shook her head as she gathered pea shells from around Gramma's feet.

Haley tapped on her iPad. "I love that one. Society ladies are like magnolia trees."

Gramma corrected her. "I said Southern ladies. Society ladies and regular people ladies all the same. All got secrets underneath they don't want nobody to see. Ain't that right, Lizzie?"

Liz's smile vanished into taut lips as she stared up at Gramma, but she quickly found it again as she stood. "Well, that sounds like a good place to stop for today. Bekah, you probably want to grab a shower before dinner. Haley, you're welcome to join us."

"Thank you, but I have plans. It was nice to meet you, Gramma."

"It was nice to meet you too." Gramma gave a slight wave as Liz helped her move toward the house.

Haley turned her camera off and half-whispered to Bekah. "Did you see that?"

"See what?"

"How Liz changed? How she shut everything down when Gramma mentioned secrets?"

"Alright, Hollywood reporter. I think you're imagining things. Must be the heat."

Haley could tell Jim and Liz were more comfortable than at the first vignette taping. They sank back into their chairs a little, shoulders relaxed as Kobi and Chad fussed with their makeup.

This time they were arranged in a seating area the crew set up at the edge of the pond. The setting would be picturesque on a TV screen, but too much real in reality wouldn't do. The "natural" feel would only work aided by four lighting umbrellas, two cameras, and various headset-wearing assistants.

"Tell me about Will." Haley settled into her chair opposite them, balancing her tablet and a mustardy-green shake.

Jim chuckled. "Will's a great kid. Well, I guess I can't call him a kid anymore. He's a fine young man. Smart. Hard-working. Good husband and father. Him and Tamika live in the brick house you pass on the way up our drive. Liz's grandparents built it when they moved to Fairview."

Haley showed her interest in this rabbit trail. "Gramma Rosamond and Woodrow? When was that?"

Liz answered. "They moved in sixty-three but built the house a little at a time over the years. Gramma still lives there. That's another way Will and Tamika are fine young people. They chose to move in to help take care of her so she could stay in her own place instead of moving somewhere on their own."

Haley said, "Quite a sacrifice for a young couple."

Liz smiled. "It's not a sacrifice; it's family."

Haley titled her head and squinted. "You haven't met *my* family." She laughed before continuing. "Tell me how Will came into your life."

Jim spoke up. "Elliot was . . . two?" He waited for Liz to nod. "Around two, anyways. We got a call from a church friend who was a social worker for the county. This woman, girl really, had showed up at the ER high on something and having contractions. They guessed the baby to be about thirty weeks. Four pounds, eight ounces. He was in NICU on a ventilator, and the mother was in a hurry to get out of the hospital. Didn't even want to see him.

"They offered counselors, a recovery program, everything they could think of, but she rejected it all . . . signed over her parental rights along with her discharge papers. Alabama's got a Safe Haven law that lets babies get dropped off in an ER without the mom being charged for abandoning."

"So," Haley prompted, "another baby God intended for you?"

With a quick glance, Jim suggested Liz answer this one. She winked at him before making eye contact with Haley. "Well, no, we didn't know it right away. Like Jim said, Elliot was about two, the business was starting to grow. Things were going good. I still wanted more babies, but . . ."

She breathed deeply before confiding, "I had another miscarriage about a year after Elliot. Hit me real hard." Jim squeezed her hand as she blinked the mistiness away. "My doctor put me on birth control so my body wouldn't even be trying. Think it helped me get out of the blues faster accepting it just wasn't going to happen. I kind of had it in my brain we'd adopt again but thinking about taking in a crack baby, that scared me. Did I want a baby who would probably have issues his whole life? Did we have the money to pay for special care? I just didn't know."

Haley typed a thought for another question on her tablet before asking, "What made you decide?"

Jim spoke up. "She saw him." They laughed and bumped their heads together.

"It's true." Liz nodded. "I told myself he had too many problems. It would be too hard. They dressed us in gowns and gloves and masks before they even let us in. I thought, *I can't do this.* Then I saw him. So tiny, with all these wires and sticky things on his body, oxygen going in his nose, machines beeping all around. Then it hit me. He was all alone. He needed a family, and it didn't matter what it cost us, we couldn't leave him without a family."

Haley grinned. "He looks perfectly healthy now. Did he have many issues?"

Liz told the story. "It took him four weeks to gain a little over a pound, but he passed all their milestone tests so he came home with no meds or machines. He was so tiny, though. I mean, Elliot came a little early, but he weighed almost seven pounds. Will . . ."

She cupped her opened hands together and held them out toward Haley. "I could hold him like this. We took him to *so* many doctors. He was in the lowest percentile of everything. They finally told us he was perfectly healthy, would just be small. Sure enough, he kept growing but still was always the smallest kid in his class."

Jim added, "And the spunkiest. From the minute he took to crawling, he got into everything. So different from Elliot. Elliot could talk a blue streak, but he always seemed kinda laid back. He liked helping take care of the baby, but once Will got to moving, Elliot wasn't quite sure what to do with him. Before you could say, 'Jack Spratt,' though, they was running around together and wrassling all the time. Will was smaller than Elliot, but he was strong."

"And fearless," Liz said.

Jim joined her. "And playing pranks and making us laugh. He always has a full tank of happy."

Haley asked, "Did he ever ask about his birth parents?"

The shift was deliberate. Casual question . . . serious question . . . repeat. The tactic threw people off-kilter enough to share things without as much of a filter. Another weapon in her emotion-wrenching arsenal. She watched the smiles fade from both of their faces.

Liz straightened her back. "I only remember him asking once. I told him what we knew, which wasn't much of anything, only what Jim said before."

"How did he take that?"

Liz cocked her head, reminding Haley of a mama bear who smelled a human near her cubs. "He took it as fine as he could, I suppose. Never asked anymore. Like we said, Will's always been a happy kid—probably our happiest."

"And now," Haley turned the conversation to Jim, "he's your right hand with the business?"

Jim straightened in his chair. "Sure is. He followed me around the greenhouses as soon as his mama would let him, like a puppy always on my heels. Seems like growing things is in his blood. And like I said, he's smart about it too. Got a real good head for the business. It'll be in good hands for at least another generation."

He winked at Liz, then peered over Haley's shoulder directly into the camera. "For more information, visit caraginfarm.com. Caragin Farm, making your garden grow since 1992."

Haley laughed. "Seems you're telling me this segment is over."

Jim had already begun disentangling himself from his microphone. "Yep. Plants ain't gonna grow themselves. Well, I guess they'll grow themselves, but they ain't gonna sell themselves. Hey, Chad, get this stuff off my face."

Haley pulled her ponytail through the back hole of the Caragin Farm cap Jim gifted her and the rest of the crew on the first day of taping. She tapped a little foundation onto imperceptible, maybe even imagined, wrinkles around her eyes.

She chided her reflection in the makeup trailer mirror. "Wake up, girl. You've started days earlier than five-thirty."

Chad leaned in over her shoulder. "Maybe you're still on LA time. You want some help with that?"

"Maybe you're right." Seeing a friendly face relieved her early morning funk. "No, thanks, though. This face is made for behind the scenes. You got Will fixed up?"

"As much as I could. Honey, I thought Jim was stubborn. I know they're not flesh and blood, but Will didn't fall too far from his adoptive apple tree. He'd only let me put the tiniest bit of powder on, and he's already sweating! Good luck getting him to sit still—or give you your teary-eyed money shot."

Haley winked. "Sounds like a challenge. Guess I'm going to need a double shot of B12 in my smoothie."

"Craftys have the tent set up already, and I think I heard blending when I got my java. Oh, and there's these humongous Princess Leia bun things that are to die for."

"You know I don't do carbs."

"Maybe you should. Would help you fill out those . . ." Chad motioned to the outside edges of her eyes and laughed.

"Thanks a lot." Haley smirked and tossed her makeup wipe at his face.

Ten minutes later, with the help of two production assistants, she had corralled Will into a corner of the main greenhouse. Sunlight streamed through the open glass roof panels. A staggering assortment of blooming petunias, daisies, marigolds, and other annuals stretched behind him like waves of a floral sea in a fantasy painting. The beauty of the location made the bear of a lighting issue worth the effort.

The darkness of Will's skin would help, but Haley could see the sweat problem. She'd set the early morning time to catch him before work. The plan was in vain. Will propped on the edge of a seedling bed table, work gloves on, dirt splatters and sweat splotches already noticeable on his neon green Caragin Farm t-shirt.

Chad pressed dry pads around Will's forehead and cheeks. He shook his head, rolled his eyes, and joined Haley. Oh, well. Guess it will put the real in reality TV. She pasted a smile over her disappointment and settled onto a stool in front of the cameras. "Thanks for meeting me so early."

"This ain't early." Will stretched his arms overhead and cracked his back. "Been up for hours; had to get the baby fed and breakfast made for Tamika. Woman don't do nothing around the house. Like she's the queen or something."

Haley could feel her smile droop. Her brain fumbled for the right words.

Will relieved her with a toothy grin. "I'm kidding. Don't tell her I said that. The camera's not on, right? Whoo . . . you should've seen your face." His whole body shook with laughter.

Haley laughed along with the rest of the crew. "Your mom and dad said you were funny." She wiped the smile abruptly and donned her producer persona. "But seriously, our cameras are always on. That will make a good sound bite."

Will's face fell, but she didn't leave him dangling long. "See, you're not the only funny one." She pointed to the bottom of the camera focused on Will. "When the red light is solid, it's on. And ready if you are."

Haley did some shuffling on her iPad before asking the first question. "Your dad is very proud of your work here. What's your first memory of the greenhouses?"

He gave it a moment of thought. "The frogs."

"The frogs? Not the flowers?"

Will laughed. "Yeah, I guess it's funny, but I suppose they were more on my eye level. I was shorter than this table I'm setting on when Dad started bringing me out here. I would play with frogs for hours. They were all over the place because it was always wet, I guess."

"Sounds like they were your pets. Did you name them?"

"Only the ones I took to the house." Will smiled. "That's when it got fun. I'd put them in the kitchen sink, in the pantry, in the girls' bathroom. Mom hated it, but she couldn't be mad at this face for long. She'd light into fussing at me, talk about spanking me, then, the next thing I knew, we'd be laughing and eating ice cream."

"Sounds like you have a truly special relationship with Jim and Liz."

"Yeah. They're the best. You know anyone else with hearts big enough to take in this many kids?"

"Can't say I do. Fifteen is a lot. When did they tell you that you were adopted?"

Will cocked his head to one side. "You know, I've thought about it before, and I don't remember them ever *telling* me. It's just something I've known as long as I can remember."

"Do you think about it a lot?"

"Think about what?"

"About having been adopted. About your birth parents."

"I guess every adopted kid thinks about it, but I don't spend much time on it."

"Do you and your siblings talk about it with each other?"

"Sure, some. Elliot and me probably the most. Our situations were really different, though. I think his was harder."

"What do you mean?"

"I mean . . ." Will took a break to drink some water. "I know the woman who gave me up was just a girl, high on drugs. She couldn't take care of herself, much less a baby. So it's like she didn't have a choice, much. Elliot's mom coulda kept him. She just didn't want to. I guess it's the same thing, more or less. You gotta find a way to deal with it."

"How did you deal with it?"

Will blew a breath out. "Well, in a family like this, you don't have a lot of time for pity parties. I guess the first time I remember thinking about it was when the twins were born."

"Beth and Sondra?"

"Yeah, Mom and Dad's only DIY babies."

"Tell me about that."

"I guess I was twelve or thirteen. I remember all of us traipsing up into the hospital to see Mom and the girls. There were ten of us by then. The nurses must've thought there was some kinda elementary school takeover. We always made a grand entrance.

"Anyway . . . I remember seeing Mom and Dad holding them, kissing their heads, smiling so big, showing them off to us. I wondered why my birth mom didn't feel that way about me."

Will broke eye contact with Haley. She took him in, this six-foot-plus bear of a man—smart, successful, funny—and her heart fluttered against her ribs. This man who appeared to have it all still longed for something that never existed. Even with loving parents and more than a football team's worth of siblings, a tinge of loneliness, and unworthiness, remained.

Chad was wrong. There could be a chance for a heartstring pull this morning. "Did you ever try to find her?"

Will swallowed and returned his attention to Haley. "Nah. Mom said there was zero trail because of the way she turned me over. She could live next door. She could be in another country by now. Back in the day, I thought about . . ."

"Thought about what?"

"Nah. It's stupid."

Haley implored him to continue with her eyes.

"When I played football—"

"Wait. What? I thought you were too small for football."

"Yeah, I was. Until the summer before junior year, when everything seemed to kick in. I grew so much, some of my friends didn't recognize me when school started. Then the coaches begged me to join the team."

"From water boy to lineman?"

Will laughed. "Yeah, something like that. They put me in at left tackle. And I was pretty good. By senior year, I thought I might be able to get a scholarship. Then—here's the stupid part—I thought I would be a college star, then maybe an NFL star. Then, one day, she'd see me . . . my birth mom . . . you know, in my *Sports Illustrated* writeup . . . hear when my birthday was and where I was born and that I was adopted. Then she'd look me up. She'd be all cleaned up and have her act together, and she'd be proud of me. Just like Mom looked with the girls."

Haley's heartbeat thudded in her ears. The impulse to give him a huge hug almost propelled her from her chair, but her journalistic goal kept her in her seat.

"And now," she continued, "you're a dad."

His thoughtful face broke into the biggest smile Haley had seen yet. "Yes, I am. And my little girl, my Zoe, is always gonna know her mom and dad are proud of her and are gonna take care of her."

"She's a lucky girl." Haley studied her notes. "Whatever happened to your football dreams?"

"Weak heart." Will balled his fist against his chest. "Passed out during a game senior year, and that's what the docs said. They guessed it was because I was born so early and only showed up when I started working so hard."

"It looks to me like you still work very hard."

"Yeah, but not football hard."

"Interesting. Your mom didn't mention the heart thing when I asked if you had health problems."

Will laughed and shook his head. "You are *never* gonna get Liz Caragin to say anything negative about her kids."

"I guess that's a mom thing." Haley had a sudden thought. "Hey, maybe your finding your birth mom dream still might work out. She could see you on this show and contact you."

Will's playfulness faded away. "Hadn't thought about that. Maybe . . ."

Here's a shot. Emotional TV is good TV. "What would you say to her if she did?" Haley invited tears to fill to the brink of her lashes with a mental image of the big guy blubbering at such a reunion. It worked the way she hoped.

Will stared into her watery eyes and small drops puddled in the corners of his own. "Well, uh, I guess . . . I guess I'd want her to know I'm okay. Great, in fact. Introduce her to Tamika and Zoe. And, uh, I . . . whew, so many things."

Haley leaned in toward him and gently prodded, "But what would you *say*?"

Will blinked, which pushed his tears over their reservoirs. "I'd say, 'I forgive you.'" Taking off a glove, he wiped his cheeks with his bare hand. His chin quivered. A big sniff and another blink as he stared at Haley.

Haley framed the shot in her head. *Hold it. Hold it. Hold it.* "And cut."

Elliot stroked Bekah's hand at the Caragin kitchen table. This made getting up before sunrise to make it for first breakfast worthwhile. Sunlight poured through the glass of the windows while a breeze carried the sweet cacophony of robins, cardinals, mockingbirds, finches, and crows through the screens.

The smoothness of her hand, the warmth of her leg pressed against his, the blush on her freckled cheeks, and the smile in her eyes as she tilted her head to touch his were a hundred times better than Liz's hash brown casserole. *No need to tell Mom that, though.*

Jim, Laurel, Marshall, and Cooper finished up their country breakfast, the sustenance to get them through until lunch, while they caught up with Elliot. Liz and their helper, Marta, ate while they cleaned and worked on second breakfast for the younger kids, who weren't expected to work full days in the greenhouses yet.

"Thanks for giving my girl the day off." Elliot grinned at Jim.

Jim pulled his faded Caragin Farm cap tight and returned the grin with a wink aimed at Bekah. "I think she's earned it. Almost outworks Will. Not nearly as delicate as she looks."

Jim yelled toward the living room. "Victoria!"

"Sheesh, I'm coming." Vee bounced into the kitchen, with full makeup, hair in a perfect messy bun, and a spotless Caragin Farm t-shirt French-tucked into her jean shorts. She kissed Liz's cheek and retrieved a Camelbak filled with green sludge from the fridge.

Liz chided. "Honey, you need a real breakfast."

"It's fine." Vee educated her mother. "It's Haley's special recipe. The craftys gave it to me. Gets her through the day. There's kale and vitamins and antioxidants."

Jim opened the door for his brood with a scoff. "What are you turning into? Craftys."

Marshall explained. "That's what they call the folks who feed the crew. They run the craft tent."

"I know what they are. Would just like to keep Hollywood outside this house."

Laurel laughed with a nod to the tiny cameras in the corners of the kitchen ceiling, "Too late for that, Daddy dear."

Liz stepped in to plant a kiss on Jim's cheek. "I'm afraid she's right. See you at lunch?"

Jim lifted his chin in his impression of a Hollywood elite. "I'll have my people call your people."

• • • •

The cool water at the base of Choctaw Falls swirled around Bekah's calves as she pressed her toes into slimy rocks. Laughter from the blond-haired family playing closer to the watery curtain blended with the gentle roar of the falls crashing to the bottom of the sixty-foot drop. Birds sang. Sun dappled. Pretty much a perfect day.

On the rocky bank, Elliot unloaded the lunch Liz insisted on packing for them. Ziploc bags of veggies, strawberries, chicken, and cookies came out of his backpack like circus clowns from a tiny Volkswagen. Everything looked yummy. The food and Elliot. An uncontrollable grin filled her face when he slipped into the pool and made his way to her.

His hands were strong and warm on her waist inches above her cutoff jeans and below her bathing suit top. He leaned in and planted the most tender of kisses on her lips.

She closed her eyes, feeling every sensation. Rippling water. Midday sun. His skin touching hers. "Mmm . . . can we live here?"

"Well, I think Mom packed enough food to last through September."

She opened her eyes to bask in his playful grin. "I see. Pretty amazing packing skills."

"It's one of her superpowers."

"What's yours?"

"Superpower?" He held her cheek in his hand. "Mind reading."

"Oh, yeah? What am I thinking?"

He scrunched his forehead and squeezed his eyes shut, whispering to himself like a clichéd psychic. "Wait. It's coming to me. Oh, yes. Very interesting. You are thinking you are a very lucky woman because the man you are in love with—hmm, I see rugged good looks and green eyes—loves you back."

"Cute."

"Wait. There's more." He opened one eye to peek at her.

"More?"

"Yes, don't disturb the winds of foretelling. Close your eyes."

She complied, then peeked to find him staring at her. Raising an eyebrow, he shook his head in playful admonition. She closed her eyes again. He caressed her face, his thumbs massaging her forehead as if he were extracting her thoughts.

"Yes, I can see it now. You wonder when this man you've been seeing for almost a year will make the next move."

"I am?"

"Yes, you wonder what you will say when he makes that move."

"What will I say, oh great mystic?"

"Hmm, the aura is cloudy."

Bekah giggled and pulled his hands from her face, holding them in hers. "Here, I'll make it easy on you. I'm thinking of my answer. You tell me."

She heard him inhale and exhale and on the verge of his next comment when a scream, followed by sobs, broke the air. The family playing near the base of the falls huddled around a distraught child.

Elliot shouted as they made their way over, "You need help?"

The dad answered, "Looks like she cut her foot on a rock."

Another child, voice trembling, yelled, "She's bleeding real bad."

Elliot stopped for a second. "Go get the backpack. I think there's some first aid stuff in there."

"What *isn't* in that pack?"

Bekah hurried to fetch the pack while Elliot made his way to the family. By the time she made it to them with the kit, the injured girl was settled on a rock, her mom holding a blood-stained t-shirt around her foot. Her younger-looking sister stood watch, sniffling. The brother, probably not more than five, played with a stick in the water, totally unconcerned. Bekah could tell this wasn't the first emergency the parents had dealt with. The dad was wading back to them with juice boxes in hand.

Elliot and the mom rifled through the supplies, pulling out a small bottle of hydrogen peroxide, antibiotic ointment, and a bandage wrap. Once the blood flow slowed, they could see the wound wasn't terrible. As they worked to bandage the foot, the patient stared at Elliot. She tilted her head to study him, then asked, "Are you black?"

"Holly," her mom reprimanded, before looking at Elliot. "I'm so sorry."

Elliot smiled. "It's okay. I get that a lot." He kneeled in the water to look the little girl in the eyes. "My mom's white and my dad's black. Believe it or not, though, the green eyes came from my dad. So I guess he's really *mostly* black. Isn't it neat how God makes people in all sorts of colors?"

Holly nodded as she sipped on her juice box. Bekah watched relief steal across the mom's face as she smiled at them.

• • • •

"Well, I never thought we would eat all of that." Bekah mushed all the lunch wrappings into a ball and stuffed them into one Ziploc.

Elliot laced up his boots. "At least it will make the pack lighter on the trek back."

"Hey, El, the way you handled the whole thing with Holly . . . the way I've seen you handle the questions before . . . are you as cool with it as you seem, or does it bother you? People talking about your color?"

He twisted his mouth and looked toward the falls where another family had taken the place of Holly's family. A separate group of young adults splashed in the basin. "What do you see out there?"

Bekah followed his gaze. "Another family, some friends, probably college kids." She took a breath and looked back at Elliot as she caught onto the question. "They're all white. Is that what you mean?"

"Do you notice it when you're in a place where the majority of people are black?"

Bekah thought back to a street fair in Atlanta and a jazz club in New Orleans. "Yes, I have to say I notice it."

"Make you feel out of place?"

She winced at the truth. "A little."

"Because . . ."

She pulled her t-shirt on, feeling a need to cover her skin and her insecurity. "I guess just because it's different from how I grew up. And when I'm in the minority, I think sometimes it feels like they're looking at me, thinking I don't belong. Is that how you feel?"

"Times ten. I mean, because, except in my family, I'm always in the minority. There are always places black people can go and be with only people who look like them and same thing for white people. There's never a place where it's a whole group of mixed people."

What could she say? *I'm sorry* didn't seem enough. Obviously, she couldn't say she understood.

"Mom and Dad set us all up to deal with it well, I think. Constantly telling us God had a plan for us, that anybody who judges us because of how we look has more problems than we do. But still, yeah, it bothers me some, especially when I'm tired or someone's mega rude or stupid with what they say. But mostly, I try to look for ways to build bridges whenever it comes up."

"Like with Holly's family?"

"Exactly. Use an awkward moment to point people to God. It's another one of my superpowers." He winked at her, stood, and offered a hand to pull her up.

"Like mind reading?"

He nodded.

"You didn't finish reading mine earlier."

"Oh, yeah. Where were we?"

She snuggled up close, drew his hands to her face, and closed her eyes. "You were trying to discern what my answer would be if the man in my life wanted to make the next move."

Her skin tingled from head to toe as he leaned his forehead in to tap hers, inhaled as if he were breathing in her soul, then pulled back a few inches. "The aura is still unclear."

Opening her eyes, she met his with a longing that threatened to pull her heart from her chest. "Yes. I'd say yes."

Elliot checked the time again. 5:42. Ten minutes later than the last time he checked. His parents were early risers. Surely they were up. Hopefully, they weren't already out. He hurried downstairs and listened at their bedroom door for signs they were awake. Yes, they were talking, but they stopped when he tapped on the door.

"Yes?" Liz answered with a smile in her voice.

He peeked in. "Y'all decent?"

Good, they were. Sitting against the headboard of their made-up bed, fully clothed, Bibles in their laps and reading glasses on, they grinned as he entered and closed the door.

"Sorry to interrupt. Wanted to talk to you about something before the day gets all Caragin."

Liz's smile spread. "Well then, you picked the perfect time."

Elliot stood at the foot of the bed, words he'd rehearsed through the night floating through his head.

Jim looked amused. "You okay, son?"

Why is my heart beating so fast? "Yeah, all good. Just wanted to tell you that I drove to the coast on Thursday to talk to Bekah's dad."

Liz shut her Bible and snatched her glasses from her face.

"I asked for his blessing to ask her to marry me."

Jim and Liz laid their Bibles on the bed and leaned forward. Jim said, "And?"

"He had a couple of concerns but bottom line, yes. He said yes."

Liz sprung from the bed. "Oh, baby."

In a flash, she was squeezing him like an anaconda, the top of her head grazing his chin, and Jim was patting his back, tears in his eyes. "That's great, son. We're real happy for you."

Liz sat at the foot of the bed. "Does she know? Have you asked her? The picnic at the falls . . . you asked her yesterday."

A quick shake of his head stopped Liz's unfiltered thoughts. "Nope. Though, that would have been a nice idea. I'm going to ask her on my birthday. That's when we had our first date last year. Making the last payment on the ring next week. It's pretty simple."

"She'll love it."

"So, her dad . . ." Jim propped on the side of the bed. "What kind of concerns?"

"Probably the same things you're wondering about. Is it too fast? Has she really healed from her past? What about her job? She'll likely need to move from Whitman to use this certificate she's worked so hard on. He just saw her give up her dreams to follow someone, doesn't want that to happen again."

"Valid questions."

"Yes, sir. Valid."

"And?"

"Well, obviously, I don't think it's too fast and do believe she's healed or I wouldn't even be asking. Y'all know I've covered this all in prayer and fasting. I believe God is going to bless us as we follow him."

"And your jobs? Your ministry is just getting going too."

"Yes, sir. I believe we can move as a team as long as we keep God first and each other's needs above our own. I've been watching you guys do it for almost twenty-six years now. You're my inspiration."

Jim shook his head with a laugh. "Well, we can't argue with you there. But I guess you knew that, huh?"

"Let's pray." Liz extended her hands to Jim and Elliot and began almost before they touched.

Her thanksgiving flowed like a song. Her petitions for unity and grace invited the Holy Spirit to work in and through them. She prayed for strength and wisdom for Elliot as he prepared to become a husband. She asked for a peace that passes understanding to fill Bekah's heart.

Elliot lifted his face as invisible energy saturated every part of his body. Every temporal concern fled from his mind as the prayer washed over him. There was only one other word necessary by the time his mother's grip loosened.

"Amen."

• • • •

Bekah meandered through the late-night mugginess to the pond. Possibilities of what "make the next move" could mean to Elliot whirled through her mind like the helicopter seeds from the maple trees spun to the ground around her. She could see the swing moving. *Looks like Haley's adopted my haven.*

The trunk of the pecan tree seemed to separate into pieces. Bekah stopped. No, it wasn't the tree, there was a man who had been leaning on the tree but who now stood in front of Haley. Should she find another refuge tonight? No need. The man walked away toward the nurseries, so she made her way to the swing. A twig snapped under her feet. Haley startled a little.

"Sorry, didn't mean to scare you."

Haley shook off the reaction. "No problem. Just had my mind somewhere else. I'm glad you're here. I brought another in case you came down tonight." She took a beer from an insulated cooler at her feet and extended it to Bekah.

"Thank you." Bekah accepted the cold glass bottle and took her place in the swing, nodding toward the man whose silhouette grew smaller by the minute. "Someone else from the crew?"

"Him? Yeah, from the crew. Production assistant." She took a long drink. "And . . . a little more."

"Do tell." Bekah curled up on the swing facing Haley.

Haley picked at the soggy part of the bottle label with her fingernail. "We've been together for a little over a year. Not sure where it's going, though." She sighed and stared across the pond. "You should know after a year, right?"

Coincidence or destiny, this conversation? Bekah settled for a shrug. "Maybe." She could tell it wasn't enough for Haley. "So . . . do you love him?"

"Yeah, I guess so. I mean, we've been through a lot together. He can be a lot of fun. But other times aren't fun at all. My roommate, Vanessa, was all like, 'Dah-ling, you shouldn't even take him on this assignment.' She's British. That's my best British accent. She'd laugh at me."

"So he works *for* you?"

"Yeah, not directly, but kind of. We were both crew until Chandler gave me the producer role."

"How'd that go over?"

"Not too good. At first, he said all the right things, but then there was a comment here, a comment there. I think it punched his male ego a little. Vanessa calls him 'the hothead.' Truth is, I was looking forward to being here without him before he was added to the crew. You know, some time to myself to think about things."

"Sounds like you have a lot to think about."

"I know. But I should know, right? After a year, don't you know whether it's time to quit or make the next move?"

There those words were again. *The next move.* "Down here, they say, 'Fish or cut bait.'"

Haley giggled. "In Texas, my daddy would say, 'Poop or get off the pot.' And he didn't always say *poop*."

"Sounds like someone my daddy would get along with."

"So . . . what about you and Elliot? How long you been together?"

"Mmm, about a year."

Haley burst out in laughter. "So we're in the same boat. Judging from the look on your face after he leaves on Saturday nights, though, you don't have any doubts. He's a good guy?"

"The best."

"Time to make the next move?"

It was Bekah's turn to work on peeling the label off of her bottle. "I think so."

"What's the holdup?"

"Stuff."

Haley pulled her legs up in the swing. "Do tell."

"There was someone else before."

"In Atlanta, that's why you left and came back to college, isn't it? I figured it was something like that."

"Dang, you're good."

"Chandler says I have superior journalistic instincts. Now, spill girl."

Journalistic instincts. The words brought tension into Bekah's shoulders. She shook her head. "Nah, I don't want my private stuff becoming a part of this story."

"I'm off the clock." Haley locked eyes with her. "Seriously, I'd never share anything someone didn't want to share. Chandler also says I have great integrity. You can trust me . . . if you want to."

"Okay, guess you could find most of this on public record if you wanted to, anyway. I married my college sweetheart, moved to Atlanta. I thought things were going perfectly until I found a hotel key in his car. He decided he didn't 'love me anymore.' Duh."

"Jerk."

"Yep. Anyway, I moved back to Whitman for a do-over—a new life and career doing something I love."

"And then you met Elliot."

"Well, not right away. Had a whole lot of bottoming out and recovering to do. But Elliot stuck with me through lots of hard places. He's definitely one of a kind and a literal gift from God."

"So . . . what's the problem?"

Could she tell Haley about Sonny? It would feel so good to get that burden out, talk it through with someone, and get some third-party advice. But still . . . nope. She settled for another answer that she'd realized contributed to her wavering thoughts.

"It's just . . . everything does seem perfect with Elliot. But it also seemed perfect to me with the ex. Looking back, I realized I missed a lot of warning signs, but I convinced myself that he was *the* one. What if I'm doing the same thing with Elliot? What if I'm just getting carried away because it *feels* so perfect? How can I know I won't wind up hurting him, hurting both of us?"

"Big questions."

"Yeah, I know. I've been stewing on it so much lately, but this morning . . ."

"What?"

"I woke up early with this incredible peace settling on me. Like a real blanket being laid on me from my feet up. You know, like your mom would lay a blanket on you when you fell asleep on the couch? I just felt this . . . assurance . . . that everything is good with Elliot."

Haley polished off her drink. "Well, sounds like an answer to me."

Subtle, Liz. Be subtle. Liz stilled her breathing, clutched the photo album to her chest, and stepped out onto the front porch.

Bekah glanced up with a smile. "Private time or alone time?"

"Private."

Bekah slowed the glider so Liz could drop on. "Whatcha got there?"

"This? It's our wedding album. Peanut was asking to look through it. She does that sometimes." *That's right. Blame it on the child.*

"Can I see?"

Thought you'd never ask. "Of course." Liz opened the cover, exposing the wedding invitation on the first page. "Nineteen ninety-one. Seems like yesterday."

"You wore hats. I've always thought that was kind of cool. You look gorgeous! And look at Jim with all that hair. And so skinny!"

"We were all skinnier then."

"And this must be your mom. Is that Gramma Rosamond?"

"Yes. And her mother, Granny Isabel."

"And your dad getting ready to walk you down the aisle."

"That's my Uncle John. Daddy didn't come to my wedding." The pain in her voice surprised her. Water under the bridge after all these years, but it still stung somehow.

"What? Why not?"

"He didn't approve of Jim and me getting married. Didn't approve of any mixed-race marriage."

"But, your mother didn't feel that way?"

"My mama was more concerned with Jim's poor grammar than his skin color." Liz shook her head with a smile. "I wish that was the biggest obstacle we had."

Bekah had stopped leafing through the book, so Liz turned the pages until she got to the group photo of the two families. Nine of Liz's family members stood on the bride's side, only five beside the groom.

"Neither of Jim's parents came. I think his father would have, but his mother put her foot down hard."

"But now . . . I mean, they're always at the family gatherings I've been to."

"Yeah, they came around. Almost everyone did, especially after the kids started coming."

"What about your dad?"

"Him too. Just held out a little longer than everyone else. Stubborn. But he did love his grandkids and, you know, Jim has a way of winning people over." A mist covered her eyes. "He died of lung cancer three years ago. Told me on his deathbed that he was sorry he acted out and wished he'd walked me down that aisle. I thought I'd forgiven him years ago but, when he said that, I cried like a baby. Guess I needed to hear him say it."

Bekah gently covered Liz's hand with hers. "Everyone seems to get along so great. Your people quilt. I didn't know there was so much drama."

"Whoo, girl! There was drama from the minute Jim Caragin asked me out. I thought my brothers were going to kill him."

"But things had been integrated for so long. People weren't used to it?"

"We had classes together, played sports together, joined the same clubs, went to the same dances, but there wasn't any mixed dating in our school until me and Jim. Prejudice dies hard."

"Was anyone violent about it?"

"Mostly name-calling. A scrape or two. Pleading from our families to come to our senses."

"But you stuck it out."

"Guess I'm a little stubborn too. And did you see how cute he was with his blue eyes and farmer's tan and wavy red hair?" She flipped to a picture of her groom and traced his face with her finger.

"You're both cute." Bekah smiled, then grew a little pensive-looking. "If your families were that divided, I'm guessing you dealt with more from other people."

Liz had made it point in her life to not dwell on bad memories. Yet, they flooded back so easily. "Oh, yes. We definitely had opposition."

"How'd you handle that?"

"When we were young, and it was just the two of us, and I caught someone's ugly stares or snide comments, I'd pull closer to Jim, call him honey, and smile at them. Until I got us in trouble."

"What happened?"

"We were going into a movie one night when I noticed a man snarling at us, so I cuddled up to Jim and thought I showed him. After the movie, though, in the parking lot, he came out behind us and yelled it was nice of Jim to take his maid to the movie."

Bekah gasped. "You're kidding."

Liz shook her head. "Before I could even think, Jim jerked away from me and flew across the parking lot and punched that guy right in the face."

"Whoa! He knocked him out?"

"Unfortunately, no. He hit back. I'd never seen Jim even a little mad. He was like a rabid tiger, face red, swinging away at that guy in between getting punched himself. It seemed like an hour, but it was probably no more than five minutes. A couple of men stepped in and stopped it."

"Must've scared you."

"Sure did. After that, I stopped antagonizing the people I caught staring. Over the years, I got better at discerning between rude people and someone who's a powder keg. Rude or ignorant people I try to win over with kindness. The other kind, I just walk the other way."

"You still get that?"

"Not around town so much. Most people here know us or know of us. Can't tell you how many times, though, people thought I must be the nanny when I would take my white babies out. And then, when we got over three kids, people assumed I was a daycare teacher."

Bekah laughed. "Well, you have to admit, you do have an unusually large family."

Liz smiled. "True. And I also admit I've probably seen racism where there was simple rudeness or ignorance. My mama would say, 'Don't assume malice for what can be explained by stupidity.'"

"That's a good one. And I'm sure I've overlooked racism, excusing it as simple rudeness or ignorance."

Liz closed the album. "What about you and El? Y'all ever stir up any drama? Anybody ever say anything ugly?"

"No. Well, not to our faces, at least. There were a couple of times early on when Elliot said he noticed us getting some stares, but he hasn't said that in a while. I mean LifeSpring is almost a hundred percent white, but they hired Elliot. I think people are trying harder to look past skin color. Don't you think so?"

"I do. Just want to make sure you keep your eyes open. There are people . . ."

"I know. There are always people looking for something negative to say or do. How do you handle it now?"

"Now? Now, I shield my children the best I can from any hatefulness, but when it can't be avoided, I try to teach them by my example. I breathe deep and remind myself out loud that I am a new creation in Christ, and I need to live like it, even when other people don't. If my life isn't showing the fruit of the Spirit, it's time to analyze myself."

Bekah ticked off fruits of the Spirit she memorized long ago. "Peace, patience, goodness . . ."

Liz helped out. "Love, joy, peace, forbearance, kindness, goodness, faithfulness, gentleness, and self-control."

"Sounds like you've got them down-pat."

"Oh, I've memorized the verses, but I have a long way to go living them out every day."

"I guess we all have a long way to go. And thank you."

"For what?'

"For coming out here with your wedding album to make sure I understand the problems that can face a mixed-race couple."

Liz rolled her eyes with a laugh. "So much for subtlety."

Jim sat at the picnic table, turning his head from side to side as Chad sponged makeup onto his face. Only a few hours ago, Liz had held his hands as she prayed he'd have patience with their "guests." Seemed like her request had worked. He felt as comfortable as a born and raised Alabama man could feel while having foundation applied. *Glad she's decided they're guests instead of intruders.*

In the third week of taping, Liz and the rest of the family appeared to be absorbing the disruptions of having strangers and cameras as a constant presence. Chandler told Jim he'd be amazed at how quickly people forgot about the interlopers, and he was, by and large, correct. There were exceptions, of course. He smiled, remembering how the impromptu revival of *High School Musical* the girls held in the living room last week had played not so subtly to the cameras in the corners of the ceiling.

Five more weeks and they would have their lives back unless they allowed the show to air and continue. That decision seemed a lifetime away. Looking at this as a summer-only adventure made it easier to process.

Chad interrupted his thoughts. "What's on your mind this morning, Jim?"

"Not much. Got a few trucks coming in today to load up for Wal-Mart. Laurel's birthday is next week. Gotta remember to tell Liz to put deodorant on the shopping list. You know . . . normal stuff."

"When you're a reality star, you can have your people make your list . . . and do your shopping and your makeup."

Jim smirked. "You know I love makeup. Maybe you can stay on and be my guy."

Chad played along. "Oh, no, honey. You can't afford me. Besides, I have to get back to the city. I miss my peeps and need my sleep."

"You ain't sleeping good?"

"No. I don't know how you do it. It's so quiet. No car horns or music from the neighbors. Just crickets . . . literally."

Liz and Haley came from the house, laughing arm in arm. Good. Liz had taken Haley in. Jim had hoped for that. He recognized a wistfulness about the young lady beneath her ever-smiling face. Maybe she needed a little mothering.

Behind the ladies strode a small cadre of production assistants. Jim took Liz's hand and kissed it when she made it to the table. "Nice of you and your entourage to join us." He laughed as Chad curtsied in her direction.

Liz rolled her eyes with a laugh and situated herself beside Jim. She snapped her fingers and assumed her best imitation of a diva pose. "And my coffee? Why is there no coffee in my hand?"

One of the younger assistants spilled out an apology and ran to the craft tent. Everyone else within hearing distance cracked up. Liz, however, had immediate compassion. "Oh, bless her heart."

Haley consoled her. "Don't worry about it. She's fine."

The young lady just made it back to the table with coffee when Haley had everything in place to begin. She settled into her chair under the main camera like a dog curling up in a cozy bed, waited for the final lighting check, and gave her first prompt. "Tell me about Marshall and Victoria."

The names surprised Jim. "Not Laurel? I thought you were going through the kids in order."

Haley smiled. "You're paying attention. I'll get back to Laurel another day. For now, tell me about Marshall and Victoria." She leaned back in her chair and took a drink of her smoothie.

Jim, as usual, felt compelled to start with the facts. "Marshall just finished community college. He's going to Whitman University next year to study farm management. Victoria may be joining him or finishing up her associates first. They're our first set of blood-related kids . . . got the same birth mother. Barely seventeen when she had Marshall. Social Services took him from her when they were called to a domestic dispute.

"She lived in a run-down trailer two counties over with a passel of other people, assorted friends and family. No electricity or running water. Squatting more than likely. Making meth even more likely. Marshall was a year old, running around in a full diaper, looked like he'd never had a bath in his life, they said."

Jim's voice cracked. Even though he hadn't seen it himself, thinking of Marshall, of any child, in such an environment brought tears to his eyes. He pinched the bridge of his nose to stop them from spilling. "Thankfully, the young lady realized she wasn't equipped and signed away her rights. Social Services found the father, and he signed away too."

"So," Haley prompted, "Social Services called you?"

Liz squeezed Jim's hand. "Yes," she laughed. "Seems like we were starting to get a reputation. He'd been in foster care for over two months. That's a long time for a baby."

"I've heard babies are in higher demand than older children."

Liz nodded. "Especially white babies. They suspect he wasn't chosen because he cried almost all the time, especially when a stranger picked him up. Once folks saw that and heard about his background, I guess they didn't want to deal with it."

Haley grinned. "But you did."

"He didn't cry," Jim jumped in. "I mean, when we got to his foster home, he was bawling. But when Liz picked him up, he stopped on a dime. It's her magic. Or maybe . . ." he winked at Haley, "another baby God wanted us to have. And then there was four."

"And soon," Liz said, "five."

"Victoria" Haley said. "The same mother?"

"Yes," Liz confirmed. "Turns out she was pregnant when they took Marshall. We got the call just about a month after we brought Marshall home. She'd had the baby, didn't want to keep it, and asked if the nice people who took her son would take his sister."

"No hesitation?" Haley raised her eyebrows.

Jim answered. "Not much. I mean, how do you think about this baby girl who has a brother she might not ever meet? And she could be the only blood family Marshall would ever know. We couldn't know about her and leave her in the system."

"I take it she favors her birth father?"

Liz giggled. "At least her skin color. Obviously, not the same father as Marshall, since he doesn't have an African American pigment in his whole body."

Haley asked, "Were the two of them especially close?"

"Not at first," Jim answered. "Not any more than the others. But as they got older and were able to understand what it meant that they had the same mother, they stuck together more. Victoria was good for Marshall. Even though his rough life was before he can really remember, it affected him for a long time."

"How so?" Haley asked.

"He was very clingy to Liz. I mean more than normal clingy. And things, too, like this stuffed tiger we gave him. He carried it everywhere would scream his head off if anyone else so much as touched it. Sometimes, he would be physically aggressive. They call it RAD, reactive attachment disorder. Lots of kids in the system have it."

"Did he outgrow it?"

"That's not how they say it. The therapists, I mean. It took a lot of work and patience. A big part of it, they think, is making sure the child feels totally secure. We tried to coddle him, but the others needed our attention too."

Liz added, "Just like all the other challenges, there was a lot of trial and error. When Marshall got old enough to properly respond, he started going to therapy. But to answer your question, it's not something you grow out of or overcome. He still has to be aware of things that might trigger an aggressive response. Will probably be a part of his whole life. He does well, though."

Haley fidgeted with her iPad, shook her head, and sipped on her smoothie like it was a security blanket. She started and stopped a question a few times as if she were searching for the right words. "When you see a child scarred from the actions of the people who are supposed to love them most, does it make you angry at the birth parents?"

"Sure, sometimes," Liz answered. "Sometimes, I've wanted to track them down and chew them out for the scars they left on my babies. But then, when I think about it, I don't have any judgment for them. Everybody's got scars. I don't know what theirs may have been. All I know is I got the privilege of calling those babies my own and loving on them the best I can."

"That's right," Jim added. "And while they all didn't feel like they were—or in truth, weren't—fit parents, at least they *had* the babies. There's lots of women would've just had an abortion, killed their babies."

Haley bolted up straight in her chair and stared intently at him. "Why do you say it like that?"

"Say what like what?"

"Abortion is killing babies."

Haley's infectious smile had vanished. The conversation had taken a dramatic shift. Jim's mind raced to figure out how they'd arrived here but he couldn't think of anything to do other than to plow ahead. "Because that's what it is. Abortion is taking life away from a usually perfect, unborn baby. It's murder, plain and simple."

He heard a low gasp from Liz. Her body grew rigid beside him.

Haley clearly wasn't ready to accept his assertion and move on. While she didn't point a finger in his face, her fierce tone did the talking. "You can't just say that. You don't know all the circumstances women are under who make that decision. Most of them don't have a choice."

Jim leaned into the table, made eye contact with Haley, and put as much tenderness as he could into his voice. "They do have a choice. It's the baby who doesn't have a choice. And it is a baby, not a glob of cells. It's a person with tiny feet and hands and a brain and a beating heart. Abortion stops all that."

Jim could see splotches of red creep up Haley's neck. The crew looked like they were caught in a bizarre game of freeze tag. Holding microphones, iPads, and coffee, they stared, unblinking. Intense silence filled the air around them. The red light on the camera demanded he say something.

Jim softened his voice further. "Look, all I'm trying to say is we value life because we believe God made all life. It's why we wanted all of our kids, why we love them and pour our lives into them. Ain't that right, babe?"

He turned his body toward Liz, expecting to see her smiling affirmation, but she wasn't smiling.

She did address Haley in a voice barely above a whisper. "Yes, we believe all life is valuable." She pushed away from the table, taking her mic off as she went. "Can we finish this later? I should start lunch."

Liz's mind concocted a dozen excuses in the seconds it took Jim to walk around the car and open her door at the restaurant. She longed to be back at home where the kids provided ample ways to buffer against a prolonged serious discussion with the man she loved most. It wouldn't be a lie to say she felt sick. Too late. Her door opened, and she accepted his hand without making eye contact.

"It wasn't very nice of us to leave Elliot and Bekah in charge tonight." She edged into an exit strategy as the hostess walked them to a table. "They don't get much time alone."

She took the chair Jim pulled out for her.

He brushed his lips over her cheek and settled in his chair. "You know who doesn't get much time alone? Us. We ain't had a date night since our anniversary. I'm sorry I let it go so long." He placed his palms up in the middle of the table.

Her hands accepted the invitation and nestled into his like they had a mind of their own. The touch wasn't electric after all these years, but the warmth of his hands caressing hers persuaded her eyes to close. In seconds, she fell into a peaceful sanctuary, a safe place she'd found with no one else in her life. His love surged through his touch. Their marriage was strong. *We can survive anything.*

"What can I get y'all to drink?"

Spell broken, Liz opened her eyes to catch a wink from Jim before they readjusted their focus to the server. Hours flew by as they chatted and enjoyed dinner. Liz relaxed into the luxury of adult conversation.

• • • •

Outside, Jim held her close at the car door and nestled his face into the nape of her neck. Heat rushed to her face. So the spark lived. She turned to face him. He cupped her face in his hands and kissed her gently, then rested his forehead on hers. With a soft sigh, he asked, "Are you mad at me?"

Serenity fell from her like Cinderella's ballgown unraveling at midnight. Her heart back in rags and ashes, she pushed away enough to accommodate the emotional wall she'd built for years. "I'm not mad."

Jim stammered. "It's just . . . since Wednesday, you been . . . I feel like I said something wrong, but I'm just not sure what it was."

She crossed her arms. "Do we have to talk about this?"

"You know we do."

Of course they did. Except for this darkest moment of hers, they shared everything. But this . . . right now? Maybe there would be a better time. She stared off into the parking lot. "I know you didn't mean to, but I think you sounded a little heartless. It just hit me wrong is all. I wish you'd found a better way to be pro-life without those words."

"Which words?"

"Killing and murder."

"I thought you believed that's what abortion is. We're supposed to speak the truth."

"The truth . . . in love. Yes, I agree with the facts, but you just don't know."

"What? What don't I know?"

"You don't know . . ." Confession stalled at the back of her throat. She swallowed it down. "You don't know what women who do make that decision go through before they get there, or how they feel during, or what they live with after. Anyone who's gone through that needs healing, not a lecture."

"Sounds personal."

"Well, yeah, it kinda is . . ."

"You know someone?"

She closed her eyes and took a deep breath. "Yes."

"It's Denise, right?"

Liz opened her eyes and fixed him with a stare. *What a stupid thing to say about her sister.*

He seemed to interpret the look as an admission. "Can't say I'm surprised. She always was the wild one, wasn't she?"

"That's not even . . ."

"Fair? You know it's fair. I mean, she's turned her life around, but back in high school . . . Is that when it happened?"

Liz rolled her eyes. Insisting it wasn't Denise would only start the roll call of suspicion. "I don't want to talk about it. I just think you could be more careful about what you say in front of those cameras. Did you even see the way Haley reacted? Like she knows someone or maybe is someone. Think about how those words could wound someone who's been through the worst time of her life and then carried it around every day.

"And I'll have you know it's not just wild girls. You and me, we didn't wait until we got married. What if . . .?"

"Well, that's an easy one, babe. We would've gotten married sooner is all."

"But what if . . . what if you weren't my boyfriend, and that had happened to me, and I thought I didn't have any other choice, and I did that?"

"Then you wouldn't be the woman I fell in love with."

There it was. The words stabbed her heart like darts from a blowgun. An urge to slap him for being so insensitive competed with the very real feeling of crumpling to the ground with the thought he really couldn't love her anymore. To keep from doing either, she sucked in and held a deep breath. Her face grew taut. *Why can't he see my pain?*

Maybe he did. Before she could say another word, he pulled her into his arms. "Come on, baby. Don't be mad at me over a hypothetical question. I'm sorry I wasn't kind, and I'll do better. Help me think of the right thing to say to Haley to smooth it over. And remind me to be nicer to Denise."

Liz's body tensed. Another lie added to the layers of lies covering the secret. "Jim, don't you dare say anything to her about this."

"You know I wouldn't. I'm not a thoughtless brute all the time." He kissed her forehead. "Thank you for telling me what you think. There's nothing sweeter to me than the way we can always talk through anything. You're my rock."

Almost eleven and still no sign of Bekah. *Guess I might as well have hers.* Haley nestled her second empty bottle into her insulated bag and pulled a fresh one out. The *phsst* of the beer opening melded with the soft patter of rain falling from the starless sky onto the pecan tree canopy.

The determined drops that made it through the dense leaves dampened her skin. When the tiniest of breezes blew through the muggy night air, chill bumps covered her arms and legs. Memories of a camping trip with her church youth group staved off more serious thoughts. There was a campfire, s'mores, a barefoot pastor playing a guitar, and a boy with the cutest dimples playing with the WWJD bracelet on her wrist.

"Mind if I join you?" Chandler stood behind her, a huge *This Land* emblazoned umbrella covering both of them.

"Sheesh! Chandler! What are you doing out here?"

He closed the umbrella and leaned it against the tree trunk. "Just wandering around looking for some possible shooting locations."

"At night, in the rain?"

"Uh-huh. I come out here a lot."

"Interesting. Because I've been out here like every Saturday night, and I've never seen you."

He winked at her. "Can't fool you, detective. I'm checking on you. Chad said he thought you'd be here. Every Saturday night, huh? Your own private getaway?"

He joined her on the swing without waiting for an invitation. She bristled at the intrusion.

"Not as private some nights." She took a drink and waited for the response she expected. "This is the part where you say, 'I'm sorry I intruded. I'll be heading out.'"

"Or I could say, do you have another one of those?"

She rolled her eyes and retrieved the last unopened bottle from her bag.

"Thanks. That's a lot of beer for one little woman."

"Last couple of Saturday nights, Bekah's been out here. You know, Elliot's girlfriend."

"We've met. Seems nice. You getting the inside scoop?"

"Just hanging. Why are you checking on me?" The breeze had vanished and thunder rumbled in the distance.

"Thought you might need checking on. Somebody may have mentioned you seemed a little emotional. And that there were some raised voices in your trailer before Alex headed out to Birmingham tonight. Trouble in paradise?"

"More often than not."

"You can tell me if you don't want him here, and he'll be on a plane tomorrow."

"Great. It would really make things better if I were the reason he lost his job."

"The reason he lost it? You're the reason he still *has* a job. I would've gotten rid of him months ago if you weren't involved. I'm like a hundred percent out of line here, but I don't get what you see in him."

"Some days, I don't either. But it's not just Alex." She took a long sip and pressed the bottle to her flushed face. "It's Jim and Liz . . . mostly Jim."

By the way he cocked his head and pulled his chin to his chest, she could tell she had confused him. *Keep it to yourself, Haley.* "Maybe I shouldn't say anything."

"Come on. You can tell me. What's up?"

"When I was doing the research before we came here, I was so skeptical that they were legit good people. I mean, honestly, who's perfect enough to adopt thirteen kids? And why, if they're so perfect, would they allow the chaos of a reality show in to potentially exploit those kids?"

"Well." Chandler removed his glasses. "They allowed it because I convinced them their story would be uplifting, potentially for millions of people."

"And a cash cow for Over the Moon Network." *Oh no. Did I say that out loud?*

Chandler's eyes widened, and he blew out a long whistle. "Ouch. Where did that come from?"

"I'm sorry. I know that's not your main motivation. But honestly, you're always on the lookout for the 'next big thing,' right? The next *Duck Dynasty* or *Fixer Upper.* A golden ticket."

"Do I want to be financially successful creating quality programming? Yes, I would like that. Do I enjoy my work and want to keep doing it until I'm old and gray? Yes."

"I know. I shouldn't have . . ."

"What's really bothering you, Haley? You said something about Jim and Liz, mainly Jim. Did he say something? Do something? Find a skeleton in his closet?"

The breath left her chest in a gush. She wiped away an escaped tear from the outside corner of her eye. "It's just disappointment, I think."

"What? Tell me."

"I said I was skeptical of their motives when you pitched the idea. But all the research and interviews we did before we left LA started to change my mind. Then, the first two weeks. They just kind of wrapped me up in down-home comfort with the way they talked, the way they are with their kids. They talk about God as easily as I talk about camera angles. I've been around a lot of hypocrites in my day. I thought they were the real thing."

"Then . . ."

"Then I found out they're like all the others, judgmental and unforgiving. Use the Bible to condemn people as sinners."

"For instance?"

"Jim said women who choose abortion are murderers." Another tear slipped onto her warming cheeks.

"Hmm."

"You don't understand. It's just . . . last year . . ."

"I know."

He didn't move, didn't look at her. Yet, she knew from his inflection, he did know. *How could he know? I hid everything from almost everyone.* The warmth in her face intensified like the heat lightning in the distant sky.

He answered her unasked questions. "You're not the only one with observation and detective skills. I knew something was wrong. I could tell by the way you walked, your face, your inability to focus. I asked you several times. Remember?"

"No, I really don't. Guess I was too wrapped up in the drama."

"That's not too wrapped up. Completely understandable."

"But how?"

"You took time off with no explanation. *So* not like you at all. I called you. Vanessa answered your phone. Said you were sleeping. Spilled the beans without realizing it."

Vanessa.

"Don't be mad at her. She assumed you'd told me. Truth be told, I felt a little guilty for knowing a secret you obviously didn't want me to know. I just care about you."

"And you don't judge me."

"Of course not."

There was no damming the tears now. They breached the wall of her lower lashes like water boiling over on the stove. She curled into a ball on the swing and buried her head in her knees.

Chandler rested his hand on her shoulder. "I don't want this to be taken as any kind of inappropriate workplace aggression, but can I hug you?"

The silliness of the culturally necessary disclaimer stopped her tears. Scooting closer to him, she dropped her head onto his shoulder, and he wrapped an arm around her.

The wobbly ceiling fans over the covered brick patio at Momma and Em's Fish House provided a slight breeze, but not enough to keep Bekah's skin from getting tacky. She could feel the wrought-iron chair impressing crisscross patterns on her legs. Elliot, Cynda, and Reuben sat in mismatched chairs around the old Formica table.

Momma and Em's was rustic long before rustic was chic. Exposed light bulbs hung from foundry pipes that supported a frayed awning. Assorted chairs and tables were salvaged as available for the last twenty years. None of it by design, but even better. The haphazardness of it all created a relaxed space.

Add to the atmosphere a pitcher of tea, fried catfish, and their best "couple friends," and the night was already a winner despite the humidity. Cynda and Bekah waited tables together at Miss Ida's diner, Ona Mae's Deli and Bait Shop, since Bekah moved back to Whitman.

Annie nicknamed them "Ying and Yang" because Bekah was white with short black hair, and African American Cynda wore short honey-blonde twists. The twinning continued over the last year as they both let their hair grow.

Cynda's husband, Reuben, and Elliot hit it off as easily as the girls had bonded. Reuben had come to Whitman on a football scholarship and still looked like the epitome of an all-star running back. In his t-shirt and shorts, it was easy to see his muscles rippling from neck to calves. His brilliant smile lit up his coffee-bean brown face in a way that would've been a sure bet to win all kinds of endorsements had he made pro. A couple of busted vertebrae and their first baby changed that path years ago.

"The gluten-free menu at the Bait Shop was *your* idea?" Bekah dropped her mouth open with a smile as she twisted her hair into a ponytail.

Cynda laughed. "Totally. Too 'new-fangled' for Miss Ida. Then I explained she didn't have to cook anything different. Grits and eggs and fruit are already gluten-free. All she had to do was add an asterisk to them and those out-of-towners coming in just to ride the bike trail would love it."

"And then," Reuben tipped his glass with a wink, "my girl told Miss Ida she could add three dollars, and they'd pay it. That did the trick."

Cynda held up a hand with a disclaimer. "Locals still pay the old price."

"So," Elliot smirked, "she doesn't mind gouging tourists but draws the line somewhere."

Cynda dipped a fry into tartar sauce and popped it into her mouth. "You know her. Says if those bikers—still haven't been able to get her to call them cyclists—have money to spend on special pants with crotch padding, they've got a few extra dollars to spend on breakfast."

Bekah stabbed her second deep-fried catfish from the platter. "You obviously get her. No wonder she feels comfortable letting you two run the Bait Shop. How's that going, by the way?"

Cynda and Reuben exchanged a look and seemed to hold their breath.

Elliot must have noticed it too. "What's up, guys?"

Reuben glanced around the room as if he were wary of eavesdroppers. "Well, we did want to talk to you about that."

Bekah sat up straight. "You're not leaving. Tell me you're not leaving."

A flash of his smile set her at ease. "Kinda the opposite. We been talking about asking Miss Ida if we can buy the place." His grin grew broader as Bekah and Elliot froze in place and stared between their friends.

Elliot found his words first. "Wow! That's awesome. I think you two would be great."

Cynda made eye contact with Elliot. "You'd be okay with it?"

"Of course. Why wouldn't I be?"

"Because Miss Ida's mom and dad started it. Wondered if you'd ever thought, you know, maybe it could come to you one day."

Elliot smiled. "Gee, no. I mean, I seriously have never given it a thought." He slowly shook his head. "But, no. My heart's in full-time ministry. That's why I turned down my dad's offer to train to take over the nursery. Nice of you to ask, but no need to worry about me."

Cynda drew out her next concern. "But . . . what do you think she'll say?"

Elliot's smile faded. Bekah could see his wheels turning. A whole host of what-ifs peppered her thoughts. *Could Elliot be thinking the same things?* He wiped his mouth, smoothed the napkin on the table, and started with a positive.

"Well, I know how much she loves both of you. And she obviously trusts you. I mean, she's left town at least three times for a whole week at a time since she gave you the reins. But you're right. Her life has revolved around the place literally all of her life. And there's Sonny."

Reuben scoffed. "Doesn't seem like the kind of place he'd care about. Unless maybe he thinks he can sell it to a casino or something."

"No. It definitely doesn't seem to fit his lifestyle. He's territorial, though, and maybe more sentimental than he seems. Remember, he grew up there too. I'm sure she'll want to run the idea by him. You'll need a business plan all laid out."

Cynda chimed in. "Already working on it. Looking into applying for a loan. Don't think that's going to be a problem. We've been more profitable all this year than last and don't see any reason that will change. We've got all kinds of ideas to make it better—you know, without changing the feel."

"It's different," Elliot cautioned, "running someone else's business than owning your own. I've seen it with my family. A lot of responsibility and not much time off."

"Yeah, I get that." Reuben nodded as he grabbed the last hushpuppy in the basket. "But we're not Caragins. Don't plan on this being a national business . . . or having fifteen kids." He grinned as the others laughed. "We do think this is where we're going to be for the long haul, though. Think it'd be cool to have something to maybe pass onto our kids one day."

Warm fuzzies filled Bekah's heart. She clutched Cynda's hand. "I think it's a great idea, and you'll be wonderful. Ask her."

Cynda returned the squeeze. "We will. Just want to have the plan completely together. Would you guys help us finish it up?"

Bekah raised her eyebrows to Elliot and waited for his nod before adding her own. "Absolutely. I'll be here for the next two weeks. We'll have plenty of time. After, of course, Elliot's Over the Moon interview is tomorrow."

Cynda hooted. "Oh, yeah. Mr. Hollywood in the house."

Elliot threw a wadded napkin at her. "Stop it. Don't even know why they want me. Probably wind up on the cutting room floor."

Bekah grinned. "It's cute how much he hates the attention. At least he'll be in a comfortable place. The Bait Shop's like another home."

Reuben chugged the last of his tea. "Just don't break anything and lock up when you leave."

From his stool at the counter of the sixty-ish-year-old diner, Elliot took in the filming crew. The whole scene reminded him of his childhood ant farm. How many people did it take for what Haley described as a "quick" interview? And how much equipment? The camera and microphones, of course, were understandable. Add to those were lights, a generator, and cables snaking across the worn wooden floors. The small space grew smaller by the moment.

The definite Queen Ant, a woman whose name he'd forgotten, scooted around Ona Mae's Deli & Bait Shop in hot pink Converse high tops. She'd positioned him at the counter for his interview, but now seemed interested in changing to a booth. With two assistants hovering over her shoulders, she framed possible shots with a photo frame-looking tool.

Lighting and camera people already set up for this angle stood, waiting for her verdict. They looked bored but not impatient, as if they'd been through this scenario a hundred times. He could see why she would want to make the booth work. The once-white horsehair plaster wall there held a running history of the town and university. Black-and-white photos arranged in no particular pattern among faded color photos chronicled the city's growth, athletic achievements, beauty queens, and visits of notable celebrities. It would look good on TV.

Still, Elliot preferred the counter. He'd met Bekah at this spot. Her raven hair, green eyes, and flirtatious smile. All captivating. That first sight made him forget why he'd wandered into the place. The memory quickened his pulse. But Bekah wasn't the only person he met in that spot that day who had changed his life.

Haley's voice from a few stools away broke his memory. "It's all pretty crazy, right?"

He realized she'd taken his smile as wonder at the sights in the diner. He swiveled so he could see her face. Just beyond her, people from the sidewalk peered through the storefront windows to see what in the world was going on. "It's kind of surreal."

"A lot of excitement for a sleepy town, huh?"

"More lighting in here, for sure. But a lot more excitement last year with the Whitman Five thing. News trucks from all over the country, FBI, curiosity seekers."

"Whitman Five?'

Really? She hadn't heard? "Must not have made the national news like I thought. Bodies of five Civil Rights workers who disappeared fifty years ago were found on an old farm in the county."

Recognition set in her eyes. "Oh, yeah. I do remember hearing something about that. Didn't remember it was here. Sorry."

"No problem. You should look into when you have time, though. My mom—Ida, my birth mom—and her best friend, Annie, run the Whitman Five Foundation for Alabama Civil Rights History over by the courthouse."

"The same Ida who owns this place?"

"Same one."

"Interesting. How did she wind up with that gig?"

"A newspaper guy from New York came down to write about the Five and happened to stop in here first and met Mom and Annie. Mom, she's white, and Annie's black. They've been friends since before integration. Annie's brother was one of the Five."

The sound of Haley's name being called stopped the conversation. Elliot turned to see the camera and light techs moving their gear. With two crooked fingers, Queen Ant requested Haley's presence.

Haley smiled like a mischievous child being summoned to the principal's office. "Nutshell version?"

"Those news articles sort of made them the faces of racial reconciliation. The city put them in charge of the memorial service. Then the state historical commission asked them to oversee the Foundation."

Haley grabbed her tablet and gave him a wink. "I'll check it out. See you in a few."

• • • •

Snugged into the corner, where booth meets wall, Elliot rested his arm on the speckled Formica tabletop. He closed his eyes as Chad dusted his face with a brush.

The makeup tech laughed. "You are nothing like your father. He can barely sit still through all of this."

Elliot laughed along with him. "I'm not really a stranger to all of it, with video production classes and preaching. But, yeah, I'd love to see him getting miked and made up."

Haley spoke from her director's chair. "That *is* some behind-the-scenes fun. Ready, Elliot?"

He nodded. The directions she'd peppered him with floated through his brain. Wait a few seconds to speak. Use complete sentences to start. Look at her face, not the camera over her shoulder. The room full of bustle grew quiet.

Haley lifted a finger. The camera light shone steady red. "Tell me about growing up as the oldest of fifteen children."

"Growing up Caragin was an adventure. Like everyone else, though, it seemed normal to me because that's just the way it was. You only know what you know, right?"

"But, at some point, you must've figured out your family wasn't ordinary?"

Elliot shook his head with a light laugh. "My family is *not* ordinary in so many ways. The first time I remember hearing anyone say anything about it was in kindergarten. Mom brought in cookies one day, and one of my white friends said, very loudly, 'Your mama's black?'"

A small shiver ran down his back. Did this really still bother him? No time to think about it. Haley waited for more.

"Everybody laughed. All the kids, at least. I don't remember what Mom or the teacher said. I just remember this look Mom had. I guess looking back and knowing her like I do now, it was her trying to repress her Mama Bear instincts. All I remember, really, is being embarrassed. It wasn't like I didn't know her skin color. I just didn't know it was something to be laughed about."

"Did that happen much?"

Elliot smirked. "You know kids are always going to pick on other kids. Too skinny. Too fat. Too ugly. Kids made fun of me because Dad is white, too. Got in a fight on the playground one time because some kid called Will a crack baby. He was so little then. You wouldn't believe it."

"How did your parents handle that?"

"They handled it all with love and grace and a lot of prayer. Tons of hand-holding and telling us how God made every person in his image with all different shades and bodies and personalities because he is a creative God."

"Sounds like a perfect response."

Elliot shook his head a little. "Mom'd never want to say she did anything perfectly. And like I said, looking back now with more mature vision, I'm sure there were things said behind closed doors she didn't want to say in front of us. That's probably every parent though, right?"

Haley nodded and typed on her pad for a few seconds. "When did they tell you that you were adopted?"

"I don't remember them ever telling me I was adopted. I just knew it."

"That's what Will said."

"I've watched them go through it with the younger kids. They were, and they always wanted us to be, very open about it. We talk about being chosen and adopted as good, loving things. We have some different backstories, but I never heard a bad word about anyone's birth parents. I truly can't think of how they could've handled it any better."

"I understand you've found your birth mother. Were you looking for her? How did that happen?"

"I've thought about who my birth parents were a lot over the years, like I'm sure every adopted kid does. But I wasn't looking for them. I came into this diner to meet a pastor for a job interview. Met Miss Ida, my mom, between here and the counter. This is her place. Her parents opened it the year she was born."

"Wow! How did you know it was her?"

"I didn't know it was her. But she knew it was me right away. She's shown me pictures of my birth dad. We're practically twins."

"And she just told you right there?"

"No. It took her a few months to get details, like my birthdate, and to work up the courage to tell me."

"Tell me about that."

Dang. His determination to not cry on camera went mushy. He pulled at the corners of his eyes with his thumb to make sure the tears didn't spill out.

The tension that filled his body as he stared at the Polaroids that day pulsed through his muscles.

"I cried like a baby. I mean, like an uncontrollable baby. Mom, Ida, showed me pictures of her and my father. Told me it was her in the picture. I don't know how long it took for what she was saying to set in. And she looked so afraid. I was finally able to push myself up and hug her. Felt like she melted in my arms. Then we were all crying."

"All?"

"We were at a pastor friend's house. Him, his wife, Bekah, Mom, and me."

"Why did she say she gave you up?"

As soon as his lips parted to explain, he sensed a warning pull in his mind. He wagged his head left to right. "I know the story. But that's hers to tell."

Haley gave him a tilt of her head, which he took as her acceptance of his answer. She tapped on her pad. "Have you met him yet?"

"I haven't. I'd rather not talk about that either."

Another tilt of her head. More tapping. "But you do have a brother you didn't know about. Sonny Friedman. Famous venture capitalist. Looks like he's about ten years older than you. What's your relationship with him like?"

Relationship. Except for sharing some DNA, there was nothing Elliot would define with that word. Sonny had been nothing more than polite with an edge of arctic coolness. *What you say could be on TV one day, Elliot.* He took two seconds to collect his thoughts and take a deep breath.

"He's a good guy. But he's really busy, so we haven't had much of a chance to get to know each other. I'm sure it will happen, though."

"Well, I can see why this place is special to you."

Special . . . quite an understatement. Walking into this diner changed his life in so many ways. Again, the corners of his mouth turned up.

"What are you thinking about?"

"I did meet another very special person here."

"Who?"

His pulse sped up again. Should he even bring this up? Yes. He wanted to tell the world. "I met Bekah before I met Ida. She's been working here and living in the apartment upstairs while she finishes up a landscaping certificate from Whitman."

Haley grinned. "You have a very big smile on your face. Must be a special girl."

"Bekah's amazing. A very big part of my life."

"And . . . maybe a bigger one soon?"

She caught him off-guard. She seemed to be asking as an interested friend, not a TV producer. He knew the two women had spent some time together. Had they talked about this? Didn't matter. The heat warmed his face so much, it could be glowing.

"I'm not supposed to ask you questions, but when is this show going to air?"

Haley cocked her head with a grin. "No sooner than September."

He shifted to straighten his back and pressed his fingers into his pants pocket enough to touch the small velvety case. *Yeah. Why not?* He fished the case out and put it on the table with a broad smile. He noticed Haley's eyes widen and gave her a wink.

"I do hope she's going to be so much more. I picked this up today. Going to ask her next week if she'll do me the privilege of being my wife."

Haley's mouth dropped open. She waited a second. "And cut." She jumped off her chair with a squeal. "Elliot, that's awesome! Let me see."

He scooted out of the booth, opened the box, and waited for her reaction.

"Oh, it's beautiful! She's going to love it."

"I hope so. Please promise me that part won't air if she says no."

"Are you kidding? You don't have a thing to worry about."

Haley settled into a chair at the kitchen table. "We're going to have to close the window, guys. Those steady, soft raindrops will sound like Niagara Falls to our mics."

Jim and Liz nodded their understanding from the opposite end of the table as a young assistant moved around the room pulling down the wooden sashes of the farmhouse windows.

They're still sitting beside each other, but somehow not as close. Was there tension between them, or was she projecting her own feelings from their last taping? She'd have to be careful to avoid injecting any kind of tone into her questions. This should be an easy interview, one of the more interesting in her series of vignettes.

"Tell me about Hope." She was right. It seemed the shoulders of both of her subjects softened.

Liz smiled. "Well, to tell you about Hope, we have to tell you about Amy. Is that okay?" She continued after a nod from Haley. "Amy came to us from Birmingham. Our friend, Reverend Taylor, brought her to us when she was only weeks old. Literally, brought her to us. Showed up in our driveway with a social worker and a baby carrier."

Jim interjected, touching his wife on the arm. "I guessed what he was up to right away, but decided to fun with him a little. As he got out of the car, I shouted out, 'It's about time you got married, Reverend. And I see you've already had a baby. Congratulations!' You shoulda seen that social worker's face."

Liz seemed amused. "Because she was barely twenty-five. Probably wondered if we were good people like Reverend Taylor told her. Luckily for us, she came on in with this beautiful child. Amy has Down syndrome. We'd never seen a baby with Down's before and didn't know anything about it, but that's the reason her birth parents gave her up."

Tears sprang to Liz's eyes, and she took a drink of tea. "Even after all we've seen, it's hard to believe sometimes . . . how someone can give up a baby, just because it's going to be hard."

"But at this point," Jim added, "I have to say I had some doubts about whether we could handle it. Six kids already. Cooper, only a year old. With the amount of time and money we were facing with his physical challenges, I wasn't sure we could handle adding Amy."

Liz agreed. "We had a lot to think about."

"But then . . ." Haley prompted, expecting to hear how Amy smiled or took Jim's finger, and they just knew God wanted them to take this baby.

Liz continued. "We told them we needed some time."

Didn't see that coming. "Really? No on-the-spot decision?"

"Doesn't much sound like us, does it?" Liz fiddled with her tea glass. "They took Amy back to Birmingham, and we prayed."

"And talked to our closest family and friends," Jim said. "They all told us we'd be crazy to take on this kind of 'burden.'"

Haley could see Liz's mental gears churning. Her eyes focused somewhere beyond Haley's face as if she were spinning the combination on a safe and removing a precious possession. Jim seemed to be aware of it, too, and didn't feel the need to fill in every quiet moment.

After a few seconds, Liz voiced the words signaling the spoiler warning of Amy's fate. "Couldn't stop thinking about that girl, though." Another silence, another sip of tea before she made eye contact with Haley. "I learned a *lot* about Down syndrome; found out there's different levels of severity, but the most important thing is to get them early intervention. Once I learned that, I could just hear the clock ticking on Amy's future.

"A week after we first met her, the social worker called to talk. She'd lined up a therapist from the Bama School of Early Education who agreed to come at least once a week to teach us the best ways to help. That same day, I remember I was sitting on the living room floor with Cooper, trying to help him roll over. Victoria, Marshall, and Laurel playing in a mountain of laundry on the couch. Jim came in and told me that he believed we needed to take Amy."

Jim smiled at Haley. "I couldn't stop thinking about her either."

Haley prompted, "And Amy led to Hope, how?"

Jim and Liz shared the first glance Haley had seen them exchange all morning. A tilt of Jim's head gave the floor to Liz.

"Well, it's kind of a bad thing that turned into a God thing. When Amy was about three, she got called a bad name."

Jim filled in a couple of blanks. "A retard. By one of our own kids."

His statement drew a frown and raised eyebrow from Liz, compelling Jim to defend himself. "I didn't say *which* kid."

Liz straightened. "It's true. We think our child must've picked it up from a kid on the school bus who saw Amy waiting with me. Of course, I jumped right in telling . . . our child . . . how it's wrong to call people names and all that. You can imagine. Then he—or she—pointed out with other less-than-kind words how Amy was different from all the rest of our family."

Jim took up the story. "It shook us up. We thought we was doing such a good job raising the kids to accept and love others. Thinking that our kids who, by the way, were about as different as they could be from each other, felt one of them was an outsider, made us wonder if we'd failed somehow. By then we had Darius and Jordan too."

Liz told the next part. "When we got the youngest ones in bed, we gathered the others up and had a long talk with them about how all people are made in the image of God and deserve respect and protection. There was lots of avoiding eye contact and crossed arms, but in the end, they all said they understood. Still . . ."

"Still," Jim added. "We knew in a way it was true. There wasn't anyone else like Amy in our house, in our town that we knew of. She'd have to deal with that, basically alone in a way, her whole life. Then, you're gonna think I'm making this up, but while we was getting ready for bed, we caught each other's eyes in the bathroom mirror and said, at almost the same time, that we needed another child with Down's."

Haley straightened in her chair. *These people can't be for real.* She typed for a few moments to gather her thoughts before her follow-up. "So you have nine children, and you deliberately seek out another child with Down syndrome? Was that difficult?"

Liz answered. "It wasn't as simple as we thought. Because of the decision Amy's birth parents made, we figured that must happen a lot. But, truth is, because of genetic testing during pregnancy, most American parents who find out their child has Down's either make a deliberate choice to keep and love the baby or . . ." She took in and blew out a deep breath. "Or they end the pregnancy."

You mean, murder their baby. Jim's words exploded in Haley's mind. She glared at him, waiting, even daring him to use the condemning words again. What would she do if he did? She didn't have to wonder long.

Jim blew out a quick breath as if he knew what she was thinking, then took the conversation back to their experience. "We found out typical adoption, which apparently none of ours had been, is very expensive. After we'd done a good bit of searching, we found it would be faster and more affordable in Ukraine, so we started the process."

At a loss for another question, Haley simply prompted, "And . . ."

Jim continued, "And *very* long story short, in six months, we were in Ukraine meeting Hope."

Liz jumped in. "We'd been able to be unusually specific. We wanted a girl between two and four with Down syndrome. When we got there, though, they spent a long time showing us other babies, acting like they didn't understand what we were talking about. We had an interpreter, and she patiently kept telling them again and again. Finally, the lady talking to us left the room and came back with Hope."

Tears filled Liz's and Jim's eyes. Haley could feel them in her own eyes. "You ever see a Down's child smile?" Liz asked.

Haley nodded as she thought of her cousin's son and grinned.

"It's something else, right?" Liz dabbed the corners of her eyes. "I have to tell you that orphanage wasn't the cleanest of places. I mean, we'd been told not to expect American standards, but there was no way to really prepare for it. It looked like a prison hospital from a bad sixty's movie. Dirty. Peeling paint. Smelled like a sewage plant.

"The children they'd shown us at first, though, looked well-cared for. Hope didn't. Looked like, and smelled like, she hadn't had a bath in a month of Sundays. Her hair was tangled, snot and drool caked on her face, dirt everywhere. But, oh, her smile. I bent down and she toddled over to me and started playing with my hair, stroking my arms. I realized I was probably the first black person she'd ever seen."

Jim took up the story. "The orphanage lady looked mad at us. I didn't understand her words, but they sounded mad too. Our interpreter said she called us stupid Americans. We could have any baby, she said, but we chose the useless one." His face reddened and tears fell as his voice broke. "Useless." He shook his head.

Liz let her head fall onto Jim's shoulder. He wrapped his arm around her and kissed the top of her head.

A cold shiver worked its way from Haley's head to her toes. She heard sniffles from more than one person in the crew.

"How did that make you feel?"

"Mad." Liz wiped her face as she sat up. "I held onto Hope as tight as I could. And, if I could've, I would've marched back into that room they brought her from and taken every other child in there they would call useless. How do you see that smile and say—" The anger forced her to squint. Her mouth tightened as her fist hit the table.

Jim slid his hand down her arm and rested it on top of her balled-up hand. "She's calmed down a lot since then."

The quip brought light laughter from all in the kitchen, including Liz. It made Haley's next question easier.

"What did Amy think?" She followed Liz's eyes to the doorway where Amy stood watching. She couldn't have planned the moment better. "Can we ask her?"

"Sure." Jim and Liz agreed.

Haley called Amy into the room, positioned her between her parents, and asked them for Amy's response again.

Liz asked Amy, "What do you think of Hope?"

A smile so big it made her eyes close spread over Amy's face as she blurted out, "I love Hope. She's my best friend!"

"Bekah, Bekah, look at me!" Annie's grandson posed on the diving board of Miss Ida's pool and begged for her attention.

"I'm watching!" Bekah turned from his two sisters to watch him for what seemed like the hundredth time. He catapulted himself into the water with a monster splash and came up grinning.

The pool couldn't be more perfect. Coolish water counteracted the muggy air. A crescent moon, a million stars, and the pool lighting made the evening serene despite the cries for attention from the kids. Elliot lingered with her in the shallow end, gently pushing the young girls on a float. Faint booms of distant fireworks punctuated the end of the day's celebration.

The others—Ida, Annie, Sonny, and Bekah's parents—lounged on the deck, brisket and potato salad hangovers looming in their futures.

"There's more flag cake," Miss Ida offered without moving.

Quiet protests came from most, but Bekah's father obliged without hesitation. "I could eat," he said as he made his way to the pool house for the dessert.

Shelby, Bekah's mom, chided in vain. "Foster Golding, you've already had three brownies." She vented to the others, "You know, it's just not fair. He eats anything he wants and still fits into his college pants. I just look at a piece of cake and add two pounds."

Annie laughed. "Then you must not look at much cake. My thigh's bigger than your waist."

Sonny winked at her. "You're perfect, Mama Two."

"Mmm hmm." Annie stood and ruffled his hair. "Time for me to take my perfect self on home." She yelled for her grandkids to leave the water as she gathered up towels and casserole dishes. Ignoring whiny protests from the children, she dispensed generous hugs and farewells to all as she herded her charges to the house.

Elliot pulled Bekah to himself through the still-settling water and kissed her cheek. "Finally, just us."

Bekah tilted her head toward the others. "Yeah, and all those people. Sorry, but I should spend some more time with them. It's a pretty big deal for them to come here instead of hosting at home, and they're leaving tomorrow."

Elliot brushed her cheek with the back of his hand and whispered, "Meet you back here tomorrow night?"

She tapped her forehead against his. "Yes, I'd like that."

"I'll go help finish up the flag cake. It'll make Mom happy if we eat it all."

"That's very sacrificial of you." Bekah laughed, wrapped a towel around herself, and joined the others. Though she avoided eye contact with Sonny, she could sense him studying her before he turned his attention to his phone.

Foster scraped the last crumbs from his plate, placed it with a flourish on the table, and leaned back with a loud sigh. "Now, I'm done. I think we may have to do this every year, Ida. Loving this pool."

Bekah's phone vibrated on the table. She turned it over to see a text from Sonny. *You are so hot in that bikini. Didn't have to cover up for me.* As fast as lightning, she deleted it. Bekah wanted to look at Sonny but couldn't risk her face betraying her thoughts. Was she turning red? Could everyone see the tension in her body? No, apparently not.

Foster turned his attention to Shelby. "Honey, we need a pool."

Shelby laughed. "Because we don't have enough to do with our miniature Butchart Gardens?"

Ida said, "Bekah's showed me some pictures. I'd love to see your place in person sometime."

Elliot sat beside Bekah, cake in hand. "I'd be happy to drive you down there."

Shelby's pride in their award-winning gardens made her beam. "And you're definitely welcome anytime."

Sonny took a break from his phone to join in. "You'd love it, Mom."

And just like that, Bekah's internal warning system went from guarded to high alert. She made quick eye contact with Sonny, a quiet glare ordering him to not say anything about his visit to the Golding home last year when he began chasing her affections. Unfortunately, she couldn't stop her father.

Foster started, "Yeah, right. I almost forgot—"

Sonny interrupted, "Forgot you were showing me all those pics earlier? Yeah, it seems like the exact kind of place Mom would love." To everyone else, it looked like he smiled, but Bekah knew the smirk. He loved making her squirm.

Relieved to find her mother waiting for eye contact, Bekah gave her a slight frown and a minuscule head shake. The mother-daughter telepathy worked.

Shelby stretched and yawned like a bear coming out of hibernation. "We'd better go, Mr. Golding, before I turn into a pumpkin." She made her way around the table, bestowing hugs and touches as she talked. "Thank you so much, Ida. It's been a lovely day. We so enjoyed being here. You're joining us for breakfast at the B&B tomorrow, right?"

"Wouldn't miss it. Here, let me get you some brownies to tide you over." Ida walked with them into the house.

They'd been gone a few minutes when Elliot noticed Foster's phone on the table. He hustled into the house to give it to him, leaving Bekah and Sonny alone.

Sonny smiled at her. The smile she found so sexy last year irritated her beyond measure. Fear and frustration spilled out in a plea. "You have to stop it."

He cocked his head, faux confusion plastered on his face. "Stop what?"

Bekah rolled her eyes and took her chances with being serious. "Really, if you do still care anything about me, stop it. Please."

Jim hummed his favorite Eagles song, "Take it Easy," as he stepped into the barn and flipped the light switch. His tomorrow self would thank him for staying up late tonight to make sure all of the paraphernalia from the picnic had been stowed properly. With so many people lending a hand after two days of feasting and fireworks, there was no telling what would be where.

The boards above his head creaked. Or the sound seemed to come from overhead. The whole place often creaked, though, especially with the way the wind had kicked up. Probably nothing. He secured lids to stew pots and moved them to the proper shelf where he found a ball of wadded tablecloths. *Really, kids?* He tossed them to the floor to take with him to the house.

Another sound from overhead. It definitely wasn't his imagination. A voice. But no one was staying in the upstairs studio apartment. At least not with permission. Adrenaline tightened his muscles. He grabbed a shovel and strode outside, making sure to slam the door to signal his departure.

He circled the barn to investigate. No lights were visible in the upstairs windows. No cars sat in the parking lot behind the barn. With a wheeze, the window air conditioner above him shuddered to life. Apparently, the interlopers had gotten too warm.

He crept up the stairs leading to the apartment. A pause outside, ear pressed to the door. Voices, at least two, one giggling. A bit of tension eased from his shoulders. Probably just some kids, but no need to let his guard completely down. Propping the shovel against the doorjamb, he tested the knob. Not locked.

Counting on the element of surprise, Jim flung the door open, swiped the light switch, and deepened his voice. "What's going on in here?"

A shriek from the pile of blankets on the bed as someone burrowed beneath them. A cuss word from the young man beside the pile, who bolted upright against the headboard, shirtless, disheveled hair. The look in his eyes said he might have just peed in his pants, if he had any on. His voice quivered. "Mr. Caragin . . . sir . . ."

Jim stifled the impulse to smile. Not so terribly long ago, youthful hormones made him reckless too. Nevertheless, this kind of behavior needed to be nipped in the bud. He kept his voice steady, as menacing as possible. "Well, I guess I don't gotta ask what you're doing here, but who are you?"

The man stammered as he pushed the covers aside and stepped from the bed, buttoning the shorts he thankfully wore. "I'm Devin, from production." His feet knocked over a beer bottle on the floor and amber liquid fizzed onto the wide planks. He stared at it as if it were an alien life form he had no control over.

"Well, for Pete's sake, pick that up." Jim jerked a kitchenette drawer open and flung a towel to the trespasser.

Devin bent to sop up the mess. "I'm sorry, sir."

"I'm sure you are, Devin from Production. But listen, you and your . . . friend," Jim tilted his head toward the motionless blanket pile, "need to get dressed and get out of here, and I don't ever want to see you here again."

Without another word, Jim stepped out and closed the door. Propping against the barn near the bottom of the stairs, he sent a quick text to Liz. *Be home soon, baby*. In his mind, he replayed the entire scene with more amusement than umbrage, enjoying the shock he knew she'd have when he told her.

The door above opened. Two sets of footsteps eased down the stairs. Devin shuffled by like a puppy caught chewing on the couch cushion. He muttered, "Sorry, again, Mr. Caragin, sir." With a glance up the steps, he walked away.

The girl. She wasn't coming down? Jim pushed himself away from the wall to see what she was doing.

Did his heart stop beating or was it about to explode? She waited two steps from the ground, staring straight into his eyes, tears spilling down her cheeks.

"I'm sorry, Daddy."

Her name gushed from his mouth with what felt like his last breath ever. "Victoria." *Is this what a heart attack feels like?* He looked after Devin from Production, all humor dashed from his mind. An overwhelming urge to grab his shovel and chase after the shadow disappearing in the darkness seized him. But he couldn't move, knee-deep in concrete of shock and grief.

• • • •

Liz hurried to the patio in her night shorts, t-shirt, and headscarf. *What in the world?* First, Jim was out way too late at the barn. Then the text that he'd be home soon. Then the text to meet "us" on the patio. Us? Who was us? Hopefully, *us* wasn't a stranger—or even a friend she wouldn't want to see her ready-for-bed self.

As she closed the door behind her, she could see two figures coming out of the darkness. So *us* was just two people then. Jim and . . . looked like a woman. Wait. It was Victoria. Jim shook his head in reply to the question in Liz's eyes and dropped into a chair. Victoria stood on the edge of the patio, arms wrapped around herself, and head down.

"Baby, what's wrong?" Liz rushed to her and held her close.

Her daughter's body stiffened, and she shrugged off the hug. "I *really* don't want to talk about this."

"Well, we're *really* gonna," Jim rasped out, voice full of weariness. "You might as well sit down, young lady."

"Daddy . . ." Victoria's weak protest hit the wall of her father's glare. She plopped onto the glider and hugged her knees to her chest. Then, the tiniest smidge of sass. "You don't have to 'young lady' me."

Jim scoffed. "Well, I guess maybe you're right. 'Lady' doesn't sound appropriate right now."

Enough. Liz pulled herself out of spectator mode and sat beside Victoria. "What is going on with you two? What happened?"

"Walked in on her and a guy from the crew using the barn apartment for a love shack."

"What? Who?"

"Devin," Jim sneered, "from production."

"Do we know him?"

"Never met him. How long have you known him, Victoria?"

"Long enough."

Liz bristled. "Watch your tone. Answer your father. How long?"

"Just a couple of weeks. I went to the trailers to see if someone would teach me more about editing for my posts, and he helped me. He's nice."

"Two weeks and you're already . . ."

Like Bruce Banner being taken over by the Hulk, contrite Victoria shifted into defiant Vee. "I don't know what you're freaking out about. We were just fooling around, nothing serious."

Jim buried his face in his hands. "I don't know if I can take this."

Liz tried to keep her voice even, despite feeling like a balloon was being blown up inside her head. "You don't think it's serious, making love with someone you just met? What about STDs or getting pregnant?"

"We weren't," Vee snarked with an eye roll and air quotes, "making love. It was just a hookup. Besides, we know how to be careful and . . . I'm on the pill."

Whoosh! The about-to-pop balloon in Liz's head escaped before it was tied off, and the air rushed out as it bounced around inside her head. *What do I say now? Dear Lord, what do I say now?*

Jim launched from his chair. "And how did *that* happen?"

"Student health center. It's free."

"Well, *that* makes it alright then. My big concern was that we was paying for it!"

"So." Liz found her voice. "This is who you are now, the girl who hooks up for fun? This is just normal in your world?"

"You're making it sound like I'm some tramp. It's not like that. I just want to be able to have fun when I want. You do want me to be careful, don't you?"

"Don't try to back me into a corner. Yes, of course, if you're going to have any kind of sex, we want you to protect your physical body. But you do realize there's more, right? Your body is tied to your emotions, to who God made you to be. When you give pieces of that away, you devalue yourself. That's why it's better to wait until you're married. Remember the whole semester your youth group spent on this?"

"I remember. True Love Waits. Purity rings. I hate to bust your bubble, but that's not reality. Maybe it worked for you and Daddy, but that's just not a thing anymore. Do you think Will and Tamika were each other's first? Or that Elliot and Marshall and Laurel are virgins?"

"Oh no, little girl, you don't get out of this by deflecting like that."

"I'm not a little girl. I'm nineteen, an adult. You can't tell me what to do anymore."

"Oh, yeah?" Jim's foot, Liz could see, was about to come down hard. "Can I tell you if you want a car to drive, you'll have to pay for it, the gas, and the insurance yourself? Can I tell you it takes a lot more money than you're bringing in from your 'Veeps' subscriptions to pay for rent, clothes, and textbooks? If you have to go to the emergency room, can I tell you that you'll have to pay the thousands of dollars that will cost if you're not on our insurance?

"There's a lot more to being an adult than choosing who you give your body to. And until you're able to live off the Mom and Dad dole, as long as you're living in this house, yes, we can tell you some things to do. First of all, I'm telling you to stay away from that boy, Devin, and from the whole production crew. If I catch you around them again, I'll send them all packing."

Victoria sprung from her seat. "That's not fair!"

"Oh, that's more than fair. You should know what I *really* want to do. And if you stay out here another minute, I might say everything I'm thinking. So I think it's best you go to bed. We can talk about this later."

"Seriously? You're sending me to my room?"

"Seriously? You should be grateful you got a room to go to."

* * * *

Liz curled up against the headboard, Bible in her lap open to the passage she'd been reading when Jim's last text arrived. It might as well be a recipe book or a magazine, though. Her concentration was shot. Closing her eyes, she implored God's wisdom only to be distracted by Jim's not-so-subtle raging in the bathroom.

Liz knew the quiet rampage was his way to vent, muttering to himself and making more noise than would ever seem possible in a nighttime routine. Instead of running the water only as needed, he let the water gush full force. Shaking his vitamins out of their container, slamming his water glass on the counter . . . every fuming sound from her mild-mannered husband made her flinch.

Finally, he emerged and sat on the side of the bed, back to her, and blew out his exasperation in one huge breath. "You were right, baby. We should've never let that TV crew into our lives. I let myself get carried away with the way the kids got so excited, convinced myself it could be a testimony for us. Now, look what we've got. We need to call this whole thing off."

Liz laid her Bible on her nightstand and slid over to wrap her arms around him, pressing her face into the middle of his shoulder blades. "I'm not saying I don't appreciate you admitting I'm right, but I don't think we can blame this all on the TV show."

"I don't think Devin from Production would've found us otherwise."

"I know. And I'm not happy about what I'm going to say, but if it weren't Devin, it was going to be someone else."

He turned to face her, head tilted and mouth slightly agape. A question he couldn't seem to formulate written on his face.

She answered the look. "You know she's always been boy crazy, sneaking out of the house with half her body hanging out of a dress we didn't even know she owned. Finding out she wasn't staying at Angelia's house like she told us that time. Those texts with that boy she met online."

"So you're saying she *is* the girl who hooks up for fun?"

"I hope that's not the way it is. But you have to admit, she's been obsessive about how she looks since she was twelve and that she enjoys the attention she gets because of the way she looks."

"She can't help that she's a beauty. Boys are gonna look. We always told her that her worth is more than that, though. We told her—"

"We told her all the right things. But you heard her. This world has told her other things, and that's the voice she's listening to. I follow all her social media. I can see it."

"So you're saying we just have to give up?"

"You know I'm not saying that. But I think we have to realize that the way we've been handling it hasn't worked. I always thought we were raising our kids to come and talk to us about this kind of thing, but now, I see she doesn't care about talking to me about it any more than I cared about talking to my mother about it. Hurts. I can't lie."

"What do we do?"

Liz sighed. "I know she's not an adult, by our definition, but she's not a little girl anymore. I don't want to lose our authority or our relationship. So I suppose we pray. We listen. We keep talking to her."

"And we ground her, right? We can still ground her?"

Liz smiled, pleased that Jim's face wasn't red anymore and his posture had relaxed. She kissed his cheek. "Maybe we can find something that will work even better. Tomorrow." She rolled to turn off her lamp, then let her head fall into her pillow facing him.

He drew his feet under the covers and kissed her. "Tomorrow."

• • • •

Jim waited until Liz's first snore to creep from their bed and out of the house. He mulled through the words he should use before pressing Chandler's name on his phone.

A sleepy-sounding Chandler answered. "Hey, Jim, what can I help you with?"

No need for apologies about the late hour or polite chit-chat. "There's a young man on your production crew, Devin."

"Yes."

"I caught him tonight in a compromising situation with Victoria. I want him off my property, off this show."

A few seconds of silence. "Yes, of course. I understand."

"Good."

"Mom and Poppa say hey," Bekah conveyed the greeting to Miss Ida as she came into the kitchen, slipping her phone into her pocket.

Miss Ida smiled as she took an ooey, gooey chocolate cake from her oven and placed it on the kitchen island. "Sure did enjoy them coming up for the fourth. You're a lot like your daddy."

"Yeah, I've been told. Usually when Mom's exasperated with me." Bekah inhaled the chocolateyness and glanced around. "Where's Elliot?"

"Sent him to the pool house for Cokes." Miss Ida tipped her head toward the French doors with a mischievous smile.

Alarm bells went off for Bekah. She hurried to the door and, hand on knob, surveyed the scene. Elliot must still be in the pool house. Sonny soaked up rays poolside. "Sonny's out there. I should go out."

"They'll be fine, honey. Ain't they been getting along good this week?"

"Yeah, when there were other people around."

"Let 'em be, Bekah. They gotta learn how to talk to each other."

"But, Miss Ida, I haven't told you—or anyone. Sonny's been calling and texting me. He says he wants to get back together with me. And Elliot doesn't even know . . ."

Miss Ida's smile faded. "You ain't told him?"

Bekah answered with a slight shake of her head.

"Well then, makes sense why you're worried." Miss Ida made her way to Bekah and put her arm around her shoulder. "But they'll be okay. Sonny wouldn't just up and tell him. Heck, he may not even talk to him. Sometimes, he's a lot like his daddy too."

Bekah's grip on the knob tightened, but she decided to stay inside. "I hope you're right."

• • • •

The Coke cans Elliot held were already sweating in his hands barely a few steps out of the pool house. He paused for a second to study his half-brother lounging on a poolside chair. Sonny looked like a model in an ad for one of those all-inclusive island resorts. Tall, toned, and tan, thumb-scrolling on his phone, head bobbing to whatever played in his earbuds. Without a doubt, Sonny had seen him and was avoiding eye contact, but Elliot had spent the last few minutes praying God would provide an opening for them to talk. Maybe this was his moment.

"Hot out here." He rolled his eyes at his own lameness. *Hot? In Alabama in July? Duh.*

Without stopping his scrolling, Sonny snarked, "Ya think?" Then, with even thicker disdain, he added, "Bruh?"

It was the opposite of an invitation, but Elliot choked back his anxiety and determined to make it work. Sitting in the chair next to Sonny, he used the snide comment as a segue. "Good, I thought this might be awkward to talk about." He extended a soda to Sonny who turned it down by lifting his own glass of tea for Elliot to see.

Elliot tried to figure out whether Sonny was looking at him but couldn't see through the dark Armani lenses. "Look, Sonny, I don't expect us to be like real brothers, but I'm hoping we can work on becoming friends. At least get to where we can talk about more than the weather."

"You're right, Elliot." Sonny yanked out one earbud and lowered his shades to make eye contact. "We're not like real brothers. I can see how much Mom loves you, so I can play nice the few times we'll be together, but I wouldn't count on the friendship thing ever working out either." He replaced his sunglasses and redirected his attention to his phone.

"I understand. I'm the interloper. I have fourteen younger siblings. Just about the time I thought Mom and Dad would have a little free time, another baby would show up. Anyway, I know it's not exactly the same, but I'm not going to give up. We may not see each other much, but I want you to be part of our lives and to be the coolest uncle ever to our kids."

Sonny whipped his head back to face Elliot. "Rebekah's knocked up?"

Elliot could only stammer. "What? No. That's not what I . . . it's just that . . . I mean, we will be getting married and, one day, hopefully . . . start a family."

"So you're engaged? Mom didn't tell me."

"Well, no, not yet." Elliot took a breath to regain his mental balance before making the decision to confide in Sonny. "Got the ring, though.

Gonna ask her on Wednesday. It's my birthday and the anniversary of our first date."

Sonny stared at the pool. "Well, well, well. Rebekah joining my family. That's great, Elliot, just great. You two will make a great couple."

Elliot's shoulders relaxed, and his smile forced his dimples to make an appearance. Sonny took a drink from his tea, faced Elliot, and issued his next sentence with jealous venom and the precision of a laser-guided bomb.

"And I know you're going to *love* the wedding night."

Elliot's smile evaporated. His body became rigid as the implication invaded his brain and heart. "What's that supposed to mean?"

Sonny swung his legs to the side of the chair, sitting up to be face to face with Elliot. "Oh. My. God. You mean she's never told you?"

The coldness of his upturned lip obliterated his pretension of disbelief. Elliot assumed it was an expression honed in boardrooms of companies he'd bought with the express purpose of breaking them into pieces. Sonny had control, and he obviously knew it. He locked his ice-blue eyes onto Elliot's green before he continued.

"Hmmm. Rebekah, what a bad girl." He smirked as Elliot's face muscles tightened and cheeks grew flaming hot, then feigned concern. "Sorry. Thought she would've told you by now. Hey, no big deal, Elliot. It won't be the first time brothers have shared."

With a rage he'd never experienced, Elliot bolted from his chair and stood over Sonny. His hands clenched into fists, his right elbow drew back, ready to release like the plunger of a pinball machine.

Sonny didn't flinch. If anything, his posture relaxed as he glanced toward the kitchen door. With one eyebrow cocked, he quipped, "You think she's watching us?" Replacing his shades, he swung his legs back onto his lounge chair and took a languid sip of tea.

• • • •

She'd seen enough. Bekah opened the door to intervene in whatever was going on. Elliot made it to the door before she could open it all the way. She stopped short when she saw his flushed face and mad tears filling his eyes.

She squeaked out his name as he brushed past her, grabbed his car keys from the counter, and stormed out the front door.

Within seconds, his Jeep screeched out of the driveway. She exchanged horrified looks with Miss Ida who threw down her dish towel and strode out the door. Bekah passed her in a flash.

"What did you say?" The words spewed out like hot lava as she crossed the short space between them, but they didn't even begin to thaw Sonny's glacial expression.

He only glanced in her direction before returning his gaze to his phone. "You said you were going to tell him. I figured by now, surely . . ."

Bekah sank to the chair Elliot had just left. Her body shook with core-wracking gasps for air. Ida paused for a second to smack Sonny's head before wrapping her arm around Bekah's shoulders.

"Why on earth, Sonny? Ain't you learned nothing about being civil with all them fancy people you surround yourself with? Sometimes you just gotta let sleeping dogs—"

"Lie? Yeah, Mom, I know about sleeping dogs." The unrepressed snark dripping from every syllable Sonny uttered made Bekah go cold. She hugged her arms around her body to overcome the trembling.

Sonny sat up to face his mother. "I thought you were through with secrets, though. Wanted everything out in the open about your little half-breed sleeping dog. Didn't matter how that affected anyone else."

He glared at Ida, then at Bekah. Their stunned silence seemed to energize him. "What? Are we only supposed to keep *some* secrets around here? Let me know because I have more I can share. Like, did you know he's planning on marrying her?" Sonny gestured to Bekah who raised her eyes to him in a silent plea to stop talking.

He steamrolled on. "Shouldn't he know that I had her first? That I loved her first? No? You're right. Let's keep all of that inside. It'll make the holidays much more bearable."

He stood with a muttered curse and turned toward the house. "I'm going to wash the Alabama off me and head back to Miami."

• • • •

Bekah curled up in the window seat of her apartment, tossing everything about the day, about the last year, back and forth in her mind with the speed and force of a squarely hit racquetball. Elliot knew. He knew about her and Sonny.

But new information had emerged. In his anger, Sonny had flung a new word. Love. He said he loved her first. She hadn't been aware he loved her at all. She'd been convinced all along he only saw her as a project, a sad sack of a girl fresh on the heels of a devastating divorce, the perfect fodder for his white-knight syndrome.

Sonny, after all, introduced her to the concept of moral relativism. There is no real right and wrong, he'd claimed with conviction. They were just enjoying each other. They didn't have to conform to what her parents or his mother or the preacher at the church thought. He made her feel beautiful and worthy with his pursuit. But love? She didn't even know the word existed in his vocabulary.

Even the confusion brought by his revelation wasn't enough to overrule the memory of Elliot's face. *He forgave you for keeping the divorce a secret for so long. He's not going to be able to forgive this. No one could. Not even Elliot. Oh, God, what am I going to do?*

"Well, good morning." Liz dried her hands on her apron as she returned Haley's cheerful greeting. She handed a soap-soaked glass to Emma and directed her, Sam, and Peanut to continue washing the breakfast dishes.

"Good morning, Liz." Kobi breezed in and set her makeup bag on the kitchen table.

He didn't tell Chandler. Should've done it myself. Knew he had too much on his mind. Liz sighed. "I'm sorry, ladies. Jim said he'd let Chandler know. He had to go to the greenhouses this morning—some trouble with a shipment. We'll have to reschedule today's vignette."

"No, he called. We decided it would be good for you to do this one by yourself. Jim said he'd let you know. Is it okay with you?"

"Well, he didn't." Liz found her cell on the island and saw the missed call and the text. "Oops, guess he did. Sure, yes, I suppose it's fine. Good thing Kobi's here. I must look a mess."

• • • •

Hair and makeup done, Liz perched as directed on a stool at the island at an angle the production assistants agreed made for the best shot. Just over Liz's left shoulder, the double-hung oversized windows at the kitchen sink framed the brilliant green leaves and shining white blooms of the magnolia tree at the edge of the patio.

"Ready?" Haley sat across the island beside the camera, flanked by the umbrella lights that now seemed as commonplace as furniture to Liz.

Liz nodded with a smile then paused and shook her head as a chill worked its way from her head to her feet. Something was wrong somewhere. She checked her phone for missed calls or messages. Nothing. Everything must be okay, but the air felt burdensome to her. She squeezed her eyes closed to pray. *Jesus, this house, this kitchen, belongs to you. Satan may roam but not here, Lord. In this house, in my heart, you alone are sovereign.*

"Liz, are you okay?"

The oppression lifted, and Liz opened her eyes to see the stares of Haley and the crew and the blinking red light of the camera. She nodded and straightened her posture. "Yes, all good."

Haley sipped her ever-present smoothie and lifted a finger to the camera operator. The red light went solid. An assistant counted down from five.

"Tell me about Cooper."

Liz's heart fluttered, and the corners of her mouth turned up. "He's a special one, isn't he? Did you know his birth mom left Cooper on our porch in a box?"

Haley gasped. "What? Who would do that?"

"That's what I said. Who would do this to a little baby? Laurel was around five. She heard the crying and saw him first. When she came to tell me, I thought she was fibbing. I sent her to get her daddy, scooped him up, and headed to the kitchen for a bottle. I used to always have bottles in this kitchen." The fond memory warmed her heart.

"Just a baby in a box. Nothing else?"

"Nope. Jim searched the box for anything that would tell us about him while I fed him, but there was nothing. Now, we were used to folks dumping cats and dogs out here, but this was hard to take in."

"I guess you noticed his physical problems right away."

"Not right away. While he drank, I pulled the blanket away. At first, we couldn't see it because of the outfit he had on, but I knew something wasn't right. After his bottle, I unwrapped him to check his diaper. Jim was with me by then. All five kids staring at him.

"That's when we saw how messed up his side was. Left arm below the elbow, left leg below the knee. They just ended in little round nubs."

Haley shook her head. "Assume that's why he was abandoned."

"No." Liz smiled. "Not abandoned. Abandoned would've been left in an alley or a dumpster. She left her baby with someone she trusted to take care of him."

"I'm sorry. I didn't mean to . . ."

"It's okay. I just don't like that word." Liz hoped her words were taken as a kind explanation, not a rebuke. "It does turn out his *challenges* were only part of the reason she left him for us."

"You found out who she was."

"It wasn't too hard for the system to find her. She was only thirteen. Her father wasn't in the picture. Her mother—on drugs—told her to 'take care of her own problems.' Her older brother worked on the farm, so she knew we'd already adopted five babies. I guess she didn't think one more would matter. Truth is, it was sweet she knew we would take care of him."

"You just kept him?"

"We had to go through the formalities, but there was never any argument from anyone in the girl's family. No one else wanted to deal with those challenges. I guess it's a good thing. He had my heart wrapped up the minute I unwrapped him. I think I would've tried to take down anyone who tried to take him from me."

Haley smiled. "Raising a child with such big disabil—" She stopped and changed the word at the sight of Liz's cocked eyebrow. "Challenges. That was something new for you and Jim."

"No, not really."

"What do you mean? The other kids didn't have physical problems, did they?"

"Oh, physical problems." Liz grinned. "You said challenges. All of our kids, everyone in the world, actually, has challenges. It's just easier to see Cooper's. Don't worry, I know what you mean.

"Yes, there were a lot of new things to learn. New doctors and specialists and therapists. Again, though, UAB came through for us. They've provided prosthetics for him since he was two. State-of-the-art. And because of Cooper, they've learned better ways to help other children and help families afford all those things."

"I imagine it's all very expensive."

"It's often prohibitive. There are foundations that help. Jim's sister started one when Cooper was a toddler and she saw the need. Organizations like hers, places like St. Jude's in Memphis, they're a Godsend to anyone dealing with children with special needs."

"I saw Cooper driving a tractor the other day. Seems like he's overcome his challenges. You and Jim have obviously done a good job helping him cope."

Memory after memory flitted through Liz's mind with the speed of hummingbird wings. "I can't tell you how hard it was *not* helping him do everything. Watching him scoot with his face in the carpet when he tried to crawl, falling over and over when he lost balance, letting him struggle with dressing himself.

"Then, of course, the bigger things like swimming, running, playing games with the other kids. They didn't seem to have any problem not cutting him slack. He had to keep up all on his own. And he did."

"Never gave up on anything?"

"Well, piano got the better of him. Other than that, he just kept plugging. There's something inside him that doesn't let him feel sorry for himself."

"Never?" Haley looked like she couldn't believe it.

"Never."

Haley paused and winked at Liz. "And cut." She closed her iPad as the red light on the camera blinked off. "I'm guessing you're okay stopping there."

It seemed like a short interview, but Liz nodded. *Good, I have plenty of things to do today.* But what was up with Haley? She seemed to be lingering, waiting for everyone else to leave. Camera operators and production assistants packed up as Kobi removed Liz's makeup.

When Kobi left, Haley sunk into a chair at the table and stared out the window.

"Can I get you some tea?" She expected Haley to turn her down as she'd already done several times since they met. The girl obviously had something against sugar.

Haley surprised her. "Sure, that would be nice."

Liz raised her eyebrows, cocked her head, and fixed a glass for both of them. She set the glasses on the table and sat beside Haley. They stared out of the window together for a while.

Liz broke the silence. "Something on your mind?"

"It's just . . . I keep thinking about what Jim said a couple of weeks ago. You know, when we were talking about Marshall and Victoria."

So this was it. Haley wanted to talk about Jim's abortion comment. That explained the uneasiness that weighed on her earlier. With no idea about Haley's past or her convictions, Liz needed to tread carefully to avoid the landmines on this battlefield. *The truth in love, Lord. The truth in love.* The silent prayer played on a loop in her head.

She made eye contact with Haley. "I remember."

Haley took a big slug of tea. Red splotches appeared as if turned up with a dimmer switch on her chest and neck. "I don't want to speak out of turn, and maybe I misread your reaction, but it didn't seem like you totally agreed with him."

"Hmm." Liz made a design in the beaded condensation on her glass with her finger. "I hope I don't disappoint you with my answer, but I do agree with him. You did see some tension, though. He just surprised me with his . . . directness."

"I don't understand. I mean, you're a woman. Don't you think women should have the right to choose what happens to their bodies?"

"I think women have the ability to choose what happens to *their* bodies."

"That's what I'm talking about."

"Not really. They're different things. Being able to do something doesn't make it the right thing to do. And, then, when a baby comes into the picture, we're not just talking about the woman's body, are we? There's another body. A weaker life that needs to be nurtured and protected. I think *that* life deserves the chance to make its own choices one day."

Liz cringed inside. Oh, if she'd only realized this all those years ago. *East from the West, Liz. Focus on this girl in front of you.* "You don't agree?"

Haley's ponytail swung as she shook her head. "It's just . . . I don't think it's so simple."

"It isn't. And . . . it is. I do mean what I said the other day. I believe all life is valuable."

"I guess that's why you have fifteen kids, huh?" Haley grinned at Liz.

Good, she hadn't pushed Haley away. Liz leaned back and brushed the hair away from her face. "Sounds like a lot when someone says it out loud."

"Why have you done it, really? Other than 'God meant them for you.'"

"I guess it sounds silly to you, but I truly do mean what I say about it. I felt called to take every child we have. I think God wants us to place the needs of weaker people ahead of our own wants."

"Weaker people?"

"Yes. From unborn babies to an elderly person who can't take care of themselves."

Haley's mouth scrunched into a bow, and her forehead wrinkled. "And people like Cooper?"

Liz nodded. "And Amy and Hope. Remember we talked about how women end their pregnancies now if they find out the baby has Down's or another challenge? The CDC loves to tell you we're eradicating Down's, but they don't tell you why it's happening."

"But what about for the single woman who can't handle a baby with challenges or any baby?"

"To tell you the truth, I believe women can handle a lot more than this culture tells them they can." Liz shook her head with a smile as a paradox popped into her brain. "Isn't it kind of crazy? So much in this country tells us that women can do anything, preaches about how strong we are. Then there's this loud voice saying we can't handle a baby we didn't plan on, like we're pitiful victims who can overcome anything except that."

The corners of Haley's mouth turned down, and she nodded as if acknowledging the point. Then she looked away, staring out the window. Liz could almost feel a confession stuck between Haley's brain and mouth. This girl was in pain. *Let her process.* Liz sipped her tea and joined Haley in staring into the backyard. *Give me wisdom, Lord.*

Haley inhaled like following orders from a doctor with a stethoscope to her chest. With her exhale, she started a sentence. "Liz . . ."

Liz turned her face back to Haley's. "Yes?"

Haley kept her eyes on the backyard. "Don't you think there's ever a time when a woman really *can't* handle everything that having a baby means?"

Liz paused to see if Haley would add more, but she didn't. "I know," Liz started softly, "that it can be so overwhelming for a woman to think about all of the consequences when she realizes she's pregnant. Especially when it's the last thing she'd planned. However . . ."

Liz waited. She wanted Haley to look at her. She gently tapped the table in a way she'd learned focused some of her kids. It worked. Haley pivoted her face, her eyes riveted to Liz's. There was a longing in those beautiful blue eyes that gave Liz the confidence to continue her sentence.

"With everything I've learned about mothers in desperate situations, I do believe the best thing a woman can do when she's unable to deal with the responsibility of raising a child is to have the baby and give it up for adoption.

I'm not saying by any means that I think it's easy. But doing the right thing often isn't."

Haley broke eye contact to focus on her tea.

Liz brought the conversation back to a happy thought. "I do hate for them the joy they're missing. I can't imagine life without Amy or Hope or Cooper or any of the others."

"It's so easy for you."

"Easy?" Liz smirked. "You've been here for over a month, girl. You know that's not the case. Every day has its own joys and challenges. You'll see someday."

It was too late to call it off. Bekah and Ida busied themselves arranging fried chicken, pigs in blankets, and other assorted extra-gluten, high-carb platters of food on the kitchen counter of the Echols' home. Brett and Karla Echols, who led the singles' ministry at LifeSpring Church, had all but begged to host a surprise birthday party for Elliot. A month's worth of planning had gone into the night.

Tonight was perfect since his birthday fell on a normal Bible study night in their bungalow-styled home. They'd all wheedled Elliot into the idea he could come to Bible study and then have dinner with Bekah and Ida.

Karla, always thrilled to put some of her Pinterest boards into action, settled on a camping theme. She'd festooned the entire kitchen and living area with swags of greenery, boat oars, fishing poles, and other miscellaneous outdoor equipment. On the kitchen table, gallons of tea and lemonade cooled in a galvanized tub of ice labeled with a *swamp juice* sign next to the birthday cake. The half-sheet cake was a work of art, a tree-lined pond with a tiny boat holding a man and a woman in fishing clothes, their lines drooped into the water.

Karla and Brett had become loving mentors to Elliot and Bekah over the last year. Their four-year-old son, Brandon, treated Elliot like a superhero. He stood at his duty station, nose against the front door glass, watching for Elliot's arrival.

Twenty-year-old Ashleigh Reed bounced into the kitchen and lowered a plate of pimento-and-cheese sandwiches onto the counter between Bekah and Ida. "Do you think he suspects anything?"

"Definitely not." Ida spared Bekah.

Ashleigh giggled. "Oh, good. I know it must've been killing y'all to keep it all secret. I could never keep something like that up. I'm a terrible liar. Momma always said so."

Ida and Bekah didn't have to look at each other to feel their mutual grief building. Oblivious to their tense bodies and reddening faces, Ashleigh grabbed a deviled egg and continued to prattle about the dangers of keeping secrets between bites.

Brett interrupted her monologue. "Elliot just called. Thought we lost him there for a minute. He said he's feeling kind of sick and wasn't going to make it. But I talked him into coming on. Did he mention anything to you two? He's supposed to have dinner with you after, right?"

Bekah cleared her throat and searched for the right words. "Yeah, I knew he was feeling a little off, but I haven't talked to him in a while. Y'all excuse me. I need to potty." She made her way to the bathroom and stared at her reflection, willing the puddles to stop gathering in her eyes. *Get it together, Bekah. Just get through the next two hours. At least you'll get to see him.*

Ida met her when she emerged, making her almost lose the façade she had talked herself into. "Oh, Miss Ida, I can't do it. I just can't."

Ida stroked her face. "Yes, you can, child. We can do it together."

Brandon's delighted squeals shattered their moment. "He's here! He's here! Eh-wee-ot's here!"

The two women made it to the living room in time to see Elliot open the door to enthusiastic cheers of "Surprise!" and "Happy Birthday!" Elliot mouthed, "For me?" in an implication he had an inkling about the party. His smile grew as he scanned the faces of his friends in the room until he got to Bekah's. Bekah read in his face and body language the indecision about how to react to them in this roomful of people. He gathered himself within two seconds, reignited his smile, and started toward Bekah.

He'd taken only one step when Brandon launched himself at Elliot like an Angry Bird flying from a slingshot. He wanted to show Elliot everything in the room, especially the cake, all at once. His excitement became the focus of the room, taking attention away from what Bekah felt was palpable tension between the two of them.

Elliot enjoyed giving Brandon his full attention until Brett insisted the birthday boy had other guests to talk to. Nudged by Ida, Bekah walked over to Elliot. Feeling everyone's eyes on them, they gave each other an awkward hug.

"Happy birthday." Bekah exuded all the fauxcitement she could gather. "Surprised?"

"Yeah. Totally," he answered half-heartedly before turning his attention to the food. "Hey, is that bacon?"

Ida came around from the counter. "You know it's not a party without bacon." She smiled as she embraced Elliot and wished him a happy birthday, taking advantage of the assumption he wouldn't shake her off and make a scene. Her bet paid off, but Elliot did no more than barely touch her until she broke the hug.

"Thanks, Ida." He moved to the counter, picked up a bacon-wrapped pretzel, and immersed himself in conversation with other friends.

Bekah moved to Ida's side, linked arms, and smiled encouragement into Ida's watery eyes.

"He called me Ida." Her voice cracked.

"I heard. He'll forgive you, and it will be Mom again. None of this is your fault. I'm the one who—"

Ashleigh, brandishing a lighter, sprang into their conversation. "Come on, you two. Let's light some candles and cut this cake!"

She corralled Bekah and Elliot to the table and set about lighting the twenty-six candles on the cake. Brett's booming voice led the Happy Birthday song.

After the last drawn-out "you," Brandon shouted, "Make a wish! Make a wish!"

Elliot glanced at Bekah and back at the tiny flickering flames. She could only guess he wished he could go back in a time machine and never meet her. He turned his attention to Brandon. "Why don't you help me, buddy?"

Like any other four-year-old, Brandon didn't need to be asked twice to blow out candles. He squeezed his eyes shut, filled his cheeks with air, and blew with all his might. Elliot came alongside him to finish the job with a more steady breath.

"Looks like your wish is going to come true!" Brett wrapped his arm around Karla and beamed at Elliot.

Elliot locked eyes with Brett and shook his head by a fraction before he forced a smile. "Guess we'll have to wait and see."

• • • •

All of the guests except Elliot, Bekah, and Ida were gone. Bekah knew their lingering had less to do with wanting to help clean up and more with not knowing how to leave separately without raising eyebrows. They'd hardly spoken to each other the whole night. Weariness showed on all of their faces. At least to her.

"We can get the rest of this." Karla brushed past Elliot with the last stack of paper plates on her way to the garbage can. "It's your birthday. I'm sure you have other things to do." She winked at him and took the box of Ziplocs from Bekah's hand to finish stashing the scant leftovers.

Elliot answered, "Yeah, I guess you're right. We all have a lot of work to get ready for the Camp Hope cookout on Friday."

"Well, not exactly what I thought you were going to say." Karla sounded disappointed. "Is something wrong? You didn't like the party?"

Brett frowned and made eye contact with Elliot with what Bekah perceived as sympathy. *Had Elliot told him? Sheesh, of course, he would've. He needed someone to talk to, right?*

Elliot shook his head and protested without great conviction. "Everything's fine. I loved the party. I'm just not feeling so good, that's all."

Bekah piped up in an effort to give Elliot an escape route. "Why don't you go on home and rest, Elliot? Ida can take me home. We do need to start organizing the supplies for Friday, so we can work in the diner for a while."

Elliot took the opportunity. "Yeah, I guess that's a good idea. Well, thanks, guys, for everything. It really was great, Karla." Elliot side-hugged Karla.

Ida and Bekah gathered their things and walked out the door with Elliot as they effused their thanks to their hosts. After Brett closed the door, Elliot strode to his Jeep without a backward glance.

"Elliot." Bekah's voice stopped him as he opened his door. She moved toward him and tilted her head back to the house. "They're watching."

Elliot waved at Brett and Karla who were peering out the glass door before locking eyes with Bekah. "I don't care."

He climbed into his Jeep, slammed the door, and backed out of the driveway.

• • • •

Please, no. I can't deal with this.

The bubbly Skype tone couldn't be ignored. Elliot took a deep breath, plastered a grin on his face, and clicked the accept button. Once he saw their faces, his phony grin transformed into a sincere one. Jim, Liz, and the thirteen youngest Caragins were piled into the screen screaming, "Happy Birthday!"

"Thanks, guys! You just made my day. And thanks for the monster cookies, Mom. I got them yesterday."

The corners of Liz's mouth turned upward into a loving mama smile. "I know you love them. So . . . tell us about your party."

"You knew about the party?"

"Sure did." Vee jumped in. "Bekah's been so excited about it. It's practically all she's talked about for weeks. Wish we coulda been there."

"I wish you could've too." Elliot longed to be with his family now, to jump into the constant fray that kept you from focusing on any one thing very long.

He saw his mother's face get serious and realized too late he'd done a terrible job of masking his homesickness.

Liz scrunched her nose and asked, "What's wrong, El?"

He shook himself out of the funk. "Nothing, Mom. Everything's fine."

"Is Bekah there?"

"Not now. She and Mom, Ida Mom, are at the diner getting ready for the cookout on Friday."

Elliot maneuvered through twenty minutes of chatter, glossing over any mention of Bekah. One by one, his siblings dropped out of the conversation until only he and his parents were still on the call.

Apparently, he'd said nothing to curb her mama's instinct that something was wrong. "El, honey, you sure you okay?"

Elliot closed his eyes with a long, slow blink. "I'm fine, Mom. Just a little tired."

Thank God for his dad. Jim stepped in, shutting down any further questions from the chief inquisitor. "Well, I'm glad you've had a good day. We'll see you on Sunday."

"Sunday?"

"Yeah, you're bringing Bekah back, right?"

Crap. He hadn't even thought about that yet. "Oh yeah, yeah. Sunday. I'll see you then."

• • • •

After the final love yous, Jim pushed the end call button and turned to face his wife. "Liz, he's fine."

She rolled her eyes at him. "He is not fine. Something's not right. When have I ever been wrong about him?"

He chuckled and kissed her cheek. "Never, baby. You've never been wrong about Elliot. Guess you're just going to have to wait until Sunday to ask more questions."

Rainy days meant indoor work. Closet cleaning started right after breakfast. Liz stood in the middle of the bedroom surrounded by stacks of clothes. The older kids were supposedly working in their rooms, but it was easier for her to do this room without the "help" of the youngest Caragins. Especially when it came to adding things to the giveaway and throwaway piles.

Sad, really, that the giveaway pile was so large. All the years of hand-me-downs were ending as the smallest outgrew their clothes. Liz felt tempted to keep some of it for her granddaughter, but she wouldn't be able to wear them for at least six more years. The need for storage space kept Liz practical.

Laurel's voice broke her concentration. "Vee and Jordan have moved on to help the middles. You need help?"

"Sure. How about pulling out whatever's under their beds?"

"You got it." Laurel peered under the double bed the girls shared. "Sheesh. This could take a while." She laughed as she pulled out a jar of peanut butter and a spoon. "Which pile do these go in?"

Liz rolled her eyes and shook her head. "I knew we were going through peanut butter way too fast. They know they're not supposed to have food up here."

"Yeah, we all know."

"Laurel, you too?"

Laurel continued to pull clothes and toys from beneath the bed. "Maybe a little. But you know I'm a rule follower. Victoria, on the other hand . . ."

Instant sorrow fell like a weighted blanket on Liz's shoulders. "Victoria." She moved to the foot of the bed and rifled through the things Laurel raked out. "That girl has her own set of rules."

"She told me what happened."

Liz glanced at the camera in the corner of the ceiling. Red light off unless specifically allowed as promised. "Really? How does her version go?"

"Dad caught her making out with a TV guy, went ballistic."

"Ballistic?"

"I'm paraphrasing. She thinks you and Dad were too harsh, your views are antiquated, and you don't understand our gen. Blah, blah, blah."

"What did you say?"

"Truthfully, not much. Mainly listened." Laurel moved to the other side of the bed. She must've noticed Liz's frown. "I did tell her she needed to slow her roll on getting physically involved with guys. Reminded her she could only get herself hurt. She deserves a man who will treat her with the respect she deserves."

"What did she say to that?"

Laurel smirked. "Said I sounded like you."

"Hope you weren't offended."

"Your mini-me? No way."

"Laurel?"

From beneath the bed, "Um hmm."

"This whole thing. It's kind of burst my bubble about thinking you all felt free to talk to me about anything. I guess I've been totally naïve."

"I talk to you."

"Not about everything, though. Like boyfriends." Hard swallow. "Sex? Victoria implied none of you older kids were virgins."

A moment of silence. "Awkward. But, FYI, she's wrong about me."

This might be pushing it. "Not even Jaron?"

A heavy sigh sputtered from Laurel as she emerged from her work and crawled onto the bed to look into her mother's eyes. "Not even Jaron."

Relief.

"Mom, I really do believe everything you've taught us about that. That God's perfect design is to wait until I'm married. That my body is a gift to my future husband and his is a gift to me."

"Victoria said nobody waits anymore."

"Of course she did. It fits her agenda. People wait. We may be in the minority, but I know plenty of people—guys and girls. Even when they don't wait, it's not the massive sexfest out there some people make it sound like."

"Well, that's good to know."

"But, Mom . . ." Laurel blew out a gush of air as she broke eye contact.

Liz knew this look. Ever-compliant Laurel wanted to tell her something about her sister without being a tattletale. Even in her twenties, she wavered between allegiance to sibling loyalty and calling out attention to a problem.

Liz plopped onto the bed beside her. "What is it, baby?"

Laurel rolled onto her back. "It's just . . . this thing with Victoria, it's more than her views on sex. She's redefining herself to appeal to more and more people. To do that, she's walking away from anything that says anything is wrong. She's walking away from her faith."

A phantom icy hand reached into Liz's chest and wrapped its bony fingers around her heart. Stinging. Stifling. Freezing wisps etched sneering words. *You've lost her now.* She grasped the cross on her necklace like a drowning person reaching for a life vest.

"Sweet Jesus." She fell to her side, facing Laurel. "What can we do? Talk to her more? Keep her home from school and off the internet? Have Pastor Ricky come talk to her?"

Laurel smiled and stroked Liz's cheek. "I know you want to fix it, but I don't think it's going to work like that."

"What do you mean?"

"I mean she's heard all the words. She's seen it lived out all her life. But telling her to behave, or not behave, a certain way because the Bible says so won't work because she's decided the Bible has no authority."

"But the Bible is Truth. That's what gives it authority. God put all the wisdom we need in there to help us live the best life we can."

"I understand. I believe that too. But what you and I see as guidelines for living the best life, she sees as limitations to her enjoyment. That's the greatest sin according to her crowd—telling them they can't, or shouldn't, do something. Judge not lest you be judged."

Liz bristled. "That's taken out of context."

Laurel smiled with gentle concern. "I know. But that's the only way her friends and followers are going to use Scripture. Selectively pulled phrases to emotionally bludgeon. That's why I say that the way to fix this isn't going to be with a sermon or a memory verse."

"What will fix it?"

"I'm not totally sure. But I know you're very good at wielding one weapon."

Liz blinked, squeezing the mist from her eyes. *Yes, Liz, you have the mightiest weapon.* "I can pray."

Laurel nodded. "That's why I told you all this. So you can pray."

Friday, July 12

Ninety degrees with a heat index of ninety-five. Not quite as hot as last year. Still sweltering by any definition, even under the park pavilion with the fans in high gear. Bekah accepted a platter of sandwiches from Reuben and whined, "Why can't they have this event in the spring . . . or winter?"

Reuben laughed, "I guess because it's called *Summer* Fun Day."

"Oh yeah, hadn't thought of that." Bekah swiped her forehead with the back of her hand. "Where's the rest of your fam?"

"In the car. Cynda's finishing feeding Jackson. Good to see you too."

"You know I love ya, Rube. It's just the boys are so squeezable."

"Whatever." He winked and left to grab more of the food for the two hundred Camp Hope kids who would swarm to the pavilion soon.

Bekah scanned the park. Miss Ida was in the next pavilion slicing watermelons and cantaloupes to set out with mountains of cookies. Bekah could tell she was talking a blue streak to her volunteers. The woman couldn't talk to a group without flailing her arms like those wacky waving inflatables outside every car dealership.

The campers grouped at various activity stations sprinkled among the bounce-house-dotted landscape. There was the obligatory face-painting station, a maze, an archery station, and more. She couldn't see Elliot, but she knew he planned to be there. Maybe he'd pulled pond duty, where they worked together last year teaching the littles how to fish.

The memory provoked a frown. How much had changed in one year . . . and the fault fell completely on her. Squeals from Reuben and Cynda's three-year-old jolted her from the funk. She turned to see him running at full throttle toward her, arms outstretched. "Aunt Bekah! Aunt Bekah!" She scooped him up in her arms, and he lay his head on her shoulder like she was his favorite blanket. Bekah nuzzled her face into his downy hair.

Seeing Cynda close on his heels with her baby in her arms was more good medicine. The two women with their arms full of love bundles embraced. The toddler pointed to his brother. "That's the baby," he explained to Bekah.

"Yes, I know." Bekah laughed as she set the boy down. He galloped away to his father.

Bekah stared after the toddler. "Can I keep him?"

"Yes! But you have to take the baby too. These boys have so much energy."

Bekah stroked the baby's pudgy fingers. "I guess Miss Ida would say that's why babies are for young'uns."

"I think I've heard that a lot in the last three years. Where is Miss Ida?"

Bekah tilted her head toward the neighboring pavilion. "Making sure there's plenty of dessert."

"Not like that's ever a problem. Sorry we had to miss the birthday party. Was he surprised?"

Chin up, Bekah. "Seemed to be."

"Is he here?"

"Hmm, not sure." Bekah busied herself rearranging the mounds of crustless PB&Js.

"Thought you might be at the pond together again." Cynda giggled. "Remember last year when those kids threw their poles into the water when you said it was cookie time?"

"Yeah. Good times." Dang, why couldn't she say it without her voice cracking? Bekah moved around the table so Cynda couldn't see her face, but her friend stuck to her like a tick on a coon hound. Bekah blinked hard and opened her eyes wide to dry the tears before she turned back so they were face to face.

Cynda didn't buy the fake smile. She took a sharp breath. "Bekah, what the—?"

Bekah rolled her eyes skyward and shook her head. "I can't. I just can't right now."

"Well, you're gonna have to." With two words and a head bob, Cynda directed Reuben to finish lunch prep and steered Bekah to a vacant swing set a few yards away. She plopped into one swing with Jackson swaddled in her arms. Bekah fell into the next and traced figure eights in the sand with the tip of her Vans.

Cynda gave her a few moments before she prompted. "What's up, girl?"

Bekah twiddled with the warm chain links for a few moments more. "I've so screwed up. He's probably never going to even speak to me again." She took a deep breath and blew it out. "He knows about me and Sonny."

Cynda brought her swaying seat to a stop. "What? How? Did you tell him?"

"Sonny did."

A four-letter word escaped Cynda's mouth followed by, "When?"

"Sunday afternoon at Miss Ida's. Then, his surprise party at the Echols' on Wednesday night—it was awful. He could barely look at me. And he's mad at Miss Ida too."

"What you gonna do?"

"What can I do? Right now, I think it's best to leave him alone for a little while, but it's *killing* me. He must hate me. I can't blame him. He's always been too good for me."

"Wait. That last thing, that's not true. Elliot's a good guy, a real good guy, but he's not perfect, and you deserve a good guy. You gotta talk to him."

"I don't know when . . . if . . . I'll ever get the chance."

As if on cue, dozens of kids popped over the horizon on their way to lunch. Shepherding them were a few counselors, including Elliot. The kids, their faces beaded with dirty sweat, piled into the pavilion. Elliot stayed on the edge of the group, scanning the volunteers under the metal roof.

His eyes finally made it to the swing set and found Bekah. Contact. She stood and begged as much as she could with her eyes. He stared at her for a moment, then turned to talk to another counselor. Leaving his charges, he sauntered away in the direction of the parking lot.

Cynda stood and rubbed Bekah's shoulder. "Woman up. You gotta at least try."

• • • •

Woman up. Easy for her to say. Bekah stood at the edge of the parking lot, staring at Elliot. He lounged in the driver's seat of his Jeep, feet propped on the open door frame, head back against the seat. Were his eyes closed? She couldn't be sure.

Faint sounds of laughter reached her from the pavilion. She turned her head back for a moment. They probably needed her help. *Stop it. They don't need you. Woman up.* One deep breath later, she stepped onto the lot. The crumbling asphalt crunched as she took one deliberate step after another until she stood within arms-length of her goal. His eyes were closed.

Another deep breath. "Hey."

He didn't open his eyes or move his head, but she saw his left hand clench and unclench. "I can't, Bekah."

His name caught in her throat. Dropping her head, she turned to leave.

His voice stopped her. "Were you not *ever* going to tell me?"

"I was. I just . . ." She turned back around and eased her way to the open driver's door. "Oh, Elliot. How was I supposed to . . . I mean, yes, I was gonna tell you, but then, Miss Ida . . . you're *brothers*. You had so much going on with your heart. I didn't want to add that on."

"No." He opened his eyes. Those beautiful green eyes, red streaks marring the whites, glared at her with the cold combination of hurt and anger she'd faced since Sunday. "You don't get to palm this off on wanting to spare my feelings. You weren't worried about me. You were worried about you."

The weight of his words hit her like a cast-iron skillet to the gut. She clung to the door to keep herself from crumbling. The meager breakfast she'd had churned in her stomach. Unable to bear his burning eyes or his accusation, she looked longingly back at the pavilion. Was it his anger or seeing the pain she'd caused? Or could it be, maybe, hearing the truth?

His voice came out rough, compassionless. "*You* is always the main thing you've ever worried about. Your divorce, your hurt, your do-over. After all I loved you through, you didn't think you could trust me?"

"Of course not. It was never that." She made eye contact, willing her tears at bay. "I just . . . I couldn't stand the thought of losing you. I didn't think you'd ever be able to forgive me."

He blinked and shook his head. "Maybe I would have, maybe not. Now, we'll never know." Elliot pulled the door away from her and slammed it. "Listen, will you tell my team I had to leave?" He turned the key and shifted to first.

Bekah wiped away the tears spilling onto her cheeks. "Please. Elliot. Tell me what I can do."

"I can't be your problem-solver on this one, Bekah. I gotta go."

Sounds of activity in the Bait Shop kitchen below her drew Bekah from the safety of her quilt fortress. Might as well get up. Not like she was sleeping, anyway. She half-heartedly tried to make herself presentable before hitting the stairs. Annie's alto, almost baritone, voice singing "You are My Sunshine" quickened her steps.

Bekah interrupted the song with an attempt at perkiness. "Good morning."

Annie, her arms full of baking ingredients, wheeled to face her. "Why hello, child. What you doing up so early?"

So much for a stoic façade. The simple sound of Annie's voice brought on the waterworks. "Oh, Annie," Bekah blubbered as she closed the space between them and fell into Annie's arms.

Almost-too-sweet gardenia perfume filled Bekah's head as she surrendered to the comfort of Annie's mothering. "I know, baby girl, I know. Ida done told me." Annie stroked her hair for a few seconds before releasing her with a mama bear hug.

Bekah sniffled to stop the crying spell. "You were so right about Sonny. You told me he only cared about himself. If I'd just listened to you . . ."

"You wasn't really in a listening place." Annie opened a tub of flour, and strew a generous amount on the butcher-block counter. "Grab a coffee and an apron. We'll have some pie therapy."

By the time Bekah made it back to her, Annie had three recipes worth of flour, sugar, and salt in the giant mixing bowl and had begun to cut in the cold butter to make the pie crusts.

Bekah trekked to the pantry for the chocolate chip pie filling ingredients. The recipe from Miss Ida's mom, Ona Mae, was a staple at the diner and had achieved legendary status in Whitman. Miss Ida shared it with Bekah last year, allowing her to hold the decades-old paper inscribed in Ona Mae's flowery cursive. Indelible stains of lard and chocolate pock-marked the paper. Quite a high honor to be entrusted with such a treasure.

Bekah laid out the eggs, flour, sugars, butter, chocolate chips, and pecans. "Mise en place." She giggled, remembering how it tickled her to hear Miss Ida use the French term.

It amused Annie too. "Mise en place. What's that mean again?"

"Everything in its place. I think she got it from watching Food Network." "Probably."

Bekah concentrated on her ingredients, avoiding eye contact that would more than likely make her cry again. "He's never going to forgive me."

Annie clucked under her breath. "He may not."

Bekah gasped and looked at Annie's face.

"Not what you was hoping I would say?"

Bekah shook her head and returned her attention to pie filling.

"I know. You wanted me to say everything's gonna be alright, but you know I always talk straight to you. It may *not* be alright. Elliot loves you. Everyone who's seen you two can tell. The Good Book says love covers a multitude of sins, but it don't say love covers everything. That's a pretty big thing you're asking him to swallow."

Big? It was huge. "I know. What do I do, though?"

Annie chuckled. "You see that movie, *The Shack*?"

Bekah nodded.

"You think I be like Octavia Spencer's big mama God? Cause I ain't."

A slight smile lightened Bekah's face.

"Well, all I can tell you right now is if you ask God to forgive you, he will. In a flash. Elliot, well he might take a little longer. Don't give up, though. It still ain't been long. But you gotta be ready in case he don't forgive you. Or, even if he does, y'all may not be able to make it past this.

"You gotta be ready to own your part and, if it comes to it, make it without Elliot. You're a lot stronger now than last year this time, but you jumped right from your ex to Elliot. Well, your ex to Sonny to Elliot."

Bekah huffed and rolled her eyes.

"Too soon?" The crinkles around Annie's eyes deepened as she smiled. "I'm just picking, girl. I know you can take it. You can take a lot more than you think you can. I know you got your heart right with the Lord and, believe me, that'll make all the difference. My husband left me twenty years ago. I wouldn't made it through without Jesus. You keep on working on *that* relationship while you wait and, Elliot or no Elliot, you gonna be fine."

Bekah sucked in a breath and typed the text. *Guess I'm heading back to the farm alone?*

The quick reply was terse. *Guess so.*

They'll be expecting you.

Blue dots . . . more blue dots . . . *I'm sure you'll find a way to cover it up.*

Ouch.

She piddled around her apartment for hours—dusted clean furniture, vacuumed dirtless floors, packed, and repacked. When the Main Street streetlights buzzed to life, she knew the procrastination had to end.

In no hurry to make it back to Caragin Farm, Bekah drove below the speed limit on the two-lane highway. Her mind dramatized scenario after queasy scenario of the questions the Caragins would ask and the answers she'd give. Probably best to keep it vague.

Jim opened her car door before she'd turned the key off. "Hey, glad you made it."

Bekah returned his hug and avoided eye contact as she went to get her bag from the trunk. "Yeah, sorry if you were staying up. Elliot—"

Jim mercifully interrupted. "Yeah, he texted. Told us he was gonna stay in Whitman and you might be late."

Her shoulders relaxed as the weight of making up excuses tumbled from them. She smiled at Jim with her best smile, an Oscar-worthy performance in her mind.

"I'll get that." He took her bag as they started for the house. "You okay, Bekah?"

Darn. Apparently, I wasn't convincing. "Yeah, fine. Just a little tired."

Jim stopped and turned to face her. "It's just that, your eyes are a little red, and Elliot, he just didn't seem right when we talked to him on his birthday. Liz—you know Liz—thinks she has this sixth sense about all our kids, but especially Elliot. I'm afraid she's waiting at the kitchen table for you."

"What did Elliot say?"

"Just that he wasn't feeling good."

167

Bekah blinked back tears. "Then that's all it is. Maybe I'm coming down with what he had."

"Okay." He nodded in a way she took as, "Okay, I know you're lying, but I'm not going to push you on it."

She'd seen the same tenderhearted look on her father's face many times. "Jim?"

"Yeah?"

"Think I could stay in the room over the barn tonight?"

Elliot tried to ignore Brett's frame in his doorway. If he kept his head down staring at the computer, Brett would see his earbuds and assume he was working on something important. Surely, he would walk away and leave a fellow pastor to concentrate.

Then came the throat clearing and the wave as Brett stood in front of his desk. No way to ignore him. After a hard blink, Elliot pulled his earbuds out and looked up. "Hey. What's up?"

"You want to tell me?"

Yes. Yes, I want to tell you. I'm dying here. Elliot shrugged. "Nope."

"Really?"

Heat rushed to his cheeks. His hands balled into fists as if they had minds of their own. "Really."

"Hmm, because . . ." Brett moved a stack of books from a chair onto the floor and sat. "I think you do. Well, better put, you may not *want* to tell me, but I think you need to."

Elliot could only stare as the battle to divulge or repress waged in his head.

Brett leaned forward, resting his forearms on his knees. "I've left you alone since Wednesday night, which, I gotta tell you, was a very weird night. Obviously, something heavy going on between you and Bekah—maybe Ida. Figured you would tell me if you wanted to. But I can tell from watching you yesterday, this thing isn't going away. You look miserable. And friends don't ignore friends' misery."

Elliot sighed and buried his face in his hands. "It's Sonny."

"Your brother?"

"*Half*-brother. He'd want to emphasize the half." Elliot's lips grew taut at the memory of Sonny's smug taunting.

"What about him?"

Elliot motioned for Brett to close the door. "He told me on Sunday . . . he told me he and Bekah had an affair."

Brett's whole frame straightened. His eyes looked like they were about to pop. "What? That's crazy! Bekah wouldn't. I mean, he's lying, right?"

169

Elliot cocked his head to one side and closed his eyes.

"He's *not* lying? Oh man, I never would've in a million years . . ."

"It was last year, before we were together. Well, we knew each other. I was already kinda into her, but we weren't together."

Brett sunk back into his chair. "Well, then that's not . . . yes, I'm sorry, it is. I know it's bad. What did she say?"

Elliot scoffed. "She's sorry. Didn't want to hurt me, so she didn't tell me."

"Well, I guess that's kinda understandable."

Elliot glared at him.

"And still wrong, totally wrong. Dude, what are you gonna do?"

"Don't have a clue. I mean, it's not like she cheated on me. And I knew she wasn't a virgin. But I told her about my prior relationship. It's not like she didn't have the time to tell me. That's the thing, I think. All this time and she didn't tell me. How am I supposed to trust her again?"

Even as the words came out, he realized the trust factor wasn't the whole problem. The true sticking point, the real thing spilled out as his shoulders tensed. "You should've seen his face. His obnoxious, smirking face. I'm telling you, I wanted to punch a hole right through it. I've never been so mad in my life. How am I supposed to live with that?"

Brett's eyes spoke in compassionate volumes. Elliot knew his friend had answers floating around in his head. A hundred different Bible verses and platitudes. A dozen ways he knew to counsel someone at a crossroads. Words of wisdom Elliot himself might offer to someone coming to him with a problem. Which made him grateful for Brett's response.

"I don't know."

"Helpful."

Brett smiled. "You don't need an answer from me. You have to find it yourself. I mean, I'm here for you, of course. Whenever you want. Just to listen or bounce things off of. Maybe you should consider talking to Doc about it."

Dr. Andrews. Elliot shook his head at the mention of the senior pastor's name. "Can't. He tried to tell me last year that I needed to be careful about being involved with her since she obviously had so much to work through. He didn't want me to complicate her life . . . afraid she might fall into using me as her savior when she needed Jesus first."

"Yeah, but I've seen him with her a lot since then. I think he really likes her and believes you two are good together."

"I know. But what if he was right? Or what if it's the other way around, and I fell into trying to be her savior because it made me feel good to 'fix' her?"

Brett smirked. "We men do like to do that, don't we?"

"Me more than average, I'm afraid."

"I just don't think that's the issue here. Don't forget Karla and I have been here the whole time. We saw Bekah's transformation *before* you two got serious about each other. No doubt, you've been good for her healing process, but I would never say a savior complex came into play."

Good to hear Brett say it, and he was right. Now back to the old devil of square one. What should he do? Sure, forgiving is the right thing. After that, though, could he live with knowing that Bekah and Sonny . . .? Can a man really get over that? Marry a woman knowing her former boyfriend isn't some generic shadow but someone who will be a part of their lives?

Brett stood and moved the stack of books back into his chair. "You just need some time, Elliot. Don't feel like you have to rush it. And if you need me—"

"You'll be here." Elliot forced a half-smile. "Thanks."

Liz plastered on a grin as Bekah opened the door, hoping the snoopy purpose of her visit wouldn't be obvious. The piled-high dinner plate, she believed, completed the subterfuge. She held it up for inspection. "Thought you could use some dinner. I'll put it on the table."

She brushed by Bekah and into the studio apartment, chattering to fill the void. "Jim said you looked like you were feeling better, but you know me. I just have to check things out myself." Liz gave Bekah a quick once-over before appraising the apartment. "I haven't been up here in a while. Looks like Jim got you set up pretty well, but it smells a little stale. I can bring you a candle and some other supplies. Anything specific you need?"

"I'm good. Thank you, though. Hope you don't think I'm being rude moving out here."

"Not at all. You made it in our crazy house a lot longer than I think I could've at your age. Just want to make sure you're taken care of and everything's alright. Is everything alright?" Liz plopped into one of the two bistro table chairs.

A dozen questions rolled around in her head, but she opted for silence. The ploy worked. Bekah took the other chair with the saddest smile Liz had seen in a while. "I'm kinda guessing you know it's not. Alright, I mean." Bekah's eyes watered, which made Liz's do likewise.

"Have you talked to him?"

"Not since Friday. Unless five-word texts count. Has he talked to you?"

"He hasn't reached out. His father told me to give him space. That's not really in my nature. I guess you know that about me by now."

Bekah's upturned lip indicated she understood. "You mean you weren't just bringing dinner to be kind?"

Liz settled for a wink when her mama bear's instincts insisted she wrap the distraught girl in her arms. "Well, that was part of it. Anything you want to talk about? You don't have to . . . unless you want to."

"I may have messed everything up with Elliot."

Liz leaned toward her. "Oh, honey. I can't believe that. You two . . . you remind me of me and Jim—years ago, of course."

Bekah wagged her head. "I don't think so. You would never . . ." She dabbed at the corners of her eyes and sniffled. "I did something I shouldn't have done, last year . . . then I tried to hide it. Elliot just found out." The tears clouded her bloodshot eyes. "I don't think we're going to be able to get past it. He must hate me."

Forget personal space. Liz pulled Bekah into her arms and rocked her gently from side to side as they cried. Through tears and sniffles, she encouraged, "You don't know that. Elliot's the most kind, forgiving child we have. And he loves you. You wouldn't believe how many girls were fawning over him all the time, but he never gave them the time of day. I knew he'd fallen for you the first time he mentioned your name."

"Maybe." Bekah pulled away and grabbed a napkin to wipe her nose and eyes. "But that was before. I should've just told him, but there never was a good time, and then I'd have a chance and push it back in, and then it was out of my hands. He found out from someone else. What I'd give to go back in time and just say it and let him decide then if he loved me. Now, it's too late."

Liz stroked Bekah's arm. "No more talk like that. At least the secret's not there anymore."

Bekah stared vacantly.

"The truth is out, right?"

Bekah nodded.

"Then what you're dealing with now is the truth. Sounds like a hard truth, but the truth's easier to deal with than a lie." *Sounds wise, Liz. Take your own advice, maybe?*

"Doesn't feel easier."

"It could be worse." Her pulse throbbed in her temples so loudly she feared Bekah could hear the steady thumping. She swallowed her hypocrisy down as she searched for helpful words that wouldn't reveal her own secret. "Y'all can work this out. You'd never want to walk into a bigger commitment with something between you . . . something that could keep you from being as close as you could be, something lurking in your heart. Fear where intimacy should be."

"I guess that would be worse. Oh, Liz . . ." Quiet tears leaked from the corners of her eyes as she begged, "You know him better than anyone. What should I do? Call him? Go see him in person? Leave him alone and let him make the next move?"

Liz shook her head. "Jim would tell me to keep my nose out of it."

"I won't tell him. Please, I need help."

What could this girl have possibly done? Don't I need to know Bekah's offense before I dispense advice? No, that's just curiosity rearing its ugly head. This is not the place. Liz pressed her back into her chair. "I'll tell you this. The day after Jordan came to live with us, El was twelve, and I found him in the tire swing in the front, not swinging, just dragging his sneakers in the dirt, head hung low. When I asked what was wrong, he said he didn't understand why a mama would give up a baby.

"For a split second, I thought he meant Jordan. But when he looked up, I could see his eyes were bloodshot, and I knew he was talking about himself. My heart kind of broke. It's the first time he'd asked a question like that. I realized real quick I'd been kidding myself if I believed he, or the others, didn't think about their missing parents a lot."

"What did you say?"

"I don't remember exactly. Just tried to explain how people are different, sin, unwise decisions, hopelessness. Tried to reassure him the children are never to blame when a parent chooses adoption. And of course, that this mama would never give up any of her babies.

"He must have seen a tear in my eye or heard it in my voice. He said he didn't want to make me sad." She felt a smidge of pride steal across her face. "That's El, always worried about other people. I told him I would only be sad if he thought he had to keep his feelings inside. Told him he could always tell me what he was feeling or ask me any questions he wanted.

"After that, it was kind of like a switch flipped, and he would start conversations with me every so often. Questions like where I thought his other mom was, and did I think his other dad knew about him; did I think she was white and he was black or the other way around. I was glad he asked, but I knew the questions meant the feeling never left his heart. Looking for a reason why he wasn't good enough for them to love him."

"Then last year."

"Then last year . . ." Liz shook her head. "I know you were there, but I can't tell you what it felt like. That day in the diner when he and Ida told us.

I stayed in a kind of shock for days, then this pride welled up in me when it hit me how he had obviously forgiven her completely in the short amount of time since he found out. In spite of twenty-five years of questions and negative thoughts, he'd been able to see her side of it and understand. The truth came out and he forgave."

Liz could see she'd made her point by the slight smile on Bekah's face.

"He did, didn't he?"

"Just give him a little time, Bekah. Not too much time, but a little. And, no . . ." she held up a hand to fend off the next question. "I can't tell you exactly how much time that means, but you'll figure it out."

Surround yourself with things that bring you joy. Haley took the advice from her positive-thinking app seriously. Acoustical guitar streaming through her earbuds blocked out all of the other noises around her on the Caragin patio. The sweet scent of wisteria hung in the morning air. A wispy breeze, the refreshing after effect of last night's thunderstorm, played around her face.

A text notice slid over the iPad notes she studied. *Sorry about last night. Lunch?*

Ugh. Sorry. Again, he was sorry. Why didn't she tell Chandler to send him home? To not even come in the first place? Vanessa was right. Alex was a hothead, and inconsiderate, and egotistical, and definitely *not* bringing her joy. She swiped away the notice and closed her eyes. *Surround yourself with things that bring you joy.*

She sensed the presence of someone in her space and opened her eyes to the welcome sight of a purple smoothie. Even better, the smile of the giver. She tapped mute on her earbuds.

Vee shook the drink in Haley's line of vision. "Açaí?"

"You're an angel. Thank you."

"No problem. That cute redheaded boy in the craft tent said you hadn't had yours yet. Told him I could bring it to you." Vee nodded to the empty bottle beside Haley's chair, residue of green clinging to its walls. "I noticed you like one after your wakeup blast."

Haley nodded toward the green smoothie Vee held. "I see you're still on the wake-up. That boy must like you."

Vee flashed a brilliant white smile as she fingered the GoPro! on her chest. "Yeah. I think they all thought I was part of the crew at first. Now, they're just used to me. The sibs are a little jelly that they give me stuff since it's only supposed to be for you guys."

"Always pays to be on the good side of the craftys."

"Hey, can I ask you something?"

"Sure." Chandler had told her why he sent Devin packing. Expecting a conversation about that, Haley closed her iPad cover and mentally fixed her face to be ready for anything.

Vee sat on the broad arm of an Adirondack chair. "What's it like living in LA?"

In a fraction of a second, Haley found herself at her favorite rooftop bar in West Hollywood. Palm trees. Mountains. The brilliant orange sunset behind the flat-topped skyscrapers, and the lights in their windows sparkling like a million diamonds, shining like the wonder in Vee's question.

"It's big. Beautiful. There's so much energy, so many people." Remembering brought a smile. "I could go on a lot. Is there something specific you want to know about?"

"I was just wondering how old you were when you went there?"

"First time, Spring Break my senior year." No need to add that she'd lied to her parents about where and with whom she went. "It was like everything you see on TV and in the movies. But you can't really tell until you're there how alive it is. Like it has its own heartbeat. I mean, I grew up in Dallas. And Dallas is big, but LA's four times as big. Always something new to see and do."

Vee's face lit up. "I'd love to go. The biggest city I've been in was DC on a school field trip. And it was so boring. I just want to get out of here, you know?"

A hundred times Haley knew. Not too long ago, her voice echoed the same wistful longing. What would she say to her nineteen-year-old self? What would Jim and Liz want her to say? Maybe a bit of caution was in order.

"I get you. However, I do have to say not every day is paradise when you live in LA. But you should definitely visit."

"Could I?" Vee's eyes widened as she sprung up. "I would love that! And I think I could talk Mama and Daddy into it for at least a week. Especially if it was with you."

Wait. What? Did she just invite Vee to visit her in LA? She didn't think so. Rewind. Oh yeah, the jump wasn't too far, but still . . . what to say to the girl with stars in her eyes? "Yeah, maybe." She glanced at her phone. "We'll have to talk about it later, though, okay? They're ready in the front yard."

• • • •

Haley could've used a few more minutes to corral her thoughts back to the interview questions, but Jim and Liz were already in place in overstuffed wicker chairs. Kobi, Chad, and the rest of the crew waited for her to fill her empty seat.

She turned on a glowing smile. "Good morning, everyone! Sorry to make you wait. Guess we need to get going before the real Alabama July shows up."

As everyone on the lawn agreed, she took a moment to mentally frame the shot. Another stellar job by the location director. The camera could zoom easily from a wide shot encompassing the Caragins and most of the farmhouse behind them down to comfortable close-ups of either or both of them. Yards of cables and cords lay camouflaged beneath faux grass that looked real enough to sink your toes in.

Haley settled into her chair with her iPad and açaí smoothie. Looking up to begin her questions, kindness in the faces of Jim and Liz stopped her. Was it something new or something about putting herself in Vee's shoes? Liz tilted her head and winked.

With a wink of her own, Haley opened the session. "Tell me about Beth and Sondra."

Liz fielded the question. "Beth and Sondra are our eleven-year-old twins. They look a lot alike, but they're really fraternal. It doesn't take long for most people to be able to tell them apart. It's even easier the last few years as their personalities have developed. They like different clothes, wear their hair differently."

"And," Haley prompted, "what else makes them unique?"

Jim obviously knew where she was leading. "The girls are our only kids Liz gave birth to. And a total surprise. I mean, not a surprise they were born because, of course, we saw that coming."

Liz placed a gentle hand on his wrist. "They were a surprise because we assumed I couldn't get pregnant after our history of miscarriages. When I skipped my cycle, I was afraid to let myself believe it. Then, the morning sickness came."

Jim laughed. "Then the afternoon sickness and the night sickness . . . didn't take long to figure out."

Haley interjected. "You must have been thrilled."

"Thrilled." Liz's smile faded. "And scared. After losing three babies and remembering what I went through, I was really scared. We went to the doctor early and often." Her hand moved to her belly like muscle memory. "I was six weeks when the ultrasound showed the two of them."

"So, Jim, you felt the same way? Thrilled and scared?"

"Whoo, boy, you know it. You heard of walking on eggshells? I was walking on eggshells over ice over glass. I wanted those babies so bad, but I didn't want to show it so much. Didn't want her to feel like a failure if something happened to them. Couldn't bear to see her go through that again."

Liz grinned. "He mothered me like you wouldn't believe. Sometimes, I had to tell him to get out of the house and leave me be. After all, we already had ten children in the house. I couldn't lie in bed all day and be waited on."

Jim clarified. "Well, she coulda laid around a lot more than she did. Once we told folks, they chipped in even more than usual. Babysitting, cooking, cleaning, driving the kids to school. I'm telling you, we're beyond blessed with the way family and friends take care of us. It ain't in her nature to be still, though. And, after her second trimester, she was running full-strength."

Liz shook her head. "At least as full-strength as you can run with sixty extra pounds and ankles the size of cantaloupes."

Haley allowed the laughter to fade. "So you went full term?"

"Thirty-seven weeks. That's considered good for twins, and I'm telling you, they were not a second too early for me. They were around five and a half pounds each. Healthy little girls."

Jim's smile lit up his face. "She stayed in the hospital for three nights. Just being cautious, doctor said. Then, we was able to take them home."

"I'll bet your other kids were excited."

Liz shrugged. "To varying degrees. You could see all of their little personalities. Elliot was really helpful, but the other boys weren't very interested. Laurel mothered. Victoria studied them like a science experiment. The rest were so young."

"So," Haley asked, "how has it been different with adopted versus natural children?" She noticed Jim glance at Liz, whose shoulders had drawn back. "I'm sorry. Did I not use the right words?"

Liz seemed to be choosing her response carefully, but her face showed irritation. "It's not the words. It's the question. All of our children are special to us. We don't like to differentiate based on how they came into our lives."

Time to tread carefully, Haley. She relaxed her posture and softened her voice while keeping eye contact with Liz. "I understand. I do. I can see that you show that every day. But it's not an unfair question, really—and one I think our viewers will be asking. This is a good time for you to educate them."

Jim spoke up. "I think I got this one. Okay, babe?"

A hesitant nod from Liz gave him a limited leash.

He took a moment. Determined, Haley thought, to not say anything in his usual ready, fire, aim manner. "The birth of the girls *was* different. The months of seeing them grow inside Liz, feeling them kick and move, being in the delivery room, and seeing them take their first breaths. Nothing like it. Pure joy.

"Raising the girls, though. The joy of that . . . really not different than the joy of raising the others. We really do believe, and try to show, that every one of them is a direct gift of God."

He looked to Liz for approval, and she granted it with a tilt of her head and a blink.

Haley checked her iPad for the quote she'd highlighted. "Will told me about visiting you and the twins in the hospital. He said, 'I remember seeing Mom and Dad holding them, kissing their heads, smiling so big, showing them off to us. I wondered why my birth mom didn't feel that way about me.' Did any of the other kids say anything like that?"

Emotional TV is good TV. A soft gasp made Liz's face tremble. Her lips grew tight at hearing the sadness in Will's words. Jim looked at Haley as if she'd betrayed their trust. Haley knew the camera had gotten the coveted reaction, but this part of her job stank.

Jim opened his mouth to answer, but Liz spoke first. "Yes." Her hand pressed to her chest as if she were trying to still her heartbeat. "We were at the table. The twins were about six weeks old. We were each holding one."

She looked to Jim. "Remember?"

He shook his head.

"Victoria asked when we were going to have their ''doption party.'"

Haley saw recollection come to Jim's face with a grimace and a quick nod.

Liz continued, "We had adoption parties for all the kids when they were officially ours. By the time the twins were born, they'd grown into pretty big celebrations. I was trying to think of the right answer when Laurel chimed in, all matter-of-fact. 'They're not adopted, Victoria. They're Mama and Daddy's *real* babies.' She didn't mean anything by it, of course. But oh, my heart!"

Haley felt tears welling. Not by any contrived effort on her part but pulled to her eyes like a magnet to Liz's love. She willed them back with a sniff. "What did you say?"

"The first thing I thought of. 'The party's two weeks from Sunday.'"

Jim's dad-radar pinged the moment Victoria stepped into the kitchen. For starters, she rarely made it there before breakfast had cooled. Second, she looked pale and her voice quivered as she clutched her iPad. "You guys, this is not good. You're trending."

"I thought trending was a good thing. What's wrong?" All activity stopped as he and Liz and the other kids in the kitchen waited for her answer.

"You don't want to trend for this. Somebody's leaked part of your interview, the one where you said abortion is murder." Vee crumpled into a chair like a scarecrow falling off its post.

As her family crowded around, she pushed play. In a heavily edited video, sound bites of Jim saying, "Abortion is killing babies" and "It's murder, plain and simple" played over and over. Video snippets from across all the days of taping made Jim and Liz look angry: Liz pointing her finger, Jim's sweat-soaked face, Liz making notes in her Bible.

The title read, *Over the Moon's Latest Reality Stars are Deep South Haters*.

"There's more," Vee squeaked out. "There are memes, a Reddit thread. It's on Insta and the Twitterverse. I can't even believe the comments from my Veeps."

Liz snatched the device from Vee and shook it in Jim's face. "This! This is why I didn't want to do this thing. I can't believe I let you people talk me into it. You know some people just *live* to bring other people down."

She couldn't say anything that wasn't storming through his brain at the same time. Jim stammered out his disbelief. "But this is so wrong. It's just a few words from a whole day of taping. Out of context. This ain't us."

Whimpers from Amy and Peanut made him realize he was yelling. Their wide-open eyes turned his churning stomach into an internal Mount Vesuvius. He lowered his voice to a degree below seething. "There's gotta be some way to take this all down."

Marshall spoke up. "Not a chance, Dad. Once it's out there . . ."

"I'm afraid he's right." Chandler stood at the kitchen doorway, looking for all the world like a dog in a cone of shame.

Liz turned her back on him and stared out the window, her fingers drumming on the sink. Jim knew her like he knew himself. He wasn't the only one ready to erupt.

Jim locked eyes with Chandler and tilted his head toward the door. "Outside."

Vee stood to follow, but Jim stopped her. "Victoria, no."

He barely heard her protest as he ushered Chandler through the door to the patio.

"Jim . . ." Chandler spoke as if he were trying to tame a wild stallion.

Jim whirled to face him and spoke through clenched teeth. "No, don't manage me."

Chandler nodded and watched him as Jim tried to call up words that would allow him to speak his mind without saying any his mama would've whipped him for. He'd like to punch the young producer. More than once. His whole body shook as he paced, running his hands through his thinning hair, wiping sweat from his neck.

"I ain't never . . . this is just so . . ." He struggled until he decided to spit out the accusation. "Is this some publicity stunt? Did you do this?"

Chandler didn't hesitate. "No. I would never. Why would I try to tank my own show? Not to mention, bring any harm to you and your family."

"Then who?"

Chandler broke eye contact and stroked his neck as if the unbuttoned collar were choking him.

"Come on! It had to be somebody on your team. Someone with access to all the video. Someone with a pro-abortion ax to grind and the ability to do it. Surely, that narrows it down."

Chandler nodded. "It does. But I can't say who for sure. Just give me a little time. I promise I'll find out, and they'll be fired. Trust me."

"Trust you? I don't think so. I want to be there."

"I don't think that's the best idea. Please, just let me deal with it."

"Alright, you wanna deal with it? I'll tell you what you can deal with. After you've fired this person, you can tell everyone else to pack up and go home. This show is over." Jim stalked to his pickup and flung gravel as he sped toward the greenhouses.

Jim wiped his sticky forearms on his shirt as he made his way back to the house. Watermelon juice from the rinds he'd dropped in the compost pile ran from his wrists to his elbows, mingling with leftover sweat and dirt from the workday.

Liz's sister, Denise, spoke to him from the picnic table, where she worked on gathering the trash from the meal. "Long day?"

He let out a heavy sigh. "The longest. Thanks for bringing dinner."

"Glad to do it. Knew all y'all could use a break. You need this?" She extended a wet towel, which he gladly accepted.

"Well, thanks anyway. Just having you guys over was almost as good as the food. Friendly faces and all that."

"Will told me y'all broke some sales records today."

"I ain't never seen anything like it. I was afraid when all this cow poop hit the fan, we might go under. Stayed awake worrying about it for the last two nights. When I saw that crowd with their signs this morning, I figured it was all them online fanatics coming to protest. Then I saw most of them was there sticking up for us. Then they started buying stuff by the truckload." He shook his head, still trying to process the events of the last three days.

"Well, shows the net can be a good thing too. Once word got out the mob was trying to shut down another honest Christian family just because of what you think, people wanted to stick up for you. Good to see folks rally around."

Even though the online attack grossly exaggerated his statements, Jim remembered Liz's admonition about his lack of tact. He hung his head. Had his words hurt Denise because of her experience with abortion? Probably. Even so, she rounded up dinner to help his huge family during this trial. Time to tuck his tail and apologize.

"Listen, Denise. I know it's good to stand up for people who get hammered because they say what they think, but some of the fault is mine. Your sister let me know after we taped that episode that I didn't exactly speak the truth in love. She said my comments could hurt people who'd been through that."

"I'm sure that was quite a discussion."

"Yes, it was. Anyway, I just want to tell you I'm sorry if my words caused you any pain. It ain't no excuse, but I didn't know."

"Didn't know what?"

"About your abortion . . . in high school."

He watched as Denise's back straightened and she cocked her head to one side. "Liz told you I had an abortion? Why would she—"

Uh-oh. Foot in mouth again. "She wasn't ratting you out or nothing. It just kinda came up when we was talking it through. I ain't judging you. I promise, I'm not. I'm just sad you went through that and want you to know I understand things ain't always so cut and dry."

Judging from the way her eyes narrowed to slits and her lips pursed together, his words weren't helping. She cinched up the trash bag full of paper goods and dropped it to the ground. "Thank you for your understanding, Jim. But I don't need it."

"I'm sorry. I was only trying—"

"I don't need it because I never had an abortion in my life, but your wife did. You talking to the wrong sister."

The soft thumps of the ceiling fan blades mimicked the pieces of Liz's heart falling apart. Thump, the anger on Denise's face when she came into the kitchen. Thump, the heated words at her car. Thump, Jim's silhouette at the picnic table. Thump, thump, thump, making excuses to each child about Dad's absence at bedtime. *Please, God, tell me what to do.*

The clock blazed 5:30 from her nightstand. No point in lying in bed anymore. Liz padded to the kitchen and pushed the button to start the brew cycle. From outside came sounds of hope—the crunch of gravel, the opening and closing of a truck door, and keys jangling on the patio. She swung the door open and searched his bloodshot eyes. He flinched when she touched his arm and shut her out with a shake of his head. He turned away and lumbered to a chair on the patio, dropping into it like a sack of concrete. Stepping out of the house, she closed the door and dragged a chair as close to him as she dared.

"What can I say?" She whispered the plea.

He closed his eyes and wagged his head. Molasses-like seconds passed. "I been wondering that all night. I guess what I need to know is why."

Why? Yes, finally she would tell him why. The words she'd practiced countless times, yearned to confide in him for decades, spilled out.

"I was fifteen. He was sixteen." She picked at a piece of peeling paint on the arm of her chair, not even daring to look at his face. "Neither of us had the sense to keep it from happening or to think what it would take to raise a baby. I wanted to tell Mama, but Denise talked me out of it. If we told Mama, she'd tell Daddy, and Daddy . . . you know how mean he was. He would've killed that boy. Maybe me too. We went to Gramma."

"Rosamond?"

Liz nodded. "I was crying so hard, I could barely say anything, so Denise did most of the talking. I really don't know what I expected Gramma to do. Would she make me tell Mama and Daddy? Would she let me move in with her and raise the baby? My heart broke a little because she looked so disappointed, even though she didn't say so. She just told me everything would be alright. Then she got her Yellow Pages out and found an ad for a doctor in Birmingham. She handed it to Denise, told her to make an appointment, and said she'd pay for it.

"I didn't figure out what they were even talking about until I heard Denise on the phone. It all happened so fast. Before I knew it, Denise was driving me to the city, and I was sitting in that chair in that dingy office. There didn't seem to be any other way."

Tears clouded her eyes. She shuddered, recalling the cool metal of stirrups cupping her feet, the blinding surgical light, the instruments between her legs. Then the horrific sound of the baby being vacuumed from her body. All done. An emotionless nurse moved her to a recliner and gave her a glass of orange juice.

"It was awful." She stopped to wipe her eyes then set them on her husband.

"I'm sorry," he said without a glance in her direction. "I'm sorry you went through that. But that's not what I meant when I said I need to know why. I need to know why . . . why you didn't tell me for all these years? Lied to me. There was a thousand times you could've told me . . . *should've* told me."

Liz sucked up a breath to steel herself. What words could smooth over a betrayal like this? "I know. I promise, I know. We just . . . I mean, I just . . . there was never a good time."

Jim scoffed and shook his head.

"I know it sounds stupid. I should have told you, but when, baby? When we were seventeen and started dating? What about when our youth groups went to purity camp weekend? They pushed us to pledge to wait until we married. You handed me a white rose in front of all our friends. I guess after that, I got scared of losing you if I told you."

She paused, hoping for a reaction, any reaction, but he didn't move at all. *Keep going, Liz.*

"When I lost our second baby . . ." The pain seared through her mind. She wrapped her arms tightly around her stomach. "I thought God . . . I thought he was punishing me—that he'd never let me have a baby because of what I did."

Her body trembled and tears rolled down her cheeks. Then, a second of solace, a glance from Jim. His face softened and mist covered his eyes, but he still didn't touch her. *Is he ever going to touch me again?*

She wiped her face and sniffled to keep her nose from running. "Then, there was Elliot. Then nine more."

"Then," Jim said, "Beth and Sondra."

"I thought God had finally forgiven me when we had those girls, when I carried them all the way, and they were healthy. I know it's not really how it works, but I thought all the good things we'd done had covered my sin good enough, and I could put it behind me. Just keep it inside."

"But a few weeks ago, you told me it was Denise who had the abortion."

"Not exactly. You asked if it was Denise. I let you believe it. I know that's a kind of lie. I did it because when I asked you, 'What if it had been me,' you said I wouldn't be the woman you fell in love with." Her voice broke with the memory. "That's what I been afraid of, I guess, all these years. If I told you, you wouldn't love me."

Jim whipped his head to face her, mouth agape, confusion in his eyes. She hung on the milliseconds. What would he say? His face flushed as pink as the rising sun had quietly painted the sky around them. Then, instead of speaking, he turned his head away. "Hmm," was the only sound that escaped.

But his expression buoyed her hope. She knew this look. He was thinking. If she could keep herself from saying anything else, he would let her know what he thought soon enough. *Not another word, Liz.* She focused where he focused, toward the pond where the sky morphed from pink to pale blue, desperate prayers zipping to heaven.

Cicadas tuned up their morning mating calls, like a thousand tiny wind-up toys stuck in the trees. The rooster crowed. Ducks on the pond called good morning to each other. Liz picked more paint off her chair.

At last, he spoke. "I shouldn't have said that. You keeping this thing, though. All these years. It does make me feel like maybe I don't know you as good as I thought. But *every* part of you is the woman I love, and there ain't nothing can ever change that."

The breath she didn't even realize she held gushed from her lungs with a cry as he reached his hand to her. She grasped it, and he drew her onto his lap. Burying her head in his shoulder, she cried as he swayed with her and stroked her cheeks to wipe away the tears.

Just as her tremors subsided, Jim's phone vibrated. "It's Pastor," he said as he slid the green button. "Morning, Ricky . . . nah, you know me, been up for hours . . . hmm, that so? . . . Yeah, probably right . . . No, you got nothing to apologize for. I'm sorry for the trouble . . . No, I get it . . . well, don't worry about us . . . I appreciate it . . . okay, talk to you later."

"So," he explained, "seems like there's a bunch of news trucks already parked at the church. He thinks it best we don't come today."

Mammoth butterflies, more like pterodactyls, churned in Haley's stomach as she trudged with Chandler to the Caragin farmhouse like a death-row inmate heading to her last meal. Her brain ached from the thousands of what-if scenarios that had been assaulting her at all hours since Thursday.

What if Chandler fired her? What if her career was ruined? What if, more and more important to her, the Caragins hated her? Chandler hadn't given her much hope to alleviate any of her worries, but this had to be done. Pay the piper. Bite the bullet. Face the music. She muttered every cliché for taking responsibility she could think of on their trek from the production trailer.

A buzz on her wrist drew her eyes to her watch. Seven o'clock. Eighty-three degrees. Heart rate, 120. When they came in sight of Jim and Liz drinking coffee on the patio, her palms broke out in a sweat. She glanced at Chandler. He gave her a firm pat on the shoulder with a look that reminded her of the way her dad would encourage her to keep going when things were tough. A kind of silent "rub some dirt on it and get back out there" nod and wink.

Jim stood to greet them and invited them to sit. Liz did nothing more than acknowledge them with a semi-polite tilt of her head. Neither smiled.

Jim spoke first. "Come to say goodbye?"

Knife. Heart. Twist. Haley was certain despair covered her face but kept quiet as Chandler had asked. Not the first tough situation he'd been in, he said. Let him do the talking.

"First," he said as he took off his glasses and made eye contact as she'd seen him do dozens, maybe hundreds, of times. "I want to tell you again how grieved we are about the whole situation. And we've found out who's responsible, and they've been dealt with."

"Fired?" Jim wouldn't be satisfied with anything less. No surprise there.

"Right now, off of this production. With HR laws the way they are, we have a whole gauntlet we have to go through to fire someone. But I promise it will be done."

"Who was it?" Jim demanded the information just as Haley knew he would.

Chandler looked at Haley. She inhaled and nodded.

"Haley's production assistant, Alex."

"Tall, skinny guy with the goatee?"

"Yes."

"All on his own?"

"Yes."

Liz spoke. "Why?"

"It was the 'abortion is murder' comment. He has a girlfriend who'd gotten pregnant last year, and they chose to end the pregnancy. He saw how your comments hurt her and decided on payback."

"Wait a minute." Jim stepped in. "He *saw* how the comments hurt her? How'd that happen? He showed her the video?"

"No, she's on set."

Haley hung her head. Silent, hot tears spilled onto her cheeks. They were going to hate her. *Suck it up, buttercup.* "It's me. I'm the girlfriend."

Liz gasped, "Oh, Haley."

Haley wiped her cheeks and made herself look at Jim and Liz. Her confession had changed everything about their posture and their faces. They both slumped into their chairs, Liz with a hand over her mouth. And their expressions . . . the same looks she'd seen when they talked about the Ukrainian orphanage calling Hope useless. Who was she to them right now? The woman who made the brutal comment that infuriated them or the innocent toddler who gained their instant compassion?

With a nod, Chandler encouraged her to explain.

"I was upset that day, for a few days. I mean, I'd thought the things you said, but no one ever said them out loud to me. Alex, my friends—they all told me it was the right thing to do for my career, for my life. I believed them; I guess because I wanted to. But when you said . . . what you said . . . I just broke a little. I swear I had no idea what he was going to do. With my credentials, he had access to everything . . . all the footage, the editing bays, the distribution channels.

"So that part of it *is* my responsibility. I'll be leaving today. I just knew I owed you a personal apology, and . . ."

She searched their faces for a clue of their thoughts. Despite her intuition and all she'd learned about them, she still wasn't sure her last plea would make any difference.

"I want to ask you to consider allowing the show to continue."

Jim scoffed.

She made eye contact with him. "I know. You've been through hell the last few days, but the truth is, this *will* blow over. I've seen it happen dozens of times. It's the cancel culture. It's really just a handful of hateful people with loud voices. If you don't cave, they'll slink away."

Haley turned her attention to Liz. "I think your stories are important . . . important enough to broadcast. I don't believe in God the same way you do but, if I did, I would say the devil is trying to keep you from telling your story because your lives, the lives of your kids, are hope personified."

Jim leaned onto his elbows and eyeballed Chandler. "You put her up to this?"

Haley answered for him. "No, he didn't. He didn't even think it was a great idea for me to come this morning."

Chandler smiled. "It's true. I've already started making preparations to leave town because I didn't think there was a chance you'd allow us to stay. But everything she just said is what I told you the day we sat at your picnic table. I do believe your story is important. And I do believe the storm will pass. With just another few weeks of shooting, we could have all we need to make the pilot. You still have the option to shelve the whole thing once you see it."

Jim turned to face Liz. "What do you say? Family meeting?"

"No." Liz shook her head. "We don't need a family meeting. This is our call."

Chandler leaned forward. "Listen, you two can take all the time you need."

"I don't need time." Liz stood with a glare in her eye. "You can stay."

Haley shared a bewildered look with Jim. *Did she just say . . .*

Liz raised her voice. "On one condition."

"Yes, name it." Chandler would've agreed to any demand.

"Haley stays."

Coffee it was. Craftys weren't even stirring at four o'clock in the morning. The Keurig proved to be Haley's only option in the production trailer conference room. Six nights of elusive sleep and gallons of tears since the social media blowup had wrecked her body maintenance routine.

She'd collapsed around seven last night, woken up around three, and forced herself out for a run around the property. Even with the electrolyte water, her legs felt like Jell-O and her face hurt. Maybe the java would help—if it didn't shock her caffeine-deprived heart into arrest.

Virtually every inch of the table was occupied by quasi-organized stacks of photos, shoeboxes of camcorder cassettes, and VHS tapes. The mention of adoption parties at their last taping intrigued Haley. She asked Liz what she could send so they could possibly weave some of these stories into the show.

Laurel and Marshall had shown up later that afternoon with all of this. A little red wagon full of memorabilia. She'd barely looked at it before the world started blowing up around her. For the last few days, after Alex's confession and expulsion, working on this rabbit trail had morphed into therapy. A handy excuse to isolate herself.

She plopped into a chair and pushed enough aside to make room for her coffee and laptop. Prep time for today's vignette. On her timeline, she'd planned to ask about Sam and how they discovered and dealt with his autism. She'd researched enough to ask intelligent questions without, hopefully, using any words that would get Liz's Mama Bear fur ruffled.

Her screen opened to her last Word doc. She stared at a handwritten poem she'd seen sprinkled throughout the photo boxes and transcribed. Short and sweet, she guessed it had been composed by Liz to welcome each child into the family.

> *Welcome precious child of ours.*
> *We all want you to know*
> *we're here no matter what you need,*
> *to help you thrive and grow.*
> *We cherish you and treasure you.*

We're thankful for this day
that God has brought you to our lives
to love in every way.

And now the tears trickled down her cheeks. Sure, her parents loved her. But did they ever feel *this way* about her? She couldn't remember ever feeling comfortable growing up. So many rules and object lessons filled her home, with no room for questions or doubts. Not like the warm blanket on a cold day kind of love of the Caragins. Not the grace and forgiveness they'd freely granted her. *Oh, to have been a part of this family.*

Jim glanced at the decades-old clock, the logo of a long-defunct seed manufacturer in the center of its face. *7:35.* Chandler said he'd come by at eight. He had time to finish reviewing the autumn mum orders for Wal-Mart. Bless his admin's heart. She knew he preferred paper even though the nursery owned updated software to handle everything. A binder of spreadsheets lay open on the dinged-up metal desk purchased for his first office, *twenty-seven years ago.*

This desk had sure seen its share of changes. Carbon copies and an electric ball typewriter. Dot matrix printers with ear-piercing whirs. From the first computer filling half the desk to the sleek laptop beside him now.

More than equipment, though. He and Liz had shared lunches, and sometimes suppers, on this desk as they made plans for Caragin Farm. One night, they shared more than that, and the memory lifted the corners of his mouth. Then, the not-so-romantic. Babies, so many babies, had their diapers changed on this desk. Thankfully, they didn't leave physical reminders, like the rusty rings of countless cups of coffee and glasses of tea.

With a tap at his door, Chandler peered in. "I'm a little early. Alright?"

"Sure. Coffee?"

"No, thanks." Chandler moved a stack of seed catalogs from a chair to a corner of the desk.

"Careful, it's a delicate balance."

Chandler returned Jim's smile as the desk wobbled. "Maybe you can get a new desk once the show gets going."

A new desk? Not a chance. "Nah, I just need to put another shim under the leg. What can I do you for?"

Chandler leaned back in his chair and took his glasses off.

Jim knew the move by now. "Uh-oh."

"What?"

"Every time you take those glasses off, you have something serious to say."

"I do?"

"Yeah. If I was a poker player, I'd say it's your tell." The surprise on Chandler's face amused him. *Had no one ever pointed this out to him before?*

"Well . . ." Chandler shook his head and replaced his glasses. "I'll be sure not to play poker. I mainly wanted to check on you. Take your temperature, so to speak, about how you're feeling."

"But . . ."

"But I also need to fill you in on the network's viewpoint and how they'd like to go forward. So how are you and Liz doing since last week?"

Jim stared into his coffee. The last seven days had been some of the most gut-wrenching of his life. Shock. Anger. Sorrow. Reconciliation was still in the works. But Chandler didn't know the reason for any of this. He only knew about the brouhaha ignited by Alex's video sabotage.

"We're hanging in there. For better or worse, you know. Not the first storm in our lives."

"All good clichés."

"Yeah, I guess I'm a cliché kind of guy."

"I know you don't love talking about your feelings. But it will really help me if I know what's going on in your head."

"Alrighty, then." Jim locked eyes with Chandler. "I'm feeling a little overwhelmed. Mad about that video. Worried about my business being destroyed by people who don't even know me. Humbled by the support of other people who don't even know me. Sad for Haley. Shocked by my wife . . ." He could still feel her trembling in his arms on Sunday morning. Maybe he needed to tell someone about it.

"I know, right? I could hardly believe it when Liz said we could stay."

"Yeah. That." Jim blinked himself back into the train of thought he knew Chandler was running on. "You have to understand; Liz is a compassionate, forgiving woman. And she's quite fond of Haley. We both are."

"That's obvious. I'm glad to see it. Haley could use a solid Christian influence in her life."

Something out of character here. "Christian? First time I've heard you mention that."

"I know I don't talk about it." Chandler started to remove his glasses then smiled at Jim and pushed them back in place. "Wow. I *do* do that, don't I? Anyway, I share your faith. The owner of the network does too. We've made conscious decisions to let our faith influence our programming without being overt about it. We feel like we can focus on clearly Christian values—faith, love, redemption, integrity—without speaking the name of Jesus and alienating an audience who needs to see those values lived out."

"So it's okay to believe in Jesus as long as you don't talk about him?"

"Not quite that cut and dry. But this does bring me to sharing how the network wants to move forward with the show."

"Hit me."

"We're committed to continuing. Based on some instant surveys, we think this whole storm will die down. Your comments weren't egregious enough to sustain the hate. And the pro-abort crowd really isn't interested in prolonging any discussion about whether a fetus is a living, feeling child right now. The science won't support their claims anymore, and they know it."

"No use in letting the facts interfere with their revenue stream."

"Exactly. So, understanding your beliefs in biblical truth, we know there are other social land mines out there we want to avoid if possible."

"Like?"

"Let's start with the current storm. Your obvious value for life. The reason you adopted all of these children and why we showed up at your doorstep. Instead of focusing on the negative, emotion-charged words—"

"Like murder." Jim flinched as he uttered the word. *How could I not have seen how harsh that is?*

"Yes, like that. We'd ask you to focus on the positives of adoption, the joys of children, the responsibility to take care of the ones who can't take care of themselves."

"Sounds reasonable."

"We also want to avoid other topics. There are groups out there combing through footage, doing research even, to ferret out people who disagree with their worldviews and make examples of them."

"More hateful than the people they target as being hateful."

"Yes. And while we can edit to suit our needs, you've had a front-row seat to see how things get out. We hire people from all walks of life with different perspectives, values, and lifestyles. We want the cream of the crop to do what they do best. Everyone from the craft folks to camera operators. It takes a lot of people to make our productions come alive. We can't guarantee someone won't leak something from the show no matter how many NDAs we have."

"Understandable. I hire a lot of people and serve a lot of people too. It don't matter to me or my company what they believe or how they live. Quality product, quality service. That's what we focus on."

"Of course, so you understand what I'm talking about."

"You don't want me to talk about hot-button issues. Or Jesus."

Chandler shifted in his chair. "With a reality show, we walk a line. We *want* to see your personal lives. It's what makes a show like this interesting. However, we don't want to let anything out that could get us canceled. Because, if we get canceled, the good things this show can do won't be seen. Honestly, your family is a microcosm of what most people want society to be. Color-blind, compassionate, hardworking, fun, authentic."

"But . . ."

Chandler tilted his head. "However, I am asking you to try to keep discussions about faith and values more generic and positive. When we're filming or when you're doing any interviews with other sources."

"I'm not sure how that would work."

"I understand. I'm not asking you to not be yourself."

"Yeah, you kinda are."

Chandler made a tally mark in the air with his finger. "Touché. Will you think about it some more and talk to Liz about it? Get back to me on Monday?"

"Of course." A thought pinged in his head. He grinned and made his own air tally mark. "I see what you did there . . . why you asked to meet with me alone. You want *me* to talk to Liz about this. You're scared of her, ain't you?"

Chandler removed his glasses and leaned in. "Yeah, a little."

He looks so tired. Heartsick. Liz diagnosed Elliot from the doorway to his tiny office. Headphones in, staring at his screen, oblivious to her presence. She waved the cooler in his line of vision. "Lunch?"

"Mom! What are you doing here? Everything okay?"

Liz smiled as Elliot jolted from his desk to embrace her. "Well, it's certainly better now." His tight hug brought tears to her eyes. The muscles in her neck relaxed as a little bit of the mama worry slipped away. At least she found him here, working, not hibernating in his apartment.

"Is Dad with you?"

"No, just me."

"Seriously, everything okay?"

She laughed. "It's okay with me. Just haven't seen you all month, and your father said you weren't coming this weekend, either. Thought we could have lunch. I brought barbecue."

"And potato salad?"

"And potato salad."

• • • •

"You laughing at me?" Liz poured tea into plastic cups and set them on the church's courtyard table alongside pulled pork sandwiches, potato salad, and succotash.

"Just wondering how much else you can pull out of your Mary Poppins cooler."

"What can I say? I've learned to be a master packer. Don't suppose you'll mind when you see this." She drew a container of something dark and gooey from the cooler. "Mississippi Mud." She winked at Elliot and reached for his hand. "You want to bless it?"

Elliot took her hand and bowed his head. "Thank you, Lord, for this food. And thank you, Lord, for my mom. In Jesus' name, Amen."

Elliot dove into the home-cooked bounty. *Good. The boy needs to eat.*

She still searched for a way to start the conversation about Bekah. None of the openers she'd rehearsed on the drive seemed right. Elliot helped her out by bringing up a different topic.

"Talked to Will. He said how crazy it's been."

"Crazy doesn't even begin to cover it. News trucks, protestors, supporters. More supporters, but you can't tell it from the angles the news people take."

"Social media?"

Liz blew out a breath of disgust. "They're like piranhas. We've told the kids to not look at it, but I think that's impossible. People are saying the most hateful, vile things. Victoria thinks her life is over."

"Of course she does. Will said business is still pretty good."

"Walk-ins, yes. Through the roof. Still don't know if Wal-Mart's going to stick with us. That'd be quite a hit."

"It's so unfair. Y'all deserve better. Been praying for you."

"We've been praying for you too."

God love him. Liz knew the definition of every tic he had in reaction to her simple sentence. The slight raise of his eyebrows as he considered feigning ignorance, the downward tilt of his head admitting his sadness, the clench of his jaw when he made eye contact, recognizing his mom knew at least something about his problems.

She plunged ahead. "I talked to Bekah."

He directed his attention to his plate, pushing the vegetables around with his fork. "Yeah? What did she say?"

"Said she did something she shouldn't, then hid it from you. Doesn't know if you will ever forgive her."

"That pretty wells sums it up."

She rested her hand on his forearm. "El . . ."

"Mom." He shook off the touch. "I don't want to talk about it."

"Okay." *Famous last words.* Liz forced herself to take a bite of her sandwich and stared into a clump of hot pink crape myrtles. She could handle a waiting game.

They finished their meals in silence. In her peripheral vision, she could practically see his mind working. Any second now, he would crack. She stacked their plates and napkins and made a move to open the dessert.

"Actually . . ." he stopped her. Time for the waiting to pay off.

"Would you mind if I just keep this for later?" He stood from his seat and reached for the container. "I mean, thanks for coming, but I should get back to work."

What? He really isn't going to talk about it? Not acceptable.

"Elliot." She cocked her head to one side and motioned with her eyes for him to sit back down.

"Mom." He stared into her eyes but didn't sit.

"Can you not forgive her?"

A violent sigh escaped, shaking him from head to foot. He dropped back to the bench and broke eye contact.

"I don't know." He swiveled to face her. "I mean, I feel like I'll forgive her, but I don't know if I'll ever get past it. And if that's the case, have I really forgiven her?

"And it's not just . . . the thing. It's the fact she didn't tell me for so long. I don't know if she ever would have if I hadn't . . . I mean, how can I trust her, knowing she could pretend it never happened? What kind of relationship would we have?"

"What on earth could she have done?" She ignored the warning tilt of his head. "I know it's none of my business. I just can't fathom what could be so terrible to you. Was she unfaithful to you?"

He shook his head. "No, it happened before me, before us being together anyway."

"So it is about another man?"

"Mom, I'm not playing this game. It's not about *what* she did, it's about the secret. A secret she was going to keep for who knows how long. The rest of our lives?"

Color rose to his face as he clenched his fists on the table. Liz's stomach tightened with the same intensity.

"Is that fair, though, son? Does anyone tell everything about themselves when they're in a relationship? Okay, so this, whatever it is, is big. Don't you think that would've made it even harder for her to admit?"

"Why are you defending her? Sure, it would be hard. Sure, I can see where she'd be scared. But after everything I've been through with her, I thought she trusted me. This is not the foundation for a successful relationship, much less a marriage. You never would have kept something like this from Dad."

Bam. Decision time. Liz stared into her son's pain-soaked eyes, the acid of barbecue sauce rising in the back of her throat.

The words came out as a whisper. "But I did."

A long blink from Elliot accompanied the shake of his head. "No, not like . . ."

"I had an abortion." The admission whooshed from her mouth like a bird fleeing a cage. Somehow, it calmed her to say it, even as she watched storm clouds of confusion cover his face. She needed to get the rest out without interruption. "I was fifteen. Scared. Thought I didn't have a choice. Then I didn't tell your father . . . all these years. It all came out because of all this television brouhaha."

"Wait. You just told him last week?"

Liz nodded then shook her head. "No, I didn't tell him. I lied about it. Your Aunt Denise told him."

"Whoa. Didn't see that coming."

"I know. It's a lot. Not sure I should've even told you, but it's right for you to know. I'm far from perfect. And I hope you'll forgive me if I've pretended to be. I know God has forgiven me."

"And Dad?"

Emotion choked out her voice, leaving her with only the ability to nod. They reached their hands to each other and squeezed tightly.

"Your dad's a good man. You're a good man too."

Trust in the Lord with all your heart and lean not on your own understanding; in all your ways submit to him, and he will make your paths straight. Bekah traced her finger over the highlighted verse, Proverbs 3:5–6, in the NIV translation on her Bible app. Looking up, she spoke into the star-studded black velvet sky over the pond.

"I'm trusting you, Lord. Please help me trust you more. Things aren't going the way I want them to, but I know your plan is perfect. There's so much hurt right now. Help me see ways I can help heal, not just Elliot, but Jim and Liz and Ida and Haley—whoever you put in my path. You know, the one you're making straight for me."

As if on cue, Haley's voice broke through the humid air. "Room for one more?"

"Of course." Bekah motioned for her to sit and took the bottle her friend offered. *That's a change.* "Sweet tea?"

"Yeah, trying to keep a clear head."

"Lot to think about. How are you doing?"

"So . . . you know . . ."

"Yeah, there was a family meeting."

"The whole fam?"

Bekah could see on Haley's face the shame and regret that had plagued her own face for the last three weeks. "For a general kind of report that the person who tried to wreck the show, the family, was gone. We prayed for him. Then, after everyone from Amy down were in their rooms, Jim and Liz told us the rest of it. We prayed for you."

"Prayed we'd burn in hell?"

"Wow. Really?"

Haley shook her head hard. "No, not really. I know Jim and Liz—none of you—would pray that. I guess I feel like it's what I deserve. To do . . . what I did, then to be blind enough to not see what Alex was up to, what kind of person he is. To judge Jim for being judgmental. I know they're sincere people. Like you said before, what you see is what you get."

"Then you know they've forgiven you."

"I do."

"And you know if you ask God, he'll forgive you for the rest?"

"Sure."

"Doesn't sound like you really believe it."

"Look, I don't want to step on anyone's faith. But I grew up in church life—was there every time the doors opened. I just outgrew it is all. So much doesn't make sense."

A memory from an earlier conversation came to Bekah's mind. "You said you had a bad experience."

"I did?"

"Uh-huh. Want to talk about it?"

Haley slugged down some tea and swallowed hard. "There was a youth pastor when I was fifteen. Took an interest in me. Totally creepy now, but at the time, I felt flattered. He was in his early twenties, good-looking, married, solid. It started out slow, telling me how pretty I was, a hug that lasted a little too long, a brush against my breast. Always, of course, when we were alone. I know now what I couldn't see at the time. He arranged those times.

"Before too long, I was in love with him—you know with a fifteen-year-old kind of love. He told me he loved me and he wanted to leave his wife, but it would take time. A kiss turned into make-out sessions turned into him sneaking into my room, into my bed." Haley closed her eyes as a visible shiver worked its way through her body.

Bekah gasped, "Oh, Haley."

"That was the clear line-crossing for me, though. All the sermons on abstinence and fornication kicked in, I guess. I was miserable watching him play happy family with his wife at church, winking at me when her back was turned. I told my mom."

"What did she say?"

"She told my dad. He stormed off to the church. Then the guy and his family disappeared. Left for 'another ministry opportunity,' they said. Wound up at a church in Florida."

"That was it? They didn't go to the police?"

"Said they didn't want me to be humiliated. It was best to forgive him and move past it. After all, I must have done something to encourage him."

"They didn't *say* that."

"They did." Her lip trembled as she squeezed her mouth in a tight line. "I did everything they'd ever taught me. Memorized Bible verses, dressed modestly, and served the community. They blamed me. A flirty teenager tempted the man of God."

"That's horrible."

Haley smirked. "And not even the worst of it."

Omigosh—how much more could happen to this poor girl? "What?"

Haley drew in a breath that seemed to suffocate her as if she'd swallowed a swarm of gnats. "I can't believe I'm telling you this. All of that aftermath, the shame, the guilt, it all brought back a memory to me. My uncle, my dad's brother, was a minister. One night when he was visiting, he came into my room. Just like that youth pastor. I was only seven. He made me . . ." Sorrow choked her voice as the memory crashed through her head. "He told me it was our secret. If I was a good girl, I wouldn't tell."

Bekah couldn't think straight. *God, help me know what to say.* "But you did tell? After you remembered it, I mean."

"How could I? My parents didn't believe what I said about a virtual stranger just because he'd been to seminary. They blamed me. There was no way they would believe me about my uncle. I couldn't face their rejection, so I never told."

"You never told anyone?"

"My therapist. And you."

Bekah's hand flew to her mouth. She moved it to Haley's shoulder, but Haley shrugged it off.

"Don't."

Bekah pulled back. "I'm sorry."

"No, I'm sorry. I appreciate it, but I can't stand the pity. I'm fine now. My therapist helped me understand that none of this was my fault. There's a patriarchy in our society that allows men to get away with these things, and it's everywhere, even in the churches. Maybe, especially in the churches. The denial, the aversion to scandal, blaming the women for the crimes of the men. That's my truth about God and the Church. It's why I can't be a part of it."

"I can understand you feeling that way with all you've been through. I'm so sorry."

"You have nothing to be sorry about. That's one thing I've learned. Women are conditioned to say they're sorry. We do it as a reflex. What that does, very subtly, is convince us that we are at fault for things that are beyond our control."

"You're right. The words popped out even though I didn't mean them that way."

"I know you didn't. It's just something I've learned to beat out of my vocabulary. I mean, it's good to apologize when I've done something wrong. But saying, 'I'm sorry,' when I feel bad about something feeds into devaluing myself."

She had a point. "I never thought about it, but you're right. What I should've said is that I'm so sad—mad, even—that you've been through those things. I'm glad you've been able to see you're not responsible for what those men did to you, but I hope, one day, you can see that kind of sin, the crime and coverups, they don't reflect the heart of God. He loves you. He made you. You are a beautiful, strong, smart woman, and you deserve to be treated with love and respect."

The corners of Haley's mouth tilted up. "Thank you. I'm learning I've been sabotaging my life with the choices I've made, the men I've chosen, since I left home because I didn't feel like I deserved the love of a good man. So Alex is gone. I'll be much more careful next time. Hope I can be as lucky as you and find someone like Elliot."

Elliot. Bekah sighed without thinking.

"What's that sound about?"

"Things aren't going so well."

"Really? That's all I get after I spill my guts to you?"

Bekah fidgeted with her empty tea bottle. "Could take a while to fill you in."

Haley scrolled to her calendar and smiled. "Turns out, I'm free. Spill."

The key verse from the morning sermon, James 1:17, played on auto-repeat in Jim's mind. "Every good and perfect gift is from above." Never had counting blessings been easier. His belly full of BLTs and sweet summer corn. Joyous squeals filled the air as young Caragins skimmed across the oversized Slip and Slide.

The Slip and Slide came from the Over the Moon Network, not directly from God. Sure, they did it for the B-roll video, but the kids were having so much fun that Jim didn't mind. Marshall and Cooper manned the hoses. Will supervised spacing the younger kids, sometimes tossing them down the slippery plastic with the flair of a professional bowler gliding a ball down the alley.

Vee followed a cameraperson around, catching her own angles with her GoPro! At the picnic tables, Laurel and Tamika cut watermelons and cantaloupes under Gramma Rosamond's watchful eye.

Thank you, Lord, for all these good gifts. Yes, even the cameraperson.

He grinned down at Zoe in her Fisher Price flower garden, gnawing on a plastic tulip. "Wonder where your Gammie Liz is. Wanna go find her?"

Jim wasn't sure the toddler understood, but she smiled and burbled as he lifted her. Nothing like a grandbaby. He'd heard his friends go on and on about how wonderful being a grandparent was and thought they were exaggerating. He was happy to be wrong.

He described every plant in the yard to Zoe's big brown eyes and chubby cheeks as he strolled around the house, finding Liz, as expected, on the front porch glider. Crazy how his pulse still sped up when he had a chance to look at her without the usual surrounding chaos. *How could that woman ever think I wouldn't love her?*

She looked up from the tablet she studied. "Hey, there."

"Got room for two more?"

She scooted to one side of the glider and reached for Zoe. Arms and legs that looked like sausage rolls flailed with excitement. Jim joined them on the glider, picking up the device Liz had tucked into a pillow.

"Reading a book?"

Liz made faces at the baby who giggled as she grasped for her grandmother's necklace. "Writing a letter."

"Yeah?"

"To Chandler and the network. You can read it."

"Okay." Jim donned his readers and lifted the tablet.

"You may be surprised."

"Hmm." Nothing he wouldn't expect in the opening sentences, except she seemed to be diplomatic as opposed to blunt. But . . . what? He blinked hard as he scrolled. It was definitely not the "take your show and don't let the screen door hit you on the way out" that he assumed would be the response after he ran Chandler's concerns by her. Not even close. He could feel her watching him for a reaction.

"*You* wrote this?"

Liz nodded. "I know. None of the things I said on Thursday night made it in there. But you're the one who asked me to think on it for a few days before we made any decision."

"I did." He stroked Zoe's head that now lay still on Liz's shoulder. "I gotta say I'm surprised."

"I know I bowed up right away, but then I thought more about exactly what they're asking. And I prayed and looked for verses to direct me. They're not asking us to deny our faith."

"But we talk about Jesus all the time. We pray. We read Bible stories. It's just part of how we live. You willing to change that?"

"That's the thing. I don't think we have to change much. For one thing, they're going to edit out whatever they want. For another, we've already learned how important it is to use words that won't come off as mean-spirited."

He felt heat rise in his face. "Boy, have we. But what would this look like?"

"Well, we still live like we always do. But when we're doing those vignettes or if we're interviewed about the show, we choose different words that mean the same thing. Instead of saying 'our Christian faith', we say 'our faith.'

"Other believers are going to know what we mean, and using more winsome words may intrigue anyone who watches. So when they look into our faith, they'll be more open to it. Like Paul said he 'became all things to all people' to win people to the Lord."

Flabbergasted. Was it simply because she'd reacted differently than he thought she would? Were her points valid? Now, he was the one who had to think some more.

"So you're saying you want this show to continue even if we can't boldly say what we think? That was the biggest reason we decided to allow this whole thing. To be a witness for Christ."

"I know. But I think there are many ways to be a witness. When I think about Haley and Kobi and Chad and all the others we've met who would never watch a show about a Christian family living out their faith but will watch a show about an unusual family struggling with ups and downs like everyone else. Then, through our examples, we show them what unconditional love is. I think we can reach people that way. Without having to quote chapter and verse."

"Hmm."

"Knew you'd be surprised."

"Yeah. I had one whole conversation with Chandler kinda planned out in my head. Now . . . I mean, I see your point. It just ain't what I was thinking."

"We don't have to decide right now." Liz leveraged herself up from the glider. "I'm going to put Zoe down and start on supper."

Jim opened the door for her then plopped back into the glider. He scanned Liz's letter again. "All things to all people," she'd said. Not normal for her to take a verse out of context. Still worth checking on. A quick Google search located Paul's words in First Corinthians. He read it himself—in five different translations of the Bible. *Hmm.*

· · · ·

Liz accepted the dripping wet pot from Victoria. The dishes were almost done and still not a word between them since Victoria stepped in to take Cooper and Amy's shift. Maybe she needed a nudge.

Liz pointed out the spaghetti sauce residue at the bottom of the pot. "What's on your mind?"

"Nothing." She swiped the bottom of the pot with her sponge.

"I thought maybe you had something you wanted to talk about since I haven't seen you volunteer for dishes since . . ."

"Ever?" Victoria laughed.

Liz smiled. "Yes. Since then."

"I guess there is something." A deep breath pulled her shoulders back as she dunked the noodle pot into the sink suds. "I'm thinking about not going back to school in the fall."

In seconds, lecture after lecture popped into Liz's brain. She fought them off like a game of mental whack-a-mole. This girl did not respond well to lectures or reason. *You're going to have to hear her out, Liz.* She plastered on a look she hoped would come off as casual interest. "What do you think you'll do?"

With a nonchalance that must have been practiced, Vee handed her the washed pot and dropped her bomb. "I'm thinking of moving to LA."

Liz couldn't stop her head from cocking. Couldn't stop the incredulity from writing itself all over her face, filling her voice. "LA, California?" Her filter did keep "Have you lost your mind?" from coming out of her mouth. A small victory.

"Hear me out." Vee took the pot from her mother's frozen hands and dried it as her master plan spilled. "I'm going to ask Chandler if I can get a job, any job, at OTN. Then I'll find a roommate. I've already been on a few message boards. In the meantime, I think Haley'll let me crash with her. I talked to her a little about it already. I'll work for a year so I can get resident status for in-state tuition. Then, get an associate's in filmmaking. There are nineteen community college campuses in LA county. Of course, I'll keep expanding my platform, get more affiliate links, and make more money that way. I'm a good saver. You know how thrifty I can be."

Liz propped on a counter stool. The words she wanted to say—starting with "If you think your father and I are letting you move to LA, you better think again"—strained the capacity of her filter. But she must have been able to corral her face into shape because she could see the hope dancing in her daughter's eyes.

Vee's words picked up speed. The girl had plans. Big plans. She sounded like she expected to waltz into Hollywood and have the town lay itself at her feet. Liz knew the city much more often chewed up dreamy-eyed kids and spit their bones out. *Balance, Liz. Inject realty without destroying dreams.*

Finally, Vee took a deep breath and asked the big question. "So what do you think?"

Buy time, Liz. "Well, that's a lot to think about."

Vee nodded and took a stool next to Liz. "I know you and Daddy may think I'm too young, but I'm older than you were when you got married."

Liz's back involuntarily straightened, and her eyes rolled before she could stop them.

"I know, you're going to say, 'It's not the same thing.' But it kinda is. That was a huge decision, and there were lots of people who thought you didn't know what you were doing, right?"

"Right. And looking back on it, they made a lot of sense. We didn't know what we were doing."

"But at the time, you were sure, right?"

A snippet of decades-old mental videos flashed in her mind. Jim's bicep strong beneath her hand as he looked her father in the eye, declaring their intention to get married with or without permission. Victoria was right. At the time, neither of them had any doubt. Dang, this girl had skills at deflecting. She managed a smile. "Not the point, Victoria."

"I'm just saying, look how great it turned out! Look at our family. Look at me and Marshall. We would've grown up with a junkie mom and no dad, or in the system, if it weren't for you telling everyone else they were wrong and you knew what you were doing."

Hackles up. "Is that what this is? You telling us we're wrong, and you know what you're doing?"

Victoria tucked her head. Slow exhale. "No, not really." Vee inhaled, raised her face, and made eye contact. "But, kinda. I want the chance to do what I really want to do. I don't see myself staying in this town, in this state."

"You have bigger plans. Want to shake this small-town dust off your feet and see the world."

"I do. But I don't really mean it in a bad way. I'm not saying your way didn't work for you. I mean, obviously, it has. And I do love it here. And I'll probably always want to come back. I just want to—"

"Make your mark on the world."

Victoria nodded.

"Here's my question for you, Victoria. What does this mark look like?"

"What do you mean?"

"Is the mark you want to make for world peace, rebelling against authority, stopping animal cruelty, finding the perfect lipstick? I've seen all of these things on your social media. What's your message? You at least need to know what your message is. What's the one thing you want to say to these Veeps of yours?"

Liz watched as her daughter changed from debate mode to serious thought. "I don't know if there is *one* thing. There's lots of things I love and want to talk about."

"Sure. We all have lots of interests, but there should always be the one thing. The glue holding them all together. Making sense of it all."

"Yeah, I get it. I want the chance to find that one thing out for myself."

"It's only . . . I see you searching for your one thing, and it seems like you're running toward fun and fame and stardust and away from your faith. That's the part that scares me."

Scared her? It terrified her. She prepared herself for Victoria to say the words the girl knew she'd want to hear. She'd never leave her faith. She loved Jesus and living in LA wouldn't change that. She could probably even find a church there.

Instead, Vee looked flatly at her and said, "I'm just not like you."

Liz thought her heart skipped. "What do you mean?"

"You've always been so certain what you believe about God. He's definitely your one thing. You're always talking about him, going to church, reading your Bible. In that way, what I'm really looking for is to be like you. To find *my* one thing and stick to it with all my heart. You never, ever, compromise what you believe is true. I want to be like that."

Ouch. Never, ever. Liz thought of her letter to Chandler. How could she even think of changing one iota of how she lived out her faith?

Victoria leaned in close, eyes pleading. "You'll talk to Daddy?"

"Oh, yes. I'll be talking to your daddy."

• • • •

Liz wedged next to Jim on their favorite living room chair. Scattered around them, all the kids from Amy down were engrossed in the TV or hair braiding or reading.

He returned her nuzzle. "I been thinking about your letter."

"Me too. I've changed my mind. We can't compromise what we say or do just to keep this show going. I don't know where my head was. What do you think?"

"Took the words right out of my mouth. I couldn't get comfortable with the idea of not saying whatever we want to about the most important thing in our lives. We'll just keep saying the truth," he grinned at her, "in love. Let the chips fall where they may."

An invisible weight lifted. Once again, she massaged his strong bicep and rested her head on his shoulder with a smile. "Then it's anonymous."

"That's gonna be a family thing now, ain't it?"

"Mmm hmm."

He smoothed her hair. "What changed your mind?"

"You won't believe it. Something Victoria said."

Elliot acknowledged Brett's sympathetic glance as the two of them and Dr. Andrews hovered over their devices in the back corner booth of the Bait Shop. If he'd only been able to screw up the courage to confide in the senior pastor like Brett suggested, surely the man wouldn't have chosen the Bait Shop for their meeting.

Brett knew everything by now and could have proposed an alternate, but lunch options were limited in town and no other had Dr. Andrews's favorite dessert, chocolate chip pie. At least Elliot wouldn't see Bekah here today. Unlikely to see Miss Ida, either..

Why did it have to be so hard? It's only a place, right? The decades-old fans powered by pulleys to the central motor turned lazily on the punched-tin ceiling. The hodgepodge of photos chronicling the town's history still needed dusting in the worst way. The same tarnished bell above the door announced each arrival and departure. But something else existed here.

Memories hung in the air as tangible as the lingering smell of fried bacon—his first look into Bekah's face by the counter, introducing Miss Ida as his birth mother to Liz, Bekah crying in his arms admitting her life was a wreck, Bekah bouncing through the swinging kitchen door to meet him for a date. Bekah.

"What do you think, Elliot?"

Hearing Dr. Andrews call his name snapped Elliot back into the conversation with the realization he'd only been watching the pastor's mouth move for the last . . . geez, how long had it been? He looked to Brett for a clue, and his friend rescued him.

"Actually, Elliot and I have already cleared the calendar for the week after Labor Day so the singles and the youth can work on all these projects together. The seniors' group has promised to help with a few too."

"Good." Dr. Andrews wiped his mouth and dropped his napkin onto his empty plate. "Serving our community is something all ages should be involved in. Good work." He glanced at his phone. "Sorry, but I need to get back. One of you can pay for the meal with the church card. Got it?"

Brett acknowledged with a nod, reached for his wallet, and waited until Dr. Andrews walked out of earshot. "You were like a zombie there."

"Yeah, thanks for the save."

"You know you should tell him. He'll understand."

Elliot scoffed. "You think so? That would be something because I still don't understand. It's just this place. I haven't been here since—"

Her voice from the door stopped him. There was no other like it. Miss Ida worked her way through the room, dripping with southernisms—"Hey, honey" and "tell 'em I said hey"—to the remaining lunch patrons. She stood beside them within moments.

"Brett. Elliot. Good to see you." She looked only at Elliot.

How fast could he get out of this place? He bolted up. "Actually, we were just leaving."

Brett stood. "That's alright. I'll settle up. You can hang here a while."

Traitor. Elliot glared at Brett, but he was striding to the counter without a backward glance.

Miss Ida scooted into Brett's vacated seat. "Please, Elliot."

With a roll of his eyes, he dropped back to the booth.

"I been hoping we could talk."

"Yeah, we can talk." Silence hung over the table. He waited until she cleared her throat to make the next move. "It's a nice day, isn't it?"

"Nice, hot but nice." She fidgeted with the reading glasses dangling from her neck.

"Did you watch the Braves' game last night?"

"Um, hmm. Until eleven, then I gave out."

"I like the new upholstery on the booths." His smile patronized her even as the tears clouded her eyes. A tug in his heart called for his sympathy, but his wounds brushed it aside. "Did you really know all this time?"

Her deep sigh and broken eye contact gave him the answer he'd already assumed.

Then her words verified it. "I knew there was something going on with them, but you gotta remember there was so much else happening. Caleb passing, the Five. Mostly, you'd waltzed in here looking like the spitting image of a man I hadn't seen in twenty-five years, and I couldn't think about much else.

"By the time I told you about being your mama, I'd figured out how much she cared about you, and I knew whatever it was with Sonny was over. You gotta know, I mean down-deep know, there was never nothing to that. She was hurting, and he's drawn to that. Wants to be the knight on the white horse and all that."

"And you were never going to tell me?"

"Well, what good would that've done? Don't you see how it's broke you up? How it's messed up everything with you and Bekah? How it's messed us up?"

"Seriously? You still think *not* telling me was the right thing to do?"

Miss Ida took a napkin to dab her eyes, folded it, refolded it, then smoothed it out on the table in front of her. "I know I should probably be setting here telling you I'm so sorry I didn't tell you. But when would've been the right time to tell you? I've thought back on it, and I just don't see it. You were so happy."

"A happy idiot."

"It ain't like that."

"Well, that's what I've been and what you were going to let me keep being. Every time he was here and we were all hanging out and everyone knew except me? How could you be happy knowing I was completely ignorant about them? Knowing now that every time he hugged her, he was looking at me thinking, knowing, I was stupid enough to not see it."

Her lips parted in silent argument. She had nothing.

Elliot leaned into the seat back. "It all makes sense now. How much he's always hated me. I mean, he said the right words but was always so cold. I'd decided it was all because he felt threatened by me coming into the picture, a long-lost brother he never wanted who would compete for your attention. But it wasn't just about you, it was about her.

"Do you have any idea how many hours I've spent praying I could have a real relationship with him? Looking for ways to start any kind of conversation just to show him we could be friends? And all this time, there's never been a snowball's chance that would happen."

Ida's hands worked her napkin to death, twisting and folding. "But don't you see? That's what I wanted too. For the two of you to be friends. I know it's my fault, and I ain't got any right to it, but to see the two of you together

. . . to have you both under my roof. It was like a dream for me. I just knew that time—"

"Heals all wounds? Nice thought, but I don't see how it can apply here."

"But can't you . . . I mean, you forgave me for giving you up. That's a mighty big thing. Can't you forgive me for this?" Her eyes pleaded, and her hands trembled on the tabletop.

"Truth?"

She drew her hands into her lap, straightened her back, and clenched her mouth shut like a child preparing for a spoonful of bad medicine to come her way. "Truth."

"I can forgive you." He watched her eyes close and her shoulders relax. "I'm not there yet, but I'm working on it. Or I guess Jesus is working on me. I know you were in a hard spot, feeling like you had to choose between your two sons. And I can see how important it was, is, to you for us to get along. But I have to tell you, Mom, I don't see how that's ever gonna be a thing."

She'd brightened considerably when the word "Mom" left his lips. "But if you can forgive me, then can't you forgive Sonny?"

Days of thinking had already answered this question in his mind. "No. I can't."

"Why not?"

"Because he doesn't need my forgiveness. He's the only one who told me the truth. Granted, it was pretty brutal, and I could see he enjoyed it. But I know there's a lot more pain in his world than he shows. I feel kinda sorry for him. I'd rather have my life here on a youth pastor's salary than all the stuff he has that doesn't bring him any real joy."

"And Bekah?"

Now she was pushing it. He covered his face with both hands and rubbed his forehead. If he pressed hard enough, maybe he could force the hurt out or, at least, separate her face from it. He parted his fingers and stared at his mother through them, wagging his head slowly. "Bekah. That's a whole 'nother thing."

"But you two love each other so much."

"I know."

"Love covers a multitude of sins." She raised her eyebrows.

He grinned despite his pain. *Oh, yes, she did just drop Scripture on me.*

"Let's talk about something else."
She leaned toward him with a smile. "Okay."
"I'm going to New York tomorrow."
"Oh, yeah? Church thing?"
"Nope. Personal. I found David. I'm going to see my birth dad."

Jim looked up when he heard Victoria's voice sweetly say, "Daddy" from the doorway to his office. Too sweetly. She wanted something. And exactly how did she still look so fresh at the end of a workday in the nurseries? Either she wasn't working hard enough, or she needed to package and sell her whatever it was she wanted to ask for.

He returned her smile. "Hey."

She got straight to the ask. "Mind if I clock out now? I want to meet some friends for dinner and a movie."

Friends? Sounded vague. Sure, you can't tighten the reins too much on a nineteen-year-old, but he still worried about her hanging around the TV crew too much. She might lie to him anyway, but at least he could ask. "What friends?"

She giggled as if it were a silly question. "Friends from school."

He knew she wasn't asking her dad for permission to go to a movie. She was asking her boss about leaving early. Still, she opened the door to talk about school. He and Liz had already decided how to handle that situation. Liz wouldn't mind if he handled it alone.

"Sure that's fine."

"Thanks, Daddy."

"Speaking of school." He took his readers off and thought for a split second about Chandler removing his glasses to make a point. He shook his head with a smile and motioned for Victoria to come in.

Her face fell a little as she trudged into the office and stopped in front of his desk.

Jim ignored the body language that filled with attitude like the fuel gauge in his car filling with gas. Knees locked. Arms akimbo. A slight huff issued through the grimace on her face.

I already know the answer, but I'll ask anyway. "You registered for classes, yet?" Her head cocked to one side, surprise on her face. "I thought Mama would've told you. I've decided not to go back to CC this year."

He leaned back. "Your mother did talk to me. She said you was *thinking* of not going back. Have a seat, Victoria."

219

With a slight eye roll, she slouched onto the edge of a chair full of catalogs, not bothering to move them. Clearly, she didn't intend to have a long conversation.

Jim shifted his weight back to the front of his chair and propped his arms on his desk. "Your mother told me about all of your plans and, while we know you're old enough to make decisions like this, we'd like you to take a little more time to think about it."

He lifted a hand to stop the argument he saw about to come out of her mouth. "Hear me out."

She pursed her lips and stared at him.

"It can't be a surprise to you to hear that we don't think moving to LA is the best idea for you. And we ain't saying that's never an option. We just think it's better if you wait, finish your associate's degree at CC, and get your BA from a college around here that has a top-notch degree in whatever part of the film industry you want to work in, then make the move to LA or New York or wherever."

Here came the first argument. "But I think that it's best to go now. Get involved in the industry, start networking while I'm young. I already have an in with Over the Moon and Haley said—"

"If you're about to say that Haley said you can live with her, let me stop you. We've talked to her and there seems to be a misunderstanding. She only remembers saying that she thought you would enjoy a visit to LA. She don't remember offering you a place to stay on that visit and certainly not a place to live while you pursue your dream."

He could tell by Victoria's look that she hadn't guessed they would check on her story. She was momentarily speechless, so he plowed on. "And you're assuming Chandler has nothing better to do than take you under his wing. Now, I'm sure he likes you and all, but he ain't promised anything like that as far as I know."

Her face fell a little, and he knew it was a good time to wave the carrot he and Liz had agreed on. "I know you got big dreams, Victoria, and I do believe you can make them come true. But you gotta realize that there are hundreds, probably thousands, of young people with dreams like yours that land in LA every day. We believe you can get a stronger foundation to help you succeed by doing it like I said. So if you'll do that . . . finish all your schooling around here . . . we'll give you five thousand dollars to help you make whatever move you decide to make."

He saw her eyes widen with the thought of that amount of money. He and Liz had agreed to ten thousand, but it was a judgment call. He watched as she pondered.

A sideways grin that he'd adored since she was a toddler brightened her face. "Ten thousand?"

That's Victoria. Now he realized why his gut told him to start at five. He hid the smile in his mind with a serious stare. "We ain't never offered anything like this to your brothers or Laurel." He allowed the smile to peek out. "Seventy-five hundred."

Her smile broadened. "I'll think about it."

Chandler's voice came from the doorway. "Sorry to interrupt. Jim, do we need to talk later?"

Victoria answered, "You can come on in. I was just leaving." She went around the desk to plant a kiss on Jim's forehead. "Love you, Daddy."

"Love you, baby girl." He watched as she sauntered out of the room, giving a fist bump to Chandler on the way. "Registration ends in two weeks."

She turned with a smile. "I know."

Time to switch focus. Chandler had already moved the catalogs and settled into the chair on the other side of the desk. He started the conversation. "You wanted to talk?"

"Yeah, for just a few minutes. Me and Liz been thinking about what you asked—you know, about how we act and talk about our faith."

Chandler held up both hands. "Not meaning, of course, that we don't want you to be your authentic selves. I want to make sure you understand that."

Jim cocked his head. "Yeah, I know that's what you meant. Here's the thing, though. Being open about our faith, talking about Jesus, is our authentic selves. Until we started thinking about not doing it, I really didn't realize how much we do it. We pray, we talk about Bible verses and principles practically every day. We don't feel right about changing that or telling the kids they gotta be careful about it. That contract says a lot about what's expected of us, but it don't say we gotta change how we talk. I'm afraid it's not up for discussion. Take us or leave us."

Chandler tilted his head down like a warrior conceding defeat. "I can't say I'm surprised. I respect your decision. I'd already told the higher-ups to expect it. There's an audience who believes as you and Liz do who will be attracted to the show. We believe they'll outweigh the negative voices. We all want to proceed."

Jim chuckled. "So that's it?"

"That's it." He stood and returned the catalogs to the chair. "I have to catch a flight back to LA. I'll be back next week for the wrap. If you need anything in the meantime, you know how to reach me."

Jim shook his hand. "Yes, I do. Safe travels."

He laughed to himself as he settled back to finish his paperwork. Less than half an hour and he'd crossed two fights off Liz's list. At least, he hoped he had.

Here we go. Elliot's shoulders tensed like a compressed jack-in-the-box when he spotted David in the café doorway. Without a doubt, it was him. Older-looking than Elliot expected, with close-cut white hair and goatee and a small paunch around his middle. Yet he moved with a fluidity that exuded the confidence and worldliness Ida had attributed to him.

His father's eyes followed the pointing finger of the hostess straight to Elliot's face. With a smile, he sauntered to the table. "Well, Elliot," the vaguest shadow of a Caribbean accent tinted his voice as he grasped Elliot's hand firmly. "I guess I can't deny those eyes very well, can I?"

Say something, stupid. All the rehearsed remarks froze together in a glob in his brain. "Guess not." *Guess not? That's all you got?*

Thankfully, the server appeared. David sat as if this were his living room, and the server was his personal butler standing ready to meet his every whim.

"What are you drinking?" His father asked him. His *father*. The man who brought him into existence. The one he'd wondered about, invented stories about, for years.

"Uh, me?" Elliot fingered the almost empty glass in front of him. "Coke."

"Would you like something else?"

"No, I'm good."

"Get him another, and I'll have a Dalmore 15, neat."

David relaxed into his chair, scratched his beard, and assessed Elliot as if he were an interesting piece on a museum wall. "Why is it you are reaching out to me now?"

Okay, no awkward small talk happening. Elliot swallowed down the ball of heat rising in his throat. "Well, I just found out about you last year. It's taken me a while to wrap my head around it, decide what I wanted to do."

"Interesting. I thought Ida would've told you long ago."

"Just found out about her last year too. She gave me up for adoption when I was born. I met her at the diner after I got a job in Whitman."

"The Bait Shop?" He cocked his head to the left and grinned, exposing the dimples he'd passed on to Elliot. "Small world. You know, I saw her name in a story in the *New York Free Press* last year. The mention of Whitman caught my eye."

"Yeah, the whole Whitman Five thing. Pretty crazy. After it was all over, the state asked her to maintain a Whitman branch of the Civil Rights museum. Her and Annie . . . you knew Annie?"

"Oh, I knew Annie. She never liked me. Maybe she was a better judge of character than Ida, yes?" He winked as if they shared an inside joke.

He'd done it again, disarmed Elliot with a smile, then put him on edge with a pointy-edged comment. The server dropped their drinks off, and Elliot took a slow sip to gather his head.

"So, Elliot, tell me about you. What is it you do in Whitman?"

"I'm the youth pastor at LifeSpring Church. It's kind of a new church; you wouldn't have known about it."

"And this will be your life's work?"

"Well, maybe not in this role, or in this particular church. But as a pastor, yes, I believe it's where God wants me to be."

David's top lip curled into a sneer around his high-end scotch. "So God, he speaks to you?"

"Not in an audible voice, no. But I've followed God for as long as I can remember, and there's a peace that comes from knowing his heart, believing in his love for me, trusting he'll always be there for me."

"Like a good father, yes?"

"Yeah. Like that."

"And, tell me, the man who adopted you, he was a good father?"

"Incredible."

"Yet . . . you still have a hole in your heart? You still need more. Do you think coming to me will fill this vacancy? Is this why you are here?"

Does he seriously want to know or is he mocking me? "I suppose so. I mean, I know Mom's—Ida's—story now. I'd like to know about you. Understand my heritage. You're originally from the Dominican Republic, right?"

David huffed and rolled his eyes as if the question was an imposition. What next? Would he just get up and leave? Elliot replied with a tilted head and raised eyebrow, a wordless "So?" The expression seemed to amuse David. He polished off his drink and motioned for another.

"My family emigrated from the DR when I was young and wound up in Flatbush in an area they recently named 'Little Haiti.' We lived a meager life, but my mother . . . she insisted we study hard and work hard. I spoke Spanish mostly, learned English in school, and French from the Haitians around me. In 1965, I joined the Army to gain my citizenship."

"Not a great time to be in the Army. Did you go to Vietnam?"

He scoffed. "Oh, no, they did not send me to Vietnam. I had better uses. They sent me to my home country to help them end the last Civil War there."

"I never learned anything about that."

"You should study it. There is more history than US history."

"Did you make a career in the Army?"

"Oh, no. The Army, they used me for my skills. I used them for a GI Bill to get my degree from NYU, then pursued my master's, then my PhD. All the while working for the UN as an interpreter, then for the State Department. I leveraged my skills and my personality to make friends and moved up quickly. Now, at seventy-five years old, I am still called on often as a consultant for international companies."

"Impressive." Elliot did the math in his head. At seventy-five, David was roughly fourteen years older than Ida. New information.

"Yes." He tipped his drink toward Elliot. "Impressive. My career has taken me around the world and shown me many things. In my travels, I met many people and had many loves, but I always, *always* returned home to New York and my family."

"Your family . . ."

"I married Maya the day before I shipped out with the Army. Her family emigrated with mine. I have loved her almost all of my life. We have four children, all of them grown with families of their own, and all who were born before my travels took me to Whitman, Alabama."

Elliot's turn to scoff. "But you didn't mention this to my mother?"

David clicked his tongue and shook his head with a smirk. "I see you are an upright, godly young man, but you must know that is not the way the game is played. Ida was strong and determined, but she had been badly hurt. I filled for her a longing as she filled for me. Then, the time came for me, as always, to return to my true love."

"And as for me?"

"I did not know she had not ended the pregnancy."

"You never asked."

David finished his second drink, motioned for another, and leaned his elbows on the table. "No, Elliot. I never asked. But I never asked any of them."

A shock as real as a plunge into icy water crashed through him. "Them?"

"My career took me around the world, often for weeks or months at a time. A man does not like to be lonely that long." David lounged back into his seat like the Cheshire Cat in a tree branch.

Blood pulsated through Elliot's temples. Why hadn't he thought about this? David as a stereotypical player, not a man torn between his wife and a vulnerable woman he'd fallen in love with in his travels. *I have totally romanticized this guy.*

"There are other . . . children . . . than your four with Maya?" Had he been able to keep his voice from cracking? What was that anyway? Hurt? Anger?

"Three, including you now. But you . . . of all my offspring, only you have my eyes." He grinned as if it were an accomplishment on his part. "Those eyes will open doors for you."

At the moment, all those eyes could do was desperately search the room for an anchor, something true to hold onto. There, on the mantel above a faux fireplace, sat a real clock. He watched the minute hand tick to its next mark. Time was still real. But what now?

David stole his thoughts. "What were you hoping, Elliot? That I would ask for your forgiveness and take you to my home and bring you into my family?"

The realization that the man was right washed over him. *Yes. That's exactly what I hoped. Despite everything I've said to anyone who knows about this meeting that I wasn't expecting much, something in me hoped for that.* Elliot returned his gaze to David's green eyes, summoning every bit of discipline he had to act like he didn't care. *Don't give him the satisfaction.*

"I am sorry, but this is not going to happen. I have built here a peaceful life and reputation. My Maya, she is not well, and my focus is on her. I will not bring disruption to her final days. Now, I know since you located me, you could also locate others in my family, your *half*-siblings. But I would ask you not do that. They, also, are focused on their mother. To bring you into the picture now would only bring confusion and pain."

He tossed the remainder of his drink back in one swallow, stood, and threw some money on the table. "I do wish you well, Elliot."

Elliot hunkered over his plate at the Manhattan diner counter, chomping the last of the overcooked bacon and dry scrambled eggs before cleansing his palate with the few mouthfuls of gooey pastry he had reserved precisely for that purpose. The food wasn't much, but the place reminded him of the Bait Shop. It was considerably more grimy and, of course, absent the parade of people saying "y'all." But the bustle, the Formica, and the heavy porcelain plates and cups warmed his Alabama heart.

He still wasn't sure whether the diner next to his hotel had a particular name. The biggest letters on the window were the ones spelling out HOT COFFEE in sun-faded blue. Eating here every morning since Wednesday made him almost as much of a regular as anyone else in this touristy part of the city. But someone else would be occupying his stool tomorrow. Adding extra days to his stay hoping his father—David, no point in calling him anything paternal now—would want to spend more time with him turned out to be a waste. Oh well. Now the mystery was over.

All he had left to do was check out of the hotel and grab an Uber to the airport. That left a lot of daylight before his redeye took off. Plenty of time to take another walk around the city. He snugged two fives with the ticket under the edge of his plate, adjusted his book bag, and slid off the stool. A step away from the door, he heard someone say his name.

You gotta be kidding me. Sonny sat in a booth, with the *Wall Street Journal* in one manicured hand and a cup of coffee in the other. He seemed out of place in his crisp shirt and blazer with the perfect pocket square. Elliot blinked, long and slow. Maybe his emotions had made him delusional.

Sonny raised his cup and his eyebrows. "Surprise."

"Unbelievable." He could only allow the one word to escape. The other words racing to his mind were ones Liz would have spanked him for uttering. He turned for the door. Sonny called out to him again.

"What brings you here?"

Elliot rolled his eyes, trudged to Sonny's booth, and crossed his arms. "Me? What brings you here? Doesn't look like your kind of place."

"Sit down and I'll tell you." Sonny waved his hand toward the opposite side of the booth as if he were a king granting audience to a vassal.

Elliot glared at his brother like a buck on a nature show who rounds a corner in the meadow and spots another buck in his territory. His feet rooted to the dingy diner floor. Sweat prickled the back of his neck.

The cockiness on Sonny's face faded into a light smile. "Please."

Elliot slid hesitantly into the booth. Sonny motioned for the waitress to bring another cup of coffee. He smiled as if they were friends, folded his paper, and stashed it in his leather courier bag. "So . . . not quite up to the Bait Shop breakfasts, huh?"

So this is how we're going to play it? Elliot chose to oblige the small-talk game. "The biscuits ain't worth a dime, but the cinnamon rolls make up for it."

Sonny tapped his fork on the half-eaten roll on his plate. "Mama Rosie's. That's why I'm here."

"They sell Mama Rosie's in this diner?"

"Sold them here first. It's Shelia's recipe. This is where I met her after a tragedy of a visit with my father. She called me 'Sonny' before I introduced myself, and it got away with me. Within months, I poured every cent the old man gave me into getting these on the market. Shelia agreed to come on board and be the face of Mama Rosie's and, before too long, the chief operating officer."

"The face of Southern comfort food from the center of New York City?"

"All in the marketing." Pride beamed from Sonny's eyes as he popped a bite of roll into his mouth.

Elliot turned his attention to the pigeons gathered around an overflowing trash can outside the smudgy diner window. Thick silence lay over the table.

"So," Sonny continued, "I always stop here for old time's sake when I'm in the city. That's my story. What about you?"

Elliot moved his stare to Sonny. Hate he thought he'd overcome burned in his heart and, he imagined, spilled out of his eyes. "I can't even talk to you." He moved to scoot out of the booth.

"Oh, come on." Sonny reached across and grasped Elliot's arm. He dropped it when Elliot's muscles tightened. "You got somewhere else to be?"

Elliot hesitated. Sonny's tone dropped to a sound of actual concern. "You look like your dog died. Wanna talk?"

Did he want to talk? Yes. To Sonny? No. To Brett or Pastor Andrews or Jim or Bekah. God, if only he could talk to Bekah. After his last heart-to-heart with Sonny, he never wanted to talk to him again. Still, he couldn't squelch the whispers in his head that this unexpected encounter had a purpose. Really. What were the odds of them both being in this diner at the same time?

Elliot sipped a little of the burnt-tasting brew from his cup. No way would he lay the tatters of his living soul on the table for this man to eviscerate. He would treat him the way he handled the many teenagers he counseled. Ask a question instead of answering one. "What's the deal with your father? You said something about tragedy."

Sonny dropped his head and blew air from his mouth like a horse resisting a bridle. "My old man. How much time you got?"

"Check out at noon." Elliot set about doctoring his coffee. In his peripheral vision, he could see Sonny shift his weight. The titan of industry squirming? Good. Elliot focused on opening minuscule plastic containers of faux cream and dumping them into his cup. If Sonny wanted to share, fine. If he got up and left, fine.

"My father," Sonny said with invisible air quotes of disgust around the words, "left Whitman when I was five years old. He was from here and, I guess, always wanted to be back here. He went to Alabama to be a part of the Civil Rights Movement. Met Mom there. Got married. I guess they were kind of all caught up in the emotions of the time. With what I know now, I can see they weren't suited for each other. Grits and escargot. Anyway, he started making more and more visits to his family here. Each one lasted longer than the last until he didn't come back one day."

"But you kept in touch?"

"Well, he would call occasionally, but I wouldn't talk to him. I could see how much he'd wounded Mom, hear her crying when she thought I was asleep. Besides, he didn't really want to be my dad . . . I didn't need him. When I got to be around thirteen, Mom talked me into coming up here to visit him. Said it was important. So I started coming up for a few weeks every summer.

"By then he'd made a big success of his father's furniture business, married a beautiful Jewish woman, had two beautiful daughters. Perfect New York success story. Except for me . . . this reminder of his past from the backwoods of the South. Maybe they tried, but they never really knew what to do with me.

"It was always about the money with him. Paid for my college and MBA. I guess that's something. Then, eleven years ago, I'm here, and he tells me he made me a vice president in his company. The role didn't come with any responsibility, but he'd put a cool two-fifty into my account."

Elliot leaned back in his seat. "Two hundred and fifty thousand dollars?"

"Pathetic, right?"

"Well, not *exactly* the word I was thinking of."

"I know it probably sounds stupid. It was a lot of money. But it was just a payoff. Something to assuage his guilt for years missed. Something to make him feel good."

"What did you do?"

"I sulked. Came here to this diner and asked a streetwise waitress from the wrong side of the Bronx for a cinnamon roll. The rest, as they say—"

"Is history." The two finished the sentence together.

Elliot relaxed for the first time since he sat down. "Wow. Quite a story. I didn't know all of that."

"Well, now you know my story. Your turn." Sonny motioned for more coffee and sopped up the sugary glaze on his plate with the last bite of his cinnamon roll. "Why are you here?"

"Interestingly enough, also father drama."

Elliot paused, his guard still up, not sure if he wanted to walk the road of trusting Sonny again. But here they were. He could either share or grab his backpack and go. Sonny raised his eyebrows and tilted his head like a golden retriever asking his owner if they were going to the park.

Elliot took in a deep breath and let it escape. "I came here to meet my birth father. Mom—Ida . . ."

"Dude, you can call her Mom. I'm gonna have to get used to it."

"I finally asked Mom about him. She told me everything she remembered. I Googled around and found out he lived here."

"And you just showed up?"

"No. I prayed about it for a while. So many questions and feelings running through my head. I found his contact info on LinkedIn. Emailed him a note with a pic of him and Mom and a pic of me."

Sonny chuckled. "Would have loved to have been there when he opened that. Must have rocked his world."

"Yeah. He didn't reply for two days. I was sweating it. Didn't know if he was in shock or mad or if I'd sent it to the right address. Then I got his reply. He basically acknowledged me but said this wasn't a good time for him. I told him I'd planned to be in New York this week and asked if we could at least have coffee."

"Elliot, *you* lied?"

"Don't even."

"Sorry. You're right. Guessing it didn't go as well as you'd hoped."

Elliot related every detail of the encounter. Sonny kept constant eye contact, even ignoring his phone when it vibrated on the table. When the story ended, there were several minutes of silence.

Sonny looked dumbfounded. "He wished you well? That was it?"

"Yeah, and I couldn't do anything but stare. I just watched him saunter out of the room like he didn't have a care in the world."

"And what now?"

"Done all I can, I guess. He knows where I am now. Ball's in his court. But I don't think I'll ever hear from him again."

"I'm sorry, man. That's rough. At least you have a real dad who cares. Jim, he seems like a nice guy."

Sonny's compassion seemed authentic. Was it because they had this dysfunctional father bond now? It could be a door to a real relationship, but there was still Bekah. Elliot's back muscles tensed. He rocked his cup back and forth on its porcelain saucer, engrossed in the movement of the room-temp java. "He's the best." Elliot glanced at his phone. "Whoa, it's eleven thirty. I need to finish packing and check out."

"When's your flight?"

"Not until midnight. Redeye."

"Hey, if you can wait until Sunday, you can fly back on my plane. I'm going to Miami, but we could make a stop in Whitman."

Was Sonny making a real overture of brotherhood or at least friendliness? Was he just showing off his wealth? Was he playing a game again, pretending to be nice so he could smack him down? Elliot blinked away the racing thoughts. "Nah, that's okay. I'm going to B'ham. My car's parked there and, uh, I need to be back for my kids on Sunday. Thanks anyway."

"Well, at least let my car take you the rest of the day. Rideshares and taxis are brutal here." Sonny spoke into his phone. "Siri, call driver."

The thoughts in Elliot's brain stepped on and over each other like hundreds of worker ants in a colony. Did accepting the lift give more power to Sonny? Could he forgive this man he had nothing in common with other than some DNA? Should he throw the dregs left in his coffee cup all over Sonny's high-dollar ensemble and tell him he could keep his stupid limousine? How could they possibly move forward?

Sonny tucked his phone into his blazer pocket. "He'll be here in five."

"Look, Sonny, this has been . . . good . . . a little weird, maybe, but good. But with everything . . . I mean . . . you're the one who said we couldn't really be friends. And . . . with all the stuff with . . . Bekah."

"Yeah. That's a tough one." Sonny stared past Elliot, his forehead scrunched. "I have to say I'm sorry about that. I was a major ass. Just jealous, I suppose is what it comes down to. It's obvious you two love each other. I wanted to ruin it for you both. And I was wrong."

Elliot couldn't force a follow-up from his brain with a crowbar. Sonny pulled at his collar as if it were tight on his neck even though the top two buttons were undone. He waited for Elliot to make eye contact before he continued. "I don't know if we can make it past that. But I hope we can. We've both been through enough. I hope you can forgive me."

Tears clouded Elliot's eyes. He opened his mouth to say he could forgive. Was it only a reflex of Christian training, or did he mean it? He was saved from deciding when Sonny glanced at his phone.

"Car's here. You go check out. I'll tell him to wait." Sonny bounded out of the booth, tossing money on the table, his benevolent millionaire persona back in play. "Go on, it's fine. Just tell him where you want to go before you have to go to the airport. Enjoy the city. I'm going to walk back to my office. It's a nice day for it."

Minutes later, Elliot stepped out of his hotel to find Sonny waiting by the car, the back door opened. The driver appeared like a genie from a bottle, took Elliot's bag from his hand, and loaded it in the trunk.

"Well, that just happened," Elliot laughed. "Thanks, Sonny."

"Happy to. Well, see you . . . around."

There was awkwardness as they settled for something between a pat on the shoulder and a firm handshake. "Yeah, see you." Elliot slid into the supple leather backseat. Sonny closed the door, waved, and turned down the sidewalk. Elliot watched him through the darkened window as the car jerked away from the curb into the crush of midday traffic.

The driver spoke. "How's your day going, sir?"

Elliot laughed and shook his head. "Strangely. *Very* strangely."

Bekah slapped another mosquito on her calf. Even the army of citronella plants circling her parents' patio couldn't keep all of them out. Her father relaxed in his chair, the newspaper he made a pretense of reading periodically dipping as his head nodded, reading glasses on the precipice of falling off of his nose. Heat lightning glowed in the night sky, and ever-so-slight thunder promised a summer shower. She sank into her cushiony chair and back into the novel on her Kindle app.

From behind her, Bekah heard the sound of the door opening and closing, then her mother's flip-flops announced her arrival. She handed a glass of lemonade to Bekah and stood over Foster. "Looks like it's time for you to turn in, Mr. Golding."

He bolted upright and examined his watchless wrist. "Hmm, yeah, I guess so. Didn't realize it was so late." He hoisted himself up, kissing Shelby's cheek and Bekah's forehead before stumbling to the house. "G'night, biscuit."

"Good night, Poppa." Bekah settled back into her book as Shelby slid into Foster's seat with her own lemonade. The charms on her bracelet tinkled together every time she took a sip. Then the slight sigh that Bekah knew signaled a conversation as sure as the distant rumble signaled rain.

"It's been a nice day."

Without looking up, Bekah murmured, "Mmm hmm."

"Made my birthday special, you coming down. And I love the bird feeder. I think I'll put it right over there."

Bekah looked up to see where she pointed and dropped her iPad into her lap. "Glad you love it. Want to talk, Mom?"

"If you want to talk."

Typical therapeutic conversation. You would've thought Shelby was a psychiatrist instead of a surgeon. Bekah shrugged.

Another slight smile from her mom. "You've filled me in on your work at the nurseries and all the drama with the TV show. Any change with you and Elliot?"

"Nope."

"Haven't heard from him at all?"

"Not directly. I do hear things, though. Jim told me he'd gone to New York this week to meet his birth father."

"That's big news."

"Yeah, wish I knew how it went." She curled her legs up in her chair and stared into the woods beyond the patio.

"Hopefully, it went well. If not, well, he may need some more time to himself. Maybe it's good for you to be apart for a little while so he can work through all of that on his own."

"What's that supposed to mean?"

"Nothing, I only . . . dealing with finding out you were adopted, meeting your birth parents for the first time and all that entails. It's just a lot of baggage."

"Baggage?" The knee-jerk defensiveness popped out of her mouth. Her jaw clenched.

"I don't mean anything by it. Nothing against Elliot personally. You know we think he's a fine young man. But sweetheart, you've gone from one disastrous event to another in the last year and some. Maybe you need this break to figure out your path without all the extra drama."

"Wow." *Dear God, help me not explode.*

"What I mean to say is—"

Heat flooded her face. "Oh, you've said what you mean. You always say what you mean. Let's talk about baggage for a moment, Mom. You know who plunged right into a whole airport full of baggage this last year without a thought for himself? Elliot.

"When I was nothing but a hot mess, he stepped in and stayed. He kept speaking truth into my life, praying for me, being so blessedly patient, and loving me unconditionally until I did find the right path. Without his presence the last year, I'd still be curled up in a ball on the floor."

"But you're on the floor now because of him."

Incredible. "I'm where I am because of *me*, what I did. I don't blame him one bit for his reaction. Sheesh, Mom. I understand you want to believe I'm the innocent party in everything. Those 'disastrous events' weren't things that simply happened. They're all consequences of my bad choices."

"Not true. Not your marriage with Jeff."

"Yeah, probably even that. If I'd been in the right place with God through college, maybe I would've seen Jeff wasn't the perfect choice for me, that he didn't love me the way he should. Instead, I just steamrolled into the perfect wedding with my college sweetheart, like I'd built up in my head since high school."

"But, Bekah, none of us could tell."

Was that a tear? Hard to tell, it happened so rarely. *Slow your roll, Bekah. Deep breath.* "I know. I'm not saying it's *all* my fault. It wasn't any one person's fault, certainly not yours or Poppa's. I'm just saying that, looking back, I can see my lack of reliance on God is the number one reason I made one bad choice after another. And the last bad choice I made was not telling Elliot about Sonny a long time ago."

The charms on Shelby's bracelet tinkled as she took another drink. The slightest breeze stirred across the patio. Songs of tree frogs, owls, and cicadas filled the void.

"So you're accepting the responsibility?"

"I think I should."

A long blink and a slight smile. "Good."

"Good?" *What just happened?*

"You're right. Sometimes, most times probably, bad events follow bad decisions. My father always said you can choose your actions, but you can't choose your consequences. Sounds like you are on the right path. The next step is forgiveness."

"I know. I've asked God, and I know he's forgiven me. I just haven't had a chance to ask Elliot yet."

"Haven't *had* the chance?"

Bekah almost smiled hearing her mom switch back to therapist mode. She was right, as usual. "Haven't *made* the chance." Another sip of lemony courage. "I'm scared he won't forgive me. I understand if he won't. And I know I'll be able to move forward eventually if he doesn't. Annie reminded me that as long as my relationship with God is right, I'll be alright."

"You sound confident."

"I am. At my core, I am. I can't let my past bad choices identify me. I know God doesn't see those when he looks at me. Hopefully, Elliot will be able to look beyond them too."

"When do you think you'll see him again?"

"Friday. There's a big wrap party at the farm. Everyone's supposed to be there."

"Then Friday. This is the Bekah that Elliot should see on Friday. Not the hot mess who will fall apart without him. The woman who loves him but knows her worth lies in her Father's love. Only let him see the confident Bekah."

Haley offered to help clean up from lunch, but Liz shooed her away, insisting the younger children needed to be responsible for that chore. Besides, she said, she was sure Haley had plenty of other things to work on.

Couldn't argue with her there. She had a lot on her plate as Over the Moon ended their time on the farm. Only one more day of vignette taping tomorrow and the wrap party on Friday. Several of the crew had already left. As she ticked off the things-to-do list in her head, Haley found herself in equal parts yearning for her LA life and wanting to stay a little longer. Liz's invitation to lunch at the picnic tables had tilted the scales toward the staying side.

For an only child, the constant activity of the Caragin family had taken a lot of getting used to. At first, she'd been completely overwhelmed as she watched Jim and Liz juggle the needs and personalities of their children with logistics that would impress any small business operator. Sometimes, their days seemed like the cacophony of an orchestra warming up. Sometimes, like today, it felt like the completed symphony.

This kind of family—that pursued virtue but embraced and encouraged each other when messes were made—was so different from her experience. She'd never felt like she could measure up to the perfection her parents expected or been allowed to ask questions. The way the sexual abuse she'd suffered was swept under the proverbial rug magnified her belief that there was something wrong with her.

The memories of the ways those two pedophiles had violated her hit her full force. Acid rose from her stomach to the bottom of her throat. They'd robbed her of her innocence and gotten away with it. She swallowed hard, willing her lunch to stay down. Her jaw clenched as heat rose from her chest to her face. *When would this end?*

She'd just finished a good meal with a family who'd welcomed her and forgiven her when she'd failed them. She had a promising career in a field she was passionate about and had a talent for. Chandler already had a new concept waiting for her when *The People Quilt* post-production work was completed.

How long would these vile memories torture her? How many therapy sessions until she believed the affirming mantras on the sticky notes on her mirror?

She turned her focus to her iPad and cleaned up some of the emails. Slowly, the bile settled, replaced by the ambient sounds of the younger Caragins on clean-up duty and the busy birds in the trees. By the time she finished and looked up, Liz and the kids were inside.

Gramma Rosamond had taken up residence on the patio, shucking corn from the bushel basket at her feet. She rocked steadily as she pulled husks and silks from the sweet yellow cobs. In her flower print muumuu and pink Skechers, gray hair pulled back from her rounded face, she looked like the epitome of a southern grandmother.

Haley stood and took a few photos with her phone, then moved closer for a better angle. As she neared, she could hear Gramma humming. A video of that peaceful moment would be a treasure. She crept closer and from an angle that would keep her out of the old woman's vision and started her video.

Ten seconds into the recording, Gramma stopped humming and rocking. "Who's there?"

Rats. Haley lowered her phone but left the video rolling as she moved closer. "It's Haley. We met a few weeks ago.

"Oh, yes," Gramma said as if she'd truly remembered.

Sweat made a line from Haley's neck to her waist. Even on the shaded patio, the air felt like a sauna. She had a hundred legitimate reasons to excuse herself and work in the cool of the production trailer. But who knew if or when she'd ever have a chance like this again?

"Can I help you?"

"That would be nice."

Haley pulled a chair close, laid her phone on the table between them, and reached for an ear from the basket. Gramma stopped her. "Let me shuck and you get the silks. My eyes ain't so good anymore. I probably leave as many as I get."

"Sounds good." Haley looked into the bucket with three shucked ears and wasn't surprised to see that Gramma was right. There were definitely more silks left than anyone would want on their corn. She picked one and began pulling off the fine strands.

Questions she'd like to ask rolled through Haley's mind. She considered and discarded them, searching for one she thought would get a good conversation started.

Gramma helped her out. "Where're you from, honey?"

"Born and raised in Dallas, Texas, but I live in Los Angeles, California, now."

"Whoo-ee. That's a long ways away. What you doing here?"

"I'm working with the TV show. Have you heard about it?"

Gramma paused her shucking and rocked. Then, as if she'd found a solution to a crossword question, she nodded and resumed her work. "Oh, yes. Jim and Liz gonna be TV stars," she chuckled.

"I've really enjoyed getting to know them and all their kids. They're really good people." A good leading question came to her. "What did you think about Jim and Liz getting married?"

Gramma wagged her head. "Hmm. I was agin it. No good can come of it. That's what I said—what most folks said. Them young'uns just asking for trouble. They was plenty of fine, young black men she coulda chose. And what was he wanting, marrying a colored girl? Didn't make no sense."

"You were worried about them?"

"Yes, lawdy. In my day, that kind of thing could cause a lot of trouble. A lot of trouble." She rocked in silence, her lips tightening into a pucker.

Haley gave her time to think, imagining the wide range of injustices Gramma had seen that could come back with clarity.

Then Gramma shook her head with a force that surprised Haley. Her lips relaxed into a slight smile. "That Lizzie had her heart set, though. Ha! I guess they was both stubborn. Looks like they was right too. They done alright. Took all them kids in. Done a lot of good. Good Christian family. Your folks church people?"

The question made Haley blink. "Yes, ma'am. But not like Jim and Liz."

"What you mean?"

How to say it? She'd had dozens of conversations with her therapist about her parents, and she still didn't feel like she could define their relationship. "I mean, we went to church all the time. Twice on Sunday, and

Wednesday night. It just always seemed like a checklist." She scoffed at a memory. "There was even a literal checklist before every Sunday school. Read your Bible. Check. Memorize a verse. Check. Bring your tithe. Check."

Gramma chuckled. "I remember those. Used to make my children fill them out too. Was that bad?"

Was it? She had to take a moment. "No. I don't guess that was bad by itself. I suppose they were an effort to teach good habits. If I missed one, though, I felt like a failure. Other things too. If my Sunday dress was wrinkled or I yawned during a sermon, I could see their disapproval."

"Hmm. Not much grace."

The sentence took Haley's breath for a second. Three words. On the surface, the words hit her as a gross understatement, but that's exactly what she'd been deprived of. She'd never doubted that her parents loved her. Never worried they wouldn't provide for her. But Gramma had put her finger on it. There wasn't much grace in her home.

She ran her fingers down the bumpy kernels on the cob in her hand. "No, ma'am. Not much at all. Nothing like what I've seen living here. It's almost like my parents aren't Christians at all compared to Jim and Liz."

"Oh, hush now," Gramma chided with a smile. "You can't judge people like that. Jim and Lizzie are fine examples, but they're far from perfect. And you can't never win comparing folks. The Good Book says there is none perfect . . . no, not one. All of us this side of heaven just trying to do the best we can 'til we can cast off these sin-wearied bodies."

Haley tucked her head. "I guess. But Jim and Liz, they would've never . . ."

"Never what?"

She ignored her impulse to say *never mind* and took a deep breath. "My parents let some people who hurt me get away with it. They made me feel like it was my fault."

Gramma rocked for a time, staring into the yard as if she could really see anything beyond a hundred feet. "Well, I sure am sorry about that, honey. There's a lot of sin going on in the world. And I know how it tears a mama up when someone hurts her baby. Your mama and daddy might not have done the best thing looking back on it, but they was probably doing the best they knew how. At some point, you'll have to forgive them and them people what hurt you."

There it was. The churchy answer. Now, it was all back in her lap. Her responsibility to make everything right. If Gramma hadn't been. . . well, Gramma. . . Haley might have blasted her and stormed off the patio. *Chill, Haley. She's trying to help.*

A voice, not audible, but more of a disembodied impression, whispered, *"Maybe she's right."*

"But Gramma, I'm not sure I can do that. You never had . . . what happened to me—"

Gramma smoothed her hand over the edge of her forehead. "You see that?"

Haley looked and saw the faintest remnant of a scar. "Yes, ma'am."

"When I was sixteen, I took a job at the shirt factory in the county after school. I wasn't the best at sewing, but it was work. My family needed the money. One day, I suppose I was doing particularly bad. Supervisor brought the third shirt back that hadn't passed inspection. Yelled at me that I was stupid and costing more money than I was worth. Then he slapped me so hard my face hit my machine."

Haley gasped.

"I was bleeding." She smoothed her hand over the scar again. "Then he yelled even more. Told me to get home before I bled all over the fabric."

"What did you do?"

"Do? I went home! I wasn't gonna backtalk him. No one else would either. You woulda thought nothing happened. Them other ladies wouldn't even meet my eyes on my way out the door."

"But that's so wrong. What did your parents do?"

"They cleaned me up. Told me to do a better job the next day so I wouldn't give him a reason to be mad at me."

Haley grasped for words. "They sent you back there? They should've called the police. He should've gone to jail."

"Probably would today but not then. A job was a job, and I was lucky to have it."

"What happened to him?"

"I don't know what happened to him. I don't care. I do know what happened to me. I carried my hate for him around for a while. Mad at my daddy, too, for not going down there and fighting that man. Then one Sunday, the preacher talked about forgiveness. How you don't do it because the person deserves being forgiven, but because the Lord demands it of us. And he demands it because he knows it's the only way to let the hurt, the anger, go."

"And you just forgave?"

"Laid it at the altar." Gramma winked.

"But you still remember it even though it happened so long ago."

Gramma laughed. "Forgiving don't mean you don't ever think about it. Lawdy, I wish that was true. It just means you've given the hurt over to the Lord, knowing he will give true justice. My mama said that bad thoughts are like birds. You can't keep them from flying around your head, but you can keep them from nesting in your hair. When I feel those bad thoughts coming, I shake my head real hard so they fly away. Then I think of the good things."

Haley remembered something from earlier in their conversation. "I saw you shake your head like that earlier when you were talking about being worried about Jim and Liz getting married."

"Hmmm. I suppose I did. You could try it sometime."

Haley smiled. "Maybe I can."

"Back to where we first met." Liz welcomed Haley to the patio with a hug, careful to keep their faces apart so Kobi wouldn't have to refresh her makeup.

Haley squeezed tightly before stepping back with a grin and fist-bumping Jim. "Seems appropriate. Thanks for meeting so early, though. Trying to get ahead of this humidity, but it's crazy, even with these humongous fans, which, unfortunately, we'll have to turn off while we're taping."

Liz watched as Haley settled into her interview routine: curling up in her chair, making some notes on her iPad, slurping her green smoothie. She noticed Jim watching her with the same affection and squeezed his hand. Haley might be leaving town soon, but she had become one of theirs now.

Finished with her setup, Haley winked at them. "I'm sure you're pleased to hear me say this is the final day of taping vignettes for the pilot."

All of the crew on the patio erupted in applause and whistles.

"Well," Jim played wounded, "sounds like y'all are more excited than us."

Liz laughed. "I have to say it will be nice to get back to normal life, but we've truly loved getting to know all of you. Thank you for your patience and kindness to our crazy family."

Was that a tear Haley wiped away? No time to wonder long. Haley grinned and clapped her hands. "Are we ready?"

The fans turned off. The camera's red light shone steady. Liz straightened her back.

"Tell me about Liz."

"Me?"

A silent nod and slight smile was all Haley gave her.

"But we haven't talked about all of the children. This is supposed to be all about them."

"Not really. It's about your whole family, and without you, Liz, and, of course, you, Jim, none of this would exist. The farm, the family, the story."

Liz squirmed and took a deep breath. "What is it you want to know?"

"Well, we know how your adoption journey began. Tell me why it stopped. Why no more after Peanut?"

Jim's left hand fell strong and steady on her lower back. Heat rose from her abdomen to her forehead as she remembered the call from her doctor. "It was cancer. Stage 3 breast cancer." Her hand involuntarily moved to her right side. "Diagnosed when Peanut was just a year old."

"But you were so young."

"Not even forty yet."

"Do you have a family history?"

"Yes, Gramma had it and two of her sisters. They never talked about it around us, though, so I didn't even know about it until my diagnosis. I'd been checking 'no' on all of those little family history boxes on medical forms my whole life."

"Treatment was rough?"

"Yes . . ."

Jim stepped in. "She won't say it, but it was brutal. The surgery, the chemo, the radiation. Just the driving back and forth to Birmingham." He grasped her hand. "She was a warrior. Always worried about everybody else. Took gift bags to the other patients and nurses in the infusion room. Always with a kind word and a smile."

Liz gave her head a tiny shake. "He's exaggerating. I had my days. It's exhausting physically but emotionally and mentally too. There were plenty of days I didn't even get out of bed, except for going to the bathroom. It's this man who was the warrior. Hired extra workers so he could be there more for me and the kids. Felt like he never even slept."

Haley asked Liz, "How did you handle it with the kids?"

"That was the hardest part. Telling the kids, trying to keep them from being scared. We were just as open as we could be with them. Elliot was at college then, but he came home a lot, and the older kids all stepped up. And, you know, we already had a built-in community of helpers. All of them—therapists, teachers, housekeepers—took such good care of us."

"And the church . . ." Jim added.

Sweet memories flooded Liz's mind. "The church *was* the Church. They brought so much good food, I told them they were spoiling everyone for when I could cook again. They chauffeured kids around to appointments, did the girls' hair, and prayed . . . sweet Jesus, how they prayed. They literally saved my life."

"Literally?"

"There's nothing figurative about clinging to a toilet bowl, barely able to hold your head up, wishing you could go ahead and die and be in heaven. Their prayers gave me hope."

"You're fine now?" A sweetness filled Haley's voice. *Sounds like she's adopted us too.*

"Cancer-free. Six years and counting."

Relief visibly stole across Haley's face. "But that influenced you to stop adopting?"

Liz nodded and swallowed a measure of sadness. "We put it on hold during my treatment. Social services actually called early on, but they were so kind when we told them. Then we wanted to wait, you know, to see if it would come back."

"But it didn't . . ."

"No, but by then, we realized it was time to concentrate on the family we had, so that's what we've done."

"You've given them so much."

Liz shook her head and smiled. "The Lord's given *us* so much, and I'm so grateful—for the battles and the victories. We have fifteen beautiful children. It's been a joy to see them grow and start to get out on their own, make their own mark, and become the men and women God made them to be. I wouldn't change a minute."

Liz closed her eyes and dropped her head to the side and felt Jim's head tilt to meet it, a muscle memory reaction by now. *Thank you, Jesus.*

"And . . . cut." Haley motioned for the camera to stop and bounced from her chair to embrace Jim and Liz. "I have to tell you guys, I wasn't crazy about this assignment when Chandler first asked. But I feel like you're my family now. I'm just so sorry—"

"None of that." Liz shook her head. "Our Scriptures say God works all things together for good for those who love him and are called according to his purpose. *All* things."

"I hope so. I think I've gotten more therapy here than all my two-hundred-dollar-an-hour sessions in LA."

"We've learned a lot ourselves." Liz moved enough to press her arm into Jim's.

He wrapped one hand around Liz's and gave Haley a quick pat on her shoulder with the other. "You know you're welcome here anytime. And we'll charge a heckuva lot less than two hundred dollars." Backing a step away, he pulled his faded Bama cap from his back pocket and snugged it on his head. "Gotta wash my face so I can get to work. See you later?"

"No later than Friday."

"Oh, yeah, Friday. I almost forgot." With a wink to Haley and a quick peck on Liz's cheek, he sauntered to the house.

Liz rolled her eyes. "You know he didn't forget."

"Yeah, I know."

"Hey, could you come inside? I have something for you."

• • • •

Haley wanted to put Liz off, her chock-full calendar forefront in her thoughts. It would be rude to refuse her, though. "Sure. Let me finish some notes while everything's fresh on my brain and I'll be there in a few minutes."

Of course, it's the last day of taping and Liz has a gift, and I haven't done anything for her. Haley fleshed out some notes she'd typed during the vignette, then spent a few minutes Googling day spas. Surely, Liz deserved a day of pampering. *But would she really enjoy that? Have to think about it later.* She closed her tablet and went into the kitchen.

Liz stood at the island grinning, as Haley's grandmother would say, like a mule eating briars. "Come on. It's actually on the front porch."

Haley followed her from the kitchen through the empty living room. How odd for no one to be here. No time to really think about it, though, as she followed Liz to the front door.

"Surprise!" The wave of voices washed over her. Everyone in the immediate family had gathered in the yard, whistling and whooping. Tied between two Crape myrtles hung a banner with her name in sparkly letters. A huge table of food festooned with streamers and balloons waited beneath it.

To say "surprise" was an understatement. Her feet rooted to the porch. Her heart pounded like she'd just finished a run. Liz squeezed her tightly.

Jim motioned from just beyond the porch. "Come on. It's your party."

Everyone chanted. "Haley! Haley! Haley!"

Sam rushed up, eyes twinkling. "You're. Really. Surprised."

Peanut was close on his heels. "I picked out the streamers. Do you like them?"

Haley noticed Vee with her GoPro!, circling while the others swarmed her with hugs. "Wow! This is so . . . I can't even believe you guys. What a great goodbye party! This is so sweet."

"It's not a goodbye party," Amy shouted. "It's an adoption party!"

"What?" Disbelief shook her head for her since she felt like she had no control over herself at all.

The younger kids yelled back, "An adoption party!"

Jordan draped a homemade beauty queen sash over her head. Glittery letters spelled out "CARAGIN."

Tears filled her eyes to the brim as she fingered each bumpy letter.

Jim held his arms over his head. "Quiet. Quiet."

All Caragin eyes turned to Liz, and Haley's followed. A piece of paper quivered in Liz's hands. "I wrote these words for Elliot, and they've been spoken at every adoption party since. This is the first time I've read them to someone who can understand what I'm saying, so I may cry."

Will teased her. "Mom, you always cry."

All laughed in confirmation. Liz smirked. "True. But here goes." She took a deep breath.

"Welcome precious child of ours.

We all want you to know

we're here no matter what you need,

to help you thrive and grow.

We cherish you and treasure you.

We're thankful for this day

that God has brought you to our lives

to love in every way."

Could a person literally turn into a puddle? Haley felt her knees buckle and prepared to hit the ground, but found herself instantly shored up by the family. They huddled around her like a giant rugby scrum. Many parts interlacing to become one living, breathing organism and enveloping her with acceptance and love that warmed her whole body, starting in her chest and radiating out.

Will broke the lovefest with a shout. "Speech!"

The chant followed quickly as the humongous hug broke. "Speech! Speech! Speech!"

Haley wiped her cheeks and fanned her face with her hand. "I'm guessing the guest of honor at these things doesn't usually make a speech."

Laughter eased the torrent of emotion coursing through her. What could she possibly say? She'd brought them so much grief. Still, every face smiled—beamed actually. If love were a tangible thing, it would've rested on the entire yard like smoky fog on a mountaintop.

Her voice trembled. "I'm not the best wordsmith. All I can say is . . . wow! I'm truly honored, you guys. I don't know what I did to deserve this."

Hope, rescued from a filthy orphanage in Ukraine, chosen by this family, not in spite of, but because of qualities that others thought rendered her useless, flung herself around Haley's waist. "You don't get in a family because you deserve it. You get in a family because you are!"

Instead of bringing more tears, Hope's wisdom brought her strength. She squeezed Hope and kissed the top of her head. "I can't say it any better than that." No more tears. Time to take the attention off of herself. She glanced toward the table. "I think I see cake. Let's have some."

As the Caragins meandered to the food, Haley surveyed the whole scene, not wanting to forget a moment. Underneath the pecan tree, stood two non-Caragins. Chandler and Bekah smiled and lifted punch glasses. She smiled and returned their salute with an imaginary glass of her own.

What a summer. Elliot gripped the steering wheel as memories from May flew through his mind like a TikTok on Red Bull. With every mile, another thought. Just like in May, he drove his Jeep, with the top and sides rolled up. Still dodging familiar potholes on auto-memory. But no Johnnyswim blaring from the radio.

They were, after all, Bekah's favorite group, and Bekah wasn't here. Her long legs weren't propped on the dashboard; her dark hair wasn't swirling around her face. No blissful thoughts of how he'd ask her, how she'd say yes, how they'd be planning their wedding by the end of summer. It'd been almost a month since he'd seen her. The angry hurt had cooled, though, clearing the way for a quiet longing to see her without a clue what he'd say when he did.

Elliot turned into the family driveway, pressing the brake as soon as he saw the golf cart in front of him. Tamika sat in the back seat facing him, Zoe in her lap. She waved the baby's hand in hello to her uncle. *There's something to smile about.*

He waved back to the baby as he scouted the front seats. Cooper in the driver's seat, Gramma Rosamond in the passenger, and Amy and Hope in the middle row along for the ride. So Cooper had ferry duty. Another happy memory from his youth—being allowed to drive the golf cart between the nursery parking lot and the house on days like this, shuttling family and friends who wouldn't have room to park at the house.

Pulling in beside the cart, he hopped out to be almost bowled over by his sisters. Their unabated glee worked its way into his bones as they wrapped around his waist, only to fall away and run to the backyard, distracted by the activity there. Tamika hugged him as he leaned over to plant a kiss on Zoe's soft baby forehead. He extended his hand to help Gramma from the cart. "Hello there, young lady."

"Lawdy. Ain't nobody called me that in a long time." Gramma chortled at the flattery. "Do I know you?"

Elliot glanced at Cooper who just shook his head with a sad grimace. Must not be a good memory day. "Elliot, my name's Elliot. I'm new here."

She took his hand and leveraged herself out of the cart, smoothing her hair and dress as her feet became stable. "Seems like they's lots of new folks today. Did you see that young man driving me? Looks like he don't have but one arm and one leg. Beats all you ever did see."

Cooper grinned and turned the cart around to return to the nursery. Tamika came up on Gramma's other side to help Elliot steer her toward the house.

Enormous white tents shaded the patio and almost every speck of the yard. Jim, Will, Marshall, and Laurel blended in with other Caragin Farm logoed shirts, setting out baskets of petunias, marigolds, and bougainvillea, the leftover inventory of summer annuals from the greenhouses. Caterers dressed all in white bustled about with tablecloths, plates, and chafing dishes.

Elliot whistled. "Wasn't expecting all of this."

Tamika grinned. "Hollywood wrap parties are obviously a step above our family barbecues. The tents went up yesterday."

"Who all's coming to this thing?"

"Family, friends, all the TV folks, and every farm employee who wants to. Jim closed the whole place for the day."

"Wow, that hasn't happened since . . . ever."

"I know, right?" Tamika linked arms with Gramma. "Come with me, Gramma. We'll take a rest inside the house for a little bit."

"Okay, honey. What in the world is going on out here? Looks like the circus is in town. Did I ever tell you about going to the circus when I was in high school? After that, I thought I wanted to be one of them trapeze girls, you know with all the makeup . . ."

It was sweet, listening to her monologue fade as she walked away. *She'll probably walk into heaven telling the Lord something she thinks he doesn't know about.* Elliot turned to survey the bustle in the yard, letting his head fall side to side working out a crick he hadn't even realized he had. He had just made the first step to move toward the tents when he heard his mother behind him.

"El!" Before he could finish turning around, she'd thrown her arms around him, rocking back and forth with gale-force mama intensity. "I'm so glad you came."

He laughed as she released him. "I didn't know it was optional."

"Well, Chandler did want everyone in the family here. It's a party and a final shoot. No hair or makeup, though. Your father's happy about that part."

"I'm sure he is."

Liz stroked his cheek with the back of her hand. "How you doing, baby?"

Her touch, her tone, melted into his heart no different from when she blew on his little-boy booboos to cool the stinging. Oh, if only she could solve his current scrapes with a little hydrogen peroxide and a kiss.

"I'm good." He half-lied, knowing she wouldn't fully believe him, anyway. "Better, at least. Lot to tell you about."

"I want to hear." She winked as she looked over her shoulder. "But I think you're about to be in demand."

Ooof! Elliot's arms were pinned to his side, and his feet left the ground. Will shook him like a dog with a chew toy. "Hey, big brother!"

Elliot talked smack as Will deposited him on the ground. "Losing your strength, He-man. Don't think you even cracked a rib."

Not much time to tease. Jim, Laurel, and Marshall surrounded him in seconds, and he could see the younger sibs heading his way from the house. They slathered him with hugs, kisses, and head rubs, and he soaked up the love. Still, someone was missing. He scanned past the beaming faces around him out to the tents.

There, at the edge of the farthest tent. Neon green Carrigan Farm shirt, blue jean shorts, dirty Keds, arms wrapped around her middle, taking in the homecoming scene. With an upward tilt of his head, he acknowledged her. She closed her eyes, tilted her head in a downward nod, and walked away toward the barn.

• • • •

Bekah's entire body tightened when the photographer asked, "Now, how about just Bekah and Elliot?"

She made eye contact with him. *Can we get out of this?* It had been uncomfortable enough when the woman directed Elliot to move from between his parents to sit by her side for the 'extended family' pic. What would he do now?

Thirty-three days since they'd touched with uncomplicated love, since he'd smiled at her with adoration, since her world had come crashing down. She opened her mouth to make an excuse, but he answered first.

"Sure." He smiled convincingly enough for the photographer, but not for Bekah.

Only let him see the confident Bekah. The mantra from her mother's advice rolled through her mind on auto-repeat. She blinked, straightened her back, and sat beside him, heart beating like a fox on the run. Ten minutes portraying a happy couple crawled by. She bolted for the fruit table to get away from the photo shoot as fast as possible.

Haley stood over an ice-sculpted bowl, spooning juicy red watermelon chunks onto her plate. "Awkward, much?"

"That obvious?"

"Well, I guess I could see it because I know what's going on. Everyone else played it real cool. Except for Liz, she looked like her heart was about to jump out of her chest when they asked you to join the family pic."

"And then just Elliot and me . . ."

"Brutal. You haven't even seen him at all today before that?"

"From a distance across the yard. I haven't even talked to him since . . . anyway, I guess he didn't want to make a scene."

"I think you both performed very well. It even looked like that one time, when she had you looking into each other's eyes . . ."

"Yeah, for just a few seconds I felt him, you know, kind of soften all over. Shoulders relaxed, smiling at me with his eyes, not just his mouth. It made me think . . . hope. You think it's possible?"

Haley tilted her head and examined the watermelon chunk on her fork. "I'd forgotten how much I love watermelon. I ate so much of this every summer of my life until I moved to LA. Then, a few times, I'd see it on a buffet, shimmering red gold. But when I put it in my mouth, it was bland, tasteless even. I stopped trying it. But this garden-grown, sun-ripened sweetness, this is the real thing." She popped the morsel into her mouth and rolled her eyes euphorically.

"Yeah, thanks for the fruit review, but—"

"Look, I know I'm not even close to the best one to give any love advice, but I'll tell you this. I've seen fake love, lots of it. It looks great on the surface but is bland, meaningless, even nasty when you take a bite. What you two have seems like the real thing to me. Yeah, I do think it's possible."

• • • •

Liz paused scrubbing on a spill one of the kids made on the punch table when Denise sidled up to her.

"You know, you don't have to do that? Today, you have people to clean up after your family."

"You're right." Liz dropped the napkin and picked up a raffia-ribboned Mason jar filled with strawberry lemonade, an oversized striped straw, and a sprig of rosemary. "Usually, if I don't clean up a mess, it stays there until I come back by the next time."

"And you needed a little break?" Denise chose her own Mason jar and pulled the rosemary out. "I know it looks pretty but rosemary? Basil would've been much better."

"Exactly. And I did need a little break. But truly, it's been a pretty perfect day." She breathed in the moment, scanning the crowd of family and friends milling underneath the tents. "Only one minor meltdown upstairs this morning. And they've been up since the sun."

"People quilt. Think they'll use that name?"

"I don't know. At first, I bristled up like a porcupine when Chandler suggested it. Like that was *my* name, and I didn't want to share. But through all these last two months, I've seen how true it is. How so many people from all kinds of backgrounds come together to make life work. Some family we choose; some we're stuck with."

Denise laughed. "Like your sister?"

"Yeah. Listen, I haven't directly told you how sorry—"

"You don't have to tell me. I over-reacted. I shouldn't have ratted you out to Jim. He just caught me by surprise."

"Nope. You don't get to take the blame. I should've told him a long, long time ago."

"Y'all good?"

Liz nodded. "We are. I actually told Elliot too. I was talking to him about forgiveness, and it came out."

"I bet you really surprised him."

"I did. But he handled it really well. Got me thinking that maybe I should tell more people."

"Why would you want to do that?"

"I think it would help women like me, living with all the guilt and shame. Help them heal like I never did." Liz sipped her drink and looked at her sister, surprised to see Denise welling up, fat teardrops falling from the corners of her eyes. "Denise?" She maneuvered them to the edge of the tent away from others approaching the table.

Denise wiped away the tears and sniffled. "You know we never talked about it, since that day. I'm sorry I made you live like that, pressing all those feelings down inside you. I thought you had just moved on. I should've asked."

"Oh, honey. You're not responsible."

"But I am. I drove you there. Drove you home. Never once asked you about it again."

"We were both so young. We didn't understand what we were doing."

"I know. Truth is, I forgot it for a long time. But when y'all started adopting those babies, especially when Cooper came along and we found out his mother was so young." She swiped more tears away. "I just wondered how it would've been if we'd talked you into putting your baby up for adoption instead of..."

Liz wrapped an arm around Denise and brushed tears from both of their faces. "Me too. That's all in the past now, and I know God has forgiven me. But this is what I'm talking about. Too many women think abortion is necessary and that it's not a person, just a choice. No one ever tells them about all the emotional pain. No one can tell it except someone who's been there. That's why I think I should talk about it. There's this organization—"

Liz stopped short at the sight of Jim striding toward her, face red, mouth taut. He grasped her arm firmly. "We gotta go. It's Cooper."

She barely heard Denise promise to take care of everyone as Jim's strong hand propelled her from the tent. Fear gripped her soul. Passing faces blurred. *Focus, Liz. What's he saying?*

"The cart flipped. Charlie saw it on his way to the greenhouses. Called 911."

Will had a death grip on the steering wheel, truck in drive, foot on the brake, waiting for them to climb in. Laurel jumped into the back seat and clutched her hand while Jim slid into the front. Soft thuds behind her. Liz turned her head enough to see Elliot, Marshall, and Victoria piling into the pickup bed. Gravel spun as Will pressed the gas.

A jillion thoughts tumbled through her brain. "Was he alone?"

Jim's syllables were clipped. "I don't know."

"How long's he been there?"

"I don't know."

"Is he—?"

"I don't know, babe."

Two SUVs blocked the street. Beyond them, red, yellow, and blue lights pulsed in the dusky sky as fire, ambulance, police—what looked like every first responder in the county—pulled up.

Charlie, their nursery foreman, met them as they piled out of the truck, sweat pouring from his beet-red face, mud covering his jeans, shirt, and hands. "The cart's on top of him. They're getting ready to winch it up."

Liz could barely breathe. "Is he . . .?"

"He's conscious."

Jim rushed to the edge of the ditch with Will, Marshall, and Elliot close on his heels. Liz's knees buckled, and she fell to the hot asphalt. Laurel and Victoria crouched beside her.

Charlie's shadow covered them as he leaned in. "I was able to lay down in the ditch, touch his hand, see his eyes." The giant of a man couldn't keep his voice from breaking. "He looked real scared, so I prayed with him. Seemed like that helped him calm down some."

Prayer. Of course. She grasped Charlie's hand. "Dear Father God, help Cooper be strong. Let him feel your peace." The whispered prayers of her daughters swirled with hers, affirming, imploring. "Help these workers get him out soon. Let him be alright. Dear Jesus, let my baby be alright."

Her wobbly knees strengthened, and peace consumed her frantic heart. She pushed herself up and made her way to the scene. Snapshots of her worst fears and greatest hopes met her there: the cart, wheels up; in the ditch, Jim on his knees, yelling encouragement into the crumpled metal; Will, Marshall, and Elliot standing watch. A small cadre of first responders milling around. A fireman affixed a huge hook to the cart, instructed the others to back away, and motioned for his partner on the truck to start the winch.

With no small amount of effort, Bekah forced her eyes open, unable to move her tingling arm. Peanut had curled into her body and was lost in deep sleep. *How could such a little girl feel so heavy?*

Swiveling her head to the door, she saw Marshall, Laurel, Vee, and Elliot in the living room. Marshall and Vee headed to the kitchen. Laurel was by her side in a moment, pulling Peanut up from the loveseat. "Come on, Peanut. Let's go to bed."

Then there were two. The first time they'd been in a room alone together since . . . when? Elliot shifted his weight from one leg to the other but made no other movement. Bekah stretched her legs out onto the ottoman. "What time is it?"

He glanced at his phone. "One forty-three. . . a.m."

"Yeah, I figured the a.m. part."

"You got the others in bed?"

"Not me. Denise and the ladies from church. You wouldn't believe. They were like ants all over the place cleaning, cooking, more cleaning. I think they have meals for the week in the fridge. Word of warning, there might be a chunk missing from the chicken spaghetti." She winked. He loved chicken spaghetti.

What was that look, though? Was he sad? Mad? He lumbered to her and fell in the chair, wrapping her in his arms. She latched onto his trembling body and buried her head in his shoulder.

"Cooper still alright? Has there been a change?"

"No. No change. Cracked ribs, concussion. He's sleeping now." Despite the reassuring words, Elliot still quivered.

She tossed out every possible question coming to her mind like swiping delete on spam texts. The wrong words might make him let go, and that was the last thing she wanted. Of course, it had been a traumatic twenty-four hours. Elliot would've been in caretaker mode the whole time. She'd seen him do it often enough. This was the exhaustion taking over.

Why doesn't matter. He feels so good. I didn't know if he'd ever . . . She squeezed her eyes shut and steadied herself. *Only let him see the confident Bekah.*

His shaking subsided, and he loosened his grip, falling back into the cushions. Her heart told her to pile under his arm, press her head into his chest, and wrap her free arm around his middle, but her head suggested she push away a little. *Head wins . . . this time.* Curling her legs beneath her, she straightened beside him, allowing one hand to rest ever so lightly on his arm.

He closed his eyes and blew out a deep breath. "I don't know, Bekah."

Wham! Her hand drew back as if it had a mind of its own, and she pushed herself further from him. Here it was, the official breakup. Wait. He said, *don't know.* Does that mean there's hope? Confident Bekah struggled to keep her head above the sea of emotions threatening to take her under.

He massaged his head and squeezed his eyes shut. "I really didn't want to come today . . . yesterday. Didn't think I could bear seeing you. But then, watching you blend in with my fam, seeing you smile, holding your hand for that picture. It just felt . . . you know? I was thinking we'd talk after the thing was over. Then Coop."

She remembered the sinking feeling when she found out Cooper could be seriously injured, or worse. Elliot must've felt that multiplied by a thousand.

"When we got down in that ditch and he wasn't answering us at all—I thought he might be gone. I think we all did. There was this overpowering grief pressing down on me. I was thinking, please God, don't let us lose him. Don't let us lose him. Then your face popped into my mind, and I thought, God, don't let me lose *her.*" He opened his eyes and rolled his head to look at her.

A chill ran through her whole body. "Elliot, I . . ."

"I had to focus on Coop, of course. Stay strong for Mom and Dad and the sibs. That's my thing."

She felt the corners of her mouth turn up. "Yes, I know."

"But through that, the being the strong one thing, all I needed was someone I could let go in front of, let my fear show. Someone who would hug me and understand I didn't need someone just to tell me it would be okay. I needed someone who knew me. I couldn't think of anyone except you."

She shook her head to stop the tears. Was this going where she hoped? Was he just worn out emotionally? She wanted to slather him with assurances that she was the one—the only one. No. That needed to be his conclusion. *Let him talk, Bekah.*

As if he were reading her mind, he said, "It's not just today and Coop. There's so much that's happened. All this mess with the family because of that video, stuff Mom told me. I met David, my birth father. And there's more. I wanted to talk to my best friend all about it. But you're my best friend, and I was so—it doesn't matter what I was. I can't stand being without you."

A gasp escaped, and tears filled her eyes. She bowed her head.

He rolled onto his side and pulled her shivering hands into his. "I want my best friend back, but I know that's not gonna be enough. I can't see us being just friends. I know we've got things to work through, but I want *us* back. I want to try. What about you?"

Confident Bekah left the building. Humble Bekah nodded and collapsed into a blubbering mess. The strength of his arms pulled her in, his hands on her face, his kisses on the top of her head. Yes, of course, they would try. And with God's help, they could make it. That much of Confident Bekah remained.

Saturday, September 14

"You don't think this is all too much?" Liz slid her hand the length of Jim's lapel as they lingered outside the limousine doors. From inside the stretch SUV, chatter and squeals of hyper Caragins seemed to keep time with flashing LED lights.

Jim winked. "Maybe. But we just spent half an hour getting them all loaded into this thing. I mean, I can go get the truck if you want, but you look waaaay too good for that old thing. You deserve to arrive at the red carpet like a movie star."

She shook her head but grinned. Between forcing her brood to handle normal Saturday chores and shoveling down an early macaroni and cheese dinner, the whole day had been Hollywood treatment. Over the Moon sent manicurists along with Kobi to pamper the ladies of the house.

Vee had begged for the job of ordering clothes for all with a network-provided Amazon credit card and proved worthy of Liz's somewhat reluctant trust. No sequined formal wear but better than normal Sunday best. The girl had a good eye. Every person from Gramma to little Zoe wore a new outfit that matched their body type and personality.

Liz's own ensemble, a pantsuit of light teal, perfectly accentuated the curves she liked while hiding the ones she'd rather keep between herself and Jim. This was the prettiest thing she'd worn since her wedding gown. She only would've made one change. She tugged upward on the neckline of the jacket.

Jim moved her hand. "It's not too low. As a matter of fact, you could undo one more of those buttons if you like." He raised his eyebrows.

"You're incorrigible."

"Yes, I am. Get in the limo, Mrs. Caragin."

Marshall extended a hand from inside the SUV. She accepted it only to feel a smack on her behind. She glanced back at Jim, eyes wide.

"What? I couldn't help it." He laughed as he hoisted himself inside and sat flush against her. He leaned in so she could hear him. "For once, I agree with Victoria. Let's just enjoy the night."

She hadn't seen him this giddy in . . . well, since before the kids started coming and they opened the business. She glanced around the cavernous interior, her eyes getting adjusted to the lights pulsing in near darkness to the beat of whatever that music was. The nearest thing to compare it to would be the nightclub she and Jim went to on their Pensacola honeymoon. Without the smoke and drunk people.

This was much better. Her whole family, including Gramma, Tamika, and Zoe, plus Bekah, in one vehicle. No telling how much it cost Chandler to get this sweet ride from Birmingham.

But enough of that. It wasn't her money. *Enjoy the night, Liz*. She leaned into Jim. "One request?"

"Anything."

"Can they play some music I can understand?"

Jim boomed over the syncopated thumping. "Hey! Who's the DJ?"

Victoria called from the front of the cabin. "Up here, Dad. Do you have a request?"

"The Queen would like some Commodores or Earth, Wind, and Fire."

"You got it! Old people music coming right up!"

All aboard laughed. Liz had no time to even feign insult before the opening horns of *Boogie Wonderland* filled the air.

All the kids were in motion. Dancing. Singing. Taking selfies. Pushing any button near them. Beth's voice came from her left. "Mom! There's a whole cooler of water in ice. Can I have one?"

Practical Liz shook her head. "It's only fifteen minutes to the theater."

Jim's hand squeezed her thigh.

Enjoy the night. "Yes, you can have water. Water for everyone!" She laughed and relaxed into the party.

In what seemed like a lot less than fifteen minutes, the car slowed to a stop in front of Fairview's Gem Theater. Liz had heard Gramma and her mother talk about how grand the place was in the fifties and sixties. By the time she saw her first show, the place was pretty broken down. In the nineties, though, some sentimental entrepreneurs fixed it up and reopened, showing second-run movies for a dollar. For a family of seventeen, it was the only way to see a movie together.

Tonight, every light bulb in the marquee glowed. OVER THE MOON NETWORK PRESENTS THE PEOPLE QUILT. Vee turned the music down and every passenger clamored to the windows so they could see. As instructed, they waited for Chandler and the chauffeur to open their doors.

The sidewalks were filled with what looked like half the town. Pair by pair, Caragins stepped onto the sidewalk to light applause. Will reached in to offer a hand to Gramma, who leveraged herself onto the sidewalk and waved like royalty on the castle balcony. The applause grew as Jim and Liz emerged. Liz tried to find familiar faces in the crowd, but most of them were obscured by uplifted cell phones. Hope and Amy pressed close against her as the family posed for official Over the Moon photos.

They were ushered into their seats in the center of the theater. Here, the friends and family who had been given tickets welcomed them with waves and smiles. Liz's heart fluttered when she spotted her mother and Uncle John in the row behind them. Tears rolled down her cheeks as she clung to her mother's neck.

Chandler's voice brought her back to the moment. "Thank you everyone for coming. What a special night."

Liz settled into her seat. The loud murmur of excitement faded away. Peanut squeezed past her siblings to sit on Liz's lap.

Chandler stood on the platform at the base of the movie screen, microphone in hand, smiling more broadly than Liz had seen. "For those of you who don't know me, I'm L. Chandler Lee with Over the Moon Network. I'm asked all the time what the *L* stands for." His eyes roved from section to section and up to the balcony. "Tonight, I'd have to say 'lucky.' I'm the luckiest guy in the world to get paid for doing this.

"No kidding. I've traveled all over this country, and I've never felt so welcome as here in Fairview and out at Caragin Farm. And I've learned a lot. I now know I'm not going to get yelled at some time in the future if I'm told someone will 'holler' at me later. 'Fixin' to' is a unit of time that could mean one minute away or next week. All sodas are 'Coke,' trucks are 'pickups,' and you're not just tired, you're 'wore slap out.'"

He waited a few seconds for the tittering to die down. "I've also learned how hard it is to get a 'born and raised' Alabama man to sit still for makeup and . . ." He swallowed hard as he made eye contact with Liz. "I've seen the faces of unconditional love. I'll tell you, there are no people finer than Jim and Liz Caragin."

Wild applause and whooping enveloped them. Little by little, every person in the room stood. *Whoo!* Liz froze in her seat, heart pumping like a startled rabbit feeling overwhelmed and humbled. Jim appeared just as stunned. He wrapped his arm around her shoulders and bowed his head. As if she had no control of her own body, she realized her hand had covered her mouth and her head shook in disbelief.

Chandler, microphone tucked under his arm, clapped right along. When she caught his eye, he resumed his emcee role. "Seriously, you guys, I mean 'y'all,' should probably stop. I think that's all they can take." After everyone took their seats, he continued. "Their humility is one thing I was drawn to. Time after time, they've turned any compliment back into praise for God, the rock of their lives."

Amens rifled through the theater.

"I could go on and on about this remarkable family, but I wouldn't be telling you anything you don't know. Instead, I invite you to enjoy this forty-five-minute glimpse into their world. On behalf of Over the Moon Network, I'm proud to present *The People Quilt.*"

House lights dimmed as the screen lit up. A narrator's voice gave an overview of their family with music playing softly in the background. A montage of photos from their wedding through last month rolled seamlessly. Each child's face appeared at least once, eliciting excited giggles around her.

The whole thing felt unreal to Liz. Her face and her family on such a big screen. She had to admit, though, the video from the Fourth of July made an impression. During these extended family events, she always focused on filling plates and making sure everyone else enjoyed themselves. This arms-length view gave her the chance to see the easy way her family mingled and played, like so many puzzle pieces glued together with respect and love. Or a quilt stitched together. Yes. She could definitely see the nickname bestowed years ago truly described her family.

From all of the days of vignettes, they'd chosen to focus on the story of Elliot. She supposed they were saving the rest for future episodes. Even though she'd prepared herself for there to be some video edited to make for more drama, Over the Moon took the high road and added no such scene.

At what seemed like the wrap-up time, the narrator's voice sailed through the speakers. "The family continues to grow, as all families do." Photos of Will and Tamika's wedding and them holding Zoe splashed onto the screen.

Then a photo of Elliot and Bekah followed by video from Elliot's interview with Haley. In the booth at the Bait Shop, a huge grin lit his face. His fingers tapped a velvet box on the table. "I picked this up today. Going to ask her if she'll do me the privilege of being my wife next week."

The audience breathed a collective, "Awwww." She heard a few hooting voices from her family. Jim's hand fell on her tensed shoulder. She leaned forward to see Elliot and Bekah staring expressionlessly at the screen.

The narrator plunged ahead. "Add another square to the quilt. See you next week at Caragin Farm." Credits rolled with behind-the-scenes photos from weeks of shooting intertwined.

House lights up. Chandler emerged from behind the screen to the applause of the crowd. "I've watched that so many times and always want to see it again. I hope you all enjoyed it as well and that Over the Moon will have an enduring relationship with this wonderful Caragin Family. Please stay as long as you like. There are drinks and snacks in the lobby. Thank you again, Jim and Liz, and everyone in Fairview who made this possible."

• • • •

Bekah stood with the rest of crowd amidst more applause and titillated chatter, her brain fixated on that last scene. Elliot looked so happy. He had a ring. What was he thinking now? Then, his strong hand squeezing hers, his voice in her ear.

"Come on."

They squeezed past family to the end of the row. His grip intensified as he pulled her to a door at the foot of the stage. Before she could gather a thought, they were in the alley. The weight of the door shut out the commotion of the theater. Except for stink from a nearby dumpster and the electric hum of a lone streetlight, they were alone. He dropped her hand and propped against the brick.

Seconds passed as she waited for whatever was coming. He stared into the back of the garage across the alley as if something very interesting was going on there.

Well, if he's not going to say anything. She cleared her throat. "Interesting exit."

He breathed out a laugh. "Sorry, I just wanted to talk to you alone before anyone could stop us."

"About?"

"About the awkward moment . . . there at the end. I'd forgotten I'd even said that. It was before . . ."

Oh, poor Elliot. Was he going through the whole conversation with Sonny at the pool? Was he embarrassed for her? There would be questions, of course, from anyone who watched the preview . . . and then the pilot . . . on national television. Sheesh, that would surpass awkward.

She propped against the wall a few feet from him. "Yeah, I kinda figured that out, during the credits. I mean, for a couple of seconds there I thought, 'He has a ring?' He's going to ask me to marry him?' Then, I remembered your interview with Haley was before . . ."

What could she say to make him feel better? She scooted closer and stroked his arm. "Don't worry about it. We can just tell people we decided to wait, or that you came to your senses and realized you could do better."

He swiveled his head and made eye contact. "I wouldn't say that."

"I know you wouldn't. Just throwing ideas out there."

"I wouldn't say it because it's not true. I'm a hundred percent certain I couldn't do better." He took her hand as he dropped to one knee. He drew his hand from this pocket and opened it for her to see a gold band with a small diamond. "Bekah, will you do me the privilege of being my wife?"

Her vocal cords felt paralyzed. Her head swam. *Is this for real?* Wobbly knees dropped her to his level. She enveloped his hands in hers. Skin to skin. This was really Elliot, on one knee, with a ring in his hands. "Elliot, you've been carrying this around since . . ."

His expression morphed from sincerity to amusement. "Yes, ever since, waiting on the perfect time to ask you."

The appearance of his dimples brought her back to the moment. She smiled. "And the dirty alley behind the Gem is the perfect time?"

He let his other knee drop to the pavement and winked. "Full disclosure?"

"Mm-hmm."

"I haven't been carrying it around. I mean, what kind of a loser would carry an engagement ring around in his pocket for three months?"

Good. He was playing. Not wanting to cross the line between playful and snarky, she resisted the urge to slap her finger and thumb in the shape of an L on her forehead. She settled for returning his smile with a slight shake of her head. *Let him talk, Bekah.*

His face turned from silly back to sincerity. "You're not the only one who did some thinking during the credits. Borrowed this ring from Tamika before I pulled you out here. She'll probably want it back."

"So, this is totally spontaneous?"

"This exact moment? Yes. Planning to ask you? No. I haven't thought about much else the last month. You're the perfect woman for me. I don't want to ever be without you."

Tears dammed up just inside her lower lashes. Her chin quivered. "You mean you've forgiven me?"

He cocked his head and his brow furrowed. "Of course. What? You didn't know that?"

She released his hands and sank back onto her heels. The tears broke past the retaining walls and raced down her cheeks. "You never told me."

Elliot draped his arms around her and squeezed. Falling back enough to wipe the tears away, he tilted her face up. Green eyes to green eyes. "Oh, girl. I thought you knew. I should've said. I have forgiven you. East from west."

Her body heaved with relief. She sniffled and wiped her face. "And now, you'll have to forgive me again."

"What for?"

"For messing up your proposal."

He laughed as he looked around them. "It's not the most romantic place. Not like you deserve."

"It's perfect." She shook the weepiness away and stood. "Ask me again."

With the cutest smile ever, he regained his balance on one knee. "Bekah, will you marry me?"

She extended her left hand. "Yes."

. . . .

Liz stroked the beautiful teal suit one last time. She'd take it to the cleaners on Monday, and it would most likely stay in the bag until Elliot's wedding. At least, she knew she'd wear it again. A funny thought of her in all the wedding albums to come with her wearing this same suit brought a smile. She closed the closet door. "We haven't stayed up this late since I don't know when."

Jim laughed from the bed. "Not without some kid puking or something."

She padded to the bed, turned off her bedside lamp, and cuddled under his arm. "Quite a night."

He pulled her close and kissed her forehead. "Yeah, it was."

"Like a fairytale."

"Mm-hmm." Another kiss. "Sure you're ready for it to end?"

"What?"

"Ready for it to end. You've decided you don't want to do the show, right?"

She propped up on an elbow. Eyes adjusted to the moonlight filtering through the window, she could see the playful smirk on his face. "How do you—"

"Know? I know you better than anyone, Liz Caragin. I could hear it while you was talking to folks at the Gem. See it in your face when the limo pulled away. The smile you had when we turned out the lights downstairs and you looked up to the spots where the cameras *used* to be."

He's got me there. She fell into her pillow and smiled as he rolled to his side to face her. Knees touching, hands intertwined. They'd had so many conversations here like this over the past twenty-eight years, in their private sanctuary.

She kissed his fingertips. "So, you know what I'm thinking. But I'm not sure how you feel about it."

"Well, I have to say I was pretty impressed with what we saw tonight. Was starting to think we should consider letting it go on. Until that part at the end."

Liz grimaced. "Elliot and Bekah looked so embarrassed. I couldn't help but think that more times like that are bound to happen. The kids have enough to deal with without having cameras on them all the time."

"I agree. Guess we're just not cut out for the reality show biz."

"Victoria's going to have a fit."

"Victoria? Think about L. Chandler Lee."

A slight pang of sadness rushed over her. "I don't take any joy in disappointing him. Even though you know I wasn't always in his corner."

Jim opened his mouth in faux shock.

She smiled. "But I did grow to like him. I hope he's not too mad at us."

"I think he'll bounce back."

"I will be happy to have my house back. Walk around in my easy pants and t-shirts. Not worrying about how much dirt all those people packing into my kitchen were tracking in."

Jim added to the list. "Big trucks making ruts in the yard. Social media hissy fits. Hollywood designers changing the front of the nursery."

She smiled. "You have to admit, the front of the nursery was an improvement. I guess there were other good things too. I liked telling our stories about the children and getting to know the crew. Haley."

"It wasn't all bad."

A sobering thought. "Not even the bad things were all bad. Like me getting backed into telling you . . ." The words stuck in her throat.

He stroked her cheek. "I know. That was tough. But I needed to know it, and you needed to tell it. No one should have to carry that kind of burden."

God, thank you for this man. "I love you."

"I love you."

After a soft kiss, he pulled her in closer. She snuggled into another comforting position, her shoulder under his arm, face on his chest, legs intertwined like a pretzel.

Jim cleared his throat. "I think Chad's going to miss me."

Her laugh bubbled out. "Oh, yeah. He's really going to miss you. If I catch you putting on my makeup, I'll know you miss him too." The thought cracked her up as the words came out of her mouth.

He laughed with her. "If that happens, you can go ahead and have me committed."

Their laughter faded into giggles then silence. A yawn shuddered its way from her chest out of her mouth. She closed her eyes and relaxed into the comfort of his arms. "So . . . no more show. We've decided?"

He kissed the top of her head. "Yep. It's anonymous."

Liz prayed silently for each soul as Jim asked the blessing for the sandwich lunch they were ready to share. All of her children, her one precious grandbaby, plus Tamika and Bekah held hands in a curvy circle among the picnic tables where their plates lay waiting.

She had a little more time than usual. Jim not only thanked God for the food, but he went on for a bit about how grateful he was for the unity of their family. Verbalizing his gratitude, she knew, was his attempt to pre-emptively smooth over any disunity that would come when they shared their decision. *Hope that works.*

As soon as he said "amen" the chatter started as everyone ate. The excitement of the premiere had carried over from last night like the breathless feeling of stepping off a wild roller coaster. Her children had been giddy all day, even during church.

Yes, she and Jim were going to burst some bubbles soon. But for now, she reveled in having her family, the center of her people quilt, all happy together within her reach. Tomorrow, Elliot, Laurel, Marshall, and Victoria would be gone again. Work at the nurseries would be back to normal as the push to get fall annuals out continued. The blessed routine of their pre-reality-show life—schoolwork, chore charts, doctor visits, sports, church—would resume. Who knew when she'd have them all here again?

Cooper, body healed since his accident, stood. "I'm done. Okay if I go to the park to meet my friends?"

How did the boy with only one hand always finish first? Jim squeezed her hand and winked as he stood. *Here we go.*

"In a minute, son. I got something I need to say before y'all start taking off." He waited for Cooper to sit. The others fixed their attention on Jim.

He smiled broadly at the group. "It's been quite a summer. I want to say how proud I am of all of you. Seeing all of your faces on that big screen last night kinda rocked me. I thought how blessed I am and what a blessing you'll be as you grow up and make your way in the world."

Liz looked around the tables, taking in the smiles—from Laurel's barely upturned lips to Amy's wide grin.

Jim continued, "Sure was a wild experience. However . . ." He hesitated and Liz met his eyes. She nodded once. "Your mom and me have decided to pull the plug. *The People Quilt* won't be on TV. We're telling Chandler this afternoon."

The hubbub started before he'd finished. Liz watched as smiles faded into surprise, confusion, and various expressions of discontent. As expected, Victoria was the most upset. They talked on top of each other, peppering her and Jim with questions and pleas to reconsider.

Liz stood. "Hold on." She waited for the murmuring to subside. "What you need to know is this is not up for discussion. We listened to your input when Over the Moon proposed this show, but the decision rested with your father and me. And the decision on whether to continue belongs to us as well. Our contract says we have to let them know within twenty-four hours of seeing the pilot if we want to stop and our minds are made up to do that."

Vee shouted from her seat. "You're ruining everything!"

Jim lowered his voice to drill-sergeant firmness. "There'll be none of that. We knew you'd be upset, but there's a lot more than that to our decision. We don't believe that the long-term exposure to everything that went on here the last few months is good for our family overall. As your parents, that's our call . . . alone . . . to make. When you're the head of your own family, you'll be able to make your own calls."

Vee slumped forward on the table with a huff, burying her head in her arms. Peanut lay her head on her sister's arm.

Elliot stood. "Uh, Dad . . . may I?"

Jim nodded his head.

Elliot cleared his throat. "I know I haven't been here for most of the action, so it may be that I don't have a place to say anything. But it also means that I've been able to look at it more impartially. I think the show was definitely a once-in-a-lifetime experience and a lot of fun.

"I also saw what a lot of work it was for Mom and Dad, who, you gotta admit, already have a lot going on. They'd love to give all of us everything we want but, as long as they're responsible for us, they have to decide when what we want isn't the best thing. They're accountable to God for the decisions they make, and I know they take that seriously."

Liz winked at Elliot when he looked at her. Thank God that he understood and was willing to speak up.

He returned her wink and inhaled deeply. "So I hope you'll all work your way around to supporting them and treating them with the respect they deserve."

Will affirmed him. "That's right, brother."

Elliot smiled. "Bekah and I need to be going soon to get back for youth group tonight, but there's one more thing. I wanted to tell you while we're all here together because who knows when this will happen again. I know I'm changing the subject."

Liz noticed him work his hands in an itsy-bitsy-spider movement he'd made when he was nervous since he was young. He looked at Bekah with a slight smile, and her face lit up. Liz felt her pulse accelerate. This could only mean one thing. *Say it, El.*

Elliot fumbled with his words. "Last night . . . after the show . . . I, uh, asked Bekah . . ."

Bekah sprang up and thrust her left hand with Tamika's ring on it into the air. "I said yes!"

In an instant, tables emptied as her children hurried to hug Elliot and Bekah. Liz rushed to them and threw her arms around Bekah. "I knew it. I knew. I'm so happy for you." She hugged Elliot. "I'm so happy for you both."

Elliot smiled and shouted out. "No posting on any social media! We still have to tell Mom Ida and Bekah's fam." Laughter and happy chaos replaced sadness and tension. Questions about dresses and venues and dates dissolved the earlier frustrations. Liz stepped back to give all of her children a chance to talk to the newly-engaged couple.

She felt Jim's arms secure around her waist as he hugged her from behind. She leaned back into him. "I love seeing them all so happy."

"Even Victoria."

He was right. Victoria had donned her GoPro! and was weaving in and out of the activity with a smile on her face.

Liz shook her head. "That girl."

"Guess we can stop the TV show, but we can't stop the drama."

Liz laughed. "That's the truth." She turned to face him and wrapped her arms around her neck. "But right now, I'm going to enjoy this. There'll be a lot going on next year. Laurel gets her undergrad."

"And Cooper graduates from high school."

"And Elliot and Bekah's wedding. You'll need to practice your dancing."

Jim swayed her in a contented slow dance. "Yep, 2020's going to be a great year." He spun her around and pulled her back close.

She nuzzled her face into his neck. "Of course it is. What could go wrong?"

Since I wrote the first paragraph of my first novel, I've felt compelled to talk about two things. The first is sin, which I believe is any action that falls short of God's best plan for our lives. Hand in hand with this problem is hurt—pain caused by our own sin and the sins of others we have no control over. Neither of these can always be wrapped up with a pretty bow when "The End" is written.

Two of the real-world problems explored in *Caragin Farm* are unplanned pregnancy and abortion regret. If you or someone you love is dealing with either of these, I implore you to seek help. Even more specifically, I implore you to seek Christian help. There is a national organization based in my home city that has resources to help. Check out lovelife.org or search for a similar ministry near you.

A friend calls my works "Real. Raw. Redemptive." I love this. Without the "redemptive" part, though, the first two descriptors would make my novels—and life—quite depressing. Sin is real. Hurt is raw. God's love is redemptive. I pray you find that love.

With deepest thanks —

Again, to my Mister. What a blessing to be married to my best friend and enjoy every day, whether we're on a fun vacay or making a Wal-Mart run! Thank you for seeing me, loving me, proofreading, and toting books and book table setups for me.

To my friend and amazing children's book author, Jill. Within minutes of my ask, she wrote the "adoption party" poem that I'd been struggling with for hours. Find her beautiful books at jillromanlord.com.

To all who offered a kind word and prayers, subscribed to my blog, and bought this book, I thank God for all of you and pray that something I've written encourages you as we share our journey this side of heaven.

About the Author

Renée Peeples Hodges is Mississippi raised, and transplanted to North Carolina so writing all things Southern comes easily. With her three children out of the nest, she's concentrated on completing her first two novels, *Ona Mae's Deli and Bait Shop* and *Caragin Farm*. She and her husband enjoy serving in their church, traveling, and hanging out in their easy pants watching cop shows and cooking competitions.

Join her journey at reneehodges.com.

Read more at https://reneehodges.com.